I0604065

The Reaper

by

Lee Cooper

'Fighting's in the Blood' series
dedicated to
My Mother, Grandmother, and
friend Leigh Henderson.

Special thanks to my editors, Alan Stephen and Rhonda Cooper who has put in countless hours on this book. Thanks also to Sheila Wink and Martin Carlin who gave it a proofread and feedback.

In him we have redemption through his blood, the forgiveness of our trespasses, according to the riches of his grace, **Ephesians 1:7**

The sins of the father are to be
laid upon the children.

William Shakespeare

Chapter 1

The Gamble:

The formidable gamble played by Jack and myself had paid off in a spectacular way. We lived as dead men for too long, sacrificed so much, but the day of reckoning had arrived. The cost to our lives and the desolation of leaving our loved ones behind became worth it. Davie Rhodes, my Father, was handcuffed, duck taped, and shocked to his core sitting in the back of the Range Rover, next to the treacherous and deceased rat Rankin. Davie was more confused over the fact I wasn't decomposing at the bottom of the Mersey, than Rankin's death. And then there was Jack's heart, which supposedly packed in a few days after my demise, was still beating, and a satisfying beat at that.

My intangible Father had finally turned up at my brother's door. It was a calculated gamble and the circumstances of this plan to phase out was so miraculously farfetched we doubted ourselves from the minute go, but two emotionally draining years had ended. The thoughts of returning to our own lives, seeing loved ones we missed, and no longer having to live in apprehension of a certain presence to appear, was utterly brilliant.

We played the long game, a game Davie liked to play, and it materialised better than we could've ever imagined. Davie's worst nightmare of decaying behind bars for the rest of his days was close to fruition. Even though Rankin had planned on handing him to C4 Millacky, where a punishing end to life was forecast, I intended on delivering that harsh end to his life, but in more poetic way. All we needed to do was hand him in to the authorities where a cruel motive drew my desire for Davie's sentence. Knowing he'd get homed inside a maximum-security jail because of his reputation, Belmarsh, the same one as C4 Millacky and all his goons served time in. A bleak future awaited him.

As Jack started the engine, I turned to double-check Rankin, or should I say Lucille, had no pulse. Recumbent, with his head tilted back and eyes pulsed open holding a surprised gaze, he was dead alright. The bullet I fired landed straight into his heart and the aftermath spurts of blood glistened across Davie's famous bomber jacket and grim face as he gazed at me like a phantom. I'm sure he reckoned we were inside the motor to save his life; how wrong he was. I had no sorrow or guilt of having to kill Rankin, he deserved it for being a rat.

The initial shock was passing as Davie began mumbling through the duct tape. At first Jack and I ignored his call of attention but after only a minute it pissed me off, I knew he wouldn't stop until he had his say. I shared a glance with Jack.

"Don't do it kid, you'll regret it. Jack insisted as we were both aware I was thinking of removing the gag. After all, this car journey would be the last moments I'd ever spend with my father. I knew Jack was right because Davie had a habit of slithering out of unforeseen situations and this was one of those it'd be typical of him to wriggle out of. I wanted to gloat over his misfortune so I hesitated no longer, swung round in my seat and ripped the tape off in one quick swipe.

"What kind o' game you playin' here boy?" His tone was sharp, and his question was more of a statement, indicating he thought I'd saved him from his impending doom or should I say, Lucille. No 'hello' or 'how are you, son', just straight into his desperation to be unconstrained.

"Game! This is no game, and if it was, I've learned from the best." I turned to look out the windscreen and focus on the road as it signified the end of a loathsome journey. The closeness of our bodies wasn't filling me with pleasantry. I could almost hear his deceitful thoughts, running through scenarios of how this was possible and how he could attempt to wriggle out of his dilemma.

"So, come on 'en boy, tell yer old man, what's goin' on here?" His voice crackled in aggravation and again Jack and I shared a look of wondering if we would play his game.

"You'll find out soon enough," I answered, absent of any empathy.

Davie leant forwards and his coarse breath on the back of my neck made me shiver. I waited for him to shout abuse as that sentence surely indicated we were handing him over to the authorities. There he knew, his capture from Joe's house was a well-constructed plan, so implausible, so mind blowing, so finely calculated, Sherlock Holmes himself would find it most improbable and all Davie was trying to do, was fathom out what the fuck had just happened.

"Son, I don't know how you've pulled this off, but I'd suggest not handin' me in just yet. And where's Millacky?" Davie made an attempt to wriggle inside my head, but he wasn't wriggling his way inside my thought pattern. I'd waited too long for this moment. Davie somehow thought C4 Millacky was part of this plan, and he was right about that.

"You don't have to worry about him," I answered coyly, slowly swivelling around on the leather seat.

"Why don't you get comfortable, Da, and I'll tell you all about it?"

Chapter 2

Max McCabe:

I was a survivor, a warrior, an addict, an absent father, and a bad bastard. My deteriorating path through life had moulded me into the unsavoury character I became, but behind the layers of a woeful exterior and emotional cowardliness, there was a reasonable man, a man who would not surface until a painful awakening. My life could be summed up as a clusterfuck of pain and agony with a few callous moments of joy that did not seem worth remembering. Years of trauma, inner torture and building anger, contaminated me from a tender age before I would be reborn, and for that to happen, I had to grace the devil's presence.

Over the years, the imprisoned problems I carried around weighed as heavily on me as trying to drag along a broken-down tank, hooked around my ankle with a dog lead. I swam across a river of hardship and it moulded me into who I would become. There were never any answers to my bleeding calls for help as my innermost pleas for mercy were a vindictive, unanswered tease, rebounding off the walls of my brains, building to an eruption of frustration that no human should have to bear. And those who did, were unlucky, and some who did, did not live to tell the tale of how they tried to dance through the Reaper's wrath.

When it came time to bear the pain of the bare knuckle, I laid my jaw on the end of a plank and my life on the line, for the thrill and that unyielding release of adrenaline that made me feel alive. Letting my fists fly through the air like deployed bullets, brought a welcomed feeling, a feeling of not remembering the castrated pain that had congregated inside me since birth, but to be truthful, that pain kept me alive. In time, I learned to release that anger in horrific ways, ways that scared me so much, it became as natural to me as passing air.

The name given to me at birth was Max McCabe, but I managed to gather a couple more in my time, The Reaper or Eclipse, depending on what night of the week it was and which loathsome character I worked for. I lived my life without a birth certificate, a National Insurance number or any form of identification in the civil world. I was a man with no identity, I didn't exist! Since as far back as my memory would stretch, I knew I didn't have a life similar to other kids. During my early years of childhood, I'd been rejected, shackled and tossed between care homes and foster parents. Inducted into various schools across Liverpool and Lancashire. I was manipulated like a pawn and controlled by meddling adults and rotten foster parents. I knew what the impact of a fist felt like before I could make a cup of tea. I didn't know what a normal or routine life consisted of, and I grew up in admiration of other kids who had that. I learned that, to survive that tough time, I had to keep my mouth shut.

The concept of a mother didn't exist for me and throughout my life, I had always wondered why I was not wanted by her. I'd been told that I had been left inside the door of a Catholic church called Our Lady of The Annunciation, located in Childwall, Liverpool.

But even I didn't truly believe that. Apparently, there was only a note left with me, spelling my name: Max McCabe. The people of the clergy took me into a house, connected with the church and soon I had a better start to life than I had been handed. There was no record of my birth, anywhere across Merseyside or England. I had a few mothering figures during my childhood years, nuns, social workers, foster parents but none of them filled the empty cavity that yearned for love. Not having a mother is what most likely led me down the road of personal destruction. I lived in a state of confined frustration, where encased anger suffocated itself inside my bones. In time, they would name me The Reaper and I learned to release that anger in horrific ways.

My father, Davie Rhodes, was a man I'd always looked up to, until the night I had fought my blood brother, Joe Marks. Davie was a formidable man who manipulated me into respecting him, from a harsh reputation and the fear of his explosive temper. From my early age, without realising, he controlled my scornful path through life.

Up to the age of 4, I was brought up by a couple in St Helens, Mrs and Mr Parker, who I believed were my real parents and called them Mom and Dad. My memory of them hardly existed anymore, the recollection of them seemed like a fantasy. I can hardly recall what they looked like, nor did I have the empathy to care. There were jubilant fragments of memories that survived and I simply recalled they were loving and kind. I lived in a lavish home where I was hugged, fed and cared for, without conditions attached. I had a hoard of toys and a colourful bedroom. They repeated regularly that they loved me, and those sacred words were what I longed to hear all the years after I left their existence. Words that wouldn't herald a use for in the underground of the degenerate worlds in which I would become enthralled. If I had been given the pleasure of staying with the Parkers, my life could have materialised much healthier than it turned out to be. I probably would never have known that I had been adopted. I had never been given an honest answer about why they gave me up; all I remembered from the social care system was that they told me they couldn't cope with being my parents.

Four years old, frightened to death, I was housed inside a god-awful, privately run care home in Wirral and little prepared for the childhood of horrors I was about to experience. In the aftermath of being ditched, I was informed by the senior figures at the home that the Parkers had adopted me from the age of a few months. That news harshly confused me and had a severe effect, as I learned what being adopted meant. I crawled into a passive shell, spoke little, and interacted even less with other kids of my age. My confidence was shattered and I tiptoed into a bleak place in my mind. Looking back, that was the first time I felt lonely and abandoned, a feeling that stuck to me like the unwanted stench of sewage.

Life had handed me an early blow and it would be the first of many.

I spent the next two years in the children's home where I began my schooling. Right from the start, I suffered from a lack of concentration or interest; it was hard to tell which. All the kids inside the home came from dysfunctional backgrounds, that we didn't dare speak or think about. It was normality for us. I differed from them in a way: they seemed to be able to forget about their past problems, laugh, caper around and learn from what the teachers taught them. At nights I could not sleep. I lay awake, locked in a trance of unwanted thoughts. I spoke to very few people and when I did, it was only through necessity. I separated myself from society.

Davie Rhodes was a figure who danced in and out of my childhood on a few separate occasions whilst I was between foster parents and care homes.

At the age of five and a half, I was under the guidance of a children's psychiatrist and pushed into private tutor lessons. In the middle of one of those tutorials, an abrupt man blatantly barged in and interrupted our session. A huge man to a young kid, dressed roguishly in a bomber jacket and denim jeans. He had a stiff, hardened scowl with a deep Scottish growl. His abrupt manner gave me a frightening dawning of intimidation. He wasn't like any other man I'd come across: he stood with an aura of strength, talked firm and straight-up without respect for authority, where he spouted a story of how he had cleared it with the head of the home, so I could accompany him for the day. I suspect now, he had bribed the person in charge for my day release. Davie had a habit of getting what he wanted in difficult situations.

It was a late Wednesday afternoon and I was sceptical as to who he was, but he spoke to me respectfully and politely as if I was an adult or his friend and not a lesser person. He told me to call him Davie, and I did. I think a part of me knew straight away who he was; my instinct tried to tell me but any logicality that could have existed in the growing egotistical part of my brain couldn't accept that.

Firstly, we headed straight into a bookie's, placed a few bets and won a considerable amount on a horse called…Eclipse. It was all so new to me and I was fascinated by the experience. It was a trip to Goodison Park after that where we watched Everton beat Southampton 3-1 in a FA cup replay. It was the most thrilling day of my life, being absorbed in the atmosphere of the crowd and I smiled all the way through it, realising that man did not want to hurt me in a physical way. He filled my pockets with money, bought me an Everton home shirt, pies and a bucket load of sweats to take back to the home. That earned me some brownie points with the other kids and took me out of my box for a moment.

Back then, it was strange, a Scottish man turning up randomly and holding me in his company. I say 'holding' because it never seemed as if there was a choice but I did not resist either. When he left, I longed for this hero to return and shower me with attention and gifts again.

This happened randomly over the years: every time he popped into town, he'd make a point of visiting, wherever I was. Little did I know that he was mingling between two lives, one from Aberdeen and one from Liverpool. He'd appear at some of the foster homes I was in and often there were awful folks I wanted to part from, like one vile couple, both alcoholics, who used to beat me and the other kids there. When I told Davie this, the day after, the police turned up and arrested them and I was returned to another home. Other random times he appeared when I was playing football for the school team or during lunch times at school. The more it occurred during my childhood years, the more I welcomed it. It was a shame that welcoming thought changed to a murderous one. For a long time, I looked up to that man with no imminent thoughts of violence and it took something out of this world to change my views.

Chapter 3

The Beginning of the End:

That cold November night on the banks of the Clyde in Glasgow will always be the night I would remember until I departed from my final thoughts. Two years prior to Davie's capture at the door of Joe's house, a legendary fight took place in the dorms of an abandoned basement in Glasgow, and it was that night that would re-write my fate on this planet.

I had been there all too many times, felt the glorious feeling of victory, witnessed the quivering sight of cowardice fall to the ground and the sinful death of men by my hands. I held no remorse for my victims, ruthlessly willing to repeat the scenario on any occasion to remain triumphant. I was relaxed in the depths of my violent thoughts, thoughts that swirled through my brain right back to my four years of age where life started to career downhill. I was at ease with rage, my mind battle-hardened to the sights of the un-human. That world was my home. There was no happy future written for men like me. I didn't think I deserved one as my life had been carved out in this direction from birth. After I tore Joe apart, I would do this no longer. My greed for victory and pain was the only thing I desired in life because it was the only thing I was good at. Looking down on my victims, broken and covered in their own blood, fulfilled my worth, the only thing I lived for was my only joy in life, others' pain. I had no idea how I'd live without it, but everything has to come to an end.

Like any other night I fought, my bulking frame was pumped with hostile meaning and the fact I knew it was my brother I was about to face, only fuelled my desire. Two sons of Davie Rhodes would compete for the crown of our father's understudy. I had to prove I was the tougher of the two; to me, anything less would be a defeat. His end had to be the same as any other and I was prepared to walk through bullets to remain unbeaten.

After that night, I conceded to a truth that I was a beast, an unholy monster who had reached the end of the road of self-destruction. I was addicted to that sole sucking environment where showing emotion is weakness. Any sane man would have taken the first turn off that scornful road and my time to take that exit was near. That was my last dance, my last flirt with death and the last time I'd have to be cast as Jacks pupil in the fighting game. He had profited from me for too long and revelled in being my manager.

After that night Jack would be finished.

My body chilled, amalgamated with the nervous jolts of uncontrolled apprehension. The release was building, where the unfair pain I'd suffered in my childhood would be unleashed with welcomed relief from the harbour of imprisoned thoughts I could never release. I would forget about everything. I had become a figure of intimidation, emanating from my size and revulsion for life. My tense build of a muscled, wide barrelled six-foot three beast, proclaimed my stature to frighten any warrior who had to face my frame. I welcomed the unfortunate men who grew too many balls and visualised de-throning me from my position and Joe was one of them like any other.

I tried to beat Joe with as much power as I could attain, with every ounce of strength I had in me and every bit of rage I could muster but it was never enough, nothing could have been enough. The last thing I'd remembered was being in a state of exhaustion and absorbing a jaw-breaking punch to the head, gathered from sheer anger and courage, driven from the gully of Joe's might. His will not to be beaten made him the most violent and unpredictable man I'd faced. Even more than the Gypsy. I collapsed onto the ground and a boot into my face sent me to a dark place, a place that I'll never forget.

I had never faced a man with as much bravery as he had. Davie must have had his hand in raising him with the same ruthlessness he conveyed. All the people I had faced before him fell, some cowardly, some took a Goliath beating, but none levelled on the same playing field as Joe, with a heart that couldn't be broken: that was the scariest thing to face, a man with guts. He was prepared to die before he'd be defeated, and I gathered strength from every corner of my being, but it wasn't enough, nothing could've been enough. Joe beat me in the only fight I had suffered defeat, or death as it became apparent, and changed my entire life. The scrap was long and exhausting between two battle-hardened bare-knuckle warriors. We cemented our history in that basement, history that had seen the hardest of men fight there over the years and nobody in that room would ever forget the names of Joe Marks and Max McCabe.

Chapter 4

What on God's Fucking Earth:

The next thing I remembered was utter confusion, sucking in a bucket of air, then punching and kicking hard steel in an upheaval of anxiety. I was static and at first, thought I was trapped inside a coffin, but then I realised I was crunched up in a tight spot. It was pitch black and I lay bare chested where my body trembled hysterically with shock, cold or probably both.

After a minute or so when some senses returned, I realised around my mouth was covered in dried blood with the right side of my lip dangling off the side. After kicking and screaming like a maniac, I became aware of a car boot opening and exposing me to the dark sky. I leapt out, roaring like a beast. I grabbed Jack by the neck and tried to choke him to death in the process. While I stood with a clenched jaw and bore a look of fury into his slithery, wrinkled eyes, the chill of the night restlessly passed through me: my hair stood on their ends, my legs twitched with weakness and my body was glazed over with a numbness. The prior events of that evening were recalled like rapid stills of slides interchanging and it dawned on me whose life I was draining. I let go and when I did, Jack fell over a gravelly surface, desperately sucking the air into his lungs.

"What on God's fucking earth?" he cried, inhaling welcomed breaths of oxygen, dragging himself backwards across the dusty ground. To him, there was a ghost in front of his confused eyes and that assessment was accurate. He struggled to his feet as I remained silent. "You're alive!" he spouted, as I ran my hands over my body, pinching and clutching my skin, coming to with a horrible unearthly feeling of being unwelcome in his world.

"Where am I?" I looked around in the dark of the early morning, only a glimmer of a mustard-coloured streetlamp shining over the remoteness of the location, on the banks of the Mersey River.

"Do you know what's happened tonight, Max?" Jack called in an anguished pitch, crackling through his Scouse tone, wondering if I knew what was going on.

"Did I die?" I responded quickly. The events of the evening weren't that clear to me; nothing was sober in my mind, but I was certain I had just died. At that point, I remembered it felt as if I had awoken from a vivid dream. I recalled a dark place, empty of light or hope and a part of me didn't want to move on from that moment, as if I might lose the memory because it seemed so outlandish. How time passed became questionable to me. It felt as if I had just spent eternity at the turnstile into Hell, but I hadn't aged. The reality was, I'd only aged hours. I could already tell, my time on the edge between life and death was slipping away. One part of my mind was still there, and another part was tuning back in.

"It's a fuckin' miracle……a miracle," Jack said, stunned and open eyed as I turned to look at his waned face before being distracted by the lamppost light. The only one I could see at the end of a narrow road that crossed a train track. In the distance over the marshy grass, I could see a pub sign, The Ferry Tavern.

"A miracle!" Jack mouthed with awe and like a thudding jab, it hit me. Jack had a date with a grave himself. It was Davie's plan, or should I say, our plan, to execute him so there weren't any ties to our past, before fleeing to Panama. The entire time, from leaving the jail up until then, I loathed the sight, the voice and idea of Jack Gallagher. I spent years hoping to serve his head on a chopping block. But realism engulfed me like a dawning epiphany, my entire life of pain was due to Davie's deceitful meddling into my affairs. The countless foster homes, my beatings in jail, my life on the street and on the end of a bare knuckle. He controlled my desires, dreams and my walk-through life. He controlled my fate and now, I was unchained.

Still feeling half dead, Jack stepped towards me, gripped my arms, and dug his fingernails into my skin. He rattled me back and forth in a quick vigorous motion. "How can this be?" Jack turned from red to a pale white and he wasn't a man who reacted to his feelings. "Get in the car, lad, you must be freezing." The thing was, I was bitterly cold, but the part of me that was still dead, did not realise it. I noticed my speech was affected by my lip split in half and then I felt the harsh pain of the duel with Joe. It was as if my feelings were coming back like notifications pinging up on a mobile phone. I glanced at the river and then at the motor that had been reversed up to an embankment through two open gates that crossed the rail line. I looked to my feet and saw a large tarpaulin, rope and a collection of heavy rocks. I fixed my eyes on Jack, knowing he was here to dispose of my body into the Mersey.

"Here," he removed a hip flask from his inside pocket and tried to distract me with it, "drink this." He handed the flask over. I stared at it for a while, only to realise, "I don't drink!"

"Shit! Here," he fumbled into the passenger side door and took out a bottle of water. "Have this."

I took it and cracked it open.

Suddenly, sirens sounded, and a red light flashed. A train came from nowhere and bolted across a train line, startling my fragile state. I became mesmerised by it going by as Jack shouted something I could not hear. Once the train had passed, I stood open-mouthed, empty of thought, staring at a woman standing at the other sides of the tracks. She was frail, vampire-white, with greased dark hair and was willing me to join her by a gesture of her hand. Her arms were littered with bleak colours with a syringe hanging loose at the curve of her left elbow, around a covering of crusty blood. It felt as if I knew her! She waved me over and I began to walk forwards her when Jack shouted, breaking me out of my trance.

"Where's Davie?" In other people's company, I always referred to my father by his first name, always having done so ever since I first met him.

"What! You're confused, Max. Nobody's seen him in years." I looked back to Jack.

"Years! I saw him a few weeks ago!

Chapter 5

Stomach Cramps:

After fights, Jack had a tradition of taking me back to his house if I didn't have prior arrangements, making sure I was comfortable and gave me a bed for the night. It became a ritual and I didn't mind that as it saved getting aggro from Courtney, my girl, by coming in the door battered at all hours of the morning. It also gave me insight into his personal life. I always thought that was for his benefit, making sure my brain still functioned correctly and I still passed breath, so I could make profit for him in future fights but maybe there was a caring side to him, respectful of me, almost. The fights I'd been in were brutal affairs, because of the beasts I fought and the lengths I was willing to go to, to be victorious. I fought, filled with rage, which suffocated me and I had no care for myself, but I fought like that to never show weakness in the eye of the enemy. Davie taught me that. I happily took a punch because it awoke something ferocious inside, something beast-like.

Jack was my manager. In the underworld of fighting, every fighter has one. There was always a deviously minded, greedy, and power-hungry person in the background. It wasn't like a professional boxer's manager who somehow, behind the lure of profit, looked out for your health and interests; these were men who lived for notoriety in the darkened underworld. I always thought the world was against me, hence the reason I was so angry my whole life but maybe Jack did have my good intentions at heart. I never dreamed that anyone could.

As we drove from Warrington, a forty-minute drive east along the A62 to Liverpool, he must have asked me twenty times if I was okay. I had no energy for small talk, and I was still coming around to my second chance in life. My head pounded, tender to touch, my nose was broken, and my weary legs had no life. Words were few as my mind tried to formulate a reality as I questioned myself, if what I remembered from being at death's door, actually happened.

"I'll phone Bev," Jack said and then insisted. "Get her to call the doc, give you a once over." Beverly, or Bev as Jack called her, was his loyal wife who knew every bent thing he got up to.

"Alright," I answered in a weary drone, and I was far from alright.

"Only an hour or so and we'll be back." I'd never seen Jack care for another man like this. His emotions were normally locked inside a chamber and despite life or family troubles, he kept a cool head. He was no doubt thinking about disposing of my body in the Mersey before I woke up.

"Where we at?" Still confused, there was a level of sanity that hadn't returned to me as the vivid memories of my brush with the other world began to fade as I eased back into my existence. I kept zoning in and out from reality and forgetting where I was. I was sane enough to know I was suffering from concussion.

"On the way home. Just chill out, won't be long." He kept looking at my lip; I must have looked in a right state. "Here's some more water, get that down you."

Normally, I wouldn't take on a man trying to aid me, but I had lost something, a piece of my personality, or maybe I left it at the gates of Hell. I gulped down the water as Jack called Bev. A woman who was a rare sight outside of their house, preferring to stay out of the public eye, well knowing her husband was a glorified pimp and drug dealer, but despite her husband's imperfections, she loved him and was as loyal as a dog.

The rest of my time on the short journey to Liverpool was spent gazing out the window, reminiscing on the events of my life and what I really wanted out of the rest of it.

By the time we arrived, the doctor, Jerry, was waiting on the ash-coloured, semi-circular sofa that faced the marble hearth, a blazing fire warming the room. It was not the first time Jerry had helped me out. Bev stood, rigid, with her right elbow perched on the corner of the varnished oak fireplace. She looked rather elegant in her black silk dressing gown, with her long curling silver hair hanging well-conditioned past her shoulders, despite her looks fading in her early fifties. Her worry for me could be noticed over her nightly moisturised hard face as she looked at me with her head tilted in pity. Not sure what drove a man to the pit of fighting, time after time. Jerry was a retired man, late seventies. Going blind, wearing thick lenses, half deaf but had no problem coming to Jack's aid at six in the morning. He would be paid handsomely.

I slumped onto the sofa as Jerry began examining me. He rested the back of his hand on my forehead. "He's as cold as a dead man. Beverly, hot tea, bring me hot tea, blankets, and a warm hat, please?" he ordered in a posh Chelsea accent with a gravelly twang.

"Sure." She stood for a moment, eyeing me with a pitiful solid gaze before pulling herself away to hurry out of the room to collect the stuff. The shock of the affair was taking its toll as my hands trembled, my body shivered and my jaw jittered. Jerry prodded and pressed around my ribs as I groaned in a pitiful agony. He tilted his head back to see through his glasses that sat at the bottom of his nose and gingerly raised my loose lip up and down with his little finger.

"This is not good!" Jerry said mundanely, shaking his head and rolling his eyes in disagreement that I had put myself through such torture.

"What, doc?" Jack asked, appearing at my rear, already with a Japanese whisky in his hand and parading around the room.

"The lip. It's in rather bad shape, Jack." If I had had the energy and wasn't shaking like fuck, I would have mocked his stupidity. "It may need an operation, plastic surgery possibly. And he'll need a dentist to fix those teeth."

"Right, get him down to the ozzy, doc." Jack insisted, crashing his glass to the table, and walked out of the sitting room towards the metal hat and coat stand near the front door. His frenzied behaviour, I suspected, was relief that my death was not to be laid on his conscience. I lifted my hand and tried to say something to Jack, but I couldn't get the words out because my jaw clashed my teeth together. Bev returned, hearing the commotion, and put a woollen hat over my head and a blanket over my body. "Jesus, Max! You're shacking like mad, this isn't normal, doc, is it? Get the car to the door, Jack!"

I tried whispering to Jack, but it was a pathetic attempt. He left the room and returned with a coat.

"We need to get a move on, he's going into shock," Jerry stated frantically, as I conversed with myself, like a mumbling mad man, trying to gain Jack's attention. Beverly rubbed her hands up and down my arms, trying to rouse some heat. I was crazed with frustration that I couldn't speak.

"We can't go to the ozzy!" I finally mumbled, clearly enough to be heard.

"Max, you heard the man. If you don't get some surgery, it'll be deformed for life, and you shouldn't be shaking like that." Bev stated the obvious. Jerry was conflicted, shifting his look between myself and Jack, waiting for more instruction.

"As for the rest of your face, young man, I'll need to straighten that nose and dip your whole body into a bath of ice." The doc stood up and bent down, over my face, blocking my view of Jack. I nudged his body out of the way.

"Jack!" I gestured for him to come closer; as he approached and bent down, so his ear was next to my mouth.

I whispered in his ear… "Davie is the Eidolon."

He wrenched away, took two backwards steps, laced his arms and stood dead. His cold eyes rebounded in disbelief, holding the expression as his brain ticked over what I had said.

"Doc, sew him up as best as you can and sort out the rest of his injuries," Jack insisted.

"Are you mad, Jack? Look at the state of him."

Jack purposefully ignored answering Bev because of the magnitude of the information I gave him unfolded in his head.

"Get it done, doc!" The doctor knew when Jack asked him to do something, he'd better do it. Jerry momentarily had second thoughts, preparing to argue my need for a hospital but quickly knew that his response would be a wasted one.

"Right, let's get him lying down, shall we?" Jerry said, as Bev gave Jack an accepting eye roll before replying to the doctor.

"Take him up to one of the spare rooms!"

Jerry cleaned me up well and gave me some Tramadol for the pain. He straightened my nose and stitched my lip back together, informing me I'd be a lucky man to keep my looks. My teeth would remain cracked and broken for a good while. Under the blanket, I began to warm up, and I was forced to drink water. Jerry checked my heartbeat and said it sounded abnormally slow in comparison to my bodily state of panic, something he'd never encountered before. In normal cases, if a heartbeat was as slow as mine, I'd be near dead, he informed me. I did not want to explain to him that I had just died. As Jerry tidied up his stuff, Jack entered the room with some ice packs. I held one over my swollen nose and stuck another one on my ribs as I became sedated from the Tramadol.

"Doc, have a seat for a minute before you leave." He sat on an armchair under the window and Jack took his place on the bed, directly opposite. My eyes glazed over, and my chin sank into my chest, trying to stay awake.

"You're an old man, Jerry, you were a good friend to my folks. I've known you longer than anyone, someone who's helped me out on more occasions than I can remember. You hold some very delicate secrets of mine and I've trusted you to abide by that and you have not to let them out." Jerry sat with his spongy chin tilted toward his chest as his eyes peered over the top of his glasses, showing his feebleness of age. He wasn't quite sure where Jack was about to go with those words.

Jack slid his elbows down his thighs, holding a very serious frown into Jerry's eyes. "You know Max," he pointed his finger in my direction while holding eye contact with Jerry. "You'll hear rumours of his death, rumours that he is now rotting at the bottom of the Mersey. That you will agree with, and this will be the last conversation about the subject."

Jerry raised his bushy eyebrows, looked to me for a few seconds and then back to Jack who handed him an envelope, thickened with notes. "That retirement lodge you've been considering buying on the banks of Loch Lomond, consider it yours, Jerry, and take this gesture as an extra gift."

The doc held eye contact with Jack for a few seconds before answering, "I hope your wife's stomach cramps ease up, Jack. I'll nip back and forth to keep an eye on her." He picked up his medical bag and scuffled to the door. "Good day, gents."

That was Jack in his prime. He could wrap anyone around his finger and he had the bank balance to do it. Jerry was one of two people who knew I was still alive, and it needed to stay like that.

Chapter 6

Breakfast Bar:

I woke the next morning, drained, without spirit, lifeless and with no memory of a dream. The house was soberly quiet, and I felt a different air in myself compared to what I usually felt. My brain was quiet and calm for the first time in years. I no longer lived inside a bleak depression or had a bitter repulsion for life. Instead, I felt reborn from a brutal end. After I had been woken for a good ten minutes, I noticed my brain was a tad sharper than the night before. My body, however, was not relaxed: I'd never been in so much physical pain.

I looked at the bedside clock. 17.43. Probably the longest I'd slept in years without insomnia or nightmares. The burdens I'd carried throughout life didn't make for sound sleep. My entire life, I'd been a fighter in the true sense of the word. I'd been at war with myself and others around me for too long. I had never once felt shame or regret for the awful things I'd done. But now I had been given the chance to redeem my life of sin and fix a situation I should have woken up to years prior. First, I had to find Jack. On my bedside table was a mobile phone. I knew Jack's number off by heart, so I picked up the phone and called him.

"Jack, it's Max. Where you at?" Jack didn't answer me for a while. "Jack!"

"Max, I'll be back soon. I'm just driving back from the bank. Beverly's downstairs. Give her a shout, she'll sort you some food." I could then hear some movement downstairs. "Are you alright?" I was shocked at the man's concern for me.

"Aye, Jack, I'm living!" You see, I was never one for conversations of politeness. I was always wound up in a bad mood, obsessed with my hatred for Jack or the lure of the bare knuckle. I'd answer questions with as little input as possible and a lot of the time, I'd just plain ignore people.

"I'll be back soon." Jack laid down the phone and I shouted for Bev.

"I'll just be up, love," she replied. I lay there feeling helpless, but I've always felt a little helpless. I was withered and weak, a feeling I wasn't used to.

Bev walked into the room with a glass of water and some painkillers.

"Here you go, love. How you feeling?" she queried in a softened dense tone, making her Scouse seem soft, while placing her palm over my hand.

"I'm alright, Bev."

"I'm making some scran. How's a homemade steak pie sound?"

"Ohh aye, I could murder one of those."

"You must be starving?" Well, she wasn't wrong. I could've eaten a horse and some but the head injuries gave me a nauseous feeling.

"Just a little," I answered.

"Jack will be back soon, and the doc's coming round later. He was here earlier but you were asleep." She was a loving woman, Beverly, despite her hard exterior. Her sorrow for my condition fluttered over her manner.

"Max, there's something you need to know." Her tone changed to fiercely serious. I didn't ask, having a new feeling of dread hover over me. "I think you need to call Courtney." My worst thoughts came to mind, was she alright? I pulled myself upright on the bed. I had fallen out with her and we hadn't talked in months.

"Why, what's happened?" She picked up the phone and handed it to me.

"Just give her a call, let her know you're alright!" Courtney used to be my other half, someone who suffered too much at the other side of my moods and temper over the years. She was the only person I felt safe with, the only person who understood me, and I took it all for granted. I was prepared to leave her, ditch her, and flee to a new life with Davie and now, I had no idea why. I was stubbornly selfish and it took until then to realise that I loved her.

Beverly left the room and straight away I tried to call the flat on the landline. There was no answer. I tried her mobile and again, there was no answer. "Beverly!" I yelled and winced in pain from under my ribs which shot into my heart, as if I was being stabbed from the inside out. I couldn't take a breath, no matter how hard I tried. as I rolled over in the bed and crashed to the ground, whispering Beverley's name. In my head I was screaming. I desperately tried to suck in oxygen, but my lungs wouldn't inhale. My body seized and turned ice cold as I pitifully panicked. I tried to slither across the floor and shout again. And then, I managed to breathe, allowing the pain to subside. It just left me, instantly, and after I collected myself, I was able to stand.

I tottered, lightheaded, into the upstairs landing, over the spongy cream carpet, and headed down the half circle stairs to the kitchen.

"Beverly, there's no answer. What the fuck's going on?" My jaw trembled with the cold that sailed through me, wearing only my boxers.

"It's not up to me to say, love!"

"Well, fuck me, you have to."

Just then, Jack entered the kitchen through the back door, looking secretive. For the past few years, every time I looked into his slithery eyes, I wanted to yank them out with a fork. I loathed his snide and nonchalant manner and that hadn't changed.

"You need to get back to your bed!" he said assertively.

"What's happened to Courtney?" There was a deliberate pause as he walked towards me. "Take a seat."

"What!"

"Take a seat and I'll tell you."

I moved over to the centre, marble-topped breakfast bar and sat down as my whole body went into another obvious shiver.

"Beverly, get Max a robe, please!" That was Jack's way of stating he needed a minute alone. I did not care for a robe, neither did he. I only wanted to hear what was going on. "What you told me last night about Davie being the Eidolon, is that true?" he asked, with a dry throat, taking a step forward.

"It's true!" Jack analysed my statement, deciphering whether I was telling the truth and he had the radar to know. Jack stepped away from me. He seemed disappointed; he couldn't believe that Davie had been so close to him and now felt inferior to Davie's intelligence. I dared not tell him I was part of his stable of men who worked for him. I wanted to hear what Jack had to say.

Right then, the landline phone started to ring. I looked out, into the open foyer, where a side table I could not see, had the phone on it.

"I don't want to be looking over my shoulder my whole life. I don't want to live knowing he could appear at any second and kill me. I want to find your father and I want you to help me." The phone kept ringing. What he said met with my agreement: I did want to find him but that was not what I wanted to hear.

Beverly walked in, a robe in one hand and the phone in the other, looking at the screen. "It's Courtney!" she mouthed, waiting to see if she should answer.

"What's it got to do with Courtney?" I barked. Beverly still held the phone in her hand. I looked at her as Jack gripped my arm.

"I have a plan, a plan to catch Davie that involves you staying dead, so if you are to help me…then everything."

Chapter 7

Breakfast Continues:

Beverly left the room to answer the phone, leaving me in two minds, whether to grab it from her or carry on listening to Jack. When Jack mentioned I had to 'stay dead', his plan intrigued me, arousing my curiosity. My first reaction should have been, 'What was up with Courtney?', but it was not. My attention was diverted.

"What's it got to do with Courtney, then?" I asked Jack again, after my thinking slowed down.

"You told me you knew where Davie will be?"

"I did!"

"Where?"

"There's a good chance he's going to turn up on your doorstep."

"What?"

"I'm dead...Right! People think I'm dead?" I asked, still bemused by the whole affair.

"Yes, everyone thinks you're dead and that's part of my plan. You have to remain dead." Jack was itching to unfold his plan but there was something he wasn't getting through his stubborn skull, and something he was holding from me.

"No, listen! Davie is planning to kill you. After the fight, he is coming here to kill you." Jack became speechless, open eyed as he glued the story together. That story included my involvement in that plan.

"You were part of this!" Jack said, as his eyes rolled away from me, sunken in disgust, but that disgust was not at my double-cross but in his inability to see anything coming.

"I was, aye." I didn't see the need to hold back on that answer since he'd already figured it out.

"That's savage, after all I've done for you. Seems the apple doesn't fall far from the Rhodes tree, Max." He had the cheek to say that, the man sent a fifteen year old to jail! "Listen, you cunt!" I gripped his throat, stood him up and backed him into the kitchen cupboards. "You put me in a fucking jail! That's right, I know about that." For the second time in a matter of twenty-four hours, I had him by the throat as he gargled for breath. My eyes spread wide as the fury cascaded through me once again, an instant transformation and something I didn't welcome any more. As the red mist spread across me, a rapid flash of the frail woman with the syringe sticking out of her arm, standing by the train tracks, suffocated me. That made me release my grip as Jack flustered backwards over the worktop and sucked in the air.

"You do that again," he yelled and removed his Walther PPK from inside his coat. "And I'll fucking shoot you, you understand?" Beverly returned, on hearing all the commotion.

"Jack…not in the house," she said, serenely calm as if seeing a gun was an everyday occurrence. He hesitated and very slowly lowered the gun to waist height. Why? Because he now needed me as much as I needed him.

"Ok, time for some home truths," he insisted. "Yes, I had you arrested, filled Carlin's wallet to bend the rules and bypass any legality proceedings. I had to get rid of any connection to your father and I didn't want to kill you, cos you were only a boy."

"So, here's a piece of karma for you, Jack." I began to walk towards him as he thought about raising his gun again. "That disgusting place turned the boy into a man and here I stand." I powered over his height and looked at him as there wasn't one hint of remorse in his eye. A technique he'd either mastered over the years, or remorse didn't exist in his mind. With Jack, it was impossible to tell.

"I can see the man, but the question is, does the man have reason not to kill me?" Jack pondered aloud, as Beverly stood, an inquisitive spectator, who only knew not to meddle too far into Jack's affairs, but she looked on, eager to know the whole truth of this matter.

"I want to find the cunt..." That was the one and only reason I had. I would not take any more aggressive action towards Jack's path to death but, like any man in his line of work, an uncomfortable death was always going to be inscribed onto the end of his timeline.

"Well, back off, sit down and tell me what Davie's plan is?"

I went through the formalities of the plan. The will I had professionally constructed and planted inside Jack's locked drawer in his office at McCartney's. The will, leaving his club, properties and cars to Ringo who was made the power of attorney, and the house on Millionaires Row to Bev. I told of the getaway to Panama, and the part that sickened Jack the most, being prepared to let Davie into his house and allow him to put a bullet into his brain while he slept beside his wife, who we intended to put to sleep with chloroform. This took some time to sink into Jack's brain. For one, Davie almost done him over in the past and the other factor he couldn't get his head around was my lack of loyalty towards him, but in reality, I was my father's son and he should have known better. But the tide of affairs had turned now. If I were to get my hands on my father, I'd need Jack's help. Jack sat speechless as I gave him a very detailed account of the plan. When I was done, he stood up and walked to the drinks cabinet, returning with a bottle of whisky and two glasses. He was cunning. I could tell there was a mouse running through a maze in his head, forging answers to questions and constructing a plan. He poured a couple of generous glasses and Beverly walked over, giving me the evil eye as she grabbed one vigorously.

"Jack's right, you're more like your father than you think." Over the years, I had to mix the hatred I had for Jack with the burgeoning need to get the better of him in the long run. It was a plan that could have been completed a lot sooner but Davie's addiction to gunrunning, and mine to the bare knuckle, prolonged the completion of that plan.

"That may have been true, but not now, now we both have a chance to get what we want." Jack re-filled his glass and asked, "So, where is he?"

"Right now, I can't be sure."

"I thought you knew?"

"I can tell you where he was last night." He waited eagerly as he lowered his glass. "He was watching, In the basement." Jack threw back his seat.

"What! He was there! How did no one see him?" "He's become a man who lives on the run. He's mastered it."

Jack was seething with annoyance as he pounded around the room and downed another drink. He couldn't believe he had been within spitting distance of his foe. Then he stopped dead, raised his head and lit a cigarette from his holder.

"Wait a minute! He thinks you're dead!" Something had hit home as his eyes gleamed a sparkle of delight.

"This is good, very good." He refilled his glass as well as Bev's. Then he decided to turn into Sherlock Holmes. "Ok, so, Mr Rhodes will still plan on killing me, that's a cert, I'm sure of it. The escape from The Eradicator, Sam Bryson, and now this…he thinks you're dead, he'll blame me, that's also good." His words battled with each other for release. "You must stay dead and…we can't go to him because we don't know where he is…We will wait…In this house for the next couple of days and he will come straight to us. Beverly, how does that sound?"

"I don't think it's Davie you have to worry about. I'd be more concerned about this lying shit sitting here." Beverly had never spoken to me like that before but who was I to argue with the truth? Jack walked back to the bar and sat down.

"Why have you so suddenly changed your mind?" he asked.

"Look at the state of my face, look at the life I've been led on. It's all down to him. I want to finish what no one else has been able to do, end him and his legacy."

"Good, then we're on the same page." From the moment Davie had escaped the Eradicator, Jack had been a paranoid mess. He would never show that side of himself on the outside, requiring to keep a level head in the public eye but instead it ate him up on the inside. Getting rid of Davie was his number one goal. Like an athlete chasing that final medal before retirement.

"Right, so no more pissing about, what's the deal with Courtney?" Suddenly, something happened, totally out of character for his personality. A grin stretched across his face.

"You're a father now. She gave birth last night. You had a boy."

"A boy!" I had never wanted a child. What did I know about looking after someone else? I didn't know how to look after myself and I didn't want to bring a child into this degenerate world I was living in. "Take me to her," I ordered frankly, surprising myself by saying that. Now, I understood what compassion was, and in my heart, it occurred that I deeply cared for, and loved, Courtney. Straight away I had to sit down and bury my head in my hands, flooded with deep regret and pangs of guilt. I had been rotten to her; I gave her nothing but worry and the cold shoulder of my inner self. Now she was with a child and heavily grieving. She would be contemplating the struggle and money worries she would have without me by her side, for the rest of her life.

"I can't, and you know that," Jack answered. The cunt of it was, I knew he was right. "You want your father's blood then you must remain dead, for that sole reason. That is reason enough for your father to drop his guard and appear somewhere. There's a massive chance he will come here for that was your plan and I'm asking you to contain yourself for only a few more days."

Everything he said was true, but there was a vast flood of shame, that I wasn't there for Courtney when she needed me and that weighed heavily on my conscience. I had not talked to her for months and I had no empathy for her pregnant state as I remained focused on battering my brother, killing Jack and fleeing to Panama.

"Is she alright?" I asked.

"She's perfect, according to what Jerry has told me and you can ask him yourself when he comes around tonight to check on you. She's still in hospital and I can send Beverly around to check on her, if that helps." He pointed to her.

"Can you take me there? I can explain everything to her." I was desperate.

"You can't go anywhere near her. Not anyone outside of Beverly, Jerry, and me can know you're alive. It's the only way this is going to work."

"Does she think I'm dead?"

Jack sobered and stared through me. Even he felt concerned about this situation.

"Everyone thinks you're dead!"

Chapter 8

For the Next Few Days:

For the rest of that evening, I spoke to Jack about the handful of times I had met Davie over the years, while he was gathering a name for himself as a proficient gunrunner who lived an obscure life in the shadows of reality. I left out the information about me being part of that franchise. It was something I didn't need to tell him, and it wasn't going to change whatever plan he had constructed. Jack was an intelligent genius when it came to plotting revenge and he was always willing to go the extra mile. I needed him as much as he needed me. If only we knew what that extra mile meant at that time.

His house, located on Millionaires Row, was fitted out with CCTV cameras and a state-of-the-art burglar alarm system. Areas across the lawn, leading to the gate and around the rear, were covered in motion detectors, setting it up so any uninvited guests would be noticed before it was too late. If set off, they triggered a silent alarm that flashed from a beacon in four different parts of his house. One of them was inside his and Bev's bedroom. Every approachable angle to the house was covered and if anyone got inside, they would have to cope with Jack's rottweilers, which had a notorious reputation for being savages, but Jack had them trained well and in a click of the fingers they would rip through anything in front of them.

Jack moved into his home study for the foreseeable future, allowing him the solitude for his criminal mind to construct a devious plan. He used a TV, two laptop screens and his tablet for live viewing of his future. All I could do was play dead. My thinking patterns were unclear. I did not know what was happening. At times, it felt like dementia and then, when I'd have a sleep, I'd waken to feel more refreshed. I had no track of the time or what day it was. That was the result of a history of head trauma and severe concussion.

Jack had all the approaching viewpoints covered at the house, but we had no eyes on the ground, except for Eiffel. He was instructed to open McCartney's and keep an eye on the place, hoping that Davie would appear. Jack was a guarded criminal; he didn't like to give anything away. He instructed Eiffel to hit a panic button in his office if any unwelcome guests appeared and he had a link to watch the cameras at McCartney's for which he used his laptop. He cowered into a man with few words, his brain concentrated on the task at hand. Jack not showing face at his club was a strange thing; it was an attachment of his arm. Automatically, those who heard of my death would think he was panicking about his own future; they certainly wouldn't think he was in a stage of grieving.

I was still in a great deal of pain and it didn't feel like letting up. I was happy to let Jack do all the cautionary thinking because it was not in me. I wasn't stupid, but Jack had lived this life for thirty plus years, knew the insides and outsides of every possible formality and probably had back up plans for everything.

The next couple days passed as if they never happened for me. During those days, I began to have mood swings caused by frustration, a part of the recovery process from the head trauma. Sleeping gave me reprieve from the confusion. When I woke from naps, briefly I had more clarity of what was occurring, but soon enough, my brain would drift away into a haze. I began to accept that the beating had changed me for the rest of my lifetime, and I held no resentment towards Joe for causing that. My ability to hold a grudge had diminished as my life had been full of hate and I had no space for it anymore. My thoughts about Courtney and young Max were vague and filled with guilt but a couple of minutes later, I couldn't fathom why I was feeling guilty. To get through the confusion, I had to hope that it was a passing phase, and I would not be like that for the rest of my breathing days.

Into the fourth day, on waking, I walked into the study. Jack sat heavy-eyed at the desk, and a tad inpatient, and not because he'd been up all night staring at a screen. It was as if he was waiting for me to enter, with an idea lying in wait. I brought him a coffee as a good gesture, laid it in front of him on his desk and sat across from him.

"Have you been up all night?" There was no response. The question, I already knew the answer to. His eyelids were hitting the desk and he didn't seem to have the energy to talk.

"Why don't you go sleep? I'll sit here for a while," while glaring at the screen, I suggested.

"I need to nip out for a few hours. you sit here and don't move."

"Why?"

"That document, the will. Where is it?"

"It's inside the bottom drawer of your desk, why?" Ignoring me, he swivelled his chair round and opened a cupboard where the security control box was. He leant down and switched off the motion detectors.

"You ask too many questions!" Just like that he stood up and walked out. I took his seat and watched a man who looked as if he was in a rush, leap into his Range Rover and spin the tyres over the gravel-filled drive as he left. I switched the alarms back on and made myself comfortable.

Bev, approaching the door, leant against the frame and folded her arms. She was in her robe again and by the look of her heavy eyes, she was sharing Jack's anxiety.

"Where's he off to?" she asked.

"Who knows!" I answered.

"Were you around the flat last night?" I asked Bev, to check up on Courtney.

"She's healthy, Max, and so is your son. He's a beautiful boy." I felt guilt like I'd never felt before, the burden of gathering a conscience was not a welcomed one. But, I was happy they were both healthy. I should have been thinking of catching Davie but all that went through my mind was that I had a child I could not hold in my arms. On top of that, because she thought I was dead, she named him Max. The irony was painful.

"How's she coping?"

"Thinking you're lying on the bottom of the Mersey, you mean?"

"Aye."

"Not well. She blames herself. Keeps saying she should've tried to make you stop fighting."

"Once this is done, I'll make it up to her…Somehow. I'm finished in this game." There was never a truer word said as Beverly gazed blankly at me, not knowing if there was any truth in my statement.

I reminisced on the ruthless environment of the fighting world I took part in. Full of scum and degenerate men, men willing to watch as their friends and foes battled it out, with rage and anger ruling their intentions, willing to let death be the result of victory in some cases. Beverly knew too well that the unsolicited world housed these men but the thing with her, she liked being on the arm of a man, smart enough to come out on top all the time and that's why I needed Jack.

"You have a second chance. Not many people are blessed with that. Use it to make amends."

"Second chance?" I asked her, as I had a memory lapse of what we were talking about and made a quick U-turn when I remembered. "I intend to!"

She noticed I was still out of it but she also saw I had changed into someone caring, and I think that was scarier to me than rotting on the bed of the Mersey.

Chapter 9

The Day the Tide Turned:

Jack arrived back at the house later that day, in a silver Mercedes Benz S class, a car I had not seen him drive before. During the time he was gone, I stayed glued to the cameras, being most interested in the ones at McCartney's. Eiffel was seeing to Jack's duties of keeping the girls in order, the staff in check and collecting the cash income from Jack's drug runners and brothels. He was performing as the loyal dog he was known to be. Something unusual happened when I watched Eiffel attending to Jack's errands. I relived the fight I had with him years ago, battling through the memory and a spire of shame suffocated me, almost unable to hide from it. I swept the feeling to the side and tried to ignore it.

Jack walked into the study and chucked an ample duffel bag onto a seat. He also had the document from his drawer. I witnessed him remove it on the live camera feed a couple of hours earlier.

The tenseness and anxiety he had exhibited before slackened somewhat and became eager to tell me something.

"Max, the plan is evolving," he said, raising his thickened brows.

"What?" I countered quickly, knowing he was itching to let it spill.

"You're dead!" I remember thinking that whatever the idea would be, it would be radical. He began striding back and forth, with elaborate hand movements. "You reckoned Davie was going to turn up here! I don't think he will now. Whatever he is doing, his thought patterns will be dealing with grief ... for you. I know he'll turn up sometime but who knows when so I'd rather he thought I was dead too. It's a play so he'll let his guard down. I'm not certain or sure if it'll work but..." he shrugged his shoulders, "it could be an advantage."

It was insane but he was right in that it could help us to deceive Davie and catch him out. And I was sure that he'd turn up for Jack's head sometime.

"You're going to fake your own death!" He began to smile, disturbingly enjoying his own smartness.

"It's a brilliant idea, kid. If he comes for me, wherever he turns up, if it's here or the club, and he finds out I'm dead, then that'll be our trump card."

"How are you going to pull that off?"

"Easily. Jerry will arrive later and sign a death certificate. I died of a heart attack. Then straight away, I'll have a big funeral, a cremation and then that's it, I'm charcoal."

Because Jack had just been seen out and about, he didn't want to pretend he died that day. He would formulate a story that he would pass away later that night.

"And what happens when someone sees you after your cremation?"

"We only need to be dead for as long as it takes to catch Davie. That won't take long and then," he dropped his palms on the study table and leaned towards me, "we can return from the dead. It'll be a thing of beauty."

"This is a bit mad, is it not?"

"Mad? It's optimistically stupid but this is how I became the man I am today. I did not become Liverpool's top asset by being simple or soft."

"What about money and where we going to stay?"

"Money is no problem. I have bank accounts in different names and I'll carry plenty of cash." The plan began to sit home with me. And the more he talked, the more I thought it could work. I thought of my own dilemma that it could still be a while before I saw my kid and Courtney. It was such a wild plan, the chances of it phasing out were impossible to calculate. But, apart from my family, there was nothing preventing me. I wanted Davie to suffer for the life he'd created for me but I don't think I was prepared to end his life. One man certainly was, and I had time to come to terms with that. I needed him to suffer but I wasn't keen on murdering him. My tale with harm and death ended after Joe finished that phase of my life. I don't think I was prepared for Jack to have his way with Davie, but I had time to talk it out of him.

Wherever Davie was at that moment, one thing was for sure, he'd be at the bottom of a bottle and contemplating on doing something erratic. Whatever ounce of goodness he had inside him would be grieving for one son and fuming at the other. That impractical situation of watching both of your sons go to war must have been nerve-racking. I had filled Jack in with lots of information over the past couple of days and he'd still be processing it. His idea of playing dead was a good one but the bigger reason for it was to get away from the carnage and think clearly.

Jack started belting out everything that had gone through his head. He already had other various bank accounts under different identities, stashes of large amounts of cash and he'd even picked out a coffin from an online brochure. He had fake identities and passports ready for a backup plan in case his empire went south. I had fake identities and a few passports that I'd gained in the past from Davie that I had never used. He used my knowledge of where I'd met him over the years since he escaped his torture episode and where I thought he might return to but honestly, I didn't know, no one knew. Well, maybe Rankin; he seemed to be the one most in contact with Davie, and then there was Turk and Barb. They would have had their own meeting points with him. I figured the best guess would be southern Ireland and I told Jack that. The one major problem I had was I couldn't contact any of them because I'd give up the con.

Finding Davie would be the major task, not faking deaths or becoming invisible and I knew the next sighting of him would be our best opportunity to catch him. If he turned up at Jack's door, then that would be like winning the lottery on a single line. I knew how masterful he was about living in obscurity, out of anyone's sight. I always imagined he had a hideaway somewhere in a place so remote, only he would know of it, like a cottage hidden in the Scottish Highlands or a tin hut in Sarajevo. Jack's plan was semi-thought out, but I wasn't sure if he had thought about what he was leaving behind or giving up; and at that point neither of us thought we'd have to sacrifice so much.

"What about Bev, your club, this house, your lifestyle? You'll be giving it all up." I was happy going along with that idea. It made no difference to me at the time, as I was already a dead man and the number one thing I wanted was to return to Courtney and young Max. If I had to play along with it, then so be it.

"You make it sound like this will take years. This will be done and dusted in a couple of weeks." He was not prepared for the dedication this would require and I don't think he had any inkling that it was about to take so long. "Bev will be sound and understand, the house will look after itself and the club…" He paused and slapped the envelope with the will in it onto the desk. "This is very smart, Max, I give you kudos for it but I suppose it was your father's idea." Jack was such a hard man to read, he spoke without emotion or attachment to anything but he was wrong about it being Davies idea. Was he revengeful towards our plan to kill him for what he had done to Davie or had he let it go, knowing there was now a bigger task at hand? I didn't answer because it was an awkward conversation to have. All I did was hold passive eye contact until he carried on. "You were going to hand the club to Ringo so let it stay the same."

"Ringo! You hate him?" Jack loathed his son and his lifestyle, and he was inviting that into his club.

"He's family…and it's time to let the past die." That was controversial and I did not believe it: he had an ulterior motive.

"He'll ruin the place," I belted out.

"No, he won't. He's always liked that place. Ever since he was little, he'd go in and play barman and pretend to be me. I'll see to it that Beverly gives him the keys on the condition that the minute she thinks he's abusing it, she can take it back. I'll make sure Beverly gets something legal to back that up. Make it concrete. I'll tell Beverly to tell him it was my dying wish he took it over. That'll buy him."

"It's your club," I nodded in agreement, accepting that this was about to happen; as Bev walked into the room, we lapsed into silence. She switched her look between us, a few times, then asked.

"What are you two talking about?"

Chapter 10

And Then We Went Away:

Bev was never taken aback by the things her husband did but that verged on the extreme for her. Jack pounded her with reason after reason as to why he had to do it but in reality, the most evident reason to him, was winning. He couldn't let it slide, he couldn't be number two, the loser, and he'd do anything to come out on top. Jack needed Bev to agree to the plan because she'd be his only contact. The only one we would be able to rely on. Eventually it was a petty reason that made her agree. She would get some time apart from Jack. They had spent the past thirty odd years together and although they loved and were devoted to, each other, the idea of some solitude from Jack greatly appealed to her. She would also be left to mend the bridge with Ringo. She wanted her son back, as the dispute in the family had driven a wedge between her and Ringo too. She would be the only person Jack would contact over the next two years; she was the helping hand in various tasks and chores that needed done that we couldn't do. It had gone eight at night and Bev called Jerry to explain that Jack had collapsed in the bathroom and died. Within the hour, Jerry had appeared at the door. Bev invited him in and took his coat. She led him to the sitting room where Jack was sitting with a whisky in hand. Jerry was confused and soon realised something else was afoot. Jack laid out the plan to him about faking his death and nothing more. I joined them in the living room as Jerry connected the dots that it was something to do with my imaginary death.

Jerry was bemused as to why someone would want to do such a thing but he never questioned the reasoning, knowing Jack had plenty of shadows in the closet. Nevertheless, Jerry agreed and he was paid to do what Jack wanted him to. After Jerry had filled out the death certificate, Jack swiftly showed him the exit, keen to make the arrangements to leave.

"That's the first step done," Jack said to Bev. "I've arranged a coffin to get here in the morning. It's bought and paid for and it's coming from Leeds. As soon as it's here, get some weight in it. I don't know what but you'll have to figure that out. Now the coffin needs to be sealed shut, that's a must, so no nosey cunts can look inside before I go into the furnace." Bev began to think about what to use as weight as Jack carried on, "When Ringo comes round, I want you to tell him that I wanted him back in our lives. Say we were talking about it a couple weeks back and then hand him the club on the conditions but get them legally written up. Everything I have is now yours for the time being. And I'll be back for it all come a few weeks."

"Please take your time," Bev said sarcastically, being overrun by her husband's compulsive disorder.

"I'll miss your humour, love," Jack countered. "Bev," I said. "I'll need you to make sure Courtney and Max are alright." When I called my son by my name, it really sank in that I had become a dad. "She can't struggle, she'll have my money but she'll need help.

She might come across tough but she's not. She's fragile and she cries a lot."

Bev stepped toward me and sighed. "What's happened to you?" she asked, bemused by my newfound nature.

"I wish I knew." She was fixated on my new-born personality.

"I'll check-up over the next few weeks, and keep you posted."

I nodded in thanks to Bev, after I convinced myself that it would only be weeks I'd be away. I shivered, thinking what reaction I'd get from her when I would return. I felt motivated to get into Jack's head.

"Have you thought about where we are going to go?" Jack spun around to me. "I have, and we're not going far. I've a flat in Waterloo, currently housed by some Albanians that I'll have evicted."

"Waterloo! That's in the middle of the city! How the fuck is that going to work? We'll be spotted in no time." "No, we won't, if we don't leave and out the back there is a secluded car park. You're still paler than an old Lada so you can have fresh air if you need it." The distraction of the situation took my mind off the pain my body was still in and the guilt about leaving Courtney with a baby to cope on her own. My brain, at times, was beginning to feel more normal, but I was nowhere near recovered.

"And how are we getting there?"

"You worry too much. I'll arrange everything." He did have it all sorted. He already had a car waiting outside. He had a host of properties to choose from so I suspect this one would be fitting. He started loading the car with a bunch of his laptops and monitors, all the necessary accessories to make them work. His bag of clothes was next, along with an assortment of things he thought would fit me. I only had the clothes on my back so I would take anything going. Bev packed the food and drink.

Once the motor was near ready to go, the rumour had to be started. Jack instructed Bev to call Ringo. She gave herself some encouragement with a couple of straight vodkas before picking up the house phone. Only serious calls were made from the house phone. We both listened to the conversation.

"Hi, love," Bev said lightly. Ringo was quiet knowing that something was up, due to Bev calling on the house phone. To Bev, it seemed as if he was already conflicted about something. Her mothering intuition told her so. They had not spoken for months before my death.

"Mum, I don't want to fight any more," Ringo said openly, as Jack raised an eyebrow. His remorseful tone was due to watching me die and the regret he was living with afterwards.

"We don't have to." Ringo did not respond as Bev took the phone to her palm and shook her head, ashamed at what she was doing. Jack gave her a sharp nod, insisting authoritatively to carry on. "Son, there's something I need to tell you."

Ringo realised the impertinence of her tone and answered sharply, "What? Spit it out. Not playing this game!" Ringo said abruptly.

"It's your Dad. I went up to the toilet a while ago and I found him on the floor...He had a heart attack and died."

"A heart attack!"

"Yeah, love. Looks like it. Jerry's not long left. I thought I'd let you know, you're the first one I've told." Bev shook her head at the insanity of what she was saying. She wanted to make amends with Ringo but there was her lying through her skin with Jack sitting right beside her. I too was conflicted with the wrongness of the moment, but I also had my own load of guilt to deal with.

"Ok. Are you alright? Want me to come over?" Bev was so touched by her son asking if she was alright, she shed a tear. Jack was waving his hands around and shaking his head, lip-syncing that Ringo was not to come over until the next days afternoon because the coffin had to be there first.

"No, you're alright. I want to be alone for a while. Come round early evening, tomorrow ok?"

"Alright, mum, I'll do that."

"Ok love, see you then." Bev was so disgusted with herself she hung up before Ringo could say goodbye and headed straight back to the drink's cabinet.

Jack, without consideration for Bev's guilt about what she was doing, turned to me and said, "Time to disappear!"

Chapter 11

No Chase:

It had been four days since our return to Liverpool and we arrived at the flat in Waterloo. Jack picked that location because it was the closest property he had in the vicinity of both McCartney's and his house in case we had to move fast. These properties Jack had dotted all over the city were usually used to house his working girls, those who danced in McCartney's and the others who worked in his brothels. All his joints were quite classy, unusual for a working girl to get that kind of hospitality in their trade. That was why Jack would never be shy of a back catalogue of good looking girls. They all literally bent over backwards to work for Jack, to get the protection and safety of his security measures.

We travelled in the early hours of the morning to avoid attention. Jack slipped his hair into a ponytail under a baseball cap and wore a knee length puffy coat. He gave me a woolly hat and a thick jacket that barely fitted me. The move over to St John's Road, off Liverpool Road, was an easy venture and we slipped into the flat from a back entrance without any interaction from people. The open-planned studio flat with a couple bedrooms was on a busy street, located above a convenience store. There was a secluded back entrance with high walls and a heavy steel gate you couldn't see through. Handy to hide the car and us.

Once inside, Jack got to work straight away, emptying the car of all the equipment. I never noticed how obsessed he was until I saw his haste in getting set up.

I suppose he knew that any missed opportunities would be instantly regretted. He had hardly slept in the past days and kept himself awake with coffee and cigarettes. Characteristically, he had the laptops and monitors set up under ten minutes over the coffee table that was primarily located in the middle of the open flat. When he was happy that he had eyes on his house and McCartney's, he put the kettle on and made a strong coffee, sparked a smoke, and settled in. He was like a kid at the cinema, all his focus on the screens, and I left him to it for the rest of the night.

With my mind still clouded and lethargic, I continued to take every opportunity for a quick nap or prolonged sleep as that seemed to be the only thing that healed the aftermath of concussion. My memory was still hazy. I couldn't tell what I did a week or a month ago. I had no idea if my mind was ever going to heal. That brought plenty of anxiety, mixed in with a dreadful hole in my gut. The whole situation was ludicrous but, somehow, I knew it was the right thing to do.

That night I slept for fourteen hours and didn't dream. It felt as if I closed my eyes and then woke up again. My body appreciated the sleep as it continued to heal. The effect of the sleep in my mind felt refreshing as if your body had been topped up with an afternoon of vitamin D.

When I awoke at around lunch time, I strolled into the open-plan room from the bedroom to see Jack standing, deathly still about a metre away from the window. The blinds were open only a tad as he was wearing a set of bulky headphones. It was a dull day, pissing rain outside, with the noise of traffic on the street filing the silence. As I approached him, I could hear The Beatles playing in his ears as I called to him a couple of times but received no answer. I walked around to a point where he should have noticed me. I called to him; again, no response. His eyes were open, his stance was solid, and then I clicked on that he was sleeping, standing up with his eyes open. He was the kind of man who could live off four hours sleep a night but that catches up with everyone at some point though. I delicately shook his shoulder as he registered and removed the headphones, gaping at me with his mouth open.

"Go through to the bed and get some kip," I demanded of him. He turned, gazing longingly at the monitors on the table before he nodded and blinked sluggishly at the same time. He handed me the headphones before strolling off to the other bedroom.

The past days of avoiding a proper night's sleep had caught up on him. I turned around and sat at the desk, turning my attention to the Big Brother screens of cameras.

For the rest of that day, I dossed around like a lethargic mess, drifting in and out of saneness. Often, I would forget the situation I was in and at times, I forgot Jack was there and who he was. Then I'd snap out of it, remembering why I was feeling like that. Flashbacks of the fight were frequent, unwelcomed and frightened me. I'd tremble with memories of my near-death experience that seemed to still be with me; and then, the next they were so distant, it felt like decades in the past, or an ancient dream. The face of that woman who stood by the rail tracks kept returning to me as if she was trying to send me a message. Randomly that day, I'd recall The Governor or The Gypsy and be disgusted at what I'd done to them. It sickened me.

I drifted around all day until Jack showed his face after it had turned dark. He ambled into the room, considerably fresher, and walked straight to the coffee maker. His first words that evening were, "Bev has given Ringo the club, and I'm being cremated tomorrow."

I sensed by his bluntness that he was not in the mood for unnecessary chat so I replied acknowledging, "Eiffel has disappeared and already the war to claim my territories has broken out. The Salford gang from Manchester has moved in and had a battle last night with The Deli mob from Kirkdale outside Big Bert's gym. An' in Dingle, big Cam Reece was gunned down by some Rastas."

He continued to mumble and mentioned a bunch of other squabbles but I simply replied.

"Ok." I was relieved with Jack appearing so I could take myself to bed.

Chapter 12

Lasagne:

The clock on the wall read quarter to ten in the morning. I strolled into the front room to see Jack wide-eyed with a spilled coffee staining both the table and a pad of paper he had been scribbling on. He was sleeping with his eyes open again. The cafetiere of coffee was nearly empty and the overflowing ashtray of butts with the surrounding area littered with ash, showed his battle to stay awake. He was displaying that even he, a man who was resilient and had a vendetta, was after all, very human. I felt a bit of sorrow for his ageing body and a part of me wanted to look after him. A man of his age should be settled in life, relaxing at home or winding down for retirement, not spending night shifts on stakeouts for the one man who was capable of outsmarting him. I looked at him calmly, aware that the hateful trend I had had for him for so many years was now gone. I took a peep at the monitor to see Ringo was in Jack's old office. It certainly looked weird for him to be there. There was no sign of Eiffel because he had taken off. He was without an employer and more importantly, he was without a regular paycheque, where his loyalty to the Gallaghers ended. Jack's drug operation would be falling apart, the runner's supply ceased, and the order Jack enforced had collapsed. His brothels would be without protection and there was space for a new operator to take the reins. A new war was about to commence across Liverpool and Jack would have fun taking it all back.

I shook Jack's shoulder to waken him when recklessly, he slipped his hand under the desk to his lap and flashed his PPK into my face. He took to his feet and stepped back before realising what was going on.

"Jesus Christ! Be more subtle next time." Jack roused himself. He mentioned that Bev had come around, when I was asleep, with food shopping and had said that Courtney and young Max were doing well, all things considered. I repeated in my head, that this situation would not last long. How wrong would I be! Jack straightened his stiffened self, pretending he was not so tired, but he was an ageing man and nothing could hide that.

He opened the fridge and pointed inside. "Bev made us lasagne, and there's plenty more in here to eat," he said, before strolling off to bed. His nonchalant manner sat well at home with him. This insane situation we both found ourselves in seemed comfortably normal to him. For me, I was more settled and ready to take things more seriously, but I was in no way relaxed about the endeavour.

As I took the shift, I noticed my head was a step closer to normality and something else I observed was that my addiction to steroids had gone. For long enough, I survived on them, relied on them for that extra burst of adrenaline. They fuelled my anger and passion to be the number one fighter and now I had no drive for any of that nonsense.

I had made myself a coffee with Jack's great Bolivian stuff and had a few slices of toast. My appetite was weak along with the recurring headaches and slight nausea I still had. Once I could hear Jack snoring, I nipped outside for a bit of fresh air.

I strolled around the car park, within the outskirts of the wall as part of me wanted to have a workout, pump some iron, beast out some press ups or pound a boxing bag. This was what I used to do with boredom, but I didn't see the point. There was nothing to train for and without steroids, I wouldn't have that extra burst of energy. But that was my first influx of energy since the fight and I had to remind myself where I was. Becoming forgetful, momentarily, I walked around the thirty square metre space for some time, long enough to begin to worry about being away from the screens for too long so I returned to my post.

Chapter 13

What's Around the Corner:

I took over the rather mundane job of staring at a screen for the next few hours with nothing much happening. Ringo was bright-eyed and at McCartney's early each morning, relishing the task of being the manager.

The news of Jack's death would be widespread now. All of his rivals' profit margins would be booming, his working girls left unemployed until another slimy lowlife would employ them, and his police informants would miss their monthly bribery. Liverpool was in carnage! Bev was in charge of the brothels and had put the buildings up for rent, much to Jack's annoyance, but it was not his place to argue that point since he was supposed to be dead.

I seized the chance to have a shower and made use of Jack's spare razor in the bathroom cupboard. The other day, when Bev dropped off the lasagne, she had brought a bag full of new clobber for me. I changed into some of it which had a positive effect in making me feel more human. I messed around for most of the day, taking my moments to check the monitors. I struggled with the concentration and looked for things to focus on. I went outside for portions of the day. I ended up having a workout after lunch time which was massively good for my motivation. I went outside later in the afternoon, enjoying the fresh air and strolled around.

Then, out of nowhere, that sharp, horrid pain struck my heart again, taking away the strength in my legs and threw me against Jack's car. I sagged to the ground as my breathing became laboured, and I struggled to inhale. I threw my hand in the air, wishing to find some leverage to help me stand, ripping off the wing mirror. I hovered around consciousness when I could see the frail lady stand above me. She stretched her hand out, offering to help me up, but she blurred into nothing as I passed out.

"Get up!" he yelled. "He's back!"

I rolled over, looking at a black sky, not realising where I was, my skin shivering from the night frost. Jack yanked me up and slapped me. "He's at McCartney's, with Ringo. We gotta move!"

I was inherently confused for another ten seconds until the dots joined and I wearily slid up the body of the car, allowing my legs to figure out what strength they had.

I noticed the sky was dark, telling me I had been out for a long while and straight away, I noticed Jack's intensity, although I didn't quite get what he was saying because I was still dazed. I jumped into the passenger seat as he handed me a laptop with the screen of the office at McCartney's on it. Jack, revving the engine, reversed the car out of the car park like a rally driver.

The screen of the laptop loaded as I flipped it open: and there Davie sat, relaxed, across from Ringo at the desk in McCartney's, sharing a drink, the moment we had been waiting for.

"How long has he been there?" I asked. Jack was bursting with purpose as he reversed the car into the wall with a wild clatter.

"I've no idea. I woke up cos I heard his voice and there he was," Jack blurted out, finding first gear.

"Has this got volume? Can I turn it up?" I asked.

"Bottom right of the screen, turn it up!" I turned up the volume as Ringo talked.

"No problem, I'll pass it on," Ringo answered Davie as Jack managed to manoeuvre out of the tight car park.

"Pass what on?" Jack asked. "What?" and sped away like Colin McRae.

"No idea," I answered. "Hold on!" Davie slid forward in his chair.

"Ringo, I can't stay. I shouldn't be here in the first place."

"I know, kid, I know," Ringo answered, as Davie leaned over the table and shook his hand …… as the picture on the laptop froze! It had reached the limits of the WiFi signal from the flat.

"Shit! What's happened? Get it back on!" Jack panicked as I realised the laptop went dead. "You let me fall asleep, you never woke me! It's fucking dark now, how long was I asleep?" He had completely lost it.

"Jack, I passed out! How the fuck am I supposed to know?"

Jack fumbled around in his pockets for his phone and called Bev. He put it on the loudspeaker on his lap to focus on driving.

"Bev, get to my study and pull up the office security camera," Jack spoke calmly but authoritatively, knowing a panicked voice was never going to make things better. Bev, aware of his haste, headed straight for the office.

"If we miss him now, we'll struggle to find him again," Jack said, waiting for Bev to answer. We were both in silent anticipation that seemed like torture waiting for Bev. Jack's full concentration was focused on running red lights and avoiding collisions. I wasn't sure what I was prepared to do once I came into contact with Davie, but Jack was.

"He's there," Bev said sharply and then quickly retracted, "No, wait, he's leaving."

"Keep an eye on the outside camera and if you hit the tab for the other security program you'll get access to the street cameras. Let me know which way he's headed and if you see him getting into a car, I need the reg." Bev went quiet as she navigated around the screen.

"Ok, I'm watching...he's on Hope Street. He's looking back at McCartney's." Bev paused, as an odd silence lingered in anticipation of what Davie was going to do next, while the car engine screamed from Jack rapping the throttle and gears.

"What's he doing now?" Jack heckled, his face turning red as if his blood pressure instantly shot through the car roof.

"Nothing. He's standing still in the middle of the road, looking down Hope Street." Bev answered calmly, despite Jack's temper randomly jacking up. "It's as if he knows he's being watched."

"How long until we get into town?" I asked.

"Around six minutes, if we're lucky with traffic and lights."

"He's moving again," Bev stated sharply, "He's walking down the middle of the street, he's turning off onto...Falkner Street."

"He's heading to a car! Get the reg!" Jack shouted.

"How far away are you?" Bev asked.

"About five minutes. I need to know what car he's in and what direction he's headed."

"I'm changing street cams, hold on. I've got him on Falkner Street." Jack knew Davie had a motor near, and he needed luck to get to him. "He's still walking...he's gone through a gate into a back garden."

"You need to figure out what back garden it is."

"It's hard to tell!" As Bev said that, Jack's temper hovered on the edge. "It's got a waist high green gate with a white transit van outside it."

"Keep an eye on it." Jack dropped a gear and gripped the steering wheel tightly, as he ran a red light, running the gauntlet of gaining unwanted attention from the feds. "Take my gun from the glove box!" he ordered. I opened it to remove his Walther PPK and looked ominously at it in my hand. Of all the guns I'd delivered in the past, this one held the biggest significance, and as I cast the thoughts through my head that a bullet in this gun could be for Davie, Jack snatched it from my hand like a selfish school kid.

We drove onto Hope Street, sped past McCartney's and drifted the car onto Falkner Street, towards the white transit and slammed on the brakes, leaving the car sitting in the middle of the road. Jack leapt out and entered the green gate, cupping the gun around his waist level. He cautiously walked down a path towards the back door of a terraced block of business units. I followed. Jack breathed heavily, and his desperation made him careless. The door was ajar and we walked in. I stayed in Jack's shadow, within arm's reach and followed him through the building. There was a glimmer of light that opened up into a heightened and wide room, lit by the tungsten yellow of the streetlights filtering in through the high windows, running parallel with the roof. The room was a spread of sewing machines, fabric rolls and old worn bulky work benches. On the far left, there were large stained double doors with one side lying fractionally open. Jack headed towards it, with his arm straightened and gun at the ready. Sharply, he pivoted and kicked the door open, having lost his caution. His hand dropped to his waist and he loosened up. I followed him through the door to see the exit door wide open. It led back out onto Hope Street and Davie was gone.

That reminded me of the last time he disappeared from my life.

Chapter 14

Davies Disappearance in 2006:

After Jack had failed in the attempt to have Davie tortured and killed, for stabbing him in the back by using the Collins brothers to cut up his cocaine, he had the police arrest me for drug dealing with the intention of wiping any connection to Davie from his life. I'm guessing I was too young to have had killed; even that would have been a new low for him, but I know he would have given that some thought. At the age of fifteen, I was about to be introduced to a whole new way of life inside a jail.

On the day after Davie had been kidnapped, a raiding squad turned up at the flat in Everton early in the morning. They were part of the specialist Merseyside drug and firearm squad who arrived in a big force and battered the door down while I still lay in bed. I heard Danielle, Davie's bit on the side at the time, and the closest thing I had to a mother figure, scream in defiance as they treated her savagely. They used their consolidation of vigour, added to their unnecessary use of power, dragging me out of my bed and pinned me down. I didn't resist, knowing it would be pointless. I'd been through all that before as a child. What was I supposed to do? Jump out of the window of the fifth-storey flat? They hauled me out the bedroom, through to the living room and into the kitchen. As they stood at least fifteen strong around the flat, vandalising anything they touched in an upheaval of panic, I peered around to find Danielle, but she was nowhere to be seen. They held me in the kitchen while outside on the balcony, there were two suited CID officers on the phone, looking cocksure and pleased with themselves. The head, Inspector Carlin, was well embedded into Jack's pockets, something I had no idea of at the time. He sighted me, returned his phone to his pocket and ambled past the door that hung on its last hinge, before squaring up to my face. He was also nothing to do with the specialist squad but his apparent interest in capturing Davie led to a joint operation between the CID and the specialist firearms and drug squad.

He was a slimy rat, with fat black greasy hair, shaped backwards with pigmented lines from his comb.

His skin was yellowed by his twenty a day habit and his podgy face grotesque by his nightly takeaways. Outside, his tall, straight shouldered male partner, Flanagan, was content, watching everything unfold and happy to be second in the door.

"Young Mr Rhodes," Carlin said, his chin locked out and lips overlapping when he spoke, making him sound as if he'd had problems with his speech over the years or he produced too much saliva to deal with. He expected me to beg or plead my case, but I wasn't satisfying his need for that.

"I'll ask because, well, I have to. Where's your father?" Even though I hadn't the slightest clue at the time, I gave the impression I was about to respond in a helpful way by stuttering.

"He's… He's…" I paused for a couple seconds, snarling at his face as it optimistically lit up.

"He's probably down the pub!" He was undoubtedly used to sarcasm in his job. The flat-faced Inspector Flanagan walked his broad frame into the kitchen at ease with his orangutan hands idling inside the pockets of his dressed trousers. Carlin turned to him.

"Want to take the lad down to the nick and get the questioning under way, while I oversee things here?"

"Absolutely. That's my favourite part of the job," he answered with a chilling smirk.

"Make it abundantly clear to him, that if he feels he'd like to help us locate his father, we shall go easy on him," Carlin said. They spoke to each other as if I wasn't there, probably an intimidation tactic they had come up with while working together. I was fifteen at the time but not a soft fifteen; I had had a challenging upbringing, yet Davie had hardened me up to life on the street. I was thankfully glad of that because it enabled me to have no fear of them.

"I'll make that abundantly clear, Inspector," Flanagan answered, looking at me assuredly in the eye. "Come on, hard man, time to take you back to school." All the time I was standing there, I wondered where Davie was. I'd been abandoned and I did not need anyone to tell me that. Flanagan gripped the underside of my triceps, above the elbow, and handed me over to two uniforms who led me onto the balcony. There, one of them stuck the handcuffs on me. Flanagan took the lead while the uniform pulled me along. I stopped and looked over the landing, onto the courtyard at the front, gasping to see the sight of someone who could help me but all there was, was a cover of flashing beacons, a police van and marked and unmarked cars. Flanagan decided he wanted to continue to gloat in the Force's success of my capture.

"If you're looking for any help out there, you won't find it, Max. From what we know, your father knew that we were onto your operation and he has done a runner." He kept his back to me as we walked. Davie hadn't done a runner. He had been kidnapped by Jack and handed to Glasgow's ex prize-fighter, Sam Bryson, who set up an execution with The Eradicator, and a very harsh lesson awaited him.

Flanagan continued, "We have lots of evidence to make sure you won't think about venturing into these kinds of affairs in the future." I wanted to ask about the evidence, but one thing Davie taught me well was to never talk to the police, even when they would offer deals or attempt to get you onto their good side. As we were about to turn the corner to the elevator, I asked a question, not because I was scared, but more to be informed.

"What's going to happen to me?" When we reached the elevator, Flanagan stopped pressed the button and turned around, halting the uniforms.

"I'll take him from here. lads." The uniforms backed off and walked away when the elevator opened and I was led in. "You're going to the big boys' jail," he said, gazing down at my gloomy outlook as the door shut.

Once out of the elevator on the bottom floor, I saw Danielle standing by an unmarked car. She started waving hysterically and shouting my name when another uniform threw her into the back. That uniform immediately took out his phone and called someone, as he gave a dubious nod towards Flanagan who led me towards the courtyard of vehicles. I suspected now that it was Jack on the other line. Even though I would see Danielle again, that would be the last time I'd recognise her.

Chapter 15

The Departure from Altcourse Jail:

Two years later from when I was locked up in Altcourse jail, in October 2008, I was released on a technicality, only a couple of weeks before my eighteenth birthday at a malnourished seventy-eight kilos. Those two years maliciously turned what was left of a boy into a man and would forever define what was about to happen to me, but as one nightmare ended, another one stood right across from the jail.

I sauntered out of the prison gates with the most beautiful feeling of freedom and relief, sucking the sweet fresh air into my lungs. The pain from that period of my life could dissolve as my shoulders relaxed but that good and calming relief was soon squashed when I spotted Davie propped up against the wall of the building across the road. He was puffing on a rollie, as he always was. He ruined my moment and turned that split instant of joy into anger. I spilled out into a rage and I wanted to kill him right there; without having any thoughts of the consequences, I marched across the road and into his face.

"Good of you to come visit, Da," I roared, losing control of my saliva, as it spluttered and spilled from my mouth. In that instant, I noticed there was something different in his mould and tough exterior. I saw regret and a touch of sorrow in his eyes where he didn't appear annoyed at my approach. I guess he suspected a backlash.

"Couldn't, son, too dangerous," he replied coolly.

"What the fuck happened? More than two years I've rotted in there!" I spat over his face as I boiled over. "How did it happen? Where the fuck did you go?" The words could not come out quick enough.

"I know who put you in there, son." He quickly tried to remove the blame from himself and pass it on. Classic Davie Rhodes in action.

"Well, why don't you enlighten me cos I've been raking my brains trying to figure out where the fuck you went!"

"It was Jack. I slipped up, son, I'm sorry. This was never my intention for you." He seemed genuinely repentant about what had happened but that didn't tame my mood at all.

"Jack! What?"

"That gear I was shiftin', most of it I skimmed off the surface…"

"You mean, the gear I shifted for you, Da?"

"Aye, that gear, Max. I had a plan to do a runner, get us away from this life, but I fucked up and Jack caught on."

"So, where the fuck have you been, cuz I've been in there!" I pointed behind me, not willing to remove my gaze from his. "Getting the shit beat out of me, starved and fucking abused!" I had to let him know how fuming I was.

"It was all Jack, son. You weren't the only one, look." He lifted his hand and showed me its deformity but staring at them, I showed no sympathy.

"Was there not a time when you told me to never show pity, Da? Why shouldn't I just do you right here, why not?" I referred to the time where Davie had held me inside an empty old bathtub on Rhiwlas Street in Liverpool, when he abducted me from the Jacksons' residence. Now I saw his eyes widen and for a brief second, they filled with a piercing numbness of wrath. In the next flash, he gripped my throat with his deformed hand and squeezed. I gargled for breath, filled with that horrible feeling of weakness, unable to do anything about it.

"Look, boy! I'm still yer old man and you better remember what I'm capable o'." He flipped me around and splattered my back up against the wall. "I've come here today to make things right, but it'll take time, you hear! A long time. We must be smart. In time, we'll take care o' Jack, but for now, we'll have to play smart, the long game." Holding his piercing gaze into my eye, I saw how he looked at me differently, as if I was now a man and not a feeble boy as I was before I walked inside that jail.

"Alright?" I muttered through the grip on my throat, so he would agree to loosen it while I kept my back firmly up against the wall.

"Ye're going to go back to Jack's and start workin' for him, get to know him and one day, we'll take everything he has." At the time, that's not what I wanted: I wanted to inflict pain on the man standing beside me. A man who had abandoned me and who I blamed for everything that had happened to me behind bars. But as he said, we had to be smart. I learned Jack was the main reason I was imprisoned. That was a bit of a reality check knowing Jack could do that to a fifteen-year-old. There was one bright side – it was better than being taken out. The respect I had for Jack died at that moment and left a belly of fury. I questioned my ability to work for him, as Davie suggested.

"How the fuck can I work for him? If I'm going to do anything, it'll be killing the spineless cunt!"

"Look, son, sometimes it's better gettin' even by being smarter, and I know ye're smart, boy."

We both began to calm down as my brain processed a plan of my own. A plan that would change directions many times over the coming years as my addiction to fighting took over my soul.

"What am I supposed to do? Act as if nothing's happened?" I answered, slightly calmer than I had been seconds earlier.

"Aye, exactly that, and in the meantime, I have a job for you." There it was, his need for me to do something for him.

"Using me as a puppet again? I don't think so, Da."

"You need to make money and we need to stay in contact, so don't be a pussy and take the work."

"What fucking work?"

"I work for the IRA, for a man called C4 Millacky. He's plannin' something big, and I make deliveries for him."

"Deliveries of what?"

"Guns."

Straight out of jail and straight back into the wrong side of the law. I had no idea what I was going to do on the outside and I had no time to give it any thought. My release from jail was a surprise and part of a compromise. One thing was definite. I had no intention of living any kind of straight down the line life, so I did not feel the need to argue with him. And plus, I needed to make money. I was not going through life cashless. I informed Davie of some of my experiences inside and he became speechless. Something I had not seen from him. His reaction told me he still cared for me. Once I finished telling him what had happened, he developed a greater hatred for Jack, but it couldn't possibly be more than the vendetta I sought.

Chapter 16

The Birth of Eclipse:

I left jail with nothing but emotional and physical trauma and the clothes on my back. There was no turning back the clock; what happened, happened, and I would never be the same boy who walked in or be able to forget the memories.

I was lost and damaged by what I went through, and I was also skint. As stubborn as I became, I needed money and Davie always seemed to have plenty siller, as he called it.

I found myself sleeping in a B&B in the area of Chinatown, congested by seedy massage parlours, poor restaurants set up to launder money and opium dens. Davie funded my stay, on the hope that I'd work for him again. A bargaining chip I could not refuse, considering I had nowhere to go. Once again, he'd harvested a level of deception to use me as his personal dogsbody and a puppet on the ends of his deceitful strings. He was never short of a pound and he handed over a decent number of notes before nicknaming me 'Eclipse' for the gunrunning duties. He named me after the horse he won a stack of money on the first time we went into a bookie's together. He insisted all telephone conversations or text messages would be used with that code name. He gave me a stack of burners and instructed me to destroy each one after a single piece of communication. That could mean after a text conversation, or a phone call between us, the phone would be destroyed or thrown to the bottom of a river.

He sorted me out with a counterfeit passport and a driver's licence, in the name, Peter Smith. Then I began to deliver his guns and arms, or should I say, the IRA's arms, up and down England in preparation for an IRA terrorism attack. I was not given the full details of what was going down nor did I care to know as I had other priorities.

Two weeks out of jail and I was sunk into a new world of crime. All the deals I ended up doing over the years put money in my pocket and allowed me to make my own connections. What I liked about the job in the beginning was that I worked on my own. In late October, I met Davie on a pier at Barrow in Furness. Before that, he had already passed through the Isle of Man and exchanged fishing vessels there. A week before, he gave me detailed instructions to buy a medium wheel-based van and forward the details of the registration papers to him via picture message. After that, I had to destroy the phone and pick up the next burner. He was very paranoid, and I followed that same level of paranoia. In Barrow, he transferred six hundred pounds of semtex and bomb making equipment into my van that was being delivered to a contact, a member of the IRA called Ratchet, in Aldershot. Along with that, a heavy collection of arms. AK47s, M16s, handguns, stun grenades, sniper rifles and scopes, were to be delivered to another member of the IRA called Micky Loose, in Tidworth. Davie's other instruction was, I had a rucksack to pick up, from a man called Vinny Deans in Southall, but he was English and inside the bag was for his own personal use. I had times, meeting points, and contact numbers and Davie insisted that his contact in London, Vinny Deans, would know who I was. I didn't ask questions and truthfully, beneath the adrenaline, I wasn't fazed about any of it. The emotional trauma of what I went through was far more daunting than what I was doing. Those tasks did not involve pain and kept my mind off the past couple of years in the slammer. It became a rehabilitation programme.

I drove to Tidworth first, since it was closest, and I wanted the consignment of arms removed from the van to salve my conscience. It was a rush, I wasn't even eighteen yet and here was me delivering a load of weaponry. It made me feel alive after the past two years of dormancy.

I called Micky Loose, just after I came off the M4 at Swindon, to inform him of my imminent arrival.

"I'll be with you in an hour." He didn't speak on the phone and hung up after I finished talking. It was a regular thing, the paranoia, in that world, as they were all suspicious of talking on phones. I already had the meeting point, a gravel patch near Sidbury Hill, a remote location in the country.

When I arrived in the pitch black, there was nobody around. I had to wait a long time before a long wheeled based van arrived. He pulled up a few car spaces apart and gave me the old undressing with the eyes.

He was a trim and nimble looking fellow, wearing a farmer's cap. He sat with the engine idling, wondering if I was the right man. I put on my cab light, so he could see me better. After a quick phone call, he exited the van and strolled over to the window. He wore a tight, long sleeved black sweater, displaying his toned body arms. His behaviour was quiet as his face mirrored a pale emptiness. A man only interested in his business.

"In the back," I said, without rolling down the window. He gave me an edgy nod and headed to the rear door. He opened the back door and shouted.

"Alright fellas." Several eager bodies spilled out. Moving swiftly, they hauled the crates of weapons out and into their vehicle. They moved as fast as a formula one pit crew, operating rapidly as if they were on a heist. Micky Loose walked back over to the driver's window and pawed his hat at me, "God bless ya, son." He said and returned to his van.

Staying there overnight, in the morning, I made my way to the address in Aldershot after a quick bite to eat for breakfast. I arrived at night, as instructed, at a garage storage facility in a small industrial area, pulling up outside a hefty security gate, with a small hut alongside but no one inside. I waited calmly and, in a few minutes, a sluggish fella, five four I'd say, in his mid-fifties, appeared from the distance and walked over coolly. He was dressed smartly in a thick, dark jacket, pressed trousers and with a woolly hat covering his head. Clearly an official security guard or appearing as one, with a Freddie Mercury moustache fitting his look. He walked towards the van as I rolled the window down a touch.

"Can I help you, Mr?" He spoke in a cheerless tone, clearly Irish, and a man who was offered too much money to say no. There was no need to beat around the bush. I didn't enjoy these meetings, that awkward human interaction wasn't for me.

"Eclipse here to see Rachet. Open the gates." He riveted me with a malicious scowl.

"Let's see your passport," he asked blatantly. Clearly, he wanted to see the Peter Smith passport, the alias I was to use, the identification he needed to confirm who I was.

"Open the fucking gate!" I replied.

His exasperated pivot indicated he didn't like my sharp manner, but I wasn't complying with his need for superiority. After a tense ten seconds of silence and acute stares, he walked into his hut and pressed a button that opened the gate. I drove into the yard, stopping in front of a low building with four big shutter doors, assuming I'd be going into one of them. I glanced in my side mirror and saw the security guard on the radio. A roller door began to open so I drove up to it as it rose painfully slowly, making screeching noises. Rachet, a sleeveless vest-wearing IRA thug, stood dead still in the middle of a vacant room, glowingly visible by the bright low bay lights. His body was tense with seriousness while a cigarette hung rigid from a tight jaw; in his right hand, a tightly gripped crowbar. I assumed he meant business. As with any other hard man, he felt the need to try and suffocate me with intimidation, waiting for me to give him a nod of some significance of respect before he moved. I didn't but he stepped to the side and allowed me to drive in. I rolled up my window and drove straight in. He walked by the door, handing me the usual

check as I remained in the van. As he opened the back doors, I watched him in the rear mirror. He pulled out a bag and trawled through it. He picked up the second rucksack and analysed that. Seemingly happy, he removed the bags and closed the door. He tried to approach the driver's door to talk to me when I reversed out of the shed, leaving him peeved at my lack of respect to even acknowledge him. I had a twenty-hour period to kill before I met the next contact so I spent the time in the back of the van, mostly sleeping. I had bought a second-hand mattress from a thrift shop, along with a couple of blankets and pillows. It was dead cold and I needed to keep warm. Accessories in that job got used and binned very quickly. It was comforting, that two years inside conditioned me to a confined room with a lock. When my mind became unoccupied without a task, I had that same build-up of aggression and overthinking that's haunted me my whole life. I felt as if I needed a release somehow. I'd often get the urge to punch walls and throw stuff around in anger. I suppose being stuck in the back of that van didn't help but I wasn't willing to converse with the public, as I hated the necessity people had for small talk and pleasantries. Alone in the back of that van, I was
hidden, and that's what I liked.

The next meeting couldn't come quick enough so I could get out of the area and back to Liverpool, where I had plans of my own. Parking the van in Southall, I walked to the address where I had to pick up the ruck-sack. The whole area was totally surreal and I couldn't help feeling as if I was in India. I found out, while I was there, that it was called Little Deli! Every soul I passed was Indian, every shop was Indian, food stalls on the street with anything deep fried and curry restaurants on every corner. It was a world I had not seen before and that's why I was so surprised when I met that guy.

My instructions were to go to a flash curry restaurant and ask for the reservation 'Reid'. When seated and because I was there, I ordered food. The contact was late, more than thirty minutes, and that plain pissed me off. I devoured a big meal while the place filled with customers. All I wanted to do was leave. Because of this man's lateness, I took out a burner and dialled number three on Davie's list of numbers. As I was about to press the call button, a seat slid out from the table and a man sat down opposite.

He seemed distant and did not introduce himself. The base of his neck was heavily tattooed and his head was covered with a thick, woolly red hat, colourfully matching a carrot orange jacket. The bright colours noticeably contrasted with his blank characteristics. He was tall, widespread, muscled with brisk shoulders and mean, dark eyes. His demeanour suggested he was tough but not someone connected with the IRA. His personality suited me due to his lack of conversation, but it was time to get on with it.

"I have a package for you," he said, in a grouchy east London accent and waited for me to respond.

"Where is it?"

He casually lifted a bag and dropped it over my plate, smearing the bottom of it in the left-over curry sauce. I riveted the guy as if he was an idiot and removed the bag from the plate, placing it on the floor. He stood up and turned towards the door, showing a brash swastika styled tattoo on the rear of his neck, that filtered into the back of his head. His walk slowed as he arrived nearer the door where a gigantic wall mirror hung. He stopped and, scowling into the mirror, he slid his hat off his bald head. He then dragged the nails of both hands through a freshly shaved scalp, spreading his eyes wide like a mad man, tensing his teeth together. He then, appearing relaxed, turned to me, tilted his head to the side and smiled.

"You can call me Skinner from now on." He left and I would never see that man again but I would hear of him.

Chapter 17

The Birth of the Reaper:

Liverpool was a gulf apart from any other city that felt more like a colony than a city in Britain. A festering cauldron of crime in any shape or form spanned the city. It was built on the back of slave trade in the early eighteenth century; it mingled into a multi-cultural establishment with a wave of immigration which brought a repulsion for authority and a natural verbal wit. It became linked to the world and the world came to Liverpool. The West Indians and Caribbeans brought a love of ganja to the doormat. The Bangladeshi and Indians opened food stores with rare and exotic fruits and vegetables, mingling with their alluring spices. The Greeks opened restaurants, the Nigerians and Kenyans brought their laidback love and a hard-working attitude while the Lebanese, Arabs and Turks opened stores that sold everything. Their multicultural ways of life and religions mixed together to form the Liverpudlian language of Scouse, a nasal intonation of clipped vowels, T-glottalization and the crackling of letters. To the uninitiated, a fine-tuned ear was needed to understand it. In the shadows of the city, that no one wanted to turn their eyes on, men and women lived a cold life of poverty and destitution that familiarised itself with my life. Davie sent me money as payment for the deliveries I'd done. The three in England and a minor drop of a padded envelope in a train station locker in Glasgow, also connected to the failed IRA attacks on the English Army Barracks.

The IRA's terrorist attack went tits up and all of the perpetrators were detained. C4 Millacky, declared to be the head of the operation, was arrested and destined to be jailed for many years inside Belmarsh. It was nationwide news and you couldn't get away from it. If I had any ounce of consciousness back then, I might have thought differently to carting around weapons that would bring lives to an end, but I did not give a shit about anything, other than my own building incentives. Davie went off the radar for a while after the attacks but that became a usual occurrence.

I joined a proper hardcore gym called Rockies, in a raw area of Birkenhead and worked out every day. I realised from working out in jail that it was a release from the daily tension. The pent-up energy would dissipate and allow my thoughts to quieten. It involved a good bit of travelling through the Queensbury Tunnel about five times a week, just to go to a gym but it felt as much like home as any other place I felt comfortable in. The place was full of meat heads, steroid junkies, and hardened eastern Europeans. The decor was raw and flaky, similar to my life. I went back on a course of steroids, supplied to me by the gym owner, Codie Gee, and started a heavy diet of meat. I had been on oxy50s in the jail, a tablet form of steroid. Codie sold me some sustanon 250 and told me to inject two doses of one millilitre a week but it was not long before I abused that. He showed me how to inject into my leg and supplied me with a box of needles. I lived on takeaways, fry ups from cafes in the mornings and bakeries during the day.

Chinese, lamb or steak kebabs at nights. I loved the extra pump from the steroids, something that made me feel alive and at the same time, sane. As I was about to find out, like fighting, it was the only thing that gave me worth. It set me alive and allowed a release from the constant bitter resentment I nurtured. Unlike my father, I didn't succumb to the lure of alcohol. I'd seen it turn people into the vilest of humans and I knew the burden of mental damage I bore was a bad combination to mix with drink.

Before I went to jail, Jack was a man I looked up to. He was the Al Capone of Liverpool. Everyone worth their mustard knew his name and everyone wise enough feared that name. Except Davie, who was as fearless as he was callous. Before I was informed that it was Jack who put me inside, I still had respect for him. He was like an uncle figure to me when Davie was running about for him, operating as his right hand man. Now I loathed the ripple of his name and I desired the one thing that drove people's motives and ambitions towards gang war…payback. Davie wanted to rip his whole life from underneath that penny grabbing fingernails of his and so did I, but he said we would only be able to do that in a patient and co-ordinated way. That, I would struggle with as my temper was loose. I would soon share that same desire and tactically, we would achieve our ambitions. It would only take time and a hell of a lot of patience. I embarked on the start of a long task, to manipulate, deceive and conquer the intelligent Jack Gallagher. I knew the truth and that would be the first edge I'd have over him.

Introducing myself into the world of the bare knuckle instead of the drug scene, was my idea. I was planting a seed for Jack to gain an interest and he'd see the potential to make money or have an inviting prospect by his side. I suppose what I really wanted, was to be like Davie and earn respect. That, and the massive chip on the shoulder I had after my two years of torture still burned.

In those two years, I had been locked behind bars; I grew to become a man driven by rage, frustration and bitterness, loaded with steroids whenever I could get them. And there, I found the only way to release it was to inflict pain, but it took a long time to figure that out. Throughout my life I'd been gullible, stupid, and let down. Abandoned and harmed by people who I thought cared or loved me and the jail was the last straw.

It was a dull night and the area sombrely quiet with only the sounds of the city echoing into the street. All alone, as I liked it, for the first time I loomed close to a derelict warehouse down at the Brunswick Docks. It used to be a food factory and the dilapidated sign of The Merseyside Food Products still hung on the walls. An entrance door to the building was being guarded by a huge man, wearing the black waistcoat cut of The Rogue Riders, and obviously there to fend off anyone not welcome to the arena. I did not satisfy his ego by looking the burly doorman in the eye and arrogantly ignored him as I placed my hand on the door handle.

"Here, here! Go 'ed boy, where do you think you're going?" His Scouse accent screeched as he surrounded my wrist with the grip of his bullish hand. I held my fix on the handle before rotating my vision towards the hand I was willing to break, and rolled my serious dagger up his chest, into his eye.

"Do you like being able to use that arm of yours?" I heckled. He stood immobile as the hardness in his eye swivelled in retreat. Alarmed by my aggressive approach, he thought he was so big, he was probably not used to being belittled and from someone so young. But I had fire and no fear of him! He stared at me for long enough to make the moment more tense as he tried to think of a suitable answer to my question. His hand still gripped my wrist tightly.

"You can't just walk in here!" "I
walk where I want to walk!"

His grip held firmly, and I exerted pressure on the door handle as I waited for his arm to be removed. I continued to glare at him and uttered the words that would get me inside. "I'm the son of Davie Rhodes."

His eyes flashed and he slowly loosened his grip, trying to decipher if I spoke the truth. I imagine that not many people would mention that name for their own benefit. He pushed the door open and nodded to me.

The door closed behind me with a thud that echoed through a vast empty area, large enough to house a football pitch, a building that had been in disrepair for decades. A look above and you could see large sections of the roof were missing, allowing the force of nature to decay the surroundings. A few of the old, corroded pendant lights hung from the roof, alighting the ground in wide circles of butter-coloured yellow around steel supports. Every step felt like an echoed movement into the unknown, as the daunting silence mimicked my edginess, being cautious of what I was approaching but I was buzzing. Buzzing to release my anger. My throat dried as my heartbeat intensified, beating through my windpipe and the reverberating stomp of my feet pulsed up my legs. I inhaled extensively, widening my nostrils, filling my chest with un-patient air. I used this motion to blank out the fear. A fear I wasn't one bit scared of, nevertheless.

These types of meetings were called 'walking the line'. There would be ten fights an evening with the winner staying on, earning £100 a pop. If they gave up before the end, then they gave up their winnings. Whoever stood at the end of the ten fights was the person collecting the total of however many fights he'd won. That meant, if you came as the penultimate challenger and won both fights, then you'd collect £200. If you went on at the beginning and won seven fights but couldn't continue, you'd have to give up the £700 you just won. It's brutal, but that's how this game works and that's how the punters were entertained. The bookie was the one who decided who went on next, formulating a trap that he was in control. It was bad enough that not only did you have to defeat your opponent and last the ten fights, you also had to beat the bookie, and lucky for me, I knew who he was.

Up ahead, a glint of flickering light, from a fitting above a door, enhanced the gateway to my future. As I crept closer, rebounding sounds of hostile cheers tried to escape through the door.

I opened it with no hesitation as the atmosphere hit me like a tornado of wind and at that moment, I knew the environment was for me. I masked the apprehension I'd had nearing the door because no doubt was welcomed. A wide circle of men and a few women surrounded a fight between two other men, as I moved, unnoticed, into a much more crowded room, alive with testosterone. Around that circle, I could spot a few men with bruises and scars, weakened, and fatigued. I figured I was a bit late to the proceedings but I was here to make my mark.

The crowd bellowed shouts and cheers, fixated by the savagery of the illegal environment. Women stood, gluing themselves to their men for the evening and equally taken aback by the barbarity of the event. By the looks of the two men in the middle, the fight wasn't far away from being over. One, wearing a sleeveless vest, Ginger Wood, was a lumbering, dead-eyed mechanical figure headed with a short crop of ginger hair. Wearing rigger boots, he plodded, casual, with a stone mask over his portly face as his guard hung, without care at his waist. Wide set, wearing cheap camouflage trousers and a bit overweight to be taken seriously, it didn't look as if he was in any bother as he picked apart a smaller man who was mentally stumped by his opponent's nonchalance. Flicking a thudding jab into his face at will, he played with his opponent and mocked him with sly grins. Ginger Wood looked vastly fitter than a man with a barrelled belly should, and it was noticeable that he had fighting experience as he kept his left shoulder high and pointed in the direction of his foe's stance. All he needed to do was plant in a big punch and the fight would be over. He was deriving joy in teasing his opponent whose inexperience caused him to trip and totter all over the place. The gathering began to disapprove of this, by booing and use of hostile language. He got the message and wasted the man with a swift right across his jaw that saw him buckle to the floor.

The loser was dragged inhumanely out of the circle by two spectators. The result saw a portion of the crowd hound the bookie at the far end of the room, who was being protected by some of The Rogue Riders, clothed in their club cut. It left me standing on my own as I began to strip down in the shadows.

As I walked over to the wall of the room, I removed my jacket and hung it up on a rusty nail on a ply board. I returned to see the bookie still being hounded by his punters as he dished out the winnings. I continued to wait patiently, still unnoticed. The programme of steroids I injected was becoming evident as my biceps tried to tear my t-shirt apart and my chest puffed out, but that was more to do with the uncontrolled intake of apprehension.

Ginger Wood had a moment to himself and a swig of water, allowing the adrenaline to wear off and his breathing to return to a controlled state. He had a couple of henchmen, also dressed in poor camouflage, feed his ego as he waited for his next victim and that wasn't going to be me.

I had no doubts about tearing him apart: what I'd experienced moulded me into a man with no hesitation or mercy. As the gathering departed from the bookie, I noticed who it was. A cigarette hung from his mouth, around a loose hanging of long ash brown hair and a flock of elegant woman gathered behind him, wearing tight dresses and kinky boots, at ease with the setting.

The bookie was Jack Gallagher's disowned son, Ringo. A man who loved the spotlight. His head jolted up from flicking through a pile of money, to me, very rapidly and returned to continue counting. He paused, slowly raising his head as I kept a blunt impression. At that moment, I realised that he had forgotten about me as the memories came rushing back to him. My changed appearance must have sent his mind into shock. Previously, I had been a shorter skinny runt, but now I was a man. The maturity he would have seen spread my face and size. As the bodies departed and took their spots in a circle formation, Ringo prepared to call on the final fighter for the night. Ginger Wood had held the line for five fights and this was the last one of the evening before the winner collected the pot. He was a seasoned fighter who travelled up and down England, looking for these types of meetings. Ringo knew that if he won, he'd have to hand over five hundred pounds and I hoped he saw me as a way out of that problem. He held his wondering attention on me as he walked into the spotlight in the centre of the circle.

"There is only one fight left tonight but who will it be?" He ran his finger over the crowd until one man stepped out. He ignored him and spun his finger around further until another man stepped out. He ignored him as well and continued, until he pointed in my direction, stood at the rear of the circle, being blocked by bodies and hidden from the cover of light that shone down into the fight area. Men parted as they realised they weren't being pointed at, and the crowd took notice as I walked forward, pulling my t-shirt over my head, throwing it to the ground. Ringo approached me.

"Do you have a name, kid?" I gave no answer, kept a solid expression, and now stared right into the game rivet of Ginger Wood's eyes. I began to tense up with aggression, almost time to let go.

"Kid, a name?" Ringo asked again. I wasn't one hundred percent sure he realised who I was, but I reckoned he wanted to ignore the fact we knew each other.

I removed my focus from my foe, onto Ringo, with a serious dig and there, Ringo knew it was me. I didn't answer.

Ringo walked backwards and turned to Ginger Wood. "Win this and you have the money." Ginger pretentiously nudged Ringo to the side as if he was of bottom class and stepped forward to stand opposite me. He saw the youth in my face and tried to faze me with a hardened stare, but it didn't have an ounce of effect.

Looking into his eyes, I could see his arrogance would be his undoing. My jaw tightened, waiting to be let go. A red-hot cauldron began to sail into my right fist. Ringo left us rooted to the spot as he began to take bets and after waiting too long, I decided I wasn't waiting for any kind of indication to start, and my victim had the same idea.

He stood solid, eyeing me as useless fodder, wondering who this new fish was. Frustratingly, I waited for him to approach as my eyes began to flash and my fist became so tight, I could have crushed rock. He lost his patience and marched forward, not bothering to take his preferred side stance. I wasn't an intelligent man, but one thing I knew, I was made for this. Even before the first drop of blood, leak of sweat, or clash of connecting bone, this was what I was born for. He took a third step forward, his right arm began to wind up; fourth step, it began to cock behind his shoulder; fifth step, his right hand began to sail through the air. I took one precise calculated step forward and head butted him on the nose.

He dropped to the ground like wasted oxygen.

Chapter 18

Roadside Café 2008:

I was buzzing after my first night of walking the line. The feeling of stripping apart someone's ego and the adrenaline buzz that took control of your body was addictive. I continued leading my bleak life as I had, since I was released from jail. I lived on eat, sleep, repeat, when there was no gun running to do but I was still focused on my task of luring Jack into my life. He would soon enough hear of my entrance into the fighting world, and I had to continue to build my reputation. But it wasn't all doom and gloom. I got used to my freedom and enjoyed having a free life.

It did become a lonely time of the year for me, Christmas, where I had no family to surround myself with, unlike everyone else. These times offered loads of questions, like who my mother was and how I ever came to be in this position. Where was my family? And where is the love that was so missing in my life? These questions always danced around in the back of my mind, and I never truly admitted what was missing.

It was Christmas Eve and Davie had summoned me to a motorway service café south of Newcastle. Davie had recently been left without an employer since the real IRA's terrorist attack went tits up and all of them were behind bars. It was nationwide news and I knew that Davie's boss, C4 Millacky, was caught. But Davie, being the conniving man he is, had C4 Millacky and the attack doomed by grassing them up; however, that was only to advance his own position up the criminal pedestal. He had ambitious plans.

I was late due to driving in bad weather conditions and when I barged into the café, Davie was sat opposite a man I would come to loathe the sight of. I hustled up to the table, took a seat beside the stranger and shoulder barged him, at the same time knocking a load of beans off his fork. I shouted to the waitress and ordered a full breakfast. "So, to what do I owe this rare pleasure?" I asked sarcastically, as I wondered who the man I sat beside was. I don't know what it was about that first meeting with him but he gave off a sour scent I didn't like. He was formal and I felt he lacked respect for me.

"Thought we'd fly over for a visit since it's Christmas, ma friend," Davie answered, speaking to me in a polite tone.

"Bullshit!" I answered. "Who's this?" I gripped the fork in a tight fist and pointed sideways to the stranger, while keeping my eyes on Davie.

"This here is Rankin, an associate of mine." Rankin nodded smartly while he continued eating his food. I glanced over to the counter to see if my breakfast was ready. "I suppose you've heard Millacky's been locked up?"

"I know all about it. I watch the news," I said quickly with no interest, as I glared over at the counter again.

"Good, that'll save me time. Pass the salt, would you?" Davie asked Rankin, "I'm looking for a man to hire from time to time."

"What you looking for, a gofer? Cuz this man to my side here," I butted in, using the fork to point again, "would fit the bill better than me." I could tell Rankin didn't enjoy confrontation as he looked away from me with an attitude. I leaned into him. "What's wrong with you!" I barked at Rankin, looking for a reaction.

"WOW! Calm down, who's ruffled yer feathers this mornin'?" Davie asked, as my breakfast arrived. Rankin returned to his food, with a sheepish approach to his eating, trying not to annoy me. "Listen, I'm lookin' for a body in England to run some merchandise when needed, just like you did before. Nothing fancy, will be pick-up and drop-off," Davie stated and I reckoned this was his way of hiring me on a more official basis.

"When? I've got another job lined up." I was fed up with playing the yes man but I was always going to agree.

"As and when needed. I haven't got a work plan to look upon." I carried on munching and shrugged my shoulders in an agreeing kind of way.

Davie had big plans in the gun running game, and he was not shy to put himself out there. Those calculated plans would earn him the name of The Eidolon, and one of the most wanted men in Europe. For me, I enjoyed the thrill, and the extra money was always welcomed. I learned things from Davie that I'd be able to use to my advantage later on in life. All four of his stable, Bard, Turk, Rankin and me, gained names for ourselves and all of our existences stayed secret.

"The drops you've done went well." I ate my food as if I'd been starved for days. The steroids did that, gave you a never-ending appetite. I hunched my arm over the plate, guarding it as you have to do in jail, squeezing Rankin into the window. "I will have nothin' to do with the IRA now, and I'm only interested in makin' money. I have two men workin' for me in Ireland, who you will meet from time to time when swappin' loads over. You will be based on the mainland o' Britain and in charge o' the drops here. Okay?" I didn't pay much attention to him and that was peeving him off.

"Aye, sounds fine," I replied, through a mouthful.

"Rankin, can you give us a minute?" He asked Rankin while he was staring at my raw eating style, waiting for me to move before he could leave. I stood and allowed him to slip out, picking up on my instinct on him. He smelled funny to me. I caught Davie eyeing my trapezius muscles, moulding out of my tight t-shirt under a tracksuit zip top.

"What's happenin' wi' Jack?" Now that Rankin was out of the café, he could ask the questions he really wanted to ask.

"I'm getting my foot in the door, still." I had not gone over my plan with Davie in any details up until that point.

"What do you mean, foot in the door?"

"I'm going to fight, win, and he'll see the potential to make money from me. That's my foot in the door."

At the time, that was only a hope, a gamble, but one I was sure that would pay off.

"You sure you want to do that? It's no' pretty," Davie said spitefully, confident that I would not be cut out for it but little did he know of my hardships in life and how they had been preparing me for such a world.

"What! You concerned for my safety, Da?"

"Not yer safety. The safety of whoever is on the other side of you I'll be concerned about."

I carried on eating, flattered by the hidden compliment. I kept quiet because I did not know how to take it.

"Who's that tit?" I referred to Rankin.

"That 'tit' will be your partner from time to time." My head pinged up; he got my attention.

"No, I work alone. What is it you used to say, you can only count on yourself." I lived by some of Davie's philosophies.

"Aye, that's true son, but in this game, you need a backup."

At the time I wouldn't know that he did have a point there.

Chapter 19

Trick and Treaters:

For the next few months, I turned up to walk the line. Ringo made casual attempts to entice me into conversation, but I kept myself to myself and stuck to my own plan. I was never sure what my intentions and feelings were towards him. Ringo never gave me any compliments on my quick-fire disposal of my foes; instead, he went about his role as the bookie as he should, collected bets and sent the next victim onto the floor. Another savage rule in this environment was if Ringo picked you out and that person refused to fight, he was sent out the door with a sense of shame and never allowed back. Every person who walked into that arena knew that he would be required to fight if he had to.

Ringo used the protection of The Rogue Riders to discourage hostile punters from having their say. Even the Riders had to fight if they were chosen, but being a collective initiated into the gang through violence, that was not an endeavour. After my first appearance, Donny Casper became a monthly sight, standing in the established position as head of his crew and watching me with a keen eye, but never offering conversation.

The task of suckering Jack Gallagher into this environment was a patient one, but I bided my time because that's all I really had, time. It was free bait, those types of fights, anybody who had an ambition to gain a name for themselves could turn up and throw a few punches and word soon spread that I'd walked through all the inspired opponents at the time. I kept reliving the jail in my head and that pattern always came back to Jack. I couldn't believe the selfish savageness of what he'd put me though, having me arrested and punished. Davie spoke of him as a calculated criminal and rightly, he was. He told me stories of how cruel he could be with the ones who crossed him, and he could never be underestimated. Like a busybody gangster, Jack had an irresistible need to know everything about what occurred in the dark of the Liverpool underworld because he owned the city, everything and everyone in it. He desired to know who the latest drug dealer on the scene was, who had been the latest criminal to be jailed for whatever illegal activity they'd been caught for and who was making a name for themselves. That last reason was the hope I carried, that he would eventually turn up at the warehouse.

It was a Friday evening, moving into Spring in 2009, and four successful months of walking the line resulted in a welcomed four grand in my pocket. Fighters with impressive reputations from all across the western cities came to have a pop. From Manchester there was Leicester Clouds, from Chester, Marty 'two punch' Clayton, and The Blackpool Tower, all top names in their cities who I disposed of.

It was standard procedure. The first fighter of the evening was always a volunteer and the victor from the previous month turned up to defend his position. I used that time to train because I did not want to lose.

I stood there that evening, ready and waiting with my shirt off, fixated in concentration at the side of the room where Ginger Wood once stood. I remember being cold at mid Spring and waiting to be warmed up with adrenaline. Unlike others, I didn't shadow box, pretending to be a seasoned campaigner. I didn't believe in all that preparation crap. In my mind, I only wished to be unleashed, so I could revel in the glory and switch my brain off.

Everyone I'd hated before that moment, I remembered with a bitter recollection of their unfound treatment of me. But neither Davie's name nor face ever popped into my thoughts at that point. I'd run through instances, fictional or sometimes truthful, of beating my past adversaries so badly they would regret their harsh treatment of me.

There were always men who were braver than they were hard, and the warehouse brought them out like Halloween brought out trick and treaters. But that night, the willing participants diminished to zero as my induction into the scene and winning streak caused the bodies to be sparse. In fact, only three of the Rogue Riders, including Donny, Ringo and two girls were present. I stood there, antisocially, ignoring the necessity to indulge in conversation, waiting for anyone to walk through the door when Ringo decided to approach me.

"Max, how's it going, kid?" He hesitantly approached, because I'd ignored his previous attempts at chit chat.

"Would be better if you had someone for me to fight," I answered, and he returned with a subdued smile.

"It would but seems like you've scared everyone away, kid."

"Don't call me 'kid'." He paused, taken by surprise. I wasn't there to make friends or small talk. Someone's phone rang from the back of the room.

"Lighten up!" Ringo said, genuinely.

"Don't tell me what I should or shouldn't do…Kid!" Right then, one of the girls walked over with Ringo's phone and drew my attention. She stopped, annoyed, by his side and handed him the phone.

"It's Lucy. You really need to talk to her, I'm not your secretary." She was a majestic sight and in that few seconds, my body turned to a blissful calm. Her flowing, light red ombre curled hair glistened down her front, pulled over her left shoulder, drew me away from her hazel eyes and a busty chest, covered over by a tight, red, knee length dress that radiated an hourglass figure.

"Hi," she said, politely breaking eye contact, showing a hint of shyness, while crossing her arms. I gulped and checked out her body again. "It's normally polite to reply!" she said, without any aggravation to her unanswered question.

"Alright," I answered sheepishly as Ringo stomped around, arguing with a girl called Lucy about giving her the cold shoulder that evening. He was uninterested in talking with her and the argument came across as being quite petty in that environment.

"Doesn't look like anyone's turning up tonight," she said truthfully, in a raw crackling Scouse accent, knowing she had spent her entire life within the confines of the city.

"No, it doesn't," I replied, while I forgot about what I was doing in the warehouse for a moment. She brought my guard down, exposing my softer side.

"Why don't you have a night off? Come join us for a drink?"

"I don't drink!"

"How do you survive?"

"What do you mean?"

"Well, if you don't drink anything, you wouldn't be able to live!"

"Ahh, you're right!" I was, frankly, flattered. I didn't have a clue how to talk to anyone, let alone that Aphrodite who decided she wanted to engage with me. Ringo hung up the phone with a couple of vibrant swear words at the end of the conversation and returned.

"Tell that ming, she's doing my head in!" Ringo said abruptly and slapped the phone into her hand.

"She's your bird, tell her yourself!" I liked her straightforward answers. What you saw, you got with her. She turned to me again, "You fancy it?"

Ringo looked at me and I knew that leaving the warehouse together would give Ringo the impression that we were friends and I didn't know if I wanted that. But, I didn't want to leave the warehouse without her.

"Sure!" I mumbled. Courtney was to become the only piece of joy in my life, and why she fell in love with a guy like me is something that I'll never understand because I was a horrible person, not to her, but towards everything and everyone else in my life. From the first moment I saw her, she filled me with a serene calmness, something I'd never felt from anyone else.

"Nice one! I've got the car outside. We're going back to Devil's for a few," Ringo said and that meant I'd be revisiting my past, creating a relationship with Donny, one of Davie's friends, and that was a path I didn't want to go down. My only concern at the time was befriending Jack. Ringo walked back to Donny   and his goons.

"Where do you stay, Max?" I was taken aback by her using my name, and I liked the way she talked to me.

"Nowhere special!" I had entirely wound down from the pent-up tension I put myself through and when I was thinking about leaving with Courtney and Ringo, the door opened.

Chapter 20

Eiffel:

Jack Gallagher stepped in, conceitedly at ease, with his hands inside his brown duffle coat pockets and behind him, Eiffel swaggered, as if he carried position at Jack's rear. Eiffel was a Danish man and a powerful figure. Dressed in a lumberjack shirt and stonewashed jeans, he looked like he should've been on a building site. Previously a man who worked for Bobby Munroe up in Glasgow, he had been hired for his minding services. After being hounded by paranoia, because of Davie's escape from the Eradicator, he needed protection from an invisible return of a foe who was once a friend.

That first sighting of Jack after being released from jail on a technicality, infuriated me. With a blank expression, he sauntered past, brushing too close for comfort, showing no hint of anxiety over his miraculous status. He had no regret about sending me to jail. He ruined my teenage years and filled my life with a storm of trauma. He thought I had no idea and I'd never let him know until I took everything from his life. We eye-balled each other as he walked past, taking an inviting look at Courtney, before fixing his gaze on Ringo, with an obvious bucket of history and hostility between the pair.

Eiffel was his shadow and proud of it. Donny remained cool as ice, keeping his hands inside his jeans pockets. His entourage became guarded and uneasy. These two very different types of people didn't like each other, and it felt like a brawl could break out at any time, even though there was no reason at that moment.

Jack arrived to stand adjacent to Ringo as he took a cautious step back, still inherently fearful of his father. They stood in total stillness and locked daggers, like a couple of boxers before the bell. The father and son combo were so contradictory of each other but at the same time, so alike. I stood and watched the pair, so far apart on personality terms but so alike in looks, almost as if they were the same person, only a generation apart. They both had shoulder length hair, both stood at the same five-foot ten height and both had the same ageing wrinkles under their eyes. Ringo's were caused by the endless partying lifestyle he led, full of potent cocaine and alcohol.

"Son!" Jack mouthed loosely. Seeing Ringo irate was an unusual thing and this was the first time they had stood beside each other since Jack had him beaten to within an inch of his life, a couple of years prior, for his involvement with Davie and undercutting Jack's cocaine empire.

"Jack!" Ringo said, an unglamorous response. He wasn't one for confrontation and didn't know how to respond to a father he hated. I knew that feeling well.

"So, you're the bookie in these parts?" He was modestly relaxed, eyes never removing themselves from Ringo, and speaking more like a punter than his own father. Almost like someone who had a hint of respect but, indisputably, Jack had no respect for his son.

"What's it to you?" This was an environment Jack wasn't welcome in as far as Ringo was concerned. Jack had his drug and prostitute empire and lived a life of bribes and payoffs. Ringo had created the nights at the warehouse for his own benefit in having something criminal to involve himself with and profit from. Like his father, he felt the need to be in control and especially without his father's devious eye looking over him.

"Well, the word on my streets is, I hear everyone's welcome here, son, and I just thought I'd check this scene out for myself."

"Who says you're welcome here?" Ringo knew his father had come into the warehouse for a reason and looking at Eiffel, standing robustly behind him, he knew what that reason was.

"A man with a lot of balls nowadays! And surely very brave with your protection here." Jack took a blank bearing towards the Rogue Riders and didn't bother to acknowledge them. Donny stood relaxed, used to the conflict with Jack, but the other crew members reacted to that comment with offence. Eiffel, who stood behind Jack, walked around him to stand by Ringo's side. Ringo looked at Jack and the reasoning for their visit became apparent.

"Shall we get this underway?" Ringo glanced towards me, and I gestured with a nod of acceptance. I gave Courtney a shallow look and walked away from her, indicating she should do the same.

Eiffel turned his back to me and began to unbutton his shirt. He removed it and handed it to the other woman who was standing beside Courtney. He circled around Jack and Ringo and stood across from me, not a hint of hesitation in his offhand body language. I hadn't seen someone so fearless until that point, which made me uneasy. He held that constant glare that bullies carry in their egos.

"Before we begin," Jack slipped his hand into his coat, "I'd like to place my bet." He flicked through a very large bundle in his hand as Ringo wondered if he had the finances to compete. As Jack finished counting and Ringo was almost sure he couldn't match the bet, he slipped his hand into another pocket. "Ten grand on my man, son."

The demeaning way he said 'son' insulted Ringo, knowing he could do nothing to overrun his old man. The last thing Ringo needed was to lose face. He could've looked at least merely confident by trying to arrange the funds inside his pocket to meet Jack's bet, but he was only too aware he only carried five grand at a time down to the warehouse.

Donny turned to his crew and held his hand out. Without reluctance, they filled it with notes. I was the son of a man the Rogue Riders respected and feared, which meant I had their support. After Donny's hand was filled, he approached Ringo while Eiffel and myself waited patiently for the formalities to be concluded. Donny was the most laid-back man you could have got, wearing a dark bandana and a leather jacket about twenty years old, with badges and scars from over the years. Without taking on Jack, he spoke to Ringo, "How much do you need?"

"Five grand."

Donny flicked through the money and started counting, until he reached a pile of five grand in total.

He handed it to Ringo while replying with a smirk of satisfaction at Jack.

"That's a sentimental gesture, Donny, isn't it, Ringo?" Ringo nodded thankfully to Donny as he returned to his crew. Including his own five grand, Ringo dropped the wager onto the dusty floor. Jack looked to the ground and took that action as a lack of respect. A subdued Eiffel took the slap on the floor as an indication to begin.

Eiffel was to be my first test in this game, and it took me a little time to sort him out.

Chapter 21

The Door Opens:

Many quiet weeks passed by and I had not heard a peep from Jack and I worried that he was not taking the bait. I made sure I left a message after I disposed of Eiffel, who was surely licking his wounds.

That time was the beginning of never knowing Davie's location or what mischievous activities he was up to. He contacted me when he needed me and that was that.

I stuck to a regular daily attendance at Rocky's and changed my steroid intake to three times a week. It brought a substantial difference to my strength and size but gathered extra side effects. Sleeping became very difficult, often having a few restless nights before I could get one good night's sleep, which became a repeating pattern. I gained a shorter temper and internally, I became angrier at life. I started to look for a flat but gave no real effort to it. The old Chinese lady who ran the B&B never bothered me and I never bothered her. I figured I had to move on because that's what people do in normal lives; they have their own place and their own privacy.

I had attended the warehouse for the two months after fighting Eiffel and nobody turned up. There were constant rumours circulating about my ruthlessness and speculation as to who my Father was. After beating a person like Eiffel, I began to crave the attention of a reputation with my fists. I knew I had become feared, and I knew I had found something I was good at. I wished for more foes to tear apart and formidable names were welcome.

The lack of attendance pissed Ringo off because his little monthly gig of pocketing a few easy grand was over. I began to be more talkative around him, his level easy going attitude was too hard to avoid and we spent a lot of time together with Courtney. He indicated that he could manage me and get me more lucrative fights, but I bypassed answering that question. I did not want him managing me and that was one reason I avoided befriending him in the first place.

Most other younger people my age were out partying or chasing their dreams but I didn't have a release from everyday life like that. My release was throwing weights around or deploying my anger and I needed my next fix.

On the way to McCartney's, I was practicing what I was going to say and told myself no matter what, I had to stay calm.

As I walked up the murky, metal plated staircase under the dank lights, I felt nervous, more than I normally would have before a scrap. I could hear the drone of Beatles music and the chatter of punters. I reached the top of the stairs and entered through the lightly hinged double doors to be confronted by a clean dressed doorman. He was a short, coloured man, with a broad width of frame. His manner was ropey with his meaty dreadlocks hanging heavily over a bristly chin, and both ears drawn out by gold hoop rings.

"£10 to get in." His light Anglo English Jamaican tongue indicated he was from a Caribbean family. A common sight throughout parts of Liverpool. I removed a tenner from my pocket and handed it over as I peeked into the main room. I saw a shapely figure with her arm around an expensive suit, dressed in a raunchy trim cut, red-laced, satin number. A further stretch of the neck revealed a few others walking around half naked with thigh cut dresses and exposed chests.

The doorman stamped my hand. "In you go, lad. Play nice, hear me!"

I continued to walk into the room and had a good scout around. There were girls talking to men in a row of booths at the far left of the room, initiating a connection with them before their intentions to empty their wallets came alive. Some were appearing from behind a rear rose-coloured curtain hiding the passage that led into the back.

The clientele were dressed suave and smart, most with their top buttons loose and their manners even looser. Their wallets were open cheque books and their wedding rings never hidden. Most were more than middle aged. These were the local significant people, councillors, solicitors, financial traders, and anyone wanting to rub shoulders with their peers to climb the ladder more quickly. More importantly to Jack, it attracted many of the local filth from the Merseyside police headquarters, about a ten-minute drive from Hope Street. They arrived to sell information to Jack in reply for wads of cash, hand jobs from the girls in the back rooms, and requests of feuds to be resolved. The decor, a mix of moss green and pale black over a dim light, was gloomy and snide, much like the mood.

I moved towards the bar, offset to the right so that it overlooked the entire room, took a pew, with my eyes focused on what was occurring around me. I heard a voice talk from behind the bar.

"Would you like a drink love or you just here for the scenery?" I turned to see Courtney's flourishing eyes look back at me.

I lost my ability to speak and misplaced my motivation for being there.

"Ohh, it's you!" she said, becoming shy, pulling over her black cardigan to cover her generous cleavage. "Would you like a drink?" She asked again as I admired the way half of her flocking hair was pulled over the left side of her face and fell down her chest.

"What?" I asked, forgetting the first question as she smiled. "A drink?"

"Aye, I'll have a coke." I snapped, being abashed and verbally timid as she grinned before walking to the end of the bar to remove a can from the fridge.

I watched her, open-mouthed, having no control over my dancing eyes. She returned and poured the coke into a glass with added ice. Her eyes clocked over my shoulder as one of the strippers approached and sat beside me, laying her palm on my lap.

"Hey, big boy!" She squeezed my thigh. Speaking English well through a thick eastern European accent, she said, "Have not seen you before. Wow, you big!" She gasped, as I exchanged her look with a less pleasant one. She flaunted her bronzed, athletic Albanian figure, wearing a lacy black cropped number, airing her rippling natural stomach under a pair of squashed breasts, making it near impossible not to look at. I rotated my look to Courtney who rolled her eyes, indicating the stripper was a pest.

"No thanks," I announced without any expression, leaving her annoyed at the lost chance to profit. She turned her nose, stabbing Courtney with a scowl as if it was her fault and left in a childish huff. Courtney surely knew I wasn't interested in the smut.

"That's Klara, she's a trier." I nodded back, struggling with the art of conversation. "What brings you here?" Courtney asked as I gazed around.

"Not sure." I didn't want to tell her anything about my life but talking to her took the edge off it.

"You're looking for Jack, uh? Can't imagine you've come for the service."

"No, the service is not for me." I agreed as the chair beside me slid out. Thinking it was another stripper coming to attempt to launder money from my pockets, I turned to see it was Jack.

"I get all sorts in my club nowadays!" Jack attempted humour to lighten the tension, sat down, and positioned his elbows over the bar, smothering it with his authority. My fist clenched while my neck tightened. Like the speed of a lightning bolt, I pictured smashing his head off the curve of the bar, when an overweight lofty man, with a swollen face and brown bushy eyebrows over bloodshot drunken eyes, butted in. His hefty gut indicated his suit kept him on his arse most of the time. "Jack, I must be off. I'll get all the paperwork written up in the next week." He offered his hand to be shaken.

Jack squashed his brows, peered at it, and ignored the offer.

"Once it's done, come to my office and I'll look it over."

The man patted Jack's shoulder, looking for a hint of acknowledgement of their friendship or at least some recognition. Towards Jack, he was polite and upstanding while being a little tipsy. Jack did not want to take him on.

"I'll see you again Jack." He walked off as Jack checked his shoulder and swept the man's prints off with his hand.

"They say you can't pick your family...that is true, but you can't pick the local councillor either. It's best to control those people who would prefer to live without acknowledging the wrongs they have done."

I lost my violent thoughts towards Jack during that moment and collected myself. Jack turned and watched the man leave. "Councillor Grant will always do what I want him to do because his career and reputation are in my hands."

I had no idea what he was talking about. I thought about my reply for some time as Courtney stood, a keen observer knowing not to butt into Jack's conversation as I exchanged a look with her. Jack picked up on my vulnerability for Courtney. He also picked up on my lack of conversation skills. "Max, join me in the office. I see you don't drink alcohol, would you like a coffee?"

"Sure," I answered, leaving my coke at the bar and following Jack to his office.

On entering, I saw Eiffel sitting comfortably on the two-seater sofa behind the door, not fazed to see the man who had beaten him up a few months earlier. Jack flicked the switch of his stainless-steel kettle and sat at his desk. I sat opposite.

"You can get yourself down to Dingle and bring that chancer back to see me!" Jack spoke straight up to Eiffel asking him to run an errand for him.

"Sure!" Eiffel agreed and left, giving me a slight brush of the shoulder.

"How do you like your coffee?"

"Strong, with sugar." He stood and turned his back, opening a fresh pack of unlabelled filtered coffee. I scanned the room, picking up any information I could. His diary lay open close to the landline phone. He had one of those revolving card holders that kept the contact details of his acquaintances. As I observed, he blurted out, "I drink Bolivian coffee. I get it from the source so it's the best of stuff." He prepared the coffee while I continued scanning. It was not the first time I'd been in there and nothing had changed. The walls were a dank red, painted over old plain wallpaper, with framed pictures of Beatles albums and Liverpool FC team photos. To the rear of his desk was his furniture rack with his coffee station; in the back corner was his reputable whisky cabinet with locked drawers. "I know why you're here, Max."

My head switched out of my analysis of the room. Did he know I was in contact with Davie? Did he have someone following me since jail? All kinds of paranoid thoughts were racing through me.

"Why's that?" I asked as he laid my cup down. Without wasting time, I took a slurp. He was right, the coffee was delicious.

Jack took his seat and faced me on with no hesitation or fear. I knew it was him I had to blame for my horrid time in jail, but he had no idea I knew and I got a kick from that.

"Before we talk about the reason you're sitting here, I need to ask you a few questions." This sounded ominous and reminded me of the police interview room. Jack wanted me to respond.

"Go on."

"When was the last time you saw your father?" I was nervous, unsure of what he knew.

"The night before he disappeared. Do you know where he went?" I tried to seem cool but inquisitive. Counter questioning was a good move considering I already knew the answer.

"Unfortunately, no one knows where the elusive Mr Rhodes has gone, but I'd like to find out, considering how much money he owes me." Jack reminded me of the cash Davie skimmed.

"I knew nothing of what he stole from you. I was just one of his gofers."

Jack was not interested in the money; he wanted to know where Davie was so he could stop living in paranoia that he would turn up and get his payback for the Eradicator's torture. I squinted at the paperwork over his desk and saw a couple stacks of property deeds with his signature on them. I glanced at the cabinet behind to see a picture of Beverly and his two rottweilers.

"I'm not sure if I believe you," Jack said, leaning back in his expensive reclining desk chair, circling his thumbs with his fingers interlocked. I showed no emotion and remained solid, as that horrid feeling of being analysed came over me. "So you like to fight!" he said, breaking the silence.

"It runs in the jeans apparently," I answered and drew a shallow smirk from him.

"I hear you've scared everyone off from the warehouse. That'll annoy my son, I expect." He opened the drawer of his desk and put the property deeds away. "You remind me a lot of Davie. I saw him fight once or twice. You've the same ruthless streak."

I found the compliment awkward to answer and hoped he would move on. "Something you might be interested in. I had Gregor Palin, a promoter from Manchester, contact me a few days ago. It's very convenient that you are now here. He's running a new age boxing show. It could be illegal, it might not, but it's bare knuckle…"

I stopped him mid-sentence.

"When?"

Chapter 22

Gregor Palin:

Discussions had taken place between Jack and Gregor Palin over purses and dates; an agreement had been made. My second concern was for the money I'd pocket. Sure, I'd collect my winnings because my blood and sweat would earn them. My first caring was to develop a great name on the circuit, to become notorious like Davie, and carry the reputation that demands a reaction of respect from people. My third caring was to get closer to Jack. The thought of losing, living with the shame, being embarrassed in front of the crowd, was more fearful to me than anything else.

I had around a month before the fight and I maintained a strong routine. I went to Rocky's five days a week, lifted weights, injected a lot of steroids, and punched a lot of heavy boxing bags. I had purpose in my life, something to look forward to and I welcomed the motivation. Some days, apart from hitting the gym, my brain was a prison of thoughts I did not desire to have. Every day I told myself that the burden of carrying the past would become lighter and I suppose, marginally, it did as I learned to live with it. At least a couple times a week I'd have outbursts of frustration, when the remote for the telly didn't work or I'd linger in a conflict of opinion with someone. Losing my keys, misplacing my trainers, minor things like that caused lots of hissy fits. Often anything that was within reaching distance would get broken. It was silly issues that caused temper tantrums. I would turn into an angry child and I could not ever see that changing.

I exchanged numbers with Jack but he rarely called me. It was a foot in the door and I was in no rush to overstep my boundaries with him. I'd be patient.

The show we were attending was a popular event and the men who fought carried pride and burned for victory. The bouts took place inside a pit of bales that formed a squared area about five-by-five metres. Hardly enough room to do a shit.

Gregor organised the show which would take place inside an abandoned cotton mill, off Bridgewater Canal, in the area of Leigh, Greater Manchester. Unlike walking the line, not any punter could have his chance - it would only be punters who had a worthy name. Fights were organised weeks in advance to aid the build-up and if there was a beef between any fighters, it would be welcomed, as it brought the crowd in.

Our fight was billed as Liverpool vs Manchester. The rivalry between the cities was bitter and detached from any reasoning, other than they were next door and had massive football clubs. Gregor Palin was brazen in spreading the word, pulling in rowdy crowds so his bookie could have more chance of profiting from the drunks.

Gregor was the Manchester version of Jack but not nearly as powerful. He dealt in the import of hash from Morocco, cigarettes from anywhere cheaper than the UK, human trafficking of prostitutes and he also ran a moderate supply chain of cocaine that was supplied to him by Jack. He was ex-British forces from the late 90's where he was jailed for drug smuggling and then given military discharge after a short stint inside the glasshouse in Aldershot.

I was matched against a menacing thug who won most of his fights due to his heavyweight size and seasoned experience. He was vastly older, in his mid-thirties, and had a lot of experience in those surroundings. His name was Bo Pat, but to everyone in the game, he was known as the Minute Mauler, because his fights did not last long.

On the day of the fight, a Saturday morning, Jack picked me up from Chinatown, the first time I'd seen him in person since I was inside his office. We embarked on the short drive to Leigh where conversation consisted of mundane chat and awkward silences. I sat in the back, leaving Jack and Eiffel to sit in the front. Eiffel learned to respect me after our scrap. I saw that in the manner he carried around me. He was Jack's bitch, willing to do anything asked, but there was an affable side to him. I sensed somewhat he didn't want to be dealing with all Jack's endeavours and chores, but being on around six grand a month won his loyalty. It differed on how much bonus money he'd get for keeping Jack's runners in check and solving any dilemmas he had. He was welcome in the car as it gave me plenty of time to zone out in the back. When you take as many steroids as I did, your mood swings and sleeping patterns are as erratic as a junkie's principles. The past few nights had been almost sleepless and I drifted off during the day to catch up.

We arrived at the destination in late afternoon when the sun began to dim on the canal. The old cotton mill, from the outside, was enormous, up to six stories high, with substantial windows filled with holes. Way too commanding for a modest fighting event.

Jack led us on foot abreast the canal, to a huddle of people and an entrance. From the smartly dressed punters in suits, newsboy hats choking on cigars, to the tracksuit-wearing thug who was already intoxicated, there was no favourable class here.

"Wait here. I'll nip inside and see what's going on," Jack insisted, as he smartened himself up, leaving me with Eiffel.

"This man you fight, I hear a lot of him." Eiffel spouted in his methodical English. "Is a tough man!"

"Tougher than you?" I responded bluntly as Eiffel checked his neck.

"I am no fighter, all I do is the job I'm asked." There it outlined how much Eiffel would be willing to do for his boss. Jack liked loyalty. "He has a reputation for being dirty, biting, low blows...watch out for that." He was trying to advise me but I was too stubborn to acknowledge and shrugged his advice off by ignoring him.

I had no patience for the waiting carry on, my legs jittered and my breathing became hard to keep at ease. I could smell blood and all I wished was to get on with it. For the previous few days, I had purposely kept away from the gym and people, allowing a build up to commence.

I entered the bottom floor of the building: rows of steel pillars under beams with some gloomy moonlight filtering in the distant rear windows. A squared area between the pillars had been swept and tidied with the pit enclosed by bales. It was tiny compared to the surroundings. And intimidating. I wondered how men could fight in such a small space.

There were around four dozen people inside, all already filled with ale at six in the evening. On my walk around and overhearing chatter, I sussed out there were to be a few fights that evening. I stopped where I could see the bodies and then I spotted him, Bo Pat. I knew it was him, from my instinctive judgement. We met eyes; he was relaxed and fierce.

His neck long, greasy curled black hair tied into a ponytail lying behind a marvellously untrimmed beard. His belly was like that of an ale guzzler and his grimy skin showed unhealthy living. He conversed with a couple of comrades, holding cans of lager. As one of them drifted to the side, I saw Bo Pat himself gripping a Guinness can.

That annoyed me. Did he have no respect for me? It did explain his butch gut. My staring interest was obvious and soon the pack of men exchanged looks with me. I did not look away and pulsed my venom towards him, so he knew I was not scared. I was merely a boy to him, a buoyant victim in his eyes. It was something ingrained into a fighter, a good instinct. I had glimpsed my opponent, which was what I wished, and I headed back out of the building, through the traffic of bodies entering, and bumped into Jack standing with Gregor Palin. He stopped me.

"Mr Palin, this is your fighter, Max." Jack barked out. Gregor Palin was butch, with a blank look of disdain under a head as smooth as a snooker ball. Standing tense, his manner indicating lack of interest in conversation, he scowled meanly. He wore a tight plain t-shirt under a body warmer that showed old-fashioned regiment type tattoos up his arms. He put out his hand for me to shake; I ignored it and walked on.

I was there to do a job, not make friends.

Chapter 23

Bo Pat:

I waited around for what seemed like a generation, in the car. I got out for short walks as my impatience drove me nuts. Eiffel and Jack did not wait with me. Why would they? I was moodier and more uncommunicative than normal. My temperament was not controllable, my imagination of what I was going to do to my foe was in overdrive. I had thoughts of being weak or getting hurt, which annoyed me, and sometimes I'd scream in denial of having them. I felt the pain of seclusion as a child and that separation from society made me feel like a loser. I feared a man of Bo Pat's size and what he could do. There was no escaping that thought. The build-up of unleashing my temper increased. Waiting was something I always detested, and never got used to.

I deployed a flurry of punches into the back passenger seat and thudded my fist into the roof. I had to leave the car. I got out, stomped around, ripped off my top layer of clothing and watched the crowd walking in and out of the shed, allowing their curious eyes to set on me. They and their intoxicated looks meant nothing to me.

The rules of the fight were simple. If you were knocked down, there was no count. If you can stand, then you continue. But you had to allow your opponent to rise before you were allowed to carry on. It was a fight until you could fight no more.

Jack came to speak to me. "You're on," he spoke gravely then returned to the shed. I stood idle, watching the door slam behind him as I glared at it harshly for a couple of seconds before I stomped towards it.

No one looked at me, the crowd was distracted, begging for their next fix of violence, as I was. People seemed to treat this as a normal occurrence. No one seemed or looked out of place. A congregation of men who lived on making bad decisions and court appearances. My eyes were open with adrenaline and my fists clammed up as I pushed through the crowd to a gap in the bales that formed the knee-high pit.

Jack stood in a corner, resting with his hands in his pockets, for sure I'd make him some cash. He gave me the nod to enter. The feelings of intoxicating adrenaline soared through me. My hair sizzled. I was young but I had been through so much until that point. That reminded me why I was there. The buzz made me forget.

As I walked into the pit, the crowd chatter fizzled down, being replaced with an air of wonder to why someone so young stood there. I gripped my fist with tensed shoulders and bit down, preparing to explode. I looked for Bo Pat and found him striding through the attendance of the shed who parted and gave him encouragement. They huddled around the pit enclosure, causing the space to become claustrophobic, roaring for entertainment.

Bo Pat lumbered over the bales in no great rush and instantly I caught the whiff of drink. His eyelids drooped but still held focus. He was a bear of a man, covered in chest hair and was mentally prepared, as I was. I felt it was a normal occurrence for him; he had been bred from a hard life like me.

A smaller man, of medium height, in a hoody, entered the pit. I wondered who he was for a few seconds before realising it was the ref. I was not expecting this to be any kind of sporting event. It surprised and momentarily distracted me before I re-focused. I saw the man across from me and wanted to hurt him, make him bleed and defeat him. He felt the same about me and I hoped my age would be enough for him to underestimate me. When you underestimate someone, it can have grave consequences as I would find out later in my fighting career.

The ref started talking to us at the same time, switching his gaze between us.

"Right, men, you break when I break you up. No eye gouging, ground fighting and no biting. Have decency and follow these rules. When you're down, you get up. There will be no counts. Once you can't stand, it's over..." The ref waited for us to agree but neither of us gave indication we wanted to. It was time. The ref looked over to Gregor Palin for clarification to begin. "Ok, get ready." His hand hung in the air, separating us.

"Fight!"

Pat dived his hulking body forward as I lined up a right hand; he smothered into my chest, butted his forehead into my face and left-hooked me in the jaw as he broke away. The space was so tight, a step here or there landed you at the edge of the pit. Reloading to explode and as quickly as I could blink, he booted my shin and jabbed me in the face.

Angered, I threw a wild wide punch with my left hand that glanced across his jaw, hardly worth acknowledging. Rapidly, he smothered me again, leaning his hefty weight over me as my knees folded and we fell over the bales. I rolled him over and wrestled him on the ground before the ref reluctantly tore us apart.

We stood again, quickly. I hit him square in the nose with my right. The punch was so rapid and hard, I felt the cartilage crunch. I entered a place in my head, full of rage mixed with frustration, and planted my feet, pulled back my head and sunk a headbutt towards his nose, but I missed and thudded his forehead. Dazed and numb momentarily with the after effect of a skull to-skull impact, I was blinded by pain. I had lost my bearings and the noise of the crowd.

A barrage of four heavy punches, whipped across my face, weakened me to sagging as another blow into my balls felt like my soul had been knocked out of my body. I fell onto the concrete ground. Two big kicks riveted my side as I struggled to suck in oxygen. The ref pulled Bo Pat off and spoke to me, but I could hardly hear him through the brain fog.

I barely rose to my feet, leaning over my hips, looking the ref in the eye.

"Carry on?" I heard him ask and bang! A thundering left whacked into my ribs and a left elbow clattered into my jaw. I staggered backwards and my weight fell over the bales. I could not get the space to move or steady myself. I was fighting on instinct, through mist. I had no idea of my stance or whereabouts.

When I pulled myself up and off the bales, Bo Pat struck me in the gut again and slipped me in a solid headlock, wrapping his forearm tightly around my throat. I gargled for breath as thundering punches smashed into my face. The ref barged in and pushed Bo Pat aside, knowing the move was dishonourable and that gave me thirty seconds to recover.

The ref returned to me as I stood to my height, breathless and weakened. "Carry on?" he asked again.

I grimaced with frustration and disgust at my weakness. I shoulder barged Bo Pat over the bales which brought an onslaught of boos. Now I had space, I could move.

Bo Pat's wide-open stance thudded over to me with his fists by his waist. Already having dealt with me so quickly, he thought he was about to finish me. His fat right hand came hurtling at me again, ricocheting off my chin. The warm-up was over; I'd become numb to any more pain. I was fuming and sent a barrage of combination punches onto his face. He dipped and swayed through them but I hurt him with a couple. He tried to rub his forehead into my face, attempting to spoil my work but I stepped to the side, allowing him to trip.

I upped the throttle and kept the pressure on as he toppled back onto the bales. I started firing punches at him frantically, pounding my weight through every punch. I could feel the bone-to-bone impact over his ribs, encouraging me to carry on. As he tried to lean to either side, I'd use the power of my punch to send him back the other way. I was deafened by the force of adrenaline that took over. I entered a haze of indignant insanity where I would turn into something empty of mercy. I had him trapped and with all the weight I could muster, I released an onslaught of howling aggression over his body and face. I could feel the grasp of hands from the rear snatch over my shoulders, trying to yank me back.

I shrugged them off, splattering them with elbows and back handers. Still, they tried and still I pummelled fists over Bo Pat's dormant body. That was when the huddle of men managed to drag me off. They pinned me to the ground. I screamed and roared, slithering around trying to get free, but I was trapped by them and by the haze. I was mad, tears of wrath streaming from my eyes.

People yelled at me, but it was all just blurred sounds. My eyes were still wide with rage. Being held down reminded me of the awful times inside the jail and there was no cure from those memories. As I calmed, Jack came into my sight, blocking the glare of a blinding light above. He pressured his arm down onto my upper chest.

"Max, it's over, it's over. These men don't want to harm you." Looking at him and listening to his words began to bring me back.

"It's over, come back." I started to calm. One by one, the men removed their grip and I stood up, almost with amnesia as to what had just occurred. I looked across to see that Bo Pat was being helped up. He was weary, pained and confused, as I caught his reluctant look. His face was mauled with blood, his legs weakened while he held the ribs I had broken. Mr Palin panicked into the pit and stood beside Jack and redirected his attention towards me with a couple of heavy steps into my chest.

"That's what we don't want to happen here, you disrespectful fuck."

I imagined grabbing his throat but Jack stepped in and separated us.

"I told ya, he was new. He doesn't know the code yet, Mr Palin. "I'll be sure to see it doesn't happen again.

Chapter 24

Two Friendly Rottweilers:

The fight was over and so was the night. The cesspit of spectators was entertained although annoyed at their local man's beating. Eiffel wasted no time in getting us out of there and back towards Liverpool. I had crossed a very fine line between respect and disrespect. Although those kinds of fights weren't exactly by the book, they did have a moral code. Jack knew that, yet never gave me one slice of advice on how to conduct myself. But would it have changed what I did? I doubt that.

Jack had seen first-hand how fucked up in the head I was and how little control I had over my temper. I had my slice of adrenaline and later, I allowed my heart and brain to return to normal.

In the back of his Range Rover, once my hyper state of stress dispensed, I conked out. I slipped into a peaceful trance after the trauma. Most men would not have been able to switch off but I was not most men. Those moments of calmness I have after a release were some of the most enduring feelings I would ever have.

I was wakened around four am by the thud of a security gate and crackling chuckies as we drove up Jack's drive in Victoria Road in Formby. Victoria Road was a line of the most expensive mansions in the Merseyside area. It was named Millionaire's Row, with an average house price of £2.4 million. You'd find footballers, managers, pop stars, property tycoons, and of course, gangsters like Jack. Steven Gerrard lived a few doors down and he'd pop into Jack's every now and again for a taste of his Bolivian coffee. There was a golf club around the corner that would cost a yearly wage to be a member. Eiffel had already been dropped off for the night.

"Morning!" Jack said as I slid up the seat, squinting my eyes to focus as the glare of floodlights dazzled my vision.

"Take me home?" I wanted to return to the B&B to be on my own.

"I'll take you back later in the day. You can kip in one of the spare rooms and get a good feed in the morning." Jack knew how much I liked food and getting in his house would allow me an insight into his other side.

Each man acts differently in his own home. You can see a side to them that others wouldn't be able to. I'd take notes and relay them back to Davie whenever I would see him next.

The car pulled up outside the doorway, with English ivy draping the sides like a post-Victorian house. The chrome-coloured streetlamps along the drive gave the dark morning some ambience. It had an old-fashioned vibe that echoed a retro-modern touch.

Jack led me inside and straight away; I could see a distant glow of a flashing orange beacon. In a lavish hall, he typed a code into the security interface. I was close enough to see the first few digits, two six two. The hallway stretched to the height of the roof which had a circular window, adding light to what was left of the moon for the morning. A curved staircase at either side led to a landing. I'd never seen such wealth before, so contradictory to the environment we had just been in.

Jack didn't need to roam in such circles as he could have retired the day after and lived a life most people dream about.

Two rottweilers limped despondently into the hall without haste or panic, as if they had just risen from a nap. They already knew it was Jack before seeing him, probably recognising the sound of his car tyres rolling over the chuckies. Both wore bulky, dark collars, stopping to sit a couple of metres away from me, giving me the shake down with their eyes.

"See, if you'd walked in here without me, they would've torn you apart." Jack moved over to pet the one on the left. "He's ok, Bruno." Bruno relaxed and slopped away with the other following.

"Don't be timid around them as they smell fear. You don't have much, they know that."

"Where's my bed?"

Jack turned, straight backed, and paused before answering. "Follow the stairs on the left and it's your second left. There's a carzie in there for you, too." He began to walk away. "I'll likely not be here when you wake up but Bev will see you alright for breakfast." Jack tapped his shoes off the marble floor and disappeared into the house, leaving my eyes to wander over his wealth. I cut Jack no slack as I was still livid about my treatment in jail. Every time I was in his company, I'd quiz myself, wondering if he knew that I knew he had me sent there. Nevertheless, I didn't want to have that conversation. Davie would be pleased I had gained access to his house and that was the main achievement of the occasion. I'd forgotten already the wrath I'd inflicted on Bo Pat and the pain he left me in. My face was tender but living with pain had become a usual occurrence for me. That night I slept well in a king-sized bed and showered in a room that was bigger than the room I rented in the B&B.

I woke in the morning with the post-fight pains. There was no adrenaline flowing to hide the aching; it was laid bare to feel, but I was young, able to heal from it. I made my way downstairs following the noise of clunking dishes and drawers. Bev stood in the streamlined minimalist vast kitchen, at a central marble-topped unit, laying some dry cutlery from her dishwasher into a drawer. She hadn't heard me sneak up, or so I thought. "You must be Max," she said, keeping her back to me, while removing dishes from the washer, surprising me that she knew I was there. She turned, "Grab a seat. Jack said you'd want some scran."

I pulled out a chair from the breakfast bar, opposite the side of her cutlery drawer. I glanced at the clock.

Bev moved around the gloss-coated cupboards, grabbing a plate and a cup and then opened the fridge, throwing food onto the counter. "You don't look like a fussy man, Max, full English do ya?"

"Aye, that'll be fine." She slowed down and tilted her head.

"You say 'aye' like your father, sounds strange from a Wollie." A Wollie was someone who stayed in the surrounding areas of Liverpool, such as the Wirral or St Helens. I spent most of my life around St Helens with the Parkers in my early years before I knew I was adopted, in foster homes and with the Jacksons, from whom Davie took me. I never sounded Scouse; I had a bit of the twang but my accent was mixed. No one had said that before and I guess she was right, something I picked up from the time I'd spent with Davie and the side of me that emulated part of him. I nodded my head in acknowledgement of the statement as she caught onto my distant nature.

"This is some house," I said, feeling as if I had to say something or else she'd think I wasn't grateful for the food and bed. She seemed like the kind of person who did not judge or care who you were. I guess being married to Jack would have that effect.

"It's good. I like it, so I do," she answered. We made small talk as she prepared breakfast. I sat shyly and took in my surroundings, waking myself up in the process. I realised I had made the breakthrough into Jack's life. I was sitting inside his house, having breakfast cooked for me by his wife.

Jack returned later in the afternoon to drive me back to the B&B.

I was looking forward to some solitude. My intention was to try and contact Davie which was never an easy task as he'd become a ghost.

It did not take long before I realised Jack was not headed for Chinatown. We were driving through Radcliffe estate in Everton.

"You're going in the wrong direction!"

"No, we're not," he answered confidently.

"My B&B is in…"

"I know. You won't be going back there, I'll put you in one of my flats. It'll be a lot more homely than that place. It's so small and way out of the way." I did not want any favours from him. "The place is clean, smells good, and the cupboards are full of food. What more does a man need!"

I toyed with the idea of refusing his offer until I comprehended it might be rent free.

"Ok," I replied, noticing we had stopped by the high rise where I stayed with Davie. He pulled into the car park and handed me the keys.

"You know where you're going!"

I was dismayed but took the keys from him. When I got out of the motor, I glanced up at the five-storey L shaped block.

"Come down to the club. Courtney's been asking for you!" Jack said, as he drove off.

I looked up again and reminisced - the last time I had been up there, I was escorted towards jail time.

Chapter 25

What to do:

I pushed open the door of the flat. Immediately I had all kinds of flashbacks, the police raid, my first conversation with Inspector Carlin in the kitchen. The flat was more or less how it was when I left. It was still unfashionable with dank brown walls matching the early 90's pine cupboards. It looked clean apart from my feet sticking to the dated vinyl floor. I opened a few of the cupboards to see plenty of supplies inside and the fridge was well stocked.

I moved into the sitting room, through the doorless frame. It was a bit cheerier because the old mouldy stained yellow wallpaper had been stripped off and been given a fresh paint of a faded dark blue. There was a new tele, sitting on a glass three-tier TV stand, with a Sky box. On the bottom shelf was an Xbox with a couple of controllers. The sofa was the same spongy, long, pecan-coloured three-seater crumpet with a newer, oak topped coffee table in front of it. Glancing at it brought back all the films I used to watch lying there, usually with Danielle close by. I realised I missed her and that simpler time where I did not live with vengeance in mind. She was easy to talk to and confide in, since there was never any conflict with her. The view out of the big rear window at the back of the sitting room was its usual depressing self. It wasn't Jack's worst flat but it was nowhere near his best.

My bag full of clothes I had from the B&B was on the floor. Jack must have had Eiffel pick it up and settle my bill. I immediately panicked! Did Jack find my hidden materials from Davie, fake phones, passports, that kind of thing? I hoped they were still in the place I'd left them, in the empty space inside the bed frame. I'd have to visit the B&B later.

I sauntered down the narrow lobby to my old room. Walking in flooded me with memories of sitting on my bed playing the PlayStation late into the night, listening out to when Davie returned home. The room had been stripped of its Everton posters and nude females; now it was mundane with a bed and a lamp sitting on a narrow chest of drawers.

I left and headed to Davie's old room. It had a bit more character with a built-in mirrored wardrobe and a tall chest of drawers. As it didn't feel right being in there, I returned to my own room and tucked myself into the bed, delighted with the solitude and had a nap.

On waking, I wanted to get in touch with Davie and to do that, I needed the burners that were in the B&B. In no haste, I travelled to the B&B, taking a bus before a long walk.

Once there, I opened the door with my key to be greeted by the innocent Miss Yang. "Max!" She was startled, confused that it was me.

"Miss Yang, I understand someone has been round here."

"Yes, a big man, tall rude man. Barged in and make demand and shouting." She spoke vibrantly annoyed and the man she was speaking about was Eiffel.

"I'm very sorry," I replied with no conviction.

"He go into room, take stuff!" Her hands waved around the air dramatically. "He filled a bag, paid bill, then left."

"Did he pay it all?"

"Too much! He gave too much." She appeared to turn to get the extra money.

"No, you keep that. There's something I left in the room…Do you mind?" She folded her arms and stiffened up.

"Go on," she said, while nodding her head up the stairs.

Miss Yang had already cleaned up. I slid underneath the bed and poked my hand up into the empty space in the bed frame. Thankfully, my shoe box I'd stashed was still there. I slid it out, dropped it onto the mattress and opened it up. It was all there, phones, passports, drivers' licences and around ten grand in cash. When I shut the box and lifted my head, Miss Yang stood in the doorframe.

"Drug money!" she suggested and marginally guilty, I paused.

"It's a lot worse than drug money!" I picked the box up, refused to enter into any more conversation and bolted out the door. Miss Yang did not deserve to have my baggage at her doorstep. Back at the flat, I went through a list of phone numbers in order to contact Davie. Whenever I met him, he gave me an updated list of numbers, from one to ten. I would go through the process of dialling the numbers one by one until one of them rang. Sometimes he would not answer and he would call me back later on. I'd also text each number with the initial E to indicate 'Eclipse'. Either way, I knew that he would have acknowledged that I'd tried to contact him.

It took him weeks to get back to me with an instruction to call number eight on the list of burners. But in those weeks, I had time to think, and I was not sure how comfortable I'd be sharing all the information of what I'd been getting up to. I decided to live my own secluded life and see how he liked to be kept in the dark, but I'd always have to give him something.

"I'm in," I said immediately as he answered the phone.

"Aye, good man, how was it done?"

"He took me on and got me a fight in Manchester." Davie gathered his thoughts for a moment. I did what I said I was going to do, fight and earn Jack's interest. A chip off my old father's block and he must have been proud of me.

"An' how did it go?" he asked.

"He took me into his house."

"No! Wi' Jack, the fight, how did it go?" I was a little taken aback that he cared, as he usually wanted to talk about business and deception. "What kind o' fight?"

"In something they call a pit."

"Bales round it?" Talking about fighting gave him a link to the past and with that came a hint of excitement.

"Aye," I answered.

"That's the old school way o' doin' it. It brings out all the sneaky fuckers who like to play dirty. Was yer man good?"

"He roughed me up a bit but he didn't last long."

"Good! Glad to hear, son. Stick in wi' Jack. Of all the time I worked for him, he never let me into his house. Ye're doin' a good job. Keep it up! One day we'll take it all. I'm makin' a lucrative trip soon. It'll be a good wee number and I'll be uncontactable for a while." It was a trip to Sweden and it became a regular thing. Often Davie would go off grid for weeks or months at a time.

"Ok."

"While I'm away, I'll be arrangin' a drop. It'll be a trip back to London and you'll be working wi' Rankin. He knows most o' the details and I'll be in touch wi' the dates."

"Alright."

With that, he hung up and I grimaced at the idea of working with Rankin. He was a snake.

For the next week or so, Jack's words about Courtney wishing to see me persistently circled my thoughts. I did wonder if it was true, as my instinct hinted Jack was trying to lure me more into his life. I welcomed that but I did not like him using Courtney as a chess piece.

The flat was freaking me out - there wasn't a day where I wouldn't think of my past there and it was not always bad times. I loved being Davie's sidekick, assisting him with drug running and collecting Jack's takes from his brothels. It was a thrill, being that young and living on adrenaline. The time he beat the Collins' brothers up in the brothel because they mocked me remained strong in my head. His willingness to protect me told me he had a caring side underneath that hard exterior.

I would remember Danielle and wonder what had become of her. Davie's lover, during the time we stayed at the flat, who looked after my needs like a mother would. I spent more time with her than I did with Davie. She disappeared at the same time Davie had and I wondered if that was a coincidence.

The flat felt empty now and it was lonely. The years of solitude in jail conditioned my brain to seclusion but my heart was different. It longed for love but I had no idea how to love someone or accept it. I shielded all that behind a wall of pain. I couldn't be seen running to Jack's every request or else he'd think he could treat me as his lapdog.

I'd continue to be patient, however frustrating that was.

Chapter 26

Flapping Around:

I settled in but I was always on edge around people, more so at Rocky's gym. I'd look for trouble, a confrontation, or anything that would allow my temper to fly. At only eighteen, I was hardly a man, but mature in the criminal world and older men didn't know how to take me on. Anyone I had come across in day-to-day life was a target too. I hadn't had a release of tension since I beat Bo Pat.

I decided to go back to McCartney's. I had a need for another fight and a desire to see Courtney. This time walking in, I bypassed any unnecessary conversation with the doorman. He now knew of my rep and I had a free pass. I walked by Jack's office door and headed straight to the bar. Even in the short time I'd been hanging around, I'd gained a reputation and the rumour had spread fast that I was the son of Davie Rhodes.

I caught a few of the loosely dressed girls' eyes analyse me as I walked across the floor on a desolate evening in the club. They showed so much skin it was hard to resist a look. I could only see two punters in the booths with company. Courtney was working and hadn't spotted me yet as I slipped onto a stool at the bar. Her eyes drew to me as she dried a glass and placed it onto a lower shelf. She wore a short cut top and caught me looking down her chest. I shifted my eyes away as she walked towards me.

"Hey," she said invitingly, "Coke is it?"

"Sure." Even that small sentence was enough to make me nervous. Her manner was more mild than other girls' and her makeup-less face matched her humble vibe.

"Haven't seen you in a while," she said genuinely while cracking open a can and pouring it into a glass.

"Aye, been busy!"

"You say 'aye' strangely!"

"Do I!" It was becoming obvious I had some familiarities to Davie. "It's because I spent a few years with a Scotsman."

"Is that your old man you're talking about?"

I silenced for a moment, wondering how much she knew of his reputation. I looked at her sullenly when she replied. "Everyone knows you're Davie Rhodes' son."

Davie still had a lively reputation around the circuit. It told me that I was being talked about behind my back. Tales were still being told of Davie and now his son was filling the missing quota.

"Aye, I'm talking about him." I shifted my head away from her eye contact. I didn't want her to think I was anything like him but there was nothing I could do to hide that.

"How old are you? I'm struggling to guess?" "Not far from nineteen the last time I checked."

"You're pretty mature looking for your age."

How was I supposed to answer that? I could have said that my youth made me old more quickly than others. Most people hadn't gone through what I had up until then.

Courtney got me into a mild tit-for-tat tat conversation, one I wanted to be in and it flowed easily. After a few minutes I asked her straight up, "How old are you?"

"I'm twenty-six, just turned twenty-six." She was well older than me and I hoped she didn't mind that.

Out of nowhere our conversation was interrupted when a pin-headed man with circled specs came screaming out from behind the velvet curtain that led through to the dancing booths.

Almost instantly, the double doors at the entrance burst open, as the doorman belted across the room. The lanky fella skipped around with his trousers and boxers around his ankles, with his willie flapping around. It was Jack's solicitor, Calvin Stuart. He was uncharacteristically leathered and seemed unsure of his actions. The doorman ran across the room as Eiffel followed from the office with his elongated steps, at quick pace. Calvin was built like the vertical edge of a flag from his toes to his pasty haircut over his pin-shaped head.

Calvin was articulate, educated and had never harmed a soul.

He stuttered, trying to pull his trousers up, when a shapely, vulgar Bulgarian stripper ran out from the curtain behind him, visibly disturbed, holding her hand over her mouth. The doorman rugby-tackled Calvin to the ground as the stripper started booting him in the guts.

When Eiffel arrived, he bear-hugged the girl, lifting her off her feet and handed her to a huddle of the other strippers who stood around watching.

"Get off me, brute!" Calvin slurred, as he kicked and thrashed. "Jack can fucking tell everyone, everyone!" He belched and then even louder, "Fucking do it! Fucking tell everyone, you cunt." He spat on the doorman, not knowing who he was. Eiffel helped the doorman take a grip of him under the armpits and dragged him across the room, his trousers still at his ankles, as his arse burned against the wooden floor.

When they got closer to the exit, Calvin shouted again, "I want my life back! Tell him I don't fucking care! Tell any fucking one, tell every fucking one." I assumed he was talking about Jack.

"Down the stairs?" Eiffel suggested, while Calvin had tears of frustration roll down his cheeks.

"Throw him down the stairs!" The doorman agreed.

At the top of the stairs, they launched him down like a missile. The standard McCartney's treatment for the extremely disliked. Calvin would be heavily pained by that in the morning.

The next thing I knew, I had travelled halfway across the room with my fists clenched, standing close by the pole that dominated the centre of the room, my breathing short and heavy, fuelled for that release.

Courtney approached me from behind, gently, so as not to startle me and touched my hand. I turned to look at her and noticed how far away from the bar I'd wandered.

She gripped my fingers and persuaded me back to my stool.

"Who's that?" I asked, as I settled back onto the stool.

"That's Calvin. Jack's solicitor."

"Surely not the way for solicitors to act!" I insisted.

"Not the first time he's done something like that."

I began to wonder what kind of hold Jack had on him to make a man act in that way. I pondered what it could be and I was curious to find out.

Courtney changed the subject, "What you doing tomorrow?"

"This and that, going to the gym, eating, sleeping, usual."

"Me and my pal Rebecca are going out for a drink. You want to come along? She'll be with Ringo and it would be nice not to be the third wheel."

Without thinking, I answered, "Sure."

From the corner of my eye, I saw Eiffel stomping over to spoil a blessed moment of joy for me.

"You could have helped Max."

"I don't get paid to clean up scraps, that's your job!"

"You're getting more pleasant by the day."

He gestured harshly to Courtney, "Give me an orange juice!"

Hold on," I said, "Say please, Cunt!"

Eiffel gawked at me while Courtney poured the fresh orange into a glass and laid it on the bar. Eiffel ignored me and as he was about to pick the glass up, I laid my palm over it.

"Say please!" I demanded.

He stood rigid, tense and socially awkward, trying to figure out how he was going to handle the situation. He looked me up and down.

"Never mind," he said and stomped away. Courtney laughed as he left.

"Rude fuck," I mouthed.

"He thinks he's the boss when Jack's away."

"Where's Jack?" I queried.

"Same place he goes whenever he disappears, South America."

Jack every so often took trips to South America to see to it that his shipments of cocaine took a different form of transport to the UK.

Keeping it fresh to keep the authorities off him. He had paid off so many people that it was nearly impossible for him to get caught.

Chapter 27

A Trip to the Big Smoke

A few weeks after his return from South America, Jack sent a message, through Courtney, asking me down to his office. After a solid work out at the gym, I travelled to Hope Street to find out what he wanted from me.

I walked in on him putting down the office phone, I sat myself down across from his desk and analysed the documents on show again, one of them was a TR1 which authorised the land registry to change the name of the owner of the land. This one was for Jacks sale of a patch of land in Allerton towards the south of the city over to a wealthy Arab who wanted to build a mansion. I paid particular interest in his signature.

"Good, good," he said, leaning back in his reclining chair, interlinking his fingers. "How's the gym work going?"

"It's fine."

"Long way to travel to Birkenhead every day."

I had not once told him anything about the gym but he knew where I trained and that I was there most days. Sitting silently, I let him continue.

"I know Codie, the owner. He used to be a close pal of mine years back, worked the door in one of my older clubs. He's a real old school tough guy."

"Ok!" I could sense Jack's manner tensing impassively, becoming annoyed with unsociable responses. He stood up, put the kettle on and began filling a big cafetiere with coffee. While he stood with his back to me, I ran my eyes across his desk to all the paperwork again, scanning it for any inside information and getting a proper look at his signature. I noticed Calvin's signature on some authorising documents. He continued speaking and fast-forwarded to the reason he wanted to see me.

"I've arranged another fight for you," he said buoyantly, as if it had been a task to arrange.

"Ok, when?"

"A couple months down in the big smoke…London. It's a little different this time."

"How?"

"It'll be in a ring, it's a bit of a rare event."

"I'm not wearing gloves!" I jumped down his throat as the kettle simmered loudly.

"Relax, there'll be no leather. But I'll tell you this for your own knowledge. You're young and hard, there's no doubt you're your father's son."

He started to point his finger into the air over his shoulder.

"This guy you're fighting is tasty. One of the promoters' men, ex-boxer, clinical and powerful, much older than you, early thirties. Knows the surroundings better than a spider operates inside a web. But, I'm asking you if you want it?"

I remained blank because I knew he wasn't finished talking.

"The prize money's good, very good. It'll be five grand."

I slid forward in my seat, the only reaction I'd made to his proposal as the kettle boiled and Jack poured water into the cafetiere.

"I'll take twenty percent of what you make from me." Jack jolted, irked and lost his words. He ceased pouring water and lightly laid the kettle down. He returned to his seat and kept a stiff face.

Coyly impressed at my request, this told him I was no fool and confident in winning. Jack would make his own side bets with the bookie or whoever wished to bet with him. It was half the reason why he was acting as my manager. The lure to beat everyone, make a killer profit off my pain and suffering and there was not one penny of that money that he needed.

"The more I look at you, the more I'm reminded of your father. But there's one thing I prefer and that's your ethics. Other men who risk their lives would ask for far more than twenty percent, but they would not consider all the work I have to put in place to make the fight happen. My connections, my negotiations, experience, transport, and my reputation, are all elements in the equation." He returned to the kettle and continued filling his cafetiere. "You can have your twenty percent!" he said, with his back to me.

"Are we done?" I stood.

"In order to protect my investment in you, I've asked Codie to take you on the bag and put you through the paces. This guy is not to be underestimated and if you do, you'll get hurt."

I was not too happy about that! I did not need any more people interfering in my life.

He waited for me to respond but I did not and he knew I was not going to.

"Yes, kid, we are done."

Chapter 28

Prep:

My relationship with Courtney took off very quickly. I wasn't sure if I was comfortable with so much company but I tried to adapt and take it in my stride. She started visiting the flat often, cooking and cleaning for me as her maternal nature demanded. I found it strange, our relationship, because I hardly offered a vibrant conversation and I had little emotional appeal. She knew I was on steroids because of my tight moods and sores that started opening over the back of my shoulders. She knew I was fighting for Jack. The topic was like the elephant in the room and never spoken about. She accepted who I was for what I was and that was the only kind of person I'd ever get on with. She knew when I did not want to talk and when I'd be open. She liked the fact I didn't partake in the consumption of alcohol or drugs. There was a sketchy family history of her mother being an alcoholic, ruining her childhood leaving her with bad memories.

I absorbed Jack's words about my opponent but they would make no real change to my preparation for the fight, except for Codie cornering me when I got down to Rocky's. At first I was distant towards his help as I thought it unnecessary, but we established a bond. Give him his due, he knew his stuff, especially the dirty side of fighting.

He kept repeating ways to fight a boxer. "Keep away from him when he's letting his hands go. When he's not, ruffle him up, smother him. Imagine you're stuck to him and play dirty when the ref's not looking."

He taught me how to fight dirty, by pulling down his head and uppercutting with the other hand, and how to grip one of his hands tight, give it a yank and hit them with the other. Bury your head into his chin, keep doing it and lever your head forward to annoy them and low blows when the ref's not looking.

Codie was a born traveller who followed trouble like a bear follows the scent of honey. He had been stabbed, shot, and beaten to a pulp on different occasions and was the right guy to run one of Jack's older gaffs. He had also done time for robbing a post office with a shotgun but now he was a reformed character.

We had both endured suffering in our lives and that's why we got on. He put me through my paces on Monday and Wednesday afternoons, he was there all day every day and when we both fancied, he would give me an extra workout, ensuring I got the full benefit of his experience.

We'd start on this heavy bag, for at least ten rounds. That's when I found out I was far from fit. After that, it was onto a hefty weight session for forty-five minutes. The weights were more like strongman contests where he'd have me throwing barrels and sandbags over my head, farmers' walks and carrying heavy loads across the room. It was far harder than the workouts I was used to but the dosage of steroids kept me filled with energy and strength. He knew the world of fighting like Pele knew the football pitch. He also knew how savage you had to be to avoid defeat or a beating.

His words of advice about steroids use: "Don't take them all the time, you have to take them in cycles, have breaks in-between, or they will fuck up your body and especially your heart."

I ignored the advice and I lived to feel the pain of that.

I trained with him for the next five weeks or so. Daily, I generated more power, strength and confidence as I continued to feel more fit. I used Codie to maximise my potential and at times I felt like a proper athlete. There was no shame in that. In many ways, we were gladiators; it did not matter if we fought in a back alley or in the Colosseum, the demand was the same. I wanted to win and win well because I had been a loser most of my life.

Chapter 29

To the Docks:

Two weeks before the fight, I had a surprise call from Davie on burner number two on the list.

"I have to keep this brief," Davie said sharply on a delayed line. "Rankin will be in touch wi' you on burner five in the next day so turn it on. You'll be makin' another trip to London. He knows the details, he will keep you right."

"What's the details?"

"You don't need to know. Ye're the muscle, son, be the muscle. Rankin will be in touch." He hung up. I was a little cranky about not receiving more information but that's how short he was most of the time. He was right enough; Rankin called the following day while I was napping on the sofa. I answered the burner vibrating on the table.

"Speak," I groaned.

"I can see where you get your personality from," Rankin rambled off the cuff in his cleanly spoken Irish accent. I slouched on the sofa.

"When and where?" I questioned as Rankin changed from his chatty opening straight into business.

"Two weeks' time, midnight on Saturday, in Brixton, with a gang called the Ghetto Gang. Twenty Berettas and a dozen pump action shotguns. I'll carry the shipment and meet you an hour before the deal. Then, I'll brief you on the formalities of the drop." I inhaled the information and rapidly comprehended I had to fight and be the muscle on a gun deal on the same night.

"Eclipse, you there?"

"Aye, I'm still here."

"There will be a new burner for you inside a car I'll have dropped off for your journey. There will be a spare set of dark clothes. You should change into these before we meet."

"Ok."

The phone went dead. These gunrunners had no manners. I wondered if Rankin knew anything about my life. Did Davie talk to him about me? I contemplated calling Davie and telling him I was fighting that night, but I wanted to keep all that private, being able to disclose what I decided, not inform him of everything. My life went from calm to hectic as I stressed about the whole affair.

I used the two weeks to come to terms with the idea but I was sceptical about being able to achieve both tasks: victory against an ex-boxer and a safe gun deal. It would be very different to the other deals I had done. There would be more factors in the equation that could go wrong. At least, I didn't have to worry about the logistics as Rankin had that covered. The major worry would be Jack. I would have to travel on my own so I could disappear afterwards. He'd see that as suspicious. I became distant in that two weeks and the one who noticed most was Courtney. It became a precedent for forthcoming fights. She saw I switched off from any kind of daily reality. She was so aware and good at guessing my need for seclusion she gave me the space without the need to ask. Not once did I ever consider telling her about my gunrunning tasks. That was a kept secret. I didn't think she knew how welcoming her company was. She was a minor distraction that kept me sane and my temper in check.

She cooked a lot of my meals but more often than not, she wouldn't stay and eat with me. Sometimes I would drift off in those distracted naps and when I woke, she would be gone. She'd stay overnight but be gone when I woke, leaving a cooked breakfast to be warmed up.

I broke the news to Jack about my solo travel. I left Liverpool three days before and told him I was going to London to meet up with an old jail buddy. He listened but I'm not sure if he bought it. He gave me the address of the fight in Canary Wharf, at the London dockyards, and said he would text me a time to meet him.

Rankin gave me his instructions on where to meet him on Somerleyton Road beside some mural walls. He said I'd recognize them. Rankin did organise a BMW motor and inside it was a sat nav. In the boot were the clothes he referred to. The gun deal was planned to take place at midnight inside the closed Brixton Village market.

I had one simple plan and one only, have the fight, ditch Jack, do the deal, and head home. I had more anxiety overachieving this than winning the fight.

I booked a cheap hotel room and travelled to London and for a few days. I took advantage of the spare time by locating the market in Brixton and the dockyards, measuring my journey between the two, which would take around forty-five minutes.

Chapter 30

The Cornish:

I had met Jack and Eiffel an hour earlier, a few minutes' drive from the venue. We arrived at the destination in the late afternoon when the sun began to dim in the heart of the London Dockyards. The industrial shed was enormous and very much in business.

The floor space inside was huge at around 100,000 ft² and was being used as an HGV lorry storage facility. Outside a heavy presence of cars had already arrived with a bustling diverse crowd. It gathered an international collection of criminals and gangs eager to flaunt their reputations and wealth. From Scandinavians to Armenians, sporting different fashions and conflicting principles.

Jack parked up and left with Eiffel to snoop around. It didn't take me long before I followed suit.

I walked inside to see a band of workers putting final touches to the preparations. Men huddled in groups of different nationalities, wary of each other's intentions and stood off.

In my sights was a goliath space, a warehouse with an avenue of stored lorries. To my right was a dull cream painted office building. Shallow with a flat roof and see-through perspex screens as windows.

Inside, on the landline, there was a serious fella, with permed shoulder length hair and a pair of lightly tinted, boxed shades, sporting a white stripped, black waistcoat over an equally black polo neck. That was the Cornish, Gunther Turner, the promoter of the show.

Offset on my opposite side, a ring sat at waist height, with a bogging, once cream canvas, cornered with shabby looking ring posts. The tattered ropes were droopier than an eighty-year-old's balls. The floor space around the ring had four rows of seats over barren dust. There was the usual bookie stand, constructed badly with a couple of unsuitable tables and upright sheets of ply, with a black board plastered on as the betting board.

My eye caught sight of a tall, elaborate man wearing a chequered fleece, talking to another bloke by the bookie stand: it was Eiffel. I contemplated approaching but I chose otherwise. Not wanting to converse with anyone, I only desired to find out the time I was on so I could escape the scene and plan my getaway to the gun deal.

Through the perspex windows to my right, Jack appeared into my vision, debating with Gunther who had just slammed the phone down. I moved closer as the argument escalated with hands raising and heads jacking out. I thudded the perspex once with the side of my fist. They both wondered who had the audacity to do such a thing as Jack reacted to my appearance. I gestured for Jack to come out and he obliged.

"There's been a problem," he said sullenly.

"What?"

"Your man, the ex-boxer, was in a hefty car crash this morning."

There was a part of me that was relieved not to be fighting the boxer but that didn't take anything away from my disappointment that I might not be fighting.

I shuffled a few steps closer to him, twitching my eyes, contemplating announcing my frustration at the problem. Then I glanced through the window.

Gunther was stressed, knotting his hands through his permed hair. I scuffed Jack's shoulder as I walked into the room.

"You the promoter?" I asked, in an abrupt and rude tone.

"Correct fucking assumption you made there!" he answered in heavy Cornish, peeved at my rudeness and lack of respect for someone who was used to being spoken to with respect. "Wipe your lip and show me your heels, boy," he insisted.

"What time am I on?"

He glanced out at Jack in disbelief, sliding his shades down his nose before removing them altogether. He returned his slack-jawed attention to me.

"What trolley did you fall off, son?"

I stepped firmly into the desk that separated us. "What time am I on, you Cornish retard?" His reaction debated between rage and confusion. Even the hardest of fighters with the worst manners respected the promoter.

"Fuck me, the trolley boy is deaf!" As with most people, they took my youth as reason to assume they could underestimate me.

I lifted the table, marginally, off the floor, side swiped it across the room with force and stepped right into him. "What time am I on?"

He had already assumed I was Jacks fighter because he had seen me talking with him.

"I don't fucking know, because your fighter is more vegetable than human at the moment you dozy cunt!" Fighters pulling out or going awol scuppered plans because the betting would change with a last-minute replacement. That meant fuck all to me.

"I'm on at NINE!!" I belted out and turned to leave the room.

"You're what?"

I stomped to the door and turned. "I'm on at nine. I'll be back at nine!"

I walked out giving Jack no response at his attempt to get my attention from his miffed attitude. I left the building and returned to Jack's car where I called Rankin on the burner he left me. The deal was still on at the same time and place. This was all the info I needed. I filled the next hours by picking up my car and driving it to the venue so I would have a quick getaway. My apprehension was heightened: not by the uncertainty of who I'd be sharing pain with but the ability to get the fight sewn up and onto the gun deal.

I was sitting in my motor around twenty to nine and watched all the activity pile into the building in anticipation of a brutal night's entertainment. I changed into loose joggers and a spare t-shirt while the wave of uncertainty mixed with tension began to take over. I had a level of uncertainty scour me because of the unknown element as to who my opponent would be but in reality, they were all unknown. You had no remote idea how tough they are until you exchange blows with them.

The gun deal played with my concentration which was usually in tune with my desire to win.

Right on the turn of nine pm, I approached the entrance to see a huddle of bodies and hear a colossal amount of boisterous noise. I opened the door and stepped in.

A rowdy fight was taking place in the ring, watched by the few hundred crowd that turned up. The place stank of discourteous individuals and cigarette smoke. I scanned the area for Jack; I needed to be certain I was fighting. As I did, someone nudged me from the side. It was Jack, the top buttons of his shirt undone and sleeves rolled up, with a patchy forehead of moist sweat.

"You're on after this," he said abruptly, pleased I had turned up. "Gunther got you a man. Don't know much about him, in his late thirties. Relevantly new to the game, I'm told."

"What's your bet?" He was aware I was asking how much he wagered on me.

"On you! I've got a ten grand bet with Gunther. Look, the rules are different here. You're in a ring, so it's six three-minute rounds, so back to the corner when the bell go's and I'll see you alright."

When bare knuckle fights worked in rounds, they would never go the distance. I could never comprehend why they had rules for fights. It's beat, or be beaten, in my book. I left Jack at that point and went to soak up the fear suffocating the room intermingling among the vultures. That fear fed my drive, fuelled my rage and brought me to boil.

All around were men who wished they had the guts to deal with that fear, wish they carried the DNA to   live like a hardened brute and experience the glory of victory. A glory I became addicted to. But most of them were cowards who lived lives unable to fill their bones with bravery and the killer instinct.

I barged and bumped through the crowd while being intoxicated with adrenaline in the midst of the smell of sweat and smoke. I built up with deep breaths and tingles of poised anxiety. This was moulding me for the first exchange of fists. When I reached the edge of the slack ropes, I huddled close to a gathering of dreadlocked Rastas with smells of hashish taking over from tobacco smoke.

The men inside the ropes were fatigued and beaten, smothered in Vaseline while they grappled together in their battle for superiority. One of them was near victory and the other would fall. It was up to themselves to drag the final punch off the floor and it arrived. In close, a sucker blow to the solar plexus dropped the other to the ground. Void of energy, he was unable to stand and the referee raised the victor's hands, something he would do for me. The beaten warrior was treated like second hand garbage, dragged to his feet and escorted out of the ring. There I saw Jack approach a corner with his earthy-haired chest on show from his unbuttoned shirt. He seemed anxious, before he spotted me, then hardened his look. The role of corner man was new to him. He knew nothing of what bare knuckle boxing felt like. Never before had he delved into this world. He nodded to me when one of the Rastas shoulder-barged me and whispered, "Sorry."

Instead of being angry, I became distracted. I squared up to him, miffed by something familiar about the man. Eiffel appeared at my side and tugged my shoulder, insisting I joined Jack. I walked away giving the Rasta a few sneering looks as he returned the same perplexed notion towards me.

The two fighters were taken from the ring.

"Get in there," Jack said.

I stepped in and lifted my t-shirt off, showcasing my ripped body. There was no opponent yet. The baiting crowd never dimmed from the last bout. Having a bare chest enhanced my adrenaline. My mind started to rattle, my palms sweated, and the cover of chills swept across me as if someone was scraping a comb across my skin.

As I pranced around, my eye shifted to the Rasta again. I noticed his build, an even six foot of a lean and upright body over a light black denim coat and short thick dreads. His eyes were hollow and dark as he watched my opponent climb into the ring. He shifted his alarm back to me, knowing who I was. He twitched between my opponent and me profusely with shock.

It clicked. It was Helder, my old cell mate. Taken out of the moment, I smiled at him, distracted by the chances of ever meeting him again, but he did not smile back. His face was reserved as he kept his concentration on my opponent. He nodded over to my foe who had entered between the tatty ropes and stood in the opposite corner with a couple of his accomplices.

He purposely held his back to me, showing his flabby overcarry under an extra-large white vest. He towered over the ring post.

My chin sank into my chest, eyes peering under the brows, glaring at him from behind, piercing him with god-awful thoughts of hurt when slowly he started to turn, showing a barrelled belly. He was a generation older than me.

Helder continued switching his head between us, hesitantly. I stepped forward as his face revealed itself to me. I stopped dead and froze. I never thought I'd see that evil man ever again.

Chapter 31

Back When Carlin Got His Way:

When I was barely sixteen years old, I had been removed from the flat and escorted to the station by Flanagan. He had me taken into a holding cell and kept me there overnight. Next day, mid-morning, I was escorted to the interview room.

As I waited, I remembered the advice Davie had given me about the police - they were never to be trusted. They were like professional con men who lied to get the tide of investigation to go their own way and make their job easier. They'd try anything and everything to get you to squeal. And despite what assurances they would give, nothing would be legit.

I had a major concern as to where Danielle was. I had been separated from her when I was removed from the flat. Was she in another cell? I had no idea and no one told me. In an illusory part of my imagination, I thought Davie would appear at some point and remove me, as he had in the past, from the care homes I was housed inside or from foster parents. It was an idealist fantasy that was never going to come true but I held onto that hope.

I felt the room close in. Time passed sluggishly as I became enslaved in the company of thoughts and worries. I sweated in the heat of the room, the roof fitted fan heater blasted out way too much warmth and the door had not been opened for a while. Surely a good tactic of the Police to make a sweaty fifteen-year-old uncomfortable.

Davie was, of course, abducted by the hands of Sam Bryson and his fate lay waiting at the hands of the Eradicator. I was not to know this until I was released and remained baffled at what was going on. That old feeling of being abandoned returned as my distressed self, increased in anxiety. When I started to pace the room, I noticed the area around the suspect's seat was heavily worn, compared to the rest of the linoleum floor. I strode across the room, kicking the toe of my trainers off the skirting boards, contemplating an outburst of punches into the walls, and continued that motion until Carlin and Flanagan walked in.

They both took their seats across the table.

"Sit down, Max," Flanagan insisted.

My insides flared with a burning disgust and I did not move.

"Sit down, Max, this will be over before you know it," Flanagan repeated, and there was the first lie. I scratched the chair back and sat across from Carlin whose vile yellowed skin made me grimace. In front of him on the table sat a thick closed brown file. He caught me gawking at it when he asked,

"You look like a coffee man," nodding his head forward, "you want a brew?"

"Shove yer coffee."

Carlin and Flanagan turned to check each other and noted my attitude.

"I'll get you some water, you'll need it for all the questions you'll have to answer." Flanagan slid his seat out, squeezed out of the space and left the room.

"Where is he?" Carlin asked.

"Who you talking about, the Dalai Lama, the Pope, Maradona? How the fuck am I supposed to know?" Carlin leaned forward out of his chair.

"Look, you second hand cunt, the more shit you give me the more this is going to hurt you!"

"You don't scare me, you fat fuck, sit down!"

His fuming cheeks retreated, the temporary fire in his eyeballs retracted and he sat back down.

"I've dealt with short stumped hard men like you before and the outcome is always the same. Your lives are going one way and that will never change. To the gutter!"

"Fuck off!"

Carlin bowed back, knowing I was not the ordinary juvenile that he could twist. "Tell me where he is?"

"Go fuck yourself," I boasted and turned towards the sound recorder. I was waiting for them to begin the interview officially. Then it sank in that I must have been entitled to a solicitor of some kind.

"Supply and possession of a class A drug, that's a long sentence. Even for a runt like you. I'd imagine you might get out for your thirtieth birthday." He got his reaction, silence. "You're not stupid, Max, you, know how this works. Give me something, tell me where he is. If you don't know then give me his phone numbers, his hideouts, what car he has been driving. Anything!"

I began to give his proposal some thought. I was way too young to go to jail but I was also naive enough to think it would not go that far. I looked away, down to the floor.

"I'll give you something… I have something in my pocket, a piece of paper with an address. Can I take it out?"

"Take it out, slowly, and lay it on the table."

I slipped my hand into my pocket and removed it in a tense fist on the table. I observed Carlin's tickled reaction.

"Go on, son, drop it on the table."

I knew giving him anything would be risky. I turned my fist around and gave him the finger.

He leapt up over the table, stretching his arm out. I slid my seat back, screeching it across the worn patch on the floor.

The door opened and Flanagan walked back in with my water. Carlin was flustered by the interruption and returned to his seat.

"He's one of those," Flanagan said, as he placed the polystyrene cup on the table. I grabbed it straight away and downed the water.

"He certainly is," Carlin quoted dryly and opened the file on the table.

Immediately, I spotted the headlined name of 'Davie Rhodes'.

"In this file is all the evidence we need to put you away." He turned the pages to many photographs of Davie doing deals with various mongrels he sold to. Then there were the street dealers he worked with. More pages later there were snaps with the Collins brothers. Some in the Collins' shoe repair store and others outside the hideout where they cut the cocaine.

Then there were all the pictures of me doing some of the running for Davie, clearly showing me handing over see-through bags of white powder in exchange for cash.

Carlin began tapping on the most evident photo of myself, handing over a bunch of small bags to a well established user. Flanagan noticed the etched antsy panic written all over my whitening face.

"Where's my solicitor? You should give me a solicitor, should you not!" I was completely ignored.

"You see, Max, we have everything. All that we need to lock you up is in this file."

I absorbed the past few minutes arduously quickly. An inspiring moment enlightened me. There was something they did not have. I lifted my posture confidently and countered, "How do you know what's in those bags? I was selling flour. Can't do much time for that, you pair of cunts."

"He has a point there, Carlin," Flanagan agreed.

I smiled sarcastically at both of them.

"Jones!" Flanagan shouted loudly, and a placid constable entered the room and leant down secretively to Carlin's mouth where whispers were exchanged. The constable left, leaving Carlin and Flanagan looking self-assured. I kept scanning them until something sounded alarm bells. I returned my look to the sound recorder which was still off.

"This is bent! Where's my solicitor?"

Carlin ignored me as if I had never spoken. Flanagan did the same.

"You cunts deaf?" Right then the constable returned with a non-transparent evidence bag and laid it in front of Carlin, smiling cocksure at me. He opened it as my attention lifted to look over the bag. From it, he took a kilo of cocaine wrapped in foil and plumped it on the table.

"Now, I may be being presumptive here, but yours is the bedroom with pics of naked ladies and Everton posters on the wall. You'll never guess where we found that, Max."

I couldn't entertain him with any remarks, so I remained quiet and that's when he had me. The coke was not mine or Davie's. He planted it. It was either that or Davie had hidden it in my bed somewhere. Either way it was not good news for me.

"So, where is he?"

I leant forward in my seat once again and flared my nostrils. "Go fuck yourself!" Carlin hissed, being more desperate than Flanagan, who was stone faced.

"What are we going to do with him?" Flanagan asked openly, while Carlin leant back and undid his top button. "We can do anything we want; the boy has no identity."

Chapter 32

Induction into the System:

It was a god-awful place, full of ill men, unknowingly discovering the art of survival. Frustration with a sour anger digested in your core like an unwanted virus. Authority reigned supreme and freedom was a distant desperation that everyone dreamed of. It would become a part of you, the institution. The bitter hostility hovered over the wings, almost certain to catch and refurbish any morals you had left.

The way of life inside would become ingrained into any soul who found himself locked inside a merciless room. It was the guts of misery. If you didn't adapt, you'd be swallowed into a vile pit of despair. I prayed I would never succumb to any kind of control over me. I wouldn't give them an inch, or so I thought, but you think differently when you have to live with it, the loneliness, the boredom, the sour resentment of life. It would break the most stubborn of men and that stubbornness is the only thing that would keep your pulse beating.

HMP Altcourse is a modern built category B local prison, filled with gangs battling for notoriety, respect and power. It had every colour of man, a multi-cultural mix of ethnicity, nationalities and a diverse list of criminals from the age of eighteen to pensioners. From the vile stench of paedophiles to the good guy who had done wrong. And then there were the likes of me, set up and abandoned by the outside world. Loyalty was hard to come by and an easy life even more so.

There were more drugs filtering through the inside than there were laced in a Howard Marks drug deal. Bagheads, the prison's name for drug users, were anyone who sniffed glue to jacking up heroin. You could get anything you asked for, if you knew the right person. The smell of grass lingered in distant corners and the drug lords dealt it to anyone willing to trade something. The biggest crooks inside the prison were undoubtedly the screws. Bent by corruption, and I guess that started at the top, with the Governor. They were the merchants, who filtered the inmates' poison inside the system. Their reason was to keep the inmates' brains dulled down so they wouldn't cause trouble, but no matter how many drugs that were taken in, a hassle-free day did not exist. Carlin kept me in that dank holding cell for a little over twenty-four hours with nothing but my thoughts where I wondered what would become of me. I was fed once with a mediocre meal and watered. Apart from that, all I had was a bed, and a toilet.

That day was only a smidgen of what was to come. Because I had no identity, Carlin manipulated the system. I was never given a solicitor and I pleaded for one each day. He kept the radar on my existence quiet. I had no rights and no one coming to my rescue. A usual feeling for my life up until that point. I complained to everyone I saw but it was no use, I was dead in the water.

Davie was right about the police; they were more bent and dishonest than criminals. Whatever happened on the outside while I was locked in that cell, I did not know, but I was fast tracked through the system and sent to Liverpool's Altcourse Jail. No trial, no rights.

As soon as I was escorted out of the prison van, my head covered by a hood and cuffed, I was taken by a screw down some echoing corridors, different heights of stairs and through locked gates until I reached a room and sat down. It smelt musty, ripe with the odour of stale wood. I was forced down onto a straight-backed hard chair with my hands still cuffed. I was notably pale, traumatised into a cold fear. I knew nothing of what was about to happen to me but even my worst thoughts could not have portrayed what was in store.

The door slammed shut behind me, causing me to jolt. There were seconds of silence before I could hear the clunks of hard soled shoes tap against the floor until they landed at my feet. My hood was pulled off and I looked onto the torso of a tall, gangly man. As my sight adjusted to the daylight blazing in from a wide prominent window, a well-trimmed man with bronzed skin stood before me. I was inside the Governor's office. It was a modernly designed, plain cream painted room but the décor and furniture was dated and robust, mimicking the Governor. He swaggered to his seat with his back to me. I had not seen his face.

He sat on his office chair, in front of the window, wearing a clean-cut, walnut striped suit that wasn't far away from the colour of his Indian skin. By then I knew the whole situation was a charade, caused by bent and deceitful men. His powdered black hair kept away from a long face, with a sullen and bleak expression over his prominent curving wrinkles to the sides of his mouth. I felt he held a disgust for his job or maybe his life but held an acceptance that this was his fate. His rock-hard gaze never offered to change as emotion seemed like a distant expectation.

"Max McCabe, fifteen, drug lord and hooligan. welcome to my prison." His speech was banally clear and direct, hiding a slender twang of Indian that had been distinctively phased out by a life of speaking English. The whites of his eyes appeared a sickly yellow, combined with harvested bags, caused by a heavy intake of alcohol taken to dull his mind from the animals he had to control. "You will behave in my system. That is not a request but a demand, young man."

At no point did I think I should talk back to his eager forwardness. My insides trembled with a bitter uncertainty. My hardness towards authority was briefly broken, I felt weak and helpless.

"After you leave this room, you will be given the necessary clothing and educated about the rules of this establishment. If I see you in this room again, it will not be beneficial for you." He glanced at a robust cupboard door, sandwiched between two bookshelves. The door was slightly ajar with the inside cupboard in darkness. "When you mingle into this society, you can ask what happens if you are sent to me and you should take what you are told, on board."

The rumour had it that he liked spending time with weak and vulnerable young men, doing sinful and dirty things to them inside that cupboard. Hanging on a hook on the wall of that cupboard was a well-used belt. I thought for a few seconds, staring through the gap into the blackness, and knew that belt was used for awful things.

I would return to that office on my own terms.

His adoption of me, with repulsion and lasting aggression, meant I had retreated to silence, knowing words would not get me out of that situation. I scanned the room and noticed on his desk was the same brown file that Carlin had of me, sitting behind the rear of his name bar that faced him, instead of the room. I thought this was strange. Did he not want me knowing his name? He had the knowledge of my life from that file. He caught me inspecting it and opened a drawer, picked it up and placed it inside. He closed the drawer vigorously. A hint that the file was not for my eyes.

"That life of yours is over. You are owned by my will and the system now." He could tell I was bricking it and loved the authoritative position he held over me, and anyone else who received his personal induction. He picked up his phone which was patched out to his secretary. "Molly, send the senior officer in please." He placed the phone down, stood up and turned his back on me, gazing out of the window.

The door creaked open; footsteps clunked across the floor until the senior officer stood by my side. I turned my head towards him. He seemed as bilious as the Governor, fixing his harsh hazel eyes, through his aviator shaped glasses, on me. I watched the Governor as I had ounces of pity filter through for the repulsion for life he held. The senior officer was named Welsh Williams and his imposing size would be fearful to any boy of my age. His wide-shouldered frame powered over a tall lumpy build. His white shirt was neatly tucked in over his gut, leaving his butch hands crossed over by his waist.

"Senior Officer Williams, show our new guest around. He's to be given the proper treatment which we talked about."

I was about to learn that Senior Officer Williams was a manipulating pawn and shameless bully. He grabbed the fabric of my jumper at the back of my neck and lifted me off my seat. His natural strength stunned me and it had to be given respect.

Williams, accompanied by a couple of other prison officers, led me into a cell which was as plain as a sheet of paper with one fluorescent light, fitted on a diagonally concave of the roof. In a light drawl that bore no similarity to Welsh, he demanded I stripped to be searched. I resisted and put up an initial fight but I was quickly overpowered and eventually agreed to be violated.

Shaken and humiliated, I was marched, naked, across some corridors, eventually arriving at a female prison officer who stood behind the store counter. She took my prints and issued me with a six-digit code that I had no idea to its relevance. Then, she handed me a bedding pack with two sets of cotton sheets and woollen blankets. I got a prison outfit, a maroon tracksuit that looked hideous. They called it 'corned beef' and usually prisoners they wanted to punish and take the piss out of, were made to wear it. I got a couple pairs of one size fits all boxers and socks. She went on to explain, I was serving an indeterminate prison sentence, meaning no date had been set for my release, and I would spend a minimum amount of time inside before I was considered for release.

I asked why and I was ignored.

From there, I was taken to the furlough wing before I would be integrated into the general population. It was standard procedure that new inmates spend at least three days there as a phasing in process.

The cell was long and narrow, barren of any personality, stale, and cold. A low-down bed with a thin mattress and a stainless-steel toilet and a sink were the only things in there. I felt a heavy landing of dread.

"Give me a moment with the inmate," Williams demanded of the other two screws. They left as Williams closed the door behind him. He turned and squared his bulbous face up to mine. I imagined he greeted every inmate in a similar fashion as he stepped closer.

"You're a dirty, dirty rodent you hear." I imagined he greeted every inmate in a similar fashion as he stepped closer. "What I say, is what goes in 'ere. You cause trouble and I'll feed ya' your scraps from the ground and bathe you with piss water. This is your new reality…boy." My body quivered, inside that tight cell I shrunk to the size of a mouse. I wanted to cry, my eyelid flickered, my jaw jittered, and I began to glaze over, but at the last moment I took control as Davie's words yelled between my ears, 'Never show weakness'.

"Fuck off, you paedo cunt!" I leathered his face with spit as I spoke, fully aware there would be a backlash and fully prepared to take it. His jaw tightened, his face crinkled, and he took a step back, calmly removing his glasses.

He smiled, with no sign of any reaction and cleaned the spit from his glasses with the inside of his shirt. He was stone cold, without empathy and had the hand of power on his side. A scary combination to obtain. "I'll see you in a few days," he said as he slammed the door behind him.

I walked over to the narrow vertical window and watched him lock it. He held the keys up teasingly, dangling them in my sight before walking away. I analysed the space outside my cell, watching all the grey track-suit attired prisoners and something surprised me: the furlough wing was full of adults and late teens. I had been put into an environment over my age group. I soon to learn that I was the only one under eighteen in the jail. I was marked as a young offender and not a Juvenile. On top of that, I had to move around in the corned beef outfit that stuck out like a glow stick.

When I looked out of the window, I noticed one guy stuck out in particular. A shifty, beany Scottish fella who was screaming and shouting at some guy while playing pool. He seemed borderline schizophrenic as if he'd be more at home in a mental institution. I watched as he lost control, cracking the pool cue in half over the table and trying to beat his innocent looking opponent while chasing him around the table. The screws manhandled him back into his cell and locked him in.

The next three days were the loneliest I'd ever had. I was under twenty-four-hour lock down. Williams starved me. Not one single breadcrumb came through the hatch and only a couple of bottles of water for each day. It was savage but it served as a precedent for my stay.

Chapter 33

Murky Drains:

After three days, a screw unlocked the door in the early morning then moved me to the young persons' Canal Wing that held about sixty inmates. I was placed in a two-man cell on the first-floor landing, called the 'twos' that only housed bunk rooms, and shared with a West Indies man, Helder Moore, a hyper and free willed streetwise con around nineteen, but all in all, a good guy.

The second I got inside, I was shown my bottom bunk bed and crashed onto it. The door was locked behind me. It was a tidy, well-kept cell with PVC plastic walls and a grey painted floor. Helder had pictures of loved ones on the walls, family and friends. There was a lot of bric-a-brac things lying around on a worktop.

I lay on the bed, curled in a ball, staring at nothing. I would not move, not for a few hours, I was too weak. My skin felt as if it was amalgamated to my bones and I must have lost a stone. I needed food. My mind was in a paralysed state of trauma. I was starved and on the verge of tears, but I did not cry. I had to hold it in, I could not show weakness in a place full of toughness. The only thing that made me move was when the door was unlocked, and a shout of "Lunch" came from a screw. Like a hungry sheep, I crawled out and followed the crowd to the server; the idea of food took my mind away from my punishment. I felt I was being treated like a wild animal.

I took my place in line, hoping no one would converse with me and waited patiently in the queue with pivoting eyes fixated on the new inmate, wearing the corned beef. I dared not look at anyone. I felt about four stone heavy and I struggled to stay on my weary feet. The queue lessened until I watched slops of sausage, potatoes and veg fill my plate from the server.

I vacuumed it up with my hands, like a hungry dog, on the way to a seat at a table with seven other inmates. As I sat, they stared at me, fully aware of the treatment I'd just received. It was a regular thing for selected new inmates and the talk of the prison. While eating, I had this constant conscious feeling I was being watched. I raised my head to see five hardy looking late teenagers, boring uninviting glares towards me from across the room. Walking observantly along the walled side of the room, Williams saw me and leant over the table to talk to those five guys.

They were known inside the jail as the Subs because Williams would have them waiting on the side-lines to do his dirty work. They preyed upon the weak and young, where I fitted the bill handsomely. I was a boy stuck in a man's world.

The Subs carried out tasks for Williams in return for privileges, like the use of mobiles, pornography, smokes, extra canteen money, and a supply of spice, a synthetic cannabis. The ringleader of the gang was Vinx, short for Vinny. A chubby, idiosyncratic inmate, a cruel nineteen-year-old. The other four, Bald Bob, Dunce, Gismo and Big Otto, the African. They were about to make my life hell and the main reason I evolved and left that jail, a man.

After that early incident, I avoided eye contact, not just with the Subs, but with anyone.

My meal was done and I could feel the energy pump through my body and brain, bringing an isolated smile of relief and hope. I wanted to disappear from their sight. I considered going back to my cell but that would back me into a corner and I was paranoid over the Subs or Williams having alternative motives. I had no idea how the system worked and I didn't fancy asking anyone. I was timid and vulnerable to any kind of manipulation, and I needed a friend.

I wanted a shower to freshen up so I approached a placid mannered female screw, Warrender, who stood around the main entrance of the canteen. She was a lax-faced, stout girl with a busty chest and had tied back blonde hair.

"Miss, I need a shower," I blurted out. I wouldn't normally have been polite but I was now at the mercy of the institution. She knew I had just been released from that cell and knew I had been starved. She stood firm, unbothered by my quaint stance. I was looking for sympathy and someone who could monitor me if I struck up a friendship. I invaded her space, pity eyed, until she agreed to help.

"Okay, McCabe, follow me."

To my relief, she escorted me out as I dipped my head to see the Subs and Williams watching my every move. On the way down a corridor, we passed a well-equipped gym with a couple of large, fixed windows. I slowed down and took a liking to it. Inside, there was a heavily tattooed, bulky man doing standing shoulder presses with the Olympic bar. The screw caught my interest.

"That's Smit," she said in her stride, "you don't wanna cross him."

His muscles were swelled out from his fatless torso under his cropped vest. Smit caught my look, held it and I guessed he felt sorry for me. A sight I had not seen until then.

We arrived at the shower block where the screw retrieved a towel and a bar of soap from a nearby cupboard.

Standing there, I asked Warrender a question. "Will you wait here for me?"

Warrender grasped the alarm I was in and knew I was fresh meat.

"Get in there, McCabe," she demanded. I thought Warrender sympathised and had seen the same look within my face as with many others.

In the white open-planed, all tiled shower room, the water refreshed me. I was without paranoia that I'd be interrupted, and it was the first shower I'd had in a week. Briefly, my mind settled with my stomach satisfied by the food. I had a moment's reprieve from the hell I'd felt for the past week. I was fed and now clean.

I milked the time in the shower, spending around ten minutes under the hot water. While the cheap soap drifted into my eyes, they began to sting, annoyingly. I reached out to grab my towel which hung on a neighbouring shower valve. I flustered around but couldn't locate it as my hand appeared to touch the familiarity of a shoulder blade.

I jumped backwards into the flow of water and adjusted my sight. In my line of vision, Vinx stood widely, in front of the other Subs in a mixed formation looking tense and mean. All of them with the body language of aggressive men.

Vinx wasted no time as I tried to focus my eyes and hooked me across the jaw. I tottered backwards, thudding into the tiled wall. I tried to grab the waterpipe to keep my balance when big Otto stepped forward and drove a thudding fist into my back. My breath escaped me as my left knee splattered onto the solid floor. Desperation filled my mind. I tried to make a getaway on my hands and knees, bobbing off the floor through a gap in their formation as a volley smashed into the side of my head where any will power I had to escape, left me. They trapped me down by leaning their weight over me and began smashing my ribs.

That's the last thing I remembered.

Chapter 34

Normality:

I was carted off to hospital with two screws for company, hardly able to move, and remained there for a couple of weeks while my ribs healed enough for me to walk freely. That wasn't what annoyed me the most; my jaw was broken in a couple of places, making speaking and eating difficult tasks. It was disappointing, but being bed-bound in hospital gave me security. I was well cared for and I didn't have to watch my back. I was fed well, mainly soup and soft vegetables. Tea was on tap and the custody officers, Wilson and Noble offered little in the way of company. In order for them to get a break from the daily twenty-four seven chaperoning, they requested the reverend from the chapel talk to me. Mostly I ignored his presence wondering what he was he going to do for me.

Once out, I was moved into the healthcare wing for a few more weeks and it was there I chose to become a hermit. The healthcare ward stank to high heaven, rotten it was, housed by the heavily sedated with methadone, mentally unstable and those on a detox from the home made moonshine. I was locked down twenty-three hours a day, only getting out for some rehabilitation yard walking. The deafening noise made the wing sound like a lunatic asylum and that hour of exercise was bliss.

I eventually got thrown back into the young persons' wing where I had notably lost a lot of weight but this time, they gave me the same plain grey tracksuit as everyone else wore.

Every morning the guards banged on the door at quarter past seven, the signal for the inmates to get up for a breakfast of cereal and toast. I randomly chose to leave my cell, depending on how brave and how hungry I felt. I figured that no one would have the energy to   start a ruck at that time in the morning and usually that was the case. I was not offered a job, nor any options to leave my cell during the day, I was locked down out with eating times and any requests were ignored.

Helder was receiving education and aimed to re-sit his maths and English exams. He always left for the classroom after breakfast, leaving me with my troubling thoughts for the rest of the day.

In the next couple of months, weekly something would occur that led to more beatings. I could never be at ease except for when I slept, and that didn't occur often as the fear caused crippling anxiety, leading to insomnia. The constant punishment was brutal on my body and mind. Most youths would have broken after a couple of weeks but I used the pain as motivation not to buckle, beg or cry.

The young offenders' wing was as hostile as the Gaza strip. These were men who wanted to prove themselves and daily there was trouble, often squabbles leading to scraps and injuries. Suicide or attempts at such were a weekly event inside Altcourse and I thought about that every day.

The time locked inside the cell wore you down mentally and every thought pattern ended up at suicide. I lived in a constant state of depression. The torment could end instantly, my pain could end, I told myself.

But they would win, I couldn't let that happen. I would win in the end and at that end, it would be that cell that aided who I would become.

During the day, under lockdown hours, in-between meals, Williams would unlock the door and allow the Subs in. The first time I was surprised and not yet healed from the shower incident. They battered me. My ribs bore most of the pain and I could hardly see out of my bruised eyes. They loved to beat you on the ground. When eventually I could see, the concussions left me double visioned and confused.

After the first time it happened, when Helder left in the morning, I'd build a barricade behind the door with the bunk bed and wedge it up against the sink. You had to learn fast inside. On occasions, it worked when Williams and the Subs were less determined, and on other occasions, it did not.

I had to eat and that was danger time for me. The journey to get food became a walk over melting coal. Often in front of the eyes of a screw, I would be pulled into a cell, slapped about and left.

I lived in survival mode but in that mode, I learned how to fight. My mind would filter back to the size of Smit in that gym. He looked menacing and the look in his eye made him appear as if he could flip at any moment. When I was not hurting too much, I began to work out, starting with press ups, sit ups, and pull ups on the window bars. I'd press the bunk bed or do anything I could think of. Some days I'd do a few hundred push ups and sit ups. It passed the time. I became committed to fighting back and not having the will beaten from my soul.

Some hope did surface for me. It took its time, but I struck up a friendship with Helder. He saw my struggle and took pity on my constant beatings. My shyness he could sense the most, conversations between us were minimal. He was the one who gave me the layout of the jail, how it was run by the Governor and Williams. He told me of all the privileges everyone else got, except me. Every prisoner who did not work had a weekly allowance of £10 to spend how they wished and I had none, nor was I offered work or education that would have passed the time.

When, the canteen came round, I asked how much money I had, they replied I did not have an account. Whenever I asked a screw a question, they fobbed me off with some bullshit answer or ignored me. I was living in a prison within a prison. I had no rights. Helder gave me the odd sweet or tin of juice. I shared his toothpaste, tea bags and toilet rolls. I literally had nothing and because of his good soul, I, at least, had some material things to use.

I learned how to get through the time or I would have ended up inside a coffin. Maybe that was the plan for whoever was pulling the strings.

Helder schooled me about the Subs and how they worked for Williams, doing his dirty work, who in turn, followed the Governor's requests. Helder felt the burden of my pain because he had to look at every day. When the Subs approached the cell, with Williams at the forefront, Helder recruited his Rasta gang of four to cause a riot on the wing, averting focus from my impending beating. The prison was mayhem each day with erratic behaviour, fights, and flaked out drug users. Helder and the Rastas knew how to push the buttons. When shit kicked off, every prisoner was sent to their cells and locked down. Helder's and the Rastas' aid gave me hope and that became a changing point for me. To change, I had to make more friends. "Yuh gotta get in da routine, man," Helder said, sensing I had hope settling in. "Get out da cell." "How do I get out?"

Living any kind of existence outside of the cell seemed impossible because every day I was locked in. "Make friends, init?" He meant that to survive outside the cell, I had to have a varied amount of people   who would look out for me. "An' another ting, orange yellow but yuh nuh know if it sweet."

I scratched my head there. Helder spoke a dialect that was hard to decode. He and his Rasta gang could chatter aloud and no-one except them would understand. What he meant was that an orange that is yellow is not always sweet. I had to act hard to avoid the bullies.

"An' yuh can't hang around with ma boys too much." His gang was willing to back me but I couldn't hang around with them for I was not a Rasta. He gave me an idea. I had to get into the gym at the same time as Smit. But how could I get to the gym? After some brainstorming, I knew I had to do a bit of acting.

The next day, when lunch was called between twelve and two, a gathering of the Rastas appeared on the ones, the ground floor, around the wing pool table. They all appeared on edge but that was the plan. At lunch, the number of screws on the wings lessened considerably as they rotated break times.

I left the cell and confronted them with a stare out before a wild game of catch started around the pool table. We tried to make it look as real as possible, so I pretended to fight back.

At the end of the wing, a locked grill gate, and the female screw, Warrender stood. She had her hand over the alarm button but avoided pressing it as I arrived at the gate. I came across leery, afraid for my life and vastly out of breath. I had little or no interaction with any screws up until then; she was trying to place me and eventually realised it was she who had led me to the showers, months previously.

"Please, you gotta let me out of here!" I said, as a couple of the Rastas pretended they had blades up their sleeves.

She believed me and willingly opened the gate. "Come with me," she said, with purpose, seemingly buoyant she had saved me from injury.

"No, I'm not going back to the showers," I pleaded, as she hoped to lead me away with a firm grip on my arm. She would have felt nervous, being the only screw around, and was not sure where to put me, deciding between corridors.

"Put me in the gym," I pleaded. She thought about her actions, knowing the two hours at lunch belonged to Smit but after thinking about it, she saw the sense.

"Alright, let's go."

I twisted around and smiled towards the Rastas, while giving them the finger, comically.

She led me to the gym and opened the door. "You have company today," she said to Smit, who had a couple of heavy dumbbells in his hand that he dropped to the floor, annoyed at the interruption.

"Fuck off, then," he muttered in a Manchester twang as Warrender closed the door behind her.

Smit edged up and rolled his fierce eyes up my feeble body that had never seen the inside of a gym before. He was an intimidating figure, his body decorated in water-coloured tattoos up to his wide neckline. His incisive gaze left you with an uneasy feeling, that at will, he could snap you in half if he wished.

"You'll need some muscle put on in this place. I've seen boys like you get murdered for being weak." His open philosophy on life could be seen by the pointing of a finger, nodding of his head or the lifting of his neck. He turned and picked a 14 kg dumbbell from the rack, passed it to me and ordered, "Get repping, son! Better build up those wings!"

I later found out Smit, who was twenty-nine, and on a different wing from me, was inside for GBH on a released sex offender who had preyed on his seven- year-old daughter. They allowed him use of the gym to himself through the two-hour lunch period to keep him away from any other paedophiles and to occupy his thoughts.

All other inmates wishing to use the gym would be allocated only a half or a full hour per day and could only use it outside Smit's time. On the outside, he was a retired MMA fighter and the head of a reputable secu-rity firm in Manchester. He appeared to be well liked by the screws, his manner and his ability to defuse hostile situations with prisoners was a welcomed resource. He was a reasonable gentleman bad guy, but when crossed, he could use his fighting knowledge to wipe out a regiment. I had the guts of ninety minutes with him in the gym that day where I did my best to appeal to his good nature.

He took a liking to my willingness to learn or maybe he sensed my desperation. I enlightened him of my predicament and pleaded to his good nature to pull some strings to allow me access to the gym. He did just that and every lunchtime, I was able to attend for the hour I was supposed to be allocated. In the second week, he gave me a small supply of oral steroids, or oxy-fifties, as he called them. That began my obsession with getting big.

My newfound friendship with Smit spurred an easier life for me. The Subs left me alone for a while, having two obstacles now, the Rastas and Smit, to get past.

I remember the day when Williams found out about my new gym membership and interrupted our session while Smit was squatting 180kg.

"Smit!" Williams barked recklessly and glanced vacantly past me, nudging his aviator glasses up. "This your new pet project?"

Smit had the Olympic bar resting on his shoulders and dropped it behind his back, crashing it onto the safety supports of the squat rack, forming an enormous dent in them. It was quite a statement to make. Williams flinched, evidently becoming alarmed at the response, and placed his butch hand on the shaft of his baton. Smit took a few steps forward to stand under the breath of Williams.

"Born in Rhyl, North Wales, mother abandoned you at seven cuz you were a cunt. Loner and loser at school, divorced and remarried with a kid, born with three toes on her right foot. Couldn't get into the police service cuz you were too thick! Abiding in the end house on Park Drive, in Hoole, Chester." Williams retreated and quietened with a shudder. He knew there was a threat to his family, becoming more wary of Smit.

Williams turned to take the measure of me, and side stepped out of the room.

"Always be ahead of those bent cunts," Smit said, returning to his squatting. That opened my eyes to the power of having knowledge over someone's weakness and how much Williams had underestimated it.

For a total of ten weeks, Smit educated me in weightlifting and gave me some fighting tips while he continued to feed me steroids of one kind or another. It gave me a real kick and I loved the extra strength they offered. I was left alone from the Subs and Williams during that time. It put a spring into my step and took away a portion of my fear, but the joy was short lived.

In ten weeks, Williams had secretly moved his family to a new town. Smit was then transferred to Wakefield in Yorkshire, under the guise of being a high security risk of escape from Altcourse. Wakefield was a category A prison and Smit had no desire to plan an escape.

I didn't know he had gone and the day after, I turned up at the gym to find the fixed window that looked into the corridor had been blacked out. I opened the door and inside stood …. the Subs.

Chapter 35

The Reverend:

From the hope of making friends and avoiding beatings to the biggest beating I'd had. They broke my wrist and three fingers on my right hand, bust my left eye socket and imaginatively slashed my thighs with a Stanley blade. My face was distorted, swollen with lumps and horrible coloured bruises and I was left with a serious concussion. My hope of an easier life had died along with my will to live. I was hardly six months inside with no idea when or how I'd get out. Time became an entrapment of a still continuum. It was wretched.

I spent the next forty-two days back in hospital. Despite the pain, I found it peaceful and I milked my stay by faking my levels of pain as it began to subside. My mind relaxed from the paranoia and uncertainty of being jumped. The nurses and doctors treated me with little sentiment, but a helping of kindness that is part of their job. At least, they were not starving or beating me. They had no investment in my wellbeing in the long run.

My ordeal inside was taking its toll on me, mentally. I became a mute. I did not want, nor need, to talk to any-one. It was a low point where I found out what depression was. What was occurring was unfair and brutal. I was put on suicide watch because I repeatedly asked the nurses and begged if they could end my life to put me out of my misery. At nights, my wrists and feet would be strapped to the bed by the same two screws who accompanied me before. To cope with my mental state, they recruited the reverend from the chapel to come and talk to me.

The reverend sat beside me, at the same time almost every day just gone ten am, while the screws went for a break, leaving me handcuffed to the bed. I was intoxicated with mind numbing drugs: those I welcomed to ease the anxiety. He muttered and babbled away in his gravelly coarse voice, to himself, because I was not interested in conversing and held my back to him. Nevertheless, he chatted and recited prayers and verses from the bible, I'm sure to give me hope during my hardship.

"The God of hope fills you with all joy and peace in believing, so that by the power of the Holy Spirit you may abound in hope. Romans 15:13." At first, hearing these words felt awkward and irrelevant but it didn't take long before I took comfort in his words that filtered into my brain through the haze of fog from the pain killing drugs. His calming coarse scratch seemed to be hypnotic but never did I turn to look at him. Each day I held my back to him as I hovered inside the darkness of my bewildering despair.

"Honour your father and your mother, that your days may be long in the land that the Lord your God is giving you. Exodus 20:12." He made reference a lot to family and loyalty, not knowing my past.

Maybe he had read my file, I didn't know, but it didn't sound as if he knew anything about my past. Days and days he went on as I recovered slowly, mentally and physically, that little bit more. His words aided me, they probably saved me. By the end of the stint, I secretly anticipated his visit. On the last day I was in hospital, he visited one last time.

"The man who had died came forth, bound hand and foot with wrappings, and his face was wrapped around with a cloth. Jesus said to them, unbind him, and let him go. John 11:44." Those words struck me with a feeling of déjà-vu and gave me tingles. He babbled on about Lazarus and his return from death. There I began to think about turning to face him when he retreated to silence for a few minutes.

Finally, he spoke the final words I would hear from him.

"The sins of the father are to be laid upon the children." I lay quiet, wondering about the significance of the quote, not knowing it was my Father's imprint on my life that led me to that bed. There was no bible reference, which I found strange and I waited for him to quote one. With no answer, I turned to ask him where it came from, but he had already left and I questioned my sanity as to whether he was ever really there.

When I was reluctantly released, I was beset with nerves. My head sagged as I walked, my shoulders slouched and I avoided eye contact with everyone.

After a few days spell back in healthcare, I was taken to my cell during lunchtime, and as I sat on the edge of my bed, I noticed Helder's pictures were no longer on the walls and his belongings were gone. Someone had replaced him as the sheets were all messed up. Helder always kept a tidy area. I dreaded to think who the new occupant was.

But soon enough I heard who it was before I saw them. He approached the cell singing a song so loud and out of tune it could have awoken the dead. He swaggered in, cocksure, and stood by the edge of his bed.

"Yi' must be ma cellmate mucker, heard yi' were in a bad way," deathly straightforward, he spouted overly loud. Stood over me with his five-five height, his blackened hair was so thickly gelled flat it could have been set with shoe polish. What he lacked in size and age, in his twentieth year, he made up for in his hard to understand, elaborate northern Scottish twang. I lay back in my bed and buried my head in my pillow, ignoring his attempts of an introduction with his awake wide-eyed stare.

"Aye, yi' don't have to speak, yi' make yerself at home, son, you've had a hard time." He stood, nakedly blasting his ego towards me, as I tried to ignore his presence. "It's lunch time." He insinuated for me to leave him alone

I swivelled around and slid my legs off the bed. I stood powering my height over him, baring my dead gaze into his beady, unshy eyes, "You want to own me as well, you Scottish prick? Then you come have your turn…Cunt."

His ego faded, contemplating the seriousness of my statement, and debated if my young age was a factor in his superiority over me. But my soul was empty of compassion or reasoning, and he sensed it, like a shark could smell blood, and backed down.

"Wow, wow, big man, I hear yi." I calmed and stepped away. "Ye're a fiery one! I like a man who speaks his mind. I can see we'll get on," he said, as he slapped my upper arm. I had set the boundaries of our relationship and returned to my bed to lie down. I wasn't having him lose the rag with me, thinking because I was young he could bully me around.

He jumped up onto the top bunk, flopped down on his back and spoke.

"The name's Micky." His last name was Macdonald and you would never have to tell anyone he was from Scotland.

Time passed methodically. Bouts with the Subs came regularly, pain was normal and help was rare. My apprenticeship in fighting had started. I was not willing to be a bitch and get beaten up all the time. I was the son of Davie fucking Rhodes and it became time I had to live up to that. I began to fight back to the best of my resilience; it was either that or bow down, and I was dog tired of doing that. I started my own assaults when I could isolate some from the group, on their own or in pairs. I found I could easily take them on individually, or in pairs, sometimes three. My drive for revenge drove my desire to take them apart.

All I wanted was to beat and hurt them as they had me. Williams would always be near when a full Subs assault was in the making. He manufactured it and watched it all unfold, following the events like a soap opera. Surely passing the info onto the Governor, whose hard exterior I never forgot. He was top of that food chain.

His sight in the wings was a rare occurrence, loathing the company of who he thought was beneath him.

I pondered as to who was to blame for all this and it became a combination of Carlin, Williams, and the Governor. I remembered the Governor's threat, about what would happen to me if I was ever sent to his office. That indulged my imagination. I learned to love danger, and I wanted to find out. He was a glorified pervert and got off on his ability to abuse whoever took his fancy. I sensed he had already lived a life of trauma and he re-lived it by taking it out on other victims.

Micky became a genuine friend. Behind his schizophrenic demeanour, he had a heart of gold. While he was erratic and wild, he had a humble side that knew I had lived a hard life, not that I confided in him or spoke about it. His accent reminded me of Davie's and that's maybe why we became pally. He taught me how to play cribbage and we shared games of pool. I was shit but enjoyed the distraction and he liked winning, so it was good for both of us.

On the outside, Micky had a cocaine addiction and was courier for a man, Carl Jenkins, in Aberdeen. He got busted on a train after he involved himself in an embargo with a group of squaddies who were on a weekend off. The hot headed and volatile Micky got in a scrap where the kilo of white powder he was carrying got ripped apart and spilled over the train carpet. He was lifted and banged up. He was the middleman doing the delivery, not a grass; he accepted the charge without argument.

He tried to protect me from Williams' coarse hand and the Subs, ending up getting as hurt as I did at times. I joined him on his rampages and often we were involved in fights with other inmates or the screws. We both used it to blow off steam and we were regularly sent to isolation or the segregation unit.

My dose of steroids was a forever changing amount and I was packing on size in bursts. Once Smit left, I had to scrape and struggle to find more and when I did get my hands on some, in turn it caused a dilemma. It made me very hungry. I had little to barter except for my dinner meals and I always laid them down in bets. One day, I had an arm-wrestling match with a guy who was twice my age, for a chocolate bar and I beat him. This kicked off a series of meetings where I wrestled for my steroids mix and extra food.

I worked out as much as I could. I got into the gym for one hour each day and no longer. They figured out I caused less trouble when I received that privilege. I did the rest of my working out in my own time. I quickly gained muscle, spurring me to have confidence in what I began to do. It also started a routine of sleepless nights of overthinking and temper tantrums. I resorted to many things to get back into the office, walking on a tightrope of other people's wrath.

One week I committed to stealing everyone's toothpaste and throwing it in the bucket. That earned me a month's stint in the segregation wing. Another thing I did was steal the ping pong balls, causing a wing-wide riot that locked us all down. That earned me a twenty four hour lock down for a couple weeks.

I wasn't gaining any favour with the screws but that was my goal: I wanted back into the Governor's office and I would shout that out in fits of anger. I rubbed my own shit over the walls and threw it off screws. I poured piss in bottles and chucked it over the control response unit when they piled into my cell and jumped me. I spat on their faces when I could not defend myself. That earned me a trip to the special intervention's unit. I did everything I could think of to disrupt the system but I soon realised if I wanted back into that office, it would have to be on my terms. I had nothing to lose, I was given no sentence and had no identity.

All the carnage I caused occurred whilst in a war with the Subs - a war I was constantly losing but a war I was determined to win. It felt as if I was preparing for something, a final outburst or redemption of some kind. I was no longer a boy; the years of innocent fun normal teenagers have, did not exist for me. I skipped those parts and turned myself into a quiet and determined hard man.

One evening, a long time into my sentence, now a grown man and so different from who I was on the first day I entered, me and Micky got deep into a conversation.

"This isn't workin', son. Yi' can cause as much grief as yi' want but you'll never get back into 'at greasy fucker's office," Micky correctly said, as we sat across from each other on our beds, elbows over knees with locked eyes. He did not have much of his sentence left and was looking forward to returning to Aberdeen.

"You're right, Micky, something drastic needs to happen."

Micky was a man who had done a god-awful amount of sinful and regretful things. He could tell so easily when another man approached his limit of logical manner and was prepared to do something of outrageous calibre that bypassed any moral compass.

"Are yi' prepared to meet the devil?" That was the most serious thing he'd ever said to me.

"What?" I assumed he meant if I was prepared to die in order to achieve what I wanted.

"I've seen it before, been there many times. The moments before yi' do somethin' 'ats beyond yer control."

I was at that junction of decision: was I prepared to lose that control? Was there some doubt? I'd already been sat at that junction, waiting for the moment, to turn onto the road of no return.

"I'd need your help." Micky was loyal, there was no conflict in his eyes questioning if he would help me.

"Aye, what the fuck have I got to lose? I'll be in and out o' places like this for the rest o' ma days."

"I'll see you good one day when we're out of this rats' nest."

"I should fuckin' think so," he said, smirking his podgy mouth. He jumped up and clapped his hands. "Right, what's the plan?"

Chapter 36

The Day of Reckoning:

A few days later when the doors had been unlocked for breakfast, and after some constructive planning, we emerged from our cell. Pumped with apprehension and the knowledge that adrenaline would soon take over, we glanced up across the twos where the first two victims could be seen. Bald Bob and Dunce, both local Scousers. Micky ambled across the twos, whistling casually with his hands inside his pockets as if he was on a Sunday stroll. As he approached Bald Bob, who was wary of Micky, he squared up to him.

"Hae, any o' yi' pair got some tobacco? I'm out 'til payday," Micky asked.

"Fuck off, you foreign leech," Bald Bob replied.

The Subs had as much dislike for Micky as they had for me and they never spoke. They were perplexed at his friendly approach and took the question as unusual. Micky scrunched his face and shook his head, kicked Dunce in the shin and legged it four doors down the corridor into Bald Bob's cell.

I followed furtively across the walkway with a spring in my step and headed to the cell. I opened the door to find Micky trapped in a headlock by Dunce, laughing deliriously at them to their confusion. I closed the door and, with no hesitation, went straight for Bald Bob, slamming my fist square onto his nose and then bounced his head off the sink repeatedly until he lacked the inspiration to retaliate. Dunce slackened his grip from Micky disillusioned by my volatile actions and barbaric nature. The element of surprise was an effective one.

While he, open-mouthed, stared at the mixture of broken teeth blended with blood pouring out of Bald Bob's mouth, I sprang over and gripped his throat, squeezed hard, rendering him unable to move. An inspired Micky battered into his stomach like a rampant featherweight boxer. Dunce struggled to breathe and sapped of the ability to fight back, he passed out and fell from my grip to the floor. We tied their hands up with bed sheets to prevent them hitting the cell alarm, and stuffed socks into their mouths. We made as little noise as possible to derail any attention, the plan being quick bursts of energy.

I opened the cell door to find a surprise! Four of the Rastas stood with their arms crossed, curious to see what we were up to. Luckily, they were the only ones who noticed our stealth-like movements but unluckily for me, Helder, the one I was closest to, had been given early release.

"Help us?" I asked. They exchanged blank expressions, uninterested at first, as they had nothing to gain. I had to persuade them. "Helder was a friend. He helped me and so have you."

They exchanged looks between them.

"We're going to do 'em all and then get to the Governor. It's Otto next." The Rastas knew what implications lay ahead if they were caught aiding us, but we were together against the screws and the system, and they liked the adrenaline as much as we did.

"Ok, we can do 'at, man."

"Good. One of you stay here and keep them quiet, rest of you follow but keep behind us. Don't want to raise suspicion."

The next target was the big African, Otto, who was inside for rape. He'd be the most daunting one to take down. At that time in the morning, Otto would be leaving his cell at the end of the block for his job assembling office furniture. We made our way to his cell, furthest one from the screws' office, and huddled outside.

Micky smiled like a crazed clown through the long slit of glass on the door. Otto's attention was drawn from his shaving. Rapidly he opened the door, his jaw still smothered in foam, showing a bare broad chest, and assumed a menacing stance inside the frame. He was unable to spot the Rastas hiding round the corner from the door.

"What the fuck are you doing, creepy white motherfucker?" he asked, in his immersed formulated English tone.

"White what…you racist cunt?" Otto leapt out of his cell to grab Micky, who stepped back onto the railing. Otto was jumped upon by all of us. A quick scramble saw us drag him back inside his cell. We climbed and jumped on him, knocking him about, but the big lump was hard to put down. In a team effort, we managed to pin him down eventually. Quickly we tied him up the same as the other two and one of the Rastas stayed inside the cell to keep him at bay.

Next it would be Vinx and his cellmate, Gismo. Now these two had the nearest cell to the wing office, and it would be trickier as it was also a congregation area for general chit chat beside the pool table on the ground floor. We had to act fast before word got out about the other three. During the morning run for breakfast, and inmates getting into their daily routine, the screws were stretched with the vast spread of movement. There was one male screw in the office, Daisy Dave we called him, and we had to get him out. Micky left us to prepare for what was the craziest and most erratic part of our plan. I hung about near the pool table for a few patient minutes before Micky burst out of the cell with his jumper on fire, screaming to high heaven. Even I was almost shouting at how unerringly scary it looked. He legged it down the stairs screaming obscenities.

The feeling of panic and fear echoed through the wing as inmates scrambled, looking for an extinguisher. Daisy Dave saw a flaming lunatic running down the stairs and burst into action. He bolted out of the office, grabbing the fire extinguisher by the door, unlocked the grill gate and legged it straight to Micky, blasting him in white foam.

Meanwhile, Gismo opened his cell door to see the commotion as the two Rastas wasted no time in barging him backwards into the cell, while I burst past, giving Vinx no warning, and started exchanging blows with him.

Vinx reacted instantly as we battled into the corner, going at it hammer and tongs, as if we were fighting inside a phone box. The surprise attack had given me the advantage. Gismo was restrained and pinned to the ground by the two Rastas. The door was closed. Vinx kept struggling, rattling me with heavy thuds and chewed on my ear as we grappled. My drive for revenge fuelled my intensity; using the power and speed at my disposal, I got the better of Vinx soon enough, after he used his last survival tactic of trying to chew my ear off. I had finally dominated him as he drifted on his feet with exhaustion when I clutched his jaw tightly with both hands and smashed his head off the hard wall. I pulled his legs from under him, pinning him with the weight of my knee over his head. The commotion and effort left me breathless and I used the time to catch it. Gismo was tied up already and the Rastas moved over and held Vinx's legs down. We tied him up and gagged them both, leaving the Rastas inside with them.

Micky had wrapped his head in a jumper, sprayed himself with deodorant and set himself on fire. He had been covered in white foam and had still overpowered Daisy Dave with the help of a couple other keen inmates. He then covered the screw with the rest of the extinguisher contents leaving him in a foamy mess on the ground.

I then had one goal left.

Warrender ran onto the wing, spotting Micky covered in the aftermath of the extinguisher and her mate on the floor. "What the Christ is going on here?" she questioned.

"Crazy bastard lit himself on fire," Daisy Dave shouted, while I sneaked behind Warrender and laid one blade of a pair of scissors, that Micky had acquired from an inmate working in the segregation unit laundry, on her neck.

"We are going to play by my rules now. Listen to me and do not disobey my orders."

A deathly silence had covered the wing after Micky's flaming outburst and all eyes were now directed on me.

"You'll get extra time for this!" she stated.

"I'll be here till I die anyways since I don't exist."

She picked up on my lack of concern for my actions as I pulled her forehead back and leveraged the blade against her throat. Daisy Dave had stood up and began to tiptoe towards an alarm.

"Micky!" I called out.

"I'll get the slithery cunt!" he answered and bolting to the screw, he chucked him into a cell and pulled the door closed. There was now a small gathering of spectators. "Any o' yi want to go in 'ere, be my guest." Micky stated firmly.

The interested parties entered the cell and soon there begging screams of mercy. I turned my attention back to Warrender who feared for her safety. I could smell it on her.

"Do you like that feeling, Miss, total fear? It brings desperation, does it not? Don't do anything desperate, you won't get mercy from me."

I edged her towards the exit gate of the wing to the left of the office. Daisy Dave was being beaten and the other inmates cheered me on. Micky and the Rastas had helped me but I was on my own now. Still no alarm had been sounded but it would happen soon. We arrived at another grill gate.

"Open this gate!" I demanded. Warrender paused as I pressed the blade into her neck, drawing blood. She opened the gate in haste. "Take me to the Governor's office!"

Another moment's hesitation before she led me down a corridor and through a few more gates. At times, she tried to talk but I pressed the scissors to discourage her. Didn't matter what she said, it was never going to derail my intentions. I could feel blood trickling down, between my fingers, and it encouraged a barbarous instinct in me to come alive.

We arrived at the base of a set of stairs. At the top was the big wooden framed double door of the Governor's office. I licked my lips in tantalising thoughts of my return between those doors. It had been a long two years.

The alarm sounded and gave Warrender hope. It made me jump but I focused. "Now, remove your keys from your belt!" She hesitated again. "Don't think because the alarm is sounding that I won't finish you." She removed the keys. "Now undo your belt and let it drop to the ground." As she did so, I spoke in her ear, "I'm going to ask you something, a question that will either kill you or save your life. You hear me?" I released a smidgen of pressure on the blade to enhance a sliver of trust.

"Ok," she muttered and I paused. "Go on," she insisted with a layer of desperation.

I persuaded her to look up the stairs, onto the office doors. We could see a shadow pacing around behind the glazed door windows.

"Describe what the key looks like that will lock that door."

"I don't have to, they're numbered, It's number one." I roughly switched my look at the keys and saw they all had numbers stamped onto them. I removed the blade from her neck and released my hold. She soared away in relief and then froze, not knowing what to do.

"Now, fuck off!" I ordered. Momentarily, she had frozen, but then legged it. I stepped up the stairs and opened the door. The Governor had his back to me, was on the phone. He turned and dropped the receiver from his ear.

"How did you get up here?" He had a link to every angle of vision throughout the prison. He was so used to the alarm sounding, he hadn't bothered to pay any attention to what was going on. I closed the door and locked it, leaving the key. I stretched for the nearest chair and trapped it between the handle and the floor. Understanding I had bad intentions, he rushed to his computer screen to see the wing I'd come from was in chaos.

"Who is it?" I growled, eyeing what I could pick up and use as a weapon. I spotted some stationary on the desk, plus a glass ashtray, but the other desk chair was the first thing that came to mind. "Who's what?" he countered, while pressing his own emergency alarm under his desk. His imposing personality had dissipated.

"Don't play dumb, you cunt, who's responsible?"

"You're a convict, you've been treated as any other would." He was playing me for a fool, something I lived to loathe. I shuffled forward a couple of steps watching him flinch as I picked up the chair, swung it over my shoulder and launched it toward him. He side-stepped out of the way as the chair hurtled through the window, covering the ground with broken glass and leaving the blinds whirling around in the stiff wind.

"You better stop now, you hear me?" he yelled, while reviewing the mess of the shattered glass on the floor. He looked at me dead eyed while the unusual feeling of gusts of wind smashed into the side of his face. He beamed down to drawers on his desk, slid one open and removed a short baton. "I'm no stranger to a temper. I was brought up with violence. If you want a fight, I'll give you one," he boasted, as the glass crunched under his feet and his thickened hair blew in the wind. I was impressed with the size of his balls. I began side-stepping around the big table, catching the wind on my face. I had seen how cautious he was attempting to play, buying time before someone came and burst the door down. His head shifted as we both heard the shuffle of footsteps.

"WHO IS IT!" I roared, deafening my own ear drums, and launched myself across the desk, leaping my weight onto him. The ricochet caused him to drop the baton when he grabbed me in a tight bear hug. I was locked in his hold as he scuffled across the glass. Trapped, I could not move so I sunk my teeth into his neck, chewing off his skin. He howled while I tasted his flesh and he slammed my back into his desk, repeating the motion with ferocity until I was too pained to hold on and fell onto the desk.

He backstepped, grasping his wound, struck by my barbarous motives. Thuds bore down on the door, but they couldn't get it. The Governor hurried his way over to the chair that held the door shut. I fumbled off the desk and glimpsed the baton on the floor. The Governor ferociously kicked the chair away, leaving only the door to unlock with the key I had left in there. I picked up the baton, bolted and jumped into the air, smacking it over his hand that was trying to turn the key. He winced and I backhanded the baton across his jaw. He weakened almost instantly and I continued with four more thudding clunks before he took a knee. I turned to haze, snarling like something inhuman, thrashing him wildly with the baton and stamping on his stomach.

The battering at the door continued, shoulders trying to break it open and feet to burst it in. I returned to his desk and investigated the open drawer that the baton came from. Lying there was that brown file of mine and a sturdy fishing knife. I removed the knife and slid the blade out. The Governor was recuperating with his second wind and managed to kneel, spotting me holding the knife. The doors were banged and banged by a heavy dose of screws outside. It was beginning to give way. He tried to stand to unlock the door but he could not coordinate himself. I rushed around the desk and kicked his hand that managed to grab the key again. I filled his face with hard hooks and jumped on top of him as I forced him to the ground. He was fatigued and confused by the thumps to the head to act with any more purpose. I pressed the blade on his throat as I sat over his chest.

"Who the fuck has done this? Who's behind it?" His darkened eyes blazed pity, begging for reprieve. He began to mumble something I could not understand.

Shards of glass scattered through the air landing all around us. The glass window of the door was smashed. "TELL ME!" I howled into his face as he mumbled more. I couldn't make out what he was saying and he eventually said something in Indian. I was furious and felt mocked.

The door burst open, Williams's hands wrapped around my body and pulled me off. He dragged me across the room to behind the desk, back into the breeze from the broken window and then to the floor where he hooked his arms around me, pining my back into his chest. The sleeves of Williams's shirt were reddened, and his hands covered in blood. Screws surrounded my vision suffocating me with vile looks of disgust. I observed the Governor whose neck squirted blood into the air like a leaking water pipe.

Warrender and another three screws pressed their hands over the wound to no avail. In the depth of the struggle, the Governor lifted his head from his shoulders and locked eyes with me. He tried to speak as he raised his hand into the air with his gangly index finger pointing down. He was trying to inform me to look into the drawer that held the file. Warrender wrapped her legs around him while trying to hold a rag over his neck. He gargled and choked, stressing to say something. Warrender nestled her ear closer as he whispered something and then his head dipped, and eyes closed. Warrender let the dead weight of his head drop, as everyone was stunned.

Warrender's vacant gaze looked up to me and repeated what the Governor said, "The sins of the father are laid upon their children."

Williams, as shocked as everyone else, released his grip and watched me pick the file from the drawer.

It was the same file that Carlin had on me but that was not what drew my attention. Underneath it were four Polaroid pictures. They were all of the Governor in his early adolescent years in the late seventies or early eighties. The first one was with his family outside a terraced housing scheme. The second was with the family's fruit and veg stall. The third was one of him posing in a boxing stance, wearing a scabby vest and a turban, surrounded by half a dozen other Indian fellows. The last one was him, wearing the turban again, in a fight with Davie.

My reaction jolted up to Williams' grimacing face as he peered at the Governor's dead body. The name tag that always faced the wrong way round towards the Governor was now facing me.

I glanced at the name…Rajeed Kapoor.

Chapter 37

Welsh Williams:

I glared at the man, Welsh Williams, whose face became overtaken with terror. Whatever his reasons were, to be in that ring adjacent to me, I did not give a damn. The opportunity was like being served karma on a plate. I realised why Helder was in shock, knowing the chances of that coincidence living out was as rare as an honest criminal. I gave Helder a dry look and his reply was an engaging nod of the head. He wanted me to hurt him as much as I did. At that point, I became distracted and I did something against my beliefs, I turned my back on Williams. Davie preached never to turn away from your challenger, whether it was inside a ring or on the street, it was a sign of weakness. But rational thought was not something that I could be aware of at that moment. I moved close enough into Jack, so I did not have to yell over the noise.

"Do you know this man?" I asked, with livid eyes and flaring nostrils. I thought he was possibly playing a game with me.

"No." He was perplexed at my question and knew I was insinuating something. "Should I?" he replied. I wanted to say bad things to him. I was furious that he didn't know Williams was the senior officer who took orders from the Governor, making my time in jail a nightmare. I wanted to spit in his face, as he acknowledged the hate emanating from my stance.

In the cramped ring, under the guise of deprived lighting, my blood began to simmer. The frightening feeling I had after I ended the Governor's life, returned and covered my skin with shudders. I did not welcome the guilt I had to live with afterwards, but I did not let it burden me because I knew he was a disgusting man. Now I had the chance for more redemption but I couldn't tell if I would be willing to inflict the same fate on Williams.

The ref tugged on my tense shoulder. I flinched and almost drove my elbow into him as I turned. I stared at Williams again, reminding me of the two and a half years of torture. He starved me, had me beaten, and deprived me to every pleasure. He was all too aware of how much wrath I carried and he looked worried.

But he was missing something from his look, other than his aviator specs. The confidence built on his bullying nature was stripped from his presence. His fear was laid bare for all to see. He knew I would be willing to kill him because that was the Governor's fate. The powerful hold he held over me would incite him into believing he could defeat me, or I hoped it would. There was no backing out, in front of a baying crowd; the shame that would follow him would not be worth the years of guilt. I could tell he debated parting with the shepherding of his unwillingness to fix eyes. I was a different person from the one he used to abuse. His confidence sagged; I could see his hulking posture weaken, knowing how much I would want to inflict pain. He would try to rely on his bullish way and strength. I could see it, the fear in his eyes. He emitted it like cattle waiting for slaughter.

Inside me was nothing but rage, a rage that could not peak. There was no end to it.

The ref pulled me into the centre with my fists gripped solid and jaw bones edging out my cheeks. I could feel the pump from the 'roids, which gave me the superior confidence I needed being the young pretender. Williams was stalled by his sweaty bull-chested corner man and eventually joined me in the middle. He tried to hide the fear by smiling at me. The room simmered; my ears bled a dead tone. The referee's words were not relevant. I had no concept of rules. In the blur I heard a bell and it snapped me into action like an aggressive canine.

As Williams kept his distance, I burned to draw anguish into his body. My desire to inflict pain drew me away from any sense. I stalked him, flatfooted, and square on with my chin buried into my chest. Williams lifted his fists to his chin, moving heavily on his toes and kept a distance. In a quick flash, he pounded two fists into my eyes, momentarily blinding me. My legs buckled slightly. I gorged the fear out of his eyes from my look as I hunted him down. He thudded me with a couple of solid jabs, hissing as he exhaled the power, each one reminding me of the past. I growled and imagined gory blood leaking from his face after I'd taken a bite. I soon figured out that Williams could fight without the backup of his screws or a truncheon in hand.

I was prepared to take it all, I would let him beat me until he tired. Punch after punch came my way as I tucked my forehead down to deflect from my nose and chin. I swung wild haymakers and missed each time, carrying on my predatory stalk afterwards. He hissed and pressed the power into every punch, determined to put me off or finish me sooner rather than later. I was only young in looks but what I held in life trauma beat most men who stood across from me.

More quickly than I imagined, the bell rang as I continued to press him. Williams did not think I was going to stop until Eiffel was sent into the ring to pull me to the corner. I was reluctantly dragged back to face Jack. "What are you doing? Hit the man!" he tried to make

eye contact with me. "Are you here, Max?"

I did not look at anyone except for the man across the ring, standing in the corner as I was. My breath was heavy and quick, my emotions were tense.

"You don't know who that is?" I asked again with a bullet stare burning across the ring at Williams. Jack peered around my body to look at Williams again.

"I don't have a clue," he answered.

"You'll need to hit him if you're going to win," Eiffel butted in. I did not need his advice; he was no match for me.

"Fucking hit him," Jack said as he tried to give me a drink. I kept my mouth shut and refused it. Williams began to look at me emptily, sorry for the rotten cauldron of anger I was trapped inside. Before the bell sounded, I stomped to the middle and clenched my fists, roaring through my throat. The room momentarily silenced and Williams' corner man was stunned.

The bell rang. I barged past the ref and charged forward with a wild right missing Williams' corner man and then Williams as he shifted away. The momentum smacked my right knee onto the solid ground. I sprang to my feet as Williams' corner man hurried out of the ring and the referee took a distance, not caring to get close. Williams was forced to defend himself when I backed him up onto the ropes, gunning for me with heavy punches that landed without registering as I countered with a barrage of wide hooks. Williams was hurt, fell to one knee and I jumped him, whipping blows across his face.

I was dragged off by the ref who kept me at bay until Williams rose. The spectators were in an uproar. This was the kind of tormented man they wanted to see, with no control over his temper. Williams rose to his feet, his boxing skills of no help to him now. Without hesitation, I pounced again. He tried to back off and threw survival punches, but they bounced off me like pathetic snowballs. I trapped him in my own corner, hailing wild overhand punches across his face until I was over the top of him again.

When the ref tried to bear hug me off, I got loose, swivelled round, headbutted him and tossed him aside. Williams was grounded, and he could not move. I jumped on top of him and drove my fists into his head, time and time again. I felt his jaw crumble as I phased out of any foundations of what I was doing. Bodies hounded me and tried pulling me away.

Flustered and annoyed, I threw my elbows and fists to free myself. I saw the pain he was in, and I was not finished. Someone had a hold of my left arm when I lifted my leg and stomped on top of his chest until there were too many bodies over me. They pinned me, face down, with too much leverage for me to move. Right to the side of my eye line was Williams' ugly face; it was battered, with his left eye closed shut. I butted my head off the ground in frustration of being held back. I spat in his face and tried to wriggle over to take a bite out of his nose. His right eye was open, and he could see the pure hatred I had of him. Not being able to move, I calmed slightly, noticing Williams was trying to whisper something.

I wanted to know what he was trying to say, so I stopped struggling. I tuned out the noise and focused on his lips until I could hear him. His jaw struggled to open and shut as he muttered…

"I'm sorry, Max."

Chapter 38

The Fast Exit

Williams was an unexpected event, and he became history. His beating sat well with me. He got his comeuppance, and I was able to put his unjust treatment of me to bed.

I thought about the chances of that occurring and it must have been colossally rare. It seemed as if an outer force laid its presence onto my path. I found out afterwards that, when I had been released from jail, Williams and half the screws were sacked; he in particular was barred from the prison service. With the Altcourse scandal rocking the area, the prison service, and the whole country, his name was linked with the Governor and he collapsed into a drink-filled mental breakdown. His wife left him, he was refused time with his kids, and he turned to fear-filled adrenaline to distract him from his depression. He moved to London and lived life as if he wanted to be thrown into a jail. I bet he wished he had after our encounter. I broke his jaw in two places, his collar bone and fractured his eye socket. His will to be a bad man was no more. When a bully is defeated, there is seldom a way back for him. The humiliation and shame took down the wall of hardness.

When he was recovering in hospital, he managed to acquire some whisky, and after lights out, he combined that with a concoction of antidepressants and sleeping pills to bring himself to death. Inside the world in which I lived, death was never far away.

After the Governor's demise, I was taken into isolation while the mess was cleaned up. I had resigned myself to the idea that the rest of my life would be spent inside, and it could have so easily been that way. I had been visited by a couple of detectives who had been assigned to the case on a few different occasions and I was pulled in and out of interview rooms for days. I did not wish to talk to anyone because either way, I knew I was fucked and I had no idea what was happening on the outside. I was burdened with an uninviting feeling of dread, that I'd done something I could never forget.

He deserved it, The Governor, but I was loaded with this horrible spell of loathsome dismay. I suppose you could call it guilt. But I also had many more questions I needed the answers to. The Governor was Rajeed who was my Father's old foe from his teenage years in Glasgow. He knew I was Davie's son because of the file. Now I wondered if Carlin knew about Rajeed and how those pieces of information found each other. Who was pulling the strings of my fate? It did explain why I was given such harsh treatment. I paid for the sins of my Father as Rajeed said.

While the authorities were figuring out what to do with me, something miraculous happened.

Well after dark on a cold October night, I was taken to an interview room. On the table was a steaming cup of coffee sitting adjacent to me. I couldn't resist and started drinking. While I took the first sip, the door opened, and in walked Carlin.

"I knew you were a coffee man," he said before sitting down. Seeing him reminded me of the start of my nightmare inside. He held a moment of a sombre quietness that matched his manner which showed a sliver of sorrow. Not the revolted look I remembered. "I know what you've had to endure in here," he said softly. I slid his coffee over the table. "No, son, you can have that." I wanted to believe in his kind, soft approach, but I was still aware it could be a trap, I remained silent until I was more convinced. "You have been locked up for a few days so I'll bring you up to date with what's been going on. Every inmate of this prison has reached out to someone, family, friends, the detectives...the newspapers as well, and they have explained how they, you and others, have been treated here. There have been stories of beatings, sexual abuse and even torture. There is now so much information filtering out, it's on the front page of every newspaper from here to Mozambique." He had my attention, but I did not respond.

"I know what you've done, but the outside world doesn't know...we would like to leave it like that." By that point, I began to perk up and the thoughts of spending most of my life in jail faded away somewhat.

"Other prisoners, and especially Micky, have told us how you had been treated and I feel personally responsible for that." Carlin relaxed and slouched back on his seat. "You have no identity, Max. To the outside world, you do not exist. In reality, no one knows you are in here, officially."

There, the door opened, and a female detective walked in. Her name was Felicity Banks. She was a pokey faced young detective, in her late twenties or early thirties, with dark rooted blonde hair. She was stout and driven, passive but heartless. She appeared to be the friendlier one but still nowhere near the nice side of personalities. Her foreign appointment to the Mersey police was a recent one and she had her own personal agenda of becoming a successful detective. She took a seat across from me and glanced at Carlin before speaking.

"You're being granted a second chance in life. If it was up to me, I'd keep you inside with the rest of the murderers. But it seems the scandal running riot has ironically come to be your saviour."

The real reason they didn't want me charged with the murder was that it was going to come at the expense of their reputations and jobs. Carlin had been paid off to bypass official channels of charges and trails.

He did not want that to come out. Carlin took over again.

"There are conditions to this, ones only you can follow. Like I said, you don't exist, so when you get outside, you have to carry on as if you were never here and in return, we will ignore the life sentence that should loom over your lucky arse."

"You're going to let me walk?" I questioned.

"In the short version of this, yes," Banks answered. "You will walk out of this prison as if you had never been here." That was ironic considering it would be impossible to forget about my time. "And we do not want to discuss anything that's gone on here."

The idea of being thrown outside after a traumatic experience inside was not one that filled me with elation. It feared me more than how I felt when I was taken in. As I pondered the advantage of not living chained to the inside, it brought me some relief from the tight band around my chest.

"You could be out of here tomorrow morning, Max," Carlin said as his phone started vibrating inside his pocket. He removed it to his ear, "Hello," he answered and stood up. "Give me a minute," he said to his caller and gave Banks the eye that he had to leave the room. Banks soon directed her intentions back to me.

"So, what's it going to be, young Mr Rhodes?"

<h1 align="center">Chapter 39</h1>

The Ghetto Gang:

The fight was behind me but I was still buzzing. Afterwards, I evaded Jack and left the building. I jumped into the motor, drove to a petrol station and entered the toilet. I used the time to allow my head to calm and recharge my thoughts onto the task at hand. I had a wash and changed into the black clothing before driving to Rankin's meeting point a few minutes from a twenty-four-hour supermarket car park. As the adrenaline wore off, my wrists and knuckles throbbed as the aftermath adrenaline trembles eventually died. My heart and body were going through the process of returning to normal. The blows I took to my face swelled up. It was something that could not be hidden.

I arrived at the meeting point Rankin had given me to see he was waiting in a medium wheel based beaten up blue van. He flashed at my approach in the black BMW. I parked close by and jumped into Rankin's passenger seat.

"Evening," he muttered.

"Alright," I tried to keep reasonable and keep the peace. I scanned the area inside the van. He had two burners sitting on the dash, an open bottle of juice in the middle cup holder by the seat, and a paper sized plastic holder slipped between the seat and handbrake. He wore all-black combat trousers and a tactical vest that had more pockets than an Asian tourist's bum bag. "You'll have to be sharp tonight; I'm expecting a small crowd of people here." I glanced at the plastic holder knowing it had the information on who we were dealing with.

"How much?"

"These guns will be getting split between gangs. No way they will all be for the Ghetto Gang unless they are starting a war, but that is who we are dealing with."

"Thought war is good for business!" I replied, as I saw one of the burners light up with a notification. Rankin picked it up, looked at it and diverted his focus.

"War is the best business," he said, as he placed the phone back onto the dash, "but too much war employs too many heroes. I've already checked out the area. We will be allowed through a security entrance from a paid-off guard. We will drive through a dispatch door and into the rear of the market. From there I will deal with one guy called Zen. The Berettas are in one manufactured gun box and the shotguns are split in two separate crates. You stay big and aware behind me, ready to pounce if they try any shifty shit. I will leave a loaded pistol hidden at the back doors to the right of the van as you open it!"

"I don't touch guns," I blurted out.

Rankin paused and gave me a second look. "A man with principles doesn't survive in this industry, young Mr Rhodes."

"Neither do men who refer to me as 'young Mr Rhodes'." I made enough eye contact with him to signal my seriousness of the statement. He should not have been using that name. He shifted forward and flicked on the interior light, about to unleash a statement he thought would have some effect on my attitude but he was quickly distracted.

"Holy Christ, boy, you've been talking while you should've been listening?"

"Something like that," I answered, not willing to give him the knowledge of what I'd just been doing. I'm sure he would have joined the dots, if not there, but at some later point. The second burner lit up on the dash as he picked it up and typed a message back. "Time to move," he said.

We both put on balaclavas and gloves and passed through a heavy steel gate at the back of a concealed yard, which was already unlocked for us. The building was old, pre-war old. The area was cluttered with overflowing industrial bins of rubbish, steel skips, and some cages of gas canisters. The paid-off security guard opened the graffitied roller shutter, just far enough for the van to enter at the rear of the market. Rankin's instructions were to leave everything open for a quick getaway if needed.

I was to follow his lead, and I was very accepting about that because it was not in me to conduct those kinds of events. I liked to watch. He had reversed and parked the van with the back facing three loading bays that stood at the height of a truck back door. There was a small gathering of coloured men standing up there. Straight away, I didn't like the set up. We were confined inside the dispatch unit and standing below them.

Inside the van, Rankin placed one of the burners inside a chest pocket and the other he left on the dash. He gave me a check and said, "Let's get this done smoothly. Stay calm, always, and follow my lead."

He opened the door and walked to the back of the van. I followed and as he opened the back doors, I stood by his side facing the gathering of men, straight away noticing the lanky Helder at the rear of the group. An individual prancing around at the front of the gathering jumped down to the van level and it was obvious he was the leader, Zen. He had that lumpy laid-back stride and so obviously showed his impatience, parading back and forth, scuffling his soles. He wore baggy trousers with lengthy pockets and a faded denim jacket. I shifted my look round to Rankin who enticed me with a sharp eyeball to help lift one of the boxes of shotguns. I obliged and we placed the box in a neutral zone between us and Zen. Rankin returned to the van and grabbed a crowbar to crack open the crate. He took some steps back and stood formally.

"There is your order to inspect but I assure you they are of great stock." Zen wasted no time in stepping forward with an ego-filled gang stride. He bent down and removed a shotgun from the straw packed box. He opened the chamber and checked the line of sight, pointing it directly at Rankin who never flinched, being a man who'd had a gun pointed at him many times. Zen held the sight for a soul sucking ten seconds without so much of a blink from Rankin. He was testing his bottle. That was a side to Rankin I had not seen.

Zen snapped the shotgun closed and pumped the chamber.

"Brand new, init?" he insisted.

"Straight out of the factory," Rankin answered. Zen turned to his gathering and gave them the nod of approval as Helder walked from the group.

"Di ammo and handguns?" Zen asked.

"In the van, in the other two crates," Rankin answered.

"Show me, man," insisted Zen. Rankin paused as Helder had jumped down with a duffle bag. He laid it beside Zen as we met looks. Before Helder walked back to the gathering, he clocked me again. I was completely hidden by my balaclava but felt I was in full view to Helder.

"Are yuh di Eidolon?" Zen directed his question towards me as Rankin shuffled his head around. Rankin waited for me to answer but I did not. That was the first time I heard the name, The Eidolon.

"No, he's not the Eidolon and neither am I. No one knows who this Eidolon is. We are merely the courier service." It was evident that Rankin was keeping as far away from confrontation as he could, swaying away from unnecessary conversation of answering questions with questions.

"I want ta see di other guns before I give yuh di money," he insisted.

Again, Rankin stalled and thought about his actions, knowing as soon as the other crate was opened, the ammo would be there for them to use. I sensed a reluctance from them to pay for the goods and so did Rankin. With an eerie silence soaking the atmosphere,

Rankin turned and walked back to the van. This time he nodded me away from the van and towards Zen. I was not totally sure of what he wanted me to do and I thought about it for a moment until Rankin gave a second nod and I began to walk towards Zen. As I did, ever so vaguely, in the corner of my left eye, I saw him go for the burner in his pocket.

As I stood across from Zen, who was keener to know our identity than receive his merchandise, I turned my head around to see Rankin fumbling.

"Tell me, what's yuh name?" asked Zen, whose only communication with me was from a hard and vacant stare. "What's yuh man doing in dat van?" Zen clearly marked that Rankin was up to something. Rankin slid the gun box of handguns from the van and carried them over, dropped it by the other crate and stepped back to my line.

"There you go, for your inspection. The other box will stay in the van until I see the inside of that bag."

Zen spotted Rankin had a handgun inside his waist holster and took firm notice. After more eyeballs of curiosity as to our identity, he threw the hefty, weighted bag over to our feet. Without instruction, I bent and unzipped the bag to see a muddled number of notes inside. Rankin shifted his head to have a peek.

"Seems organisation is not your strong point, Mr Zen! We will have to count that before anything else happens."

Rankin stood coolly as I lifted the bag of cash to the rear of the van and started counting, standing with a side view of the action. It was two grand short of the twenty.

I didn't want to speak and tapped on the metal of the van door, instructing Rankin to come back, keeping a dominant view of Zen and the gang.

"It's two g's short," I said.

"Are you sure?" Rankin countered.

"You saying I'm thick?" Rankin thought quickly.

"Let's make them think we are okay with this. Help me with the other crate."

I was a bemused but I played along. Rankin unbuttoned the holster of the gun, ready for use. We carried the crate and dumped it on the ground. A massive thud vibrated through the building, as if a door had been booted open. It happened simultaneously with the crate being dropped. Rapidly, bodies in swat uniforms holding tactical weapons flooded into the area from two doors located to either side of the unloading section on the landing. The frontal entrance roller door of the loading bay opened, and bodies entered in their dozens. I exchanged wide eyed looks with Rankin. Those seconds of shock, when something so random happens, rooted me to the spot. Rankin reacted instantly and legged it towards the way we entered, the only foreseeable exit route. I did the most stupid thing and remained frozen. I watched as the gang members went into a chaotic state of alarm. I turned round and looked into the inside of the van, right through to the front dash, where I could see the phone Rankin left.

Acting on instinct, thinking the phone would have my details in it, I grabbed the bag of money, jumped into the back and beelined for the driver's seat. Without so much as a thought, I started the engine and began to floor it when one of the armed cops jumped in the back. Instilled with panic and fear, I pressed my foot to the floor as I made to exit the dispatch room with a handbrake turn, smashing into some industrial shelving. I stalled and swiftly started the engine again, seeing the cop rolling across the floor in my rearview mirror. In a momentary moment of calm in the carnage, I waited for him to stand and floored it again watching him fly out of the back. I sped out of the shed and evaded four more oncoming cops on foot and smashed through a convoy of police cars who were not tooled up to stop a speeding van.

Outside, the security gate was still open, and I bolted away, noticing the security guard sprinting too. There was no way I was returning to jail.

Chapter 40

Time Passes:

That was a close shave and I would endeavour for it to be my only one. After the episode, I decided to try and contact Davie to relay the information to him. But the problem was I didn't have a clue as to where he was. He was a man who could not be found and only contacted me when he required me to do something. I figured Rankin had more contact with him and I knew he would hear about it.

I spent two months trying to get a hold of him and in the end, I decided I was going to keep the information to myself, along with some other information I had picked up through the phone left on the dashboard of the getaway van.

Davie lived his own existence. He would call randomly and have a light chit chat, never revealing where he was. I knew he was not in the UK because of the hissing sound on the phone or the delay in talking. I started to keep a note of when he called because at times he boasted about the exchanges, deals, and money he was making across Europe. He mentioned regular deals with a Swedish man who worked within the network of arms factories in his country, and a dangerous deal in the Chechen Republic, along with other countries like Germany and Armenia. But I felt he would only mention them after they were completed so he could boast about his growing legacy.

I had the odd tasks to do in England but they were mediocre, like opening a bank account with a false name, only so cash could be filtered through it, or delivering ammo. I had not at any time any real knowledge of where he was and I would ask on the phone only to be diverted onto another subject. Sometimes I managed to pick up on background accents if, at the rare times he called, in public, or if he had the TV on in the background, I could try and gauge what country he was in by the chatter.

I recorded everything on paper because I wanted to try and outsmart him. I knew he spent a lot of time in Northern and Southern Ireland. There were two arms dumps and I was determined to find out where, for my own benefit. I knew if I asked these questions, he would avoid answering, and I knew he would become suspicious of the interrogation because he was a paranoid mess. The reason being he had set up the most notorious and violent member of the IRA, who was going to rot inside Belmarsh Jail for the rest of his days. But C4 Millacky would be a man who was always going to come back into Davie's life and mine, so it happened.

The other members of his stable, Turk and Barb, were as elusive as Davie. I was only once in their presence, during an exchange of arms on the Isle of Wight, and they only spoke when they needed to and did not reveal their identity. And Rankin, I did not wish to talk to. Something was off about that deal, the two phones and texting on both, and the impeccable timing of the police raid; I could smell the wrongness in that man, but I would keep all the information to myself for the time.

Some things began to frustrate me. It felt as if everyone around me was keeping secrets from me. Davie, Rankin, and then I had to deal with my hatred for Jack. I had to up my game on gathering information that I could use against him. The idea of outsmarting Liverpool's most notorious criminal since Curtis Warren was an appealing prospect. The more knowledge I gained about Jack, slowly I began to build confidence that one day I would have redemption. Ideas began to brew in my head, like burning down his club and his properties across Liverpool, or other things, like having his dogs killed or kidnapping his wife but none of those thoughts came to fruition.

My yearning for revenge grew regularly and I became patient about it. I learned that my fists were not the only way to fight a battle. It struck me that everyone saw me as thick because I had only a little education while growing up. I was street smart and that's all I needed inside that world. It did make me feel inferior at times, not being able to do the simplest things, like reading letters or filling out forms, whether it was online or written. That's why I adopted some help with reading and writing.   I located a structured English course at a nearby school and joined night classes for two months. I didn't need to become the next Charles Dickens but I kept this secret because I was embarrassed. It was hardly a place a hardened bare-knuckle fighter should be found.

I had a couple of mediocre fights in a six-month spell after the battle with Welsh Williams. They were over quickly and painlessly. I had my purse and a percentage of Jack's winning bets. A trip to the Isle of Man and a jaunt to Cardiff for them. It all topped up my earnings and tucked inside the shoe box. Plus, I kept the twenty grand from the gun deal and stashed that away inside a bank account.

The longer I went without a fight, the more the kettle boiled; I needed one every couple of months. It became therapy, to allow the red mist to dawn and the momentary joy of switching off my mind. After those two fights, I longed for bigger challenges. I learned fast when I was dropped into the den and the more I exchanged fists, the more ruthless I became, following Davie's famous trait. At times it felt like rage consumed my life, sheathing inside my bones like a pressurised valve until it was time to deploy my wrath like dropping a bomb.

There was only one person I felt relaxed with and that was Courtney. Everything I was involved in, she took in her stride. She reminded me of a younger Beverly. Someone who knew that their man was not exactly a straight down the line nine to five kind of person. At times I contemplated that I was forming one man from Jack and Davie's influence. I made sure when my rage was nearing overspill, I evaded spending time with her. I'd seen from some of my fostered days, women of the house being beaten by drunk and aggressive husbands and I did not wish that for her. She was the one person I did not have a barrier against and I had no shame in telling her how I felt. She was the only one who knew about the night school and she did not judge me. That is why I was taken by her. Often, I would think about the family I didn't have,   like aunts, uncles, cousins and siblings, and that made me scared that I'd grow old by myself, like a sad man whose only friends are those who congregate inside the pub, that your loneliness forces you to visit every day. Strange thoughts for someone on the right side of his twenties to think about.

It was safe to say I had settled into a life when Courtney moved in, however uniquely unorthodox it was.

Chapter 41

Straight Forward:

I was not long shy of my twenty-first birthday and I had arrived at the understanding that the comings and goings of my life were going to be classed as normal to me. I was money-motivated and greedy. Guess that ran in the family.

I received instruction in a text message that an upcoming deal was on the horizon. In all honesty, anything that filled me with adrenaline appealed and I loved the rush of gun deals. The sensation of doing something so secretive and dangerous gave me a kick. Rankin and I had done a small handful of deals since the Brixton job with no complications and the next one was on the horizon.

Davie called - a request of a gun deal with a Scottish gangster, Steve Dean, was announced. It was supposed to be straightforward!

"How's it goin', son, keepin' well?" That was his idea of chit chat. I don't think he gave a shit about how I was keeping.

"Surprised you still know who I am!" I lethargically answered.

"You got a hankie? …Better give yer eyes a rub." A few seconds into a conversation and he already had me in a mood.

"What is it!" I bitched.

"There's a deal comin' up with an old friend of mine in Dundee. Rankin will accompany you."

"Who's the friend?"

"A slimy rat called Steve Dean. He has a man who never leaves his side. A Hungarian, Lukas. Rankin knows all about him. He's someone you don't want to cross and don't think about it either." It intrigued me to think that Lukas was a dangerous character and judging by Davie's nervous tone about Mr Dean, I felt there was a history there.

"What's the deal?" I could tell from Davie's tone of response that he was taken by my interest.

"Outdated stalk I want out of the church bunker!" I wanted to find out more information about the bunker but decided to veer away from asking, when he carried on. "After this deal, I want you over to Ireland. I want to show you around."

I was flattered with his offer and decided to change the subject to suggest I was not interested.

"Jack! When are we following through with this?" I asked forwardly. There was a long pause, as I listened to a muffle of heavy breathing over some background traffic noise.

"We should wait a while. Leave him to whatever it is he's doin'." Davie was so addicted to the world of gunrunning, getting payback on Jack for his disfigured hands and dodgy knees was well down his list of priorities. He was more accustomed to building the reputation of The Eidolon. I knew the day would come when I would have to take the plan into my own hands and that was the moment when I began to take that idea seriously.

"Where are you?" I asked.

"Rankin will be in touch shortly." And with that, he hung up the phone.

The deal with Mr Dean went down dreadfully. It was conducted on a patch of farmland he had on the outskirts of Dundee where he tried to fob us off with fake notes that were more than likely supplied by Skinner, the counterfeit expert whom I met in London when I first started peddling weapons for Davie. In a burst of action that happened so fast without thought, Lukas got knocked out by a wheel wrench as I jumped Mr Dean, overpowered him and dragged a knife across his face, leaving him permanently scarred.

As we rushed away from the scene in a rampage of upheaval, in the distance, rapidly approaching sirens sped towards the farmland. Rankin clicked onto them before me with a mute reaction. It was a unit of cops, speeding onto the scene to bust the deal.

I did not know what to think of this situation.

Chapter 42

Trips:

"Welcome to Ireland, son!" Davie said, as he met me off the Belfast ferry, on a wearily grey and wet afternoon. "Fucking hate boats," I moaned with an upset stomach, having been sick over the side a few times. "You'll get used to it, son!"

Davie wandered around the port with me for a while, to allow my seasick legs to stabilise. When he saw a bit of life come back into my cheeks, he patted my shoulder. "It's good to see you. Come on, let's go for a drive. I've somethin' to show you."

On the journey, we discussed the Dean deal and how it all went tits up. He explained his past relations with him during his fighting days and that he was a slithery con man. He put the slippery attempt at using fake money, down to Mr Dean's annoyance at dealing with ghosts and shadows. Davie had acquired a fabled nickname of The Eidolon and Steve Dean decided he wanted to be the man to unravel who it was. Davie thought that he had conspired with the authorities to swoop in and catch all parties involved in the pretext that The Eidolon would be there. I suspected some more suspicious behaviour from Rankin but I withdrew from saying anything. I assumed Rankin told him about the incident!

"Maybe that scar you gave him might wise him up, son," Davie said, in admiration of my assault.

"Should we not be worried about this Lukas character?" I countered, as Davie's reactions delayed when that name was mentioned. The same thing that happened when C4 Millacky's name was uttered. I saw that these were two men he feared and he wasn't this indestructible figure I had structured inside my brain. There was a different side to him from the one who abducted me from The Jacksons.

"We should be worried. That man could find out how Moses split the Red Sea if he looked long enough." That did not fill me with much festivity. "But you wore balas?"

"Aye, both of us."

"En he'll never know. Those plates on the van are not registered so he canna trace us."

"He can't trace the plates of the van?"

"No, untraceable."

We headed for the church on Falls Road. My first experience of Belfast was a trip to the Republican territory in the west of the city. The murals on the gable ends of the buildings were interesting and I found the new sights a welcome solitude from my racing thoughts. I knew nothing of the conflict, except for snippets from Davie and what I'd heard on the news when C4 Millacky had been arrested: an incident and name that Davie never mentioned, knowing full well he grassed on them for his own benefit.

We parked across the road from the grand St Paul's Church and Davie led me, wandering in without hesitation, as if he had a spare key for the place.

"Son, have a pew here." He opened his palm for me to sit down and I accepted, sitting into the cramped pew two rows down from the back. He sat beside me as I gazed at the marvel of the decoration and the wonder of the huge space. It was dead quiet and I noticed how the surroundings calmed me.

"What are we doing here?" I asked as I watched a priest walk into a confessions box.

"Ye're here for my insurance!" That was a bold statement but I did not reply, not knowing what he was on about. "Ye're the only one o' the stable that hasn't been into the basement."

I turned my head towards him; he remained shy about it.

"Wait here for a while. I'll be back. I must talk to the priest!" Davie took off across the pews at the opposite side, into a confessions box, leaving me on my own. I was left in quietness, something that made me feel awkward and unsure of myself. I marvelled at the structure as my eyes were repetitively drawn to the grand cross at the altar of the church.

Out of nowhere, someone sat down behind me. I did not turn around because I did not want to acknowledge anyone. Out of all the empty pews, he chose to sit in that one.

"People are drawn to the church for the solitude," his voice was gravelly, like that of the reverend who visited me in the infirmary. It had a typical deep melody to it like that of a religious hymn. "And then they are drawn here to coincide with the wrongs that they wish to right!"

I could tell he was trying to bring out an emotional side of me that I never admitted existed.

"Just think, out of all the places that you could have chosen to go today, you, son, have decided to visit God's cathedral."

The door of the confessions box creaked open and Davie marched back to me, just in time to stop the ramblings of the voice behind me. As Davie walked towards me I turned to visualise the man but he had gone.

Davie plumped back down beside me. "Right, follow me." He got up excitably and walked off down the middle aisle towards the alter. I followed to the baptismal font, then to a thick and hardy wooden door, to the left. It opened to reveal a maze of circular stairs heading downwards, poorly lit with low wattage bulkhead lights. A few more corridors, before we finished at a strong steel door at the bottom. It was evidently dark as my eyes tried to adjust, with the nearest light too far down the corridor to have an effect. Davie fumbled with a set of keys and then the door opened. Again, it was pitch black before Davie switched the lights on.

It was a mini medieval cell block of six cells. On looking into the first, I saw a collection of metal gun lockers with steel mesh panels, filled with shotguns and rifles slotted into open upright racks. Industrial shelving had an assortment of pistols and attachments adjacent them.

"Have a walk down. Take it all in." It was a satisfyingly impressive set up.

The next cell had a total fifteen, compartment shoe box sized electronically fitted lockers and an overall similar set up to the first call but with more of a used collection of arms. The third cell had a couple of work tops with vices, some hanging tools, lots of different miniature brushes and an assortment of cleaning products and oils.

The next two cells were more like bedrooms: cooking implements like camping gas stoves, microwaves and kettles, bunk beds, sheeted with pillows, picture art on the walls and somewhere to hang your coat. A television set hung up on the wall and some sockets wired into the cell.

Davie trotted up behind me. "It's a good place to come and relax and it keeps me focused on work." I was speechless as I admired his set up, looking into a two-bed cell.

"I need two beds in case the twins need a hideout," he said, pointing to the bunk beds and referring to Turk and Barb. Up until then, I didn't know how big his operation was and I was impressed. His life on the road and in hideout became appealing to me because of the sheer freedom of it. There, I imagined what my life would be like, working as a top gunrunner. Davie walked into one of the bedroom cells, opened a mini fridge and held out a tin of export. I repaid his look blankly and he kept the tin for himself. "Cola?" he offered.

"Aye, that'll do."

Davie made for the first cell and I followed him. On walking in, he immediately cracked his tin open and said, "You know where it is now, you've been wonderin'," as he sat on a heavy-duty gun box. "If I disappear or if anythin' happens to me, 'en you can do whatever you please wi' it. Turk an' Barb are good men but they're no' my blood. Once I'm out o' this life, I won't give a fuck."

I looked around passively as he gulped from the tin. "I didn't know fuck all about weapons when I started, and I know little now. They make money, tax free money, and that's all you need to know."

I was taken with his 'don't give a fuck' attitude for the first time. Davie went on about many things he had been organising within his gunrunning empire and I was happy to listen but some of it was trivial to my ears. The mystery of what he was getting up to and not knowing was frustrating when I was stuck in Liverpool and I thought I'd appreciate the significant insight into his operation but it became inconsequential the longer he went on. At least I knew more than I did before. He continued to speak of a Swede and the regular arms deals with him. He repeatedly mentioned Rankin as if he was his best pal from the playground and how efficient and reliable he was with any request he passed for information or supplies he needed. I did not mention my suspicions of him. I did not think it would register with him.

He had a list of matters he wanted to discuss. It wasn't often we got the chance to speak person to person and Davie hated talking on phones. "I need to cash in on what I'm doin' before I return for Jack. That could be a while but the patience will pay off, ye're in the door now." It seemed Davie's secretive trait rubbed off on me. I needn't want or need to tell him anything of my life over there, with Courtney or fighting, but I had to tell him something.

"I'm doing some work for him, when I like."

"Does that leach trust you?" Davie rose stiffly from his pew on a gun crate and tensely stared at me.

"I've been into his house, met his wife. She's cooked me breakfast, lunch and supper. I've worn his slippers and I'm often in the office in Macartney's having coffee with him."

"Good," he turned away, loosened up and sat back onto the gun crate. "Ye're proper pally then, that'll make it easier. I want it all, his money, his house, his club, his motors, his property, everything he owns. I want it and then I'm going to chuck it…His life, too" His eyes turned cold, as hollow as they would be, like someone with no empathy for his most hated rival. There was no respect and I had no reply. I agreed with the hatred he bore for Jack. I loathed Jack's role in having me binned to the jail but I loved to fight; it was my one exit from torture and it was a walkway for my future. It was what I was born for. I needed Jack at that time!

"How are we going to do that?" I asked.

"There will be a way, and there will be a time, son," he squinted his tight gaze and twisted his stiff neck. He must have seen my doubt. "All 'at pain you felt in jail was down to him and no other. Always remember that because, as time passes, you'll forget a slice o' that pain each day and each day you will become softer."

I absorbed that word, 'soft'. It infuriated me. "SOFT!" I yelled, and stepped over, "Fucking soft, you cunt!"

"Better," he replied firmly. "Now, are you on board here?"

"Aye…I'm on fucking board. I'm on the fucking board!"

Chapter 43

A Knock on the Door:

I came to realise that happiness was an illusion, and my life would never succumb to any kind of level that could relate to it. My mind would never settle and I would always live in wonder of what could have been. I burned for that next release of adrenaline from the underworld of bloody fists. I knew another bout was going to present itself before long. I had told Jack I wanted a real challenge from a top name and he took that request seriously because I had no upcoming opponents. I burned to have the respect that Davie had and more, I wanted a real challenge. A name that would cement my arrival in that world and what an arrival it would become. The idea of carrying on Davie's legacy and becoming top dog in the game drove my ambitions. I had fuck all else to live for and I had no other desires to achieve. Anybody else would want to achieve promotions, build a family or move into nice neighbourhoods. Not me. I lived for pain whether it was inflicting it or living it.

Courtney was a Godsend to me. Forever she looked after me. I never wished for a meal and never complained about her company. Not once did she question why I fought. It was something she accepted and never questioned. Sometimes I wished she did question it so I could unload some of the weight of my thoughts.

One of the things she adored about me was the clean abstaining from drink because of a rocky childhood with her parents and both of their addictions to alcohol. It killed her father, Ricky, who fell into the water down at Codie docks after a long day on the ale. That wrecked her childhood. Courtney had a good relationship with her mother, Sylvia, but it was never always like that. She was far worse than her husband ever was and after his death, she spiralled into the gutter where she took her bitter frustrations out on Courtney with spats of violent abuse. I knew that hardship only too well after a childhood with rotten foster parents who still burdened my memories but I would learn to forgive in time. Courtney's mum, Sylvia, had been sober for seven years and in that time, she mended the bridges with her daughter. Their rocky years were behind them and Courtney would very seldom touch alcohol or any other drug. It always reminded her of awful times that she did not want to recollect.

She continued to work for Jack and there was never an issue with that. Often it was a good excuse for me to spy on him at work. I did it strategically, getting the odd opportunity to snoop around his office and overhear his phone calls. I often would check for his signature and after buying a phone with a decent camera, I would take pictures. If I could not take photos, I was able to store the information in my brain.

Not having a good education over the years, I was able to utilise something that was close to a photographic memory. Once I saw something, I could remember it easily. I had finished with my English night classes and I'd gained so much confidence in my writing and reading ability. I would need that to take everything from Jack.

I became more relaxed in my skin and moderately accepted what and who I was. There was a hiatus from the gunrunning after the Dean deal which led to no contact from Davie for around six months. I had not heard from Rankin either. I wondered what kind of tricks Davie was up to. It grated on me that I was left to figure out what to do to Jack but that became a challenge, something I had to overcome by being smart.

My night classes certainly gave me a boost in confidence. There was one way of knowing of his reputation and that was checking out Interpol's most wanted list where he sat inside the top five. Quite a surreal situation seeing your father's alias of The Eidolon on an international Wanted list and even more strange was knowing that you were one of a small collection of people who knew who The Eidolon was.

A strange thing occurred at my flat one Wednesday evening. The sky was tar black at round one thirty in the morning, with a deluge of rain pelting off the windows and the flat roof of the building. Courtney was sound asleep as I stayed up watching the telly as I suffered from a bout of insomnia.

Firstly, I heard a couple of light taps coming from the kitchen under the lashing of rain. I thought nothing of it at first. Then a couple of minutes passed before it happened again. It would stop and start methodically. Then I heard harsh scratching. It went on for a while and eventually I had to walk through to the kitchen where

I switched on the lights.

It was silent for a moment before I heard the scratching noise again. It came from the front door so I switched the outside light on and peeked out of the side window, onto the landing. There was a lady lying in a twisted position, stomach down with her head perched on the door, wearing a manky black, medium length skirt with badly ripped stockings and an oversized leather jacket that the rain rebounded of. Just some drunk trying to find her door on the way home from a big session, I suspected.

"Piss off!" I muttered coyly, trying to keep it quiet but she would have hardly heard me over the battering noise. She twitched slightly and I knew straight away she was wasted. As I opened the door, her head fell onto my kitchen floor. She was soaked through as she gargled and grumbled some words I could not make out. Overwhelmingly, she reeked of piss.

"You're at the wrong flat!" I said, as she showed a little more movement and tried to crawl inside. The rain soared into the kitchen, dragged by heavy gusts of wind as I turned cold.

Her hair was dirty black, greasy and untidy, over a gaunt body, skinny enough to be anorexic. Her head hovered under a slack neck that she did not have the energy to lift.

I shook her. "You don't stay here, lady."

She was not compos mentis enough to know what she was doing or saying. I hated drunks for this reason but I suspected she was more than drunk. I did not want her in the flat and especially nowhere near Courtney and it would be a matter of time before she woke.

She reeked so much it made me choke on the air and I didn't want to touch her, but I had to get her out of the kitchen so I could close the door. I stepped over her on the balcony, picked her up under her arm pits, spun her around and dragged her back, perching her against the balcony wall. Her head dangled over her chest, unable to raise itself. I knelt down, feeling pity for her, lifting her chin as a stream of sickly drool fell from the side of her mouth. Her eyeballs were vacant of life as I slapped her across the cheeks a few times but she was too far gone on heroin, it was obvious to me then. She was far enough away from the door though so I could close it. Even with the foul night, I wanted her out so I dragged her onto the balcony. I took a last look at her and began to close the door when she mumbled something that made my head turn. When I heard it, I thought my mind was playing a trick on me. I opened the door again to face her.

"What did you say?" She babbled again and this time, I knelt and lifted her chin, "What did you say?"

"Help me, Davie!" Straight away, the dots joined in my head and it dawned on me who I was looking at.

"Danielle!" I gasped, "Is that you?" I cupped her chin, as her eye makeup ran down her troubled face, and drew back her sticky hair behind her ears.

"Danielle, look at me!" It was not until she showed me her traumatic brown eyes that I knew it was her. Eyes that were void of anything compos mentis.

"Who's that?" Courtney had appeared behind me. I spun around with a gasped expression that she picked up on.

"I don't believe it…It's Danielle, Davie's ex!" She knew who it was because I had talked about her a few times.

"Look at the state of her!" she commented with a tight face. Danielle was a heroin addict. "What is she doing here?" she asked, as curiously as I felt.

"I don't know…We have to help her!" Judging by the state of her, Danielle needed help, lots of help.

"I'm not having that in this flat," Courtney hissed with resentment, knowing by experience that alkies and smack-heads were bad news. "We let that in here, and you can count on one thing, she will steal everything she can from us."

"This used to be a friend of mine. I'm not going to kick her onto the street, look!" I pointed to her,

"She's wrecked." Truth was, I needed her because she held answers to questions about what had happened when I was arrested and she disappeared. I had not seen her since that day. Courtney's past experiences with her mum were all too close for comfort. It brought back memories she did not want to relive.

"You don't know what you're getting into. This won't end well for no one, including her."

"Then that will be on my head. I need to know what happened to her and letting her back on the street is not an option. She's probably going to die if I close that door on her."

For the first time, Courtney's approach to me changed, revolted at the thought of sharing a room with Danielle.

She pondered responding and gazed at Danielle with revulsion and returned to the bedroom. That was brutal retaliation for me that Courtney could be so callous and have no empathy for someone in that state but I had no time to dwell on that.

I lifted Danielle's petite body over my shoulder, rushed into the sitting room and laid her on the sofa. I returned to close the door to the rain, grabbed some tea towels and began to dry her off in a panic. I had no idea what to do with her. I looked at her and became packed with compassion for her condition. She was majorly malnourished; she had destroyed herself. I could have taken her to hospital but I didn't know if that would kill her because she was so weak so I called the one person who could help me, Jack.

The phone rang for some time…

"It better be worth the call at this time," Jack moaned and I was not sure if he had been asleep or awake.

"I need a doctor, at the flat, as soon as possible."

"People who call to say something like this should really explain in the first sentence as to why!"

"It doesn't matter! Can you get one?"

"You call at one thirty, demanding an action from me without reason." Jack had to know; there was no other way of getting him to help me.

"An old friend of mine has turned up at the flat. She needs a doctor, she's one step away from dying."

"Take her to the hospital, that's what they're for." I rubbed my head with frustration as Danielle vomited over the sofa.

"You hear that! I can't take her to the hospital cos it might kill her, she's too weak!"

Jack quietened, debating if he would help. There was no benefit in him helping me.

"Give me a short description of what's wrong with this woman."

"She's skin and bone, fucked on the brown, drink or God knows what." Jack gave thought as to who this female could be that I'm friends with in such a state.

"Is it a friend of Courtney's? She's got a couple loose rags that like to dabble," Jack carried on as if he was gossiping and in no real concern.

"No! It's not a friend of Courtney's! Can you get a doc to here?" Jack became miffed at my raised voice.

"Who is it?" I was not keen on telling him but I had to. Jack had a nice knack at knowing when he was being lied to and even if I did lie, he'd find out somehow.

"It's Danielle!" Jack retreated in silence. "Jack!"

I wondered if he was still there and then I understood that Jack was weighting up the options of helping me.

"Davie's ex?" Jack asked.

"Aye." There was another long pause.

"I'll give Jerry a call."

Chapter 44

More Questions:

Jerry arrived about thirty minutes after the call and straight away, I noticed the alarm in his usual calm exterior. I had stripped Danielle of her clothes and put on some of Courtney's on who kept coming back and forth while she made phone calls in her bedroom, probably to her mates to moan about what was happening.

The first thing Jerry did was pull back the blankets I had put over her and then slipped the sleeves of her jumper up. Her hand was noticeably swollen against her anorexic wrist and the track marks on the inside of her elbow were a gross slaver of a dark brown and purplish bruising. He rolled up the other sleeve which revealed the same. He shook his head, something he had seen before and something that the mild-mannered doctor disliked.

"She needs to go to hospital straight away, Max, and I mean now." He stated that, without opening his doctor's bag or taking a more serious evaluation. I took the seriousness of his tone to mean something.

"Okay," I agreed and was startled and taken aback by the state Danielle was in, a far cry from the woman I remembered. Jerry fumbled in silence briefly before he shot into action.

"Right! Can you drive?"

"Aye."

"Okay, let's get moving. You can drive my car. Pick her up and get to the elevator."

I did straight away. I was heartbroken about her condition but I was driven by the need to get some answers from her. As we marched to the elevator with Danielle over my shoulder, Jerry started describing her state.

"She's malnourished, God knows the last time she had a meal," Jerry paused to catch his breath. "She may have liver disease or maybe hepatitis. Her body's shutting down."

Above the natural caring need I had for her to recover, I hoped she would have some answers for me. As I carried her to the elevator, she began vomiting down my back as her stomach pressed into my shoulder. I manhandled her into the back of Jerry's car.

"You drive and I'll sit in the back," Jerry insisted and cleaned her chin and neck of sick while I sped away in the car making for the hospital. Danielle started slipping in and out of consciousness while Jerry tried his best to keep her awake by slapping her in the face and splashing some water from a bottle over her. "I don't think she is going to make it through the night," he said abruptly in his formal Chelsea accent.

"What!" I belted back.

When we arrived at Liverpool Hospital A&E, Jerry said, "I'll jump in. They know me here." He leapt out the door and moved fast for an old guy. "It'll speed things up!" he yelled. I jumped into the back with Danielle and lifted her chin.

"Danielle, you awake? Danielle!" I said, shaking her whole body frantically. Her eyes shyly opened with the glimpse of some sanity in her tormented and fatigued face. She squinted at me and spoke with disbelief.

"Max, what are you doing here?" She peered past my shoulder, fixating on something drawing her attention. I shook her again and drew her look back to me.

"Aye, it's Max, you remember me."

In a daze, her eyes wandered, often into the air and nothing more.

"Course I remember you, you were a good boy." Her cold palm touched my cheek and then she looked away again past me onto the hospital entry doors. Her other palm, she gently laid over the rainy window.

"Where did you go? What happened?" I asked, hoping she knew that I referred to the time when we parted company. I turned to notice a flock of nurses running towards the car. Danielle's pupils began to drift into the back of her head. Anxiously, I grabbed her shoulders firmly and violently shook her when she mumbled, "Davie." And I stopped.

"No, it's Max," I answered.

"Davie," she whispered again. I felt she wished to tell me something about him but I could not be sure. Just before Jerry and the nurses arrived at the car, I threw my arms across the front seats and locked the doors, along with the rear ones. I grabbed her vigorously, tightly.

"Danielle, listen to me. What did Davie do? Is he responsible for this?" Danielle laid her palm onto my cheek again.

"You were such a sweet boy, handsome, a handsome boy...."

Excessive thuds, accompanied by screams, started banging on the windows and I blanked them. I was close to an answer as to what happened to her.

"What do you want to tell me?" I yelled. "What happened to you!"

"You remind me of your mother. She had a sweet heart, just like you."

I paused, my ears blocking out the noise of the thuds and the pelting rain on the roof. My thoughts came to a standstill as I gazed at the harrowing pain in her tired eyes. I gripped her arms tightly and watched her eyelids close, a sole tear rolling down her gaunt cheeks. The windows and doors of the car were being constantly buffeted as I could only be saddened by her stillness, unaware of the panic outside. Whatever pain she was in had ended. I guided her head onto the window and released my grip, knowing she had gone to peaceful place.

Watching a life leave the world like that, created a new belief for me - that there was something much more peaceful than living…Death.

Chapter 45

Fist on the Table:

It took me some time to process what had happened. Danielle had no one else in the world, no one except what became her only accomplice, heroin. I did not have the answers that I wanted, only a questioning of what happened to her. How did she end up in that mess and was it self-inflicted? I remembered her as a stable and sensible person. I learned the painful burden of grief and regret. These emotions, I did not like dealing with. I had been abandoned and hurt plenty of times but never did I have to deal with grief. She knew who my mother was and the chance of sharing that information, left the world with her. I knew instinctively that Davie had something to do with it but I did not feel that he was the cause. I didn't know how, but there was a connection there. It was the way she uttered his name, as if she wanted to tell me something evident about him. That moment passed, and I could not go back so I had to move on; but there was one man I could query about the situation.

There was no one to identify the body. She had no living relatives that I knew of and she could only officially be identified by her prints that the police ran to identify the body. She was born in Liverpool and had a sister who also died at a young age, by the same poison. Both grew up around Toxteth and lived through the riots in 1981 between the black community and police. Embedded into their upbringing was a fortitude of drug taking; they understood they had to lean on that in order to numb their brains from being reared in poverty and lack of opportunity. It was an addiction that would never leave them alone.

Because she had no one, I took care of all the formalities, arranged the cremation, and paid the bill. I was never short of a coin, so it didn't bother me one bit. I thought it was the least I could do. There were only three people attending the cremation: Courtney, who became quite supportive after her dissociation with Danielle at the flat; myself, and the other one was Ringo, who knew Danielle well enough from when Davie kicked about with her. His appearance surprised me and I began to cut him some slack, finally.

After the cremation, Ringo, Courtney and I went for a strong coffee at a nearby dingy café. Ringo mixed his with whisky of course and had a white cocktail of powder in the toilets.

As we sat at the table, a hollow moment stained the air so I decided to quiz Ringo about a few things. "Who was she?" I asked. He knew who I was talking about but he still questioned me.

"Who?" He held a slightly loose face while he honked his nose, trying to assume he didn't know what I was talking about. "I know a couple of things about her," he finally said.

"Go on," I said, as Ringo gave Courtney the cold shoulder. "Courtney, give us two a minute!"

She hesitated because she wished to know what Ringo was hiding but eventually, she left.

"I'll go out for a cigarette."

Ringo watched her stride away before answering. "Danielle, she worked for Dad for a lot of years. In one of the brothels. Got her out of bother a lot of times. Well, you know, she liked the brown and some of the punters were giving her lay ons an' she would never have the cash to pay so she would give 'em freebies." I drew back in my seat not knowing that she used to be a working girl. "Dad found out about this," he stopped.

"And?"

"He did something kind and I don't know why, something that's not in his system to do and to this day, I don't know why. He took her out of there and locked her inside a room in the house for thirty-one days, to get her clean and it worked. I was young an' I remember a little. Mum did most of the work but it was all Dad's idea."

"What did he want from her?" "To

this day, I don't know what."

"Your father does nothing for free. She must've done or known something,"

"You're not wrong. He's a vindictive fucker and he had his reasons, whatever they were."

"And what do you know of me?"

Ringo never lacked in words but I put him on the spot where he did not want to answer. He began to stand.

"I'm just running to the khazi, back in minute."

I slammed my fist onto the table, jolting the cups into the air, spilling the coffee from them, igniting the whole café's attention and yelled. "SIT!"

He froze. I grabbed the neck of his jumper and yanked him down. "Answer me!"

"Max, I don't know…Honest."

"You know, you cunt, and whatever you know, you tell me now!"

"I probably know what you know. You were left at that church as a kid and when Davie found out you'd been abandoned, he started visiting you." That was the first time I asked someone that question.

"And my mother. Who's my mother?"

"I've no idea. Swear on my life and all that matters to me, I don't know."

"Someone must know!" I had spoiled the calmness that we had shared and now I was furious. I could not look at Ringo after that. I scowled, "Go on! fuck off!"

After I calmed down that day, I became more friendly with Ringo, to Jack's annoyance, but I figured being friendly with a person Jack had so much animosity towards could only end up being an advantage.

I took my frustration out the only way I knew how. In the gym. On the bag and throwing weights around but the biggest escape was at the end of a bare knuckle.

In the next eight months, I had a few fights. All three of them I finished under a couple of minutes to men who could not lace my boots. I was leading up to a big show down. Those second-hand muppets I fought were of no challenge to me and I let Jack know my feelings on that. I told him to find the toughest man in the country and I would face him without hesitation, no matter who it was. It was a ticking clock. Jack came around to betting his house on me, I was that much of a cert to him. There was a big name on the circuit, one avoided by most and talked about in relative secrecy. That was Belcher Oakley or The King of the Gypsies, as he was known. More often than not the travelling community did not associate with the outside world of bare-knuckle boxing and it was only on special occasions that they did. The name had been mentioned a few times in the shows I had gone to and Jack always refused to answer my questions on him. One thing I knew was that the Gypsy was deaf and had been since birth, for reasons unknown, because those people were not registered on the NHS to visit doctors. They had their own holistic therapies that they followed and nothing would change that.

The difficult short spell of grief I had with Danielle wore off more quickly than I expected. I put that down to my family's inability to feel empathy towards others and my dire need to keep busy to distance from thinking. One day after I had finished at Rockies, I drove into the city to have a chat with Jack. It was mid evening around the seven mark after McCartney's had opened. Walking up the stairs, I could hear a refrain of mulled shouting. When I reached the top of the stairs, I saw Courtney and the doorman huddled around the office door.

"What's going on?" I asked Courtney and looked at her hands trembling; she was filled with apprehension. She gripped my wrist tightly.

"It's the solicitor, Calvin. He's in there, with a gun." I turned my head towards the doorman.

"He's got a pistol in there," he answered, as Calvin shouted from behind the door.

"Keep out! All of you, keep out!" His voice was plagued with panic and rage.

"What's he want?" I asked Courtney.

"This has been going on for ages. Jack's got something of his, something he wants back!"

I reached out and tried the door. It was not locked but something was wedged behind it.

"Jack?"

"I'm here," he answered calmly. I assessed the sturdiness of the door and decided there was only one way in. I paced back to the swing doors that took you through into the main hall of the club. I sprinted forward and burst through, shattering the door from its hinges. I crashed to the ground, quite embarrassingly.

"Stay there, you hear! Don't fucking stand up," Calvin demanded, peltered in sweat and seething. His eyes were burst while his left hand wobbled like crazy as he still pointed the gun at Jack. I got up to a kneeling position and caught a look of Jack. His hands were tie-wrapped to his office chair. He was unusually serene.

"You're paying for that door, Max!" Jack joked, to Calvin's annoyance.

"Shut it, just shut it!" Calvin shuffled towards Jack with a couple of shimmying steps forward. It seemed Jack had been winding him up for a good while. It was easy to tell Calvin had never pointed a gun at someone. My sanity around them came from my exposure to the gunrunning. I managed to stand up to my full height, with my arms at my sides, indicating I was no threat to Calvin, but I was not sure how that would come across since I had come crashing through the door.

"Calvin, what the fuck are you doing?" I pleaded. "You're pointing a gun at Jack Gallagher," Jack squinted his brows and probably got a hard on with that compliment. "I don't care anymore. Once I kill him, I'll kill myself." "Fucking hell, Calvin, that's a lot of blood to be cleaning up. I only hire one cleaner," Jack said.

"Quiet!" Calvin yelled, flinching forward, lifting his arm at the same time. I dived across the air and smashed his body into the wall as a shot was fired across the room into Jack's framed picture of Liverpool FC behind his desk. The gun fell out of his hand on the way down. He was weak and had no strength to wrestle with me. Almost immediately he began to weep.

"You pathetic man, no dignity, fucking private schooled wimp!" Jack uttered as Courtney and the doorman ran into the room. The doorman took over from me on the ground.

"Better search him," I insisted. "Might have something else on him."

Courtney ran around the desk and cut Jack's ties. Without standing or thanking anyone, Jack commanded, "Everyone get out of my office!"

I knew very well what that meant but no one wanted to leave Jack in that room with him. "Out!" he said.

We all looked at each other. There was something about the way he conducted himself, without rage or being rude, he commanded so much power. After he met everyone in the room's worried gaze, we all began to walk out.

"Courtney," he asked, and she turned around. Jack put his hand into his dressed trousers and threw her the keys. "Lock the doors. We won't be open tonight."

Chapter 46

Holiday Blues:

Calvin was never allowed inside the club again and no one quite knew what went on in that room that night. He was spared his life because Jack had a use for him as his solicitor. After that, there would be no more outbursts.

The incident with Danielle and the unanswered questions continued to burden me and it was only leading to my own outburst.

One late spring night, I had nipped down to the club after being at the gym. I was particularly on edge around that time and while in conversation with Courtney at the bar discussing some stuff I didn't care to discuss, she nagged me about paying for a holiday in the summer and had done for months.

"You can afford it, a break in some sun somewhere!"

"I'm not the holiday type."

"You don't like heat!"

"Listen, this is doing my head in. You've been going on about this for ages…I'm not going on holiday."

"I'll go myself then," she huffed.

"That's a great fucking idea, give me some peace," I said, walking away from the seat at the bar. What did I need a holiday for? That was never something I would consider. The plan to take everything from Jack had grown some legs and I had already begun to organise it.

I wandered past the doorman and stopped at Jack's door before I walked in.

Jack had his feet up on the desk, a cigarette in hand, while he watched the midweek football. I stood there detached, tense, and awkward. Jack took his feet off the desk and saw I was in a funny mood.

"Are you sitting or standing?"

"What happened to her?"

"Who!"

"Danielle. After I was nicked, what happened to her?"

Jack stubbed his smoke out and took his feet off his desk.

"I see you're still upset about her passing. Holding onto grief is a cruel motive, Max. It's best to let it go before it eats away at you."

"I'm not grieving. I want to know what happened to her. Davie disappeared, I was jailed, and Danielle disappeared. What happened to her?"

Jack stalled and sat forward.

"Have a seat. You're making me feel uncomfortable in my own office." He held an antsy expression with me until I sat down. "Heroin always carries with it, a cruel story of despair. And the thought of taking heroin binds to you for life. Only the most determined of people can live without the pull towards it. Danielle was no different. She used it from an early age to cope and that never changed." I leant forward in my seat.

"This isn't story time! What happened to her that day I was nicked?"

"When you were nicked, so was she. She did a couple years inside and in there is where she rekindled her taste for the brown."

"And what happened when she got out?"

"She lived as any other addict lived, from day-to-day looking for their next hit. I helped her once before and I wasn't going to help her again."

That gave me some closure on the affair, and I guess that satisfied me for a time. Jack quickly changed the tide of the chat.

"I have been in contact with some people and I have found out where the Gypsy is. They are willing to have you fight him. I had to use your father's name to seal the deal. The Gypsy doesn't fight any odd man out there."

As soon as he said that, my arms rose in a wave of goosebumps.

"So, it's a done deal?"

"The details are being ironed out but you will have to go to Ireland for the fight. They said if you want him then you must go to him…You see, there isn't a man sane enough who wants to go to him and especially not in their backyard."

"Make it so, then," I stood and left his office. I looked through the double doors at Courtney who was serving a punter. For the first time I felt guilt when I looked at her. It must have been all the secretive thoughts I carried around and had no one to tell but it was more to do with the fact that in the not-so-distant future, I would be running away from her.

The rules of the fight were different somewhat. Once you were put down, you got space to stand up again. No counts or interruptions of breaks - it was the bleakest of raw occasions. I never feared the Gypsy but the anticipation of walking into his den weakened my confidence.

Chapter 47

Belcher Oakley:

My life became consumed with the notoriety I would receive if I defeated the Gypsy, Belcher Oakley. Someone my father avoided when his name became famous in the fighting world when Belcher was a youngster. The tales about him were crude and true. Born without hearing, he proceeded to adapt to life without insecurities or woes about his condition. From an early age it was recognised that he had a special ability to fight. As he grew older, his size aided that ability. Belcher knew nothing less and nothing more than fighting. When he was a teenager, he battled with grown men. Men were wary of him because Belcher did not react to words or gestures. He grew up using instinct and had that sixth sense that he used to read people's body language. He did not contest with accusations or egos and only reacted to the competition of the man who stood against him. He lacked concern for loss and like me, would not allow it. If there was such a thing as a God of the bare-knuckle fighting world, then Belcher Oakley could have been one. It was known that he had not been defeated at any time in his life, right back to when he was thirteen.

His will to win was inherited from his father who once lost a fight to settle a feud between him and another family. The dispute was caused by an argument over a patch of land between two travelling families. Belcher was only thirteen at the time where he watched this unfold and vowed to his father that he would get redemption for their family. And four years later he did. They all thought he was young and brave to be victorious fighting a man thirty years his senior but to those who knew him better than everybody else, they knew that was his coming of age. Later, he became a known name in the travellers' circuit as the young pretender and became hooked on the thrill of exchanging punches. It seemed that the fate he had been handed to at birth, set him up in good stead. Being noticeably different moulded him, without his knowledge, into a real tough bastard. It became his sixth sense.

His enthusiasm helped him to embark on a road of glory and demand a fight with the toughest man in each community among their travelling circles, which ventured from Ireland to Romania. He grew from strength to strength and in size until he was crowned the King of the Gypsies around four years later.

There were men who made false claims to this throne and Belcher found them and defeated them. Particularly those from England and the rest of the UK. To a traveller, being the top fighter meant as much in riches as owning the entire contents of the federal reserve's gold store. They carried enough pride and desire as entire armies could muster. Backing away from a fight would riddle them with shame and the most dedicated would lie and rot in the pool of their own blood before they would admit defeat.

But he was getting on now, creeping into his forties and by no means the fresh youngster he once was. The desire and ability to remain at the top when you age is a problematic feature in life. That gave me the edge and, in my early twenties now, I was more than a man and ready for him.

The fight was to take place inside a circus tent in Tuam, Galway, in Ireland and to get there, Jack took the motor over in the ferry to Dublin which gave me a lot of time with him. One side of me wanted to engage with him to continue the deception but the other hated him to the core. The only reason he was still alive was he served a purpose for me.

It was weird thinking Davie might be close since he hopped between places in Ireland. But there was more chance of him hopping around mainland Europe and there was no chance he had thought about me during that time. I knew he was making plans for a permanent home for us abroad but where, at that point, I wasn't sure. He spoke about purchasing some property, kitting the home out with furniture and a fleet of expensive vehicles.

Whatever he was doing, I hoped he had that side of things sorted for when we did Jack over. I had played the game long enough and I was ready to get rid of him. I had worked hard on the documents that would transfer all his assets over to Ringo. Jack's signature was copied and had two witnesses, me, and a forgery of Ringos, on a counterfeit will. Davie saw it fitting that Ringo got everything because of the beating Jack ordered on him. He reminisced at that being his fault and wanted to pay him back.

Ringo was not a bad guy, and I was happy with that. All I desired for Jack was for him to be dead, rid of the world so I could start a new life somewhere else. Courtney was not a part of that plan, and I could not see a way of making it work. It was best for her sake and life that she had no part of mine. Inside I was a monster who only thought of himself, and I don't think I could ever change that. I awaited Davie contacting me to finalise things but that could take some time.

In the meantime, I had a legacy to cement and only that would take my immediate focus.

Chapter 48

The Fight:

I became obsessed with thoughts of the encounter with Belcher once we arrived in Tuam. Unlike any other fight, I was hailed with strange thoughts that were derived from anxiety. I was devastated with fear, more so than before. Although it was normal to me, I couldn't control what was going on.

It was pitch black and dead calm at around ten pm. The circus tent was situated on a large patch of grass interlinking with a local fair and flicking of light could be seen through the red tent. They waited for us. It had not opened yet and it seemed our fight was the opening ceremony.

We wandered in. I stood behind Jack and let him do the talking, allowing me to deal with the fear. It was then when it dawned on me where the fear came from. I was scared of losing and as I realised that, something inside me relaxed. Admitting it caused the anxiety to shrink. But I had never faced such a task as this which was about to present itself.

There was a large circular sand pit in the centre of the tent. That was the stage, lit by an outline of flaming torches on the tops of poles. It made the environment seem ancient, rather like a gladiators' Colosseum. Around the outside of the pit, there was a semi-circle of seats. Just off to my right, I spied him, through the mass of bodies; he was draped in a big black coat to keep warm, with his elbows resting over his knees on a stool.

Around him was a gathering of serious-looking, unfashionably dressed travellers, all showing confidence.

Belcher sat with his side to me, oblivious of what was going on around him, going through his own mental ritual. He had a rough topping of bushy, black hair and even though he was sitting down, I could tell he was massive.

Jack was having some debate with Belcher's father, Danny, about wagers and rules. They were talking about referees. When the travellers fought, there was a ref for each man, supplied by the rival's corner. But Jack did not wish for this and insisted that both men were respectful enough not to have one.

I took some of it in, but I'd reached the limit of my patience about the affair. I removed my jacket and hooded top and threw them to the side. The dew of the cold night evaporated from my mouth as I moved casually past everyone. I stepped over the border into the sand pit wearing my black joggers, the only thing keeping me warm. I was sculpted, forearms tight with popping veins, shoulder caps bulked over a heavy chest. Anyone who looked at me knew I was visually prepared, at the peak of my physique, and it was easy to tell I was loaded with steroids. I looked like a pumped bodybuilder. I noticed straight away how heavy and sluggish my feet felt moving over sand.

Belcher eyed me, forming an impression as he watched me. He stood up methodically and let me see his full size as he brushed his coat off his shoulders. A tremendous size of a man, scary to contemplate being on the end of one of his beatings. His body was covered in thick black hair, with a solid gut, wide intimidating shoulders, and massive hands, almost gorilla like. His dead-eyed expression was frightening. So at ease with his actions.

Danny and Jack continued to argue and left us to set about each other with daggers. Belcher's manner was cool, whilst the discussions were going on. His grave aura was different from any other human I had met until then. It was as if only a darkness lingered inside him.

Jack had settled discussions with Danny and it transpired that there would be an involvement of only one referee if it was needed.

Prior to the meeting, they had agreed a forty grand bet. Unlike at other events, there were no drunks or bookies on the go. It was a closed doors affair and that suited me.

Belcher gave an irate signal, using sign language, to his father to which he responded and then Belcher began to move around as if the fight had begun.

With no words said, I gathered that was the fight under way. He was a heavy lump who kept a straight back leaned marginally over his front foot. He towered above everyone, his nose squashed to the side by the barrage of punches he'd endured. That beaten face remained concentrated with a tense jaw, blending with fixing stares that tried to peek into my soul. We continued to mimic our movements, rotating in small circles while changing direction to feel each other out. I could sense he was getting in the mood to test me out. He was no fool and kept a level of caution. I could not get used to the heavy drag of the sand and it slowed me down, as if my reactions were delayed.

He had enough of the opening stares, manoeuvred closer and threw a jab into my face, then another one, stepping through the sand easily. I realised then that it was an advantage to him because he had fought in sand many times. Another couple of blows hit me as I buried my head and countered with wide hooks. Both connected with him as he barged into me, leaning his weight over my body as he buried his head into my neck. I tried to move back but the sand beneath my feet slowed me down. Then he landed a solid blow into my gut that took my breath away and backhanded me as soon as I raised myself. I surrendered to the ground, the ferocious power he could generate, I had not felt before. Belcher was respectful of the rules and let me stand.

Jack became alarmed at the ease of how Belcher put me down.

I stood to confront him with a fresh drive and started again. I tried to close him down and move my feet more quickly as I longed to draw blood. He was old and I knew I had to use my youth to advantage. I lifted my legs and moved rapidly, going forward, and I rained a barrage of punches over his face. He parried a couple, dodged one and then all I felt was a massive blow over the left side of my jaw. I blacked out and found myself fallen on the sand. My ears rang and after a few dazed seconds, I looked up to him, a beast of a creature who only knew one thing…Brutality.

I questioned everything about myself while I knelt in the sand; it was déjà vu, as if I knew my life had taken me to that point and all I had to do was stand up.

Before I did, I collected my thoughts with an eerie silence in my ears. I looked down to my feet and the trainers I was wearing. I decided to take them off so I could move more freely.

Belcher squinted and looked at his father, who had not seen that done before. But Belcher had to let me stand. It felt abnormal inside the tent because, unlike the hostility of the crowd that usually derived from these events, they did not cheer or shout. That made every slap and clatter of bone echo the arena. Straight away I felt lighter on my feet. Now I could move more freely and set to work. Belcher taunted and shadowed me to figure out what I was going to do. This time, I crouched on my knees and pointed my shoulder in his direction, making the target tighter. Belcher hurled his fists towards me while I stayed short, weaving from his hammering punches. He broke away from the effort, requiring to think and I stalked him until I got inside the brute. I let my arms deploy like pivoting pistols, grunting and hissing while landing many blows and still he stood there, exchanging punches with me. His strength was like no other. As my combo slowed, he clocked me across the side of my neck with a swinging right hand and set my neck into a spasm.

Through instinct, I buried my head and countered a left hook that splattered across his temple with a crunching sound, ruining my wrist. It happened in a split second, the ferociousness and speed, devastating to be a part of. Without knowing, he had fallen to the ground with me and I had broken a bone in my left hand.

As I gathered myself, I watched Belcher rise and spit a hock of blood over the sand. We both breathed heavily like tired lions but I was only warming up.

I rejoined Belcher by standing a couple of metres away from him as he nodded in respect of the punch, I had landed on him.

The travellers were shocked to see him fall. We had both felt each other out and then we met and battled like Spartans, blow after blow landed and with each blow, I returned my own. When we clinched, he slithered over me, and held or pushed my head down to uppercut me. His punches felt as if I was being hit by iron bars and each one weakened me. They put me on the back foot time and time again.

We paused and broke apart so we could both have a breather. The broken bone in my hand could not be felt through the soaring adrenaline pumping through me but I knew the pain was there. We both leaked sweat and blood and I knew this was the real thing. That man was worthy of a fight. He had no weakness, no sign of backing down and I loved it. The blood drove through my veins like a wolf's which had tasted gore. I stopped dead still and roared inside the sandpit, drawing everyone's attention.

Belcher could not hear me, but he had seen the fury; he could feel what I felt. He ran at me with wild purpose and stomped on my bare left foot, left hooked me in the solar plexus and drove an uppercut into my chin that embedded itself onto my jawbone. I sagged briefly, with little breath and punched him in the gut, followed by a right hook to his head and four grunting punches into his stomach before he took me in a head lock. He squashed tightly, leaving me choking and breathless. He could have stayed there to finish me but I got out by doing something Codie taught me. I pinched the inner skin on his thigh and uppercut his balls. He tossed me to the side where I brushed the sand. I rose quickly to absorb more pressure. His barrage continued with bone crunching punches to my body and then a knuckle into my lips burst them open.

I backtracked away and ran my tongue around my lips, devouring the blood. I dropped my arms, shuffled up to him and unleashed a bombardment, finishing with a big blow to the gut. He dropped to one knee and I bore the bone of my knee into his jaw.

The gathering of travellers booed and hissed, knowing that was not honourable. Belcher stood up and this time, I saw that he had been weakened. That was the tide of age catching up on him as he struggled to see through one of his swollen eyes. He did one thing I was not expecting - he smiled.

He paused, gathering his thoughts, and I welcomed the rest. He breathed deep and hard, louder than a normal person because he had no concept of sound.

In the centre of the circle, a support pole stood the height of the tent, and we were approaching it. Stalking him, I felt I had the advantage because he moved slower. I hunted him like prey and got close, to pound him with another attack as he replied with his own barrage. Knuckle rebounded off bone and skin slapped against each others as if it was nothing to either of us but they all hurt.

We were warriors and would not back down. We both took a breather and I repeated the motion, steaming and powering in painful blows to his face that cut open and bruised easily. I was seething and continued my assault with ferocity. He countered me and hit me freely, but the haze had covered me. I cared not for what pain I would endure, and I knew only death would stop me.

Belcher was depleted in energy and he dropped to the ground on both knees after I pounded him with blows, using the pole to hold him aloft. He was exhausted and badly hurt, and I only wished for him to stand so I could finish him off. He leaned his head towards me, breathing forcefully. He wanted to stand but was hesitant, although his pride would get him to his feet.

I turned around to witness the travellers standing still, in shock, with Jack equally stunned. The wolf inside me was there for all to see. The intoxicating rush of the release from life ruled me. Belcher used the pole to pull himself up as he considered a last assault. He would never give up voluntarily.

I respected his honour, allowed him to stand and gave him the opportunity to remove his hand from the pole before I deployed my next onslaught. He wasn't stupid and he had already foreseen the capture of his title. My fists clenched for a last time as my teeth gripped together, my body filled with ecstasy and possessed by the haze that controlled me. The second he took his hand off the pole, I pounced, wilfully taking a sole punch from him that I walked through. I dipped down and punched up into his ribs, repeating it a few times.

He weakened as did his seat on the throne. As he bent over, I rifled in, hook after hook, across his face, watching it whip back and forth as he found the pole to lean against to stop him from falling. If he fell, he would not rise again and he knew that. I held him up after each punch, wishing to bury any idea of a revival. I watched his teeth fly out of his mouth, felt his jaw break against my knuckle and witnessed the blood spill from his toothless gums.

Still, he stood. I recoiled for a last time, allowing his head to dangle over his chest. He was already gone as I followed through with every ounce of fury I had; I drove that punch across his jaw as his head pinged like a chicken's neck that had been snapped. I watched him flop to the ground as nothing but the air could be heard. Some of the travellers leapt into the pit as I felt on a high with pride over their beaten warrior. I was now top dog and it would stay that way.

Approaching was Danny, Belcher's father, while another guy took his pulse and felt nothing. He shook his head in the direction of Danny who was motionless with shock. I stood there doused in blood, sweat and pain looking down at his body. I felt nothing.

Jack approached me without words and handed me my hooded jumper. I put it on and he urged me towards the exit of the tent. He approached Danny, put his hand on his shoulder and said, "Danny, my condolences." Danny was ill with horror, frozen to nothing with the death of his boy and so was everybody else.

Jack, in haste, knew that moment was the one to get out of there quickly.

Chapter 49

Remorse:

I knew what I had done but he knew the risks. I was known as the Reaper after that, and I was not sure how at ease I was with that. I had accomplished something Davie had achieved; now both of our names would live with the notoriety brought about by the tales that would be told about us. The idea that I was a monster rebounded off the walls of my brain as if a ball was being thrown against a wall and caught simultaneously. But like every other pull of emotion, I sent it into a dark place and locked it there.

After the fight, Jack drove us to the ferry port straight away and we caught the first one in the morning. He had turned his phone off and appeared to come across edgy, worried about repercussions from the Travellers. Luckily for both of us, we never heard from them again. I assumed, because of the seal of honour they live by, that the Gypsy King was beaten fairly and I'm sure it was not the first death they had witnessed.

Jack hardly said a word to me. Talking about what happened didn't feel like anything, either of us wanted to do. I had to let my adrenaline die down and Jack had to have it sink in that he had created something. Something I am not sure we were proud of. I kept telling myself I was now king, but there was not the glorious feeling I had expected.

As we returned home, the usual happened. Jack took me to his house and Jerry came and gave me a once over. I slept there for five days that time. I did not allow

Courtney to visit me nor did I talk to her on the phone. That was the longest time, apart from when I was inside that I never talked to anyone. The harbouring realisation that I had then taken two lives ate me inside out. The remorse weighed heavy on my stomach and the battling thoughts of regret plagued me. The inner punishment does not leave you. Never would you be without the guilt, and I tried to send it to the furthest away part of my brain but it would never be far enough away for it always returned. Only time lessened the burden. The Governor deserved his end, that was absolute, but Belcher did not. He knew what world he dabbled in and he himself had taken the lives of other men. I went weeks without injecting too and I became majorly withdrawn from it. A flood of depression overcame me, with heart palpitations, the shakes and an unwelcome feeling of weakness. Nevertheless, I needed to return to the flat.

I went back on a Thursday evening when I thought Courtney was working. I asked Jack before I returned home and he confirmed that so when I walked into the kitchen with my arm in plaster, face bruised and body still in plenty of pain, I was shocked when Courtney steamed in from the sitting room.

"Where the fuck have you been!" she yelled, scaring the shit out of me.

"Jack's!" I said, after I drew a sharp breath.

"I know you've been at Jack's. It was a rhetorical question."

"Why did you ask, then?"

"Don't play the comedian with me. You could've called or messaged."

"Since when have I done that?" I brushed past her into the sitting room, hoping she would shut up, and sat on the sofa. "Thought you were supposed to be working?"

She ignored my query.

"Since when have you killed someone, Max?" she replied. I was not happy that she knew but I could hardly deny it and hearing it like that from her mouth made me feel ashamed. I ignored her and turned the telly on.

"Max! Why did you not come home?" I continued to ignore her, wishing she would give it a rest and leave me in peace. She marched around to the front of the tele. "I've been worried sick, and I've had to put up with Jack telling me to shut up every time I asked about you."

"Can you move out of the way?"

"Max!"

"QUIET!" I yelled and sprang to my feet. "I decide what I do and when I do it. If I don't want to come home, then I don't come fucking home." I launched the remote past her head, into the wall, watching her flinch. "Now, I want to watch the telly in peace so fuck off!"

Immobilised, she gawked at the floor open mouthed, with a tremble in her hands while I stood penetrating her with fear. She grabbed her bag in a hurry and left the flat. I was glad of the peace and the silence that enveloped the room once she was gone.

That started a hairy period between us where we could not speak to each other without something hostile happening. I remained flat-bound for a couple of weeks as I left my body to heal and my mind to forget. On occasions, I'd nip out for a walk, in an attempt to clear myself from worry and it worked marginally but the reality, I could never run from. I hated the withdrawal symptoms and the feeling of sadness and depression I got from not injecting. It made me lifeless and weak.

Courtney moved between her friend Rebecca's flat and mine until we both came to a point where we calmed enough to have sensible conversations. It had been a couple of days since the last argument, and we were both cuddled up on the sofa. I struggled with closeness and her touching me for I felt ashamed of who I was; there was no goodness in me. She had hovered around my mood and was avoiding asking me something for a few days. I thought she was leading up to breaking up with me. I would not have judged her for it.

"Max, I want something from you," she asked optimistically and immediately I felt awkward about what she wished for. My first thought was that she was going to ask me to stop fighting and you know if she did, I probably would have agreed then.

"What's that?" I asked.

"I'm almost thirty now and I'm ready for a change."

I said nothing and waited for her to carry on as she cuddled into my chest, facing the tele. "I want to settle, and I want you to settle."

"How do you mean?"

She raised her head from my chest and turned to look at me, with her hair hanging over the right side of her face.

"You have lived a hard life, a life no one should choose to live ..." She was correct. "Wouldn't you like to change your life?" She was being remarkably tactful in her moderate tone, trying not to fuel a temper. "I know you have money, and I don't want any of it but could we not buy a house in a nicer part of the city? It feels like I'm rotting here. I'm dead inside."

There was no inkling before this that she felt that way but even if she did, I would not have noticed, being wrapped up in my own problems. All the time she was speaking, I knew I was going to be walking out on her and that would not be a long time away once Davie had got in touch with me.

"I can look into it!" I said, watching a submissive smile appear and a glint of joy in her eye. "Jack knows all about that kind of stuff. Next time I see him, I'll ask him." I was, of course, lying through my teeth.

"I want something else from you." Now she knew she was dancing on the verge of causing a mood swing,

"What?"

"I want a kid to run around this house with and a dad who will start to look after himself."

I was taken aback and silenced. I could not raise a child. I couldn't look after myself, let alone a kid. I removed eye contact with her and switched my focus to the tele.

"Max," she said, while slapping me on the chest.

"One thing at a time, woman," I answered bluntly, ending that conversation. She did have a point. I had lived a cruel life up until that point and I wished I had listened to her logic, but I could not. I had a debt to pay.

Chapter 50

No Contact:

I had taken a sabbatical from going to the gym, speaking to Jack or appearing at his club. In my early twenties, I had taken the throne from Belcher, proved my worth and reached the top of the fighting tree. I had moved forward and made progress in the plan to take everything from Jack. My part had been done and I awaited Davie to show face or get in touch to follow through. There had been no contact with him for several months. I had gone through every phone number that I had for him and got no response from text messages and missed calls. I had tried Rankin and I was given the same cold shoulder.

Next, I had a few odd numbers for Turk and Barb that I had never tried and I was only given them in case of emergencies. On one number, they responded to me, by calling on a secure line from a fresh burner. For the first time, I spoke to Turk who was heavily Irish but articulate and straight forward. Once he had clarified who I was, their simple answer was, "The Boss is on mainland Europe and we are in the same position as you…In the dark." I stuck out at each turn and decided to resort to some fresh tactics.

I decided to check the one place that might give me some clues and that was, the arms bunker in the basement of St Paul's Church. Davie had informed the priest who I was and to give me jurisdiction of the bunker if it was required.

I took the ferry from Holyhead in Wales and hopped over to Dublin where I drove north to Belfast. I entered the church on a late windswept afternoon that came with a turn of rain. Straight away, the swirling noise of the wind disappeared behind the closing of the thick door. Immediately, I felt serenely peaceful when I sat down, a few rows down from the rear pew, smudging the seat with my wet clothes. I figured that I returned home when I entered a Catholic Church, knowing I had been left at the door of one in Liverpool. It was not long before I heard the clunk of shoes behind me, approaching at ease; the wearer sat down methodically in the pew behind. I did not need to look behind me for I knew it was a member of the clergy.

"Hello, son of God, are you here to pray?" The voice spoke lazily and gravelly behind me.

"I don't think a prayer would help me, father." I began to turn around when I felt a palm on my shoulder that told me I did not have to turn.

"A prayer will help us all! Even the blessed lived with sin once and had to ask for forgiveness."

"You couldn't correct my sins, Father. I'm as rotten as you'd get."

"I could not, but the Lord could. Pain must subside somehow and then it must die along with the darkness that collects people. Forgiveness is the key! Jesus forgave those who sinned and he did not forget their pain. He only healed it by forgiveness."

"I am lacking of any goodness,"

"Certain people can gain from the pain of others when redemption is raised. Lazarus was raised from the dead because Jesus felt anger for not appearing sooner to help him. So good was created from pain and then forgiveness prevailed."

"Who am I to forgive?" I asked, mystified by his words as I saw the priest of the church appear from the distance. I watched where he was going as it was from him I needed the key.

"You must first forgive your mother," the voice uttered, while I waited for him to expand on that. He left me surprised and distant to a reaction where I watched the priest enter the confessions box. I turned around to question the voice but he was gone. Not a sign of him anywhere. I stood and looked around but he had disappeared, like Batman on a rainy night.

I made my way to the box and sat down. I said nothing and waited for the priest to talk.

"All mortal sins must be confessed, son. I am here to offer counsel."

I remained silent, intrigued about being inside the box for the first time.

"Each person who turns to God in genuine repentance and faith will be saved, my son."

"Not each person requires God to be of some help. Some only require the key to the bunker!"

A silent moment passed before the slot that separated the two sides opened and a key was slid over.

"Can you send down supper? I've had a long day, Father!"

The Priest grouched a "Mmh" and left the box.

Once downstairs, I paraded around for some spare clothes to change into so that I could dry my own over the heater. In a locker in the third cell, I found a pair of denim jeans, a plain black t-shirt and a thin black jacket. I dried myself with some other loose clothing and changed clothes. When I walked past a mirror, I realised my attire was the carbon copy of Davie's. I suddenly fantasised about being this gunrunner character and was drawn to the life of secrecy and solitude it brought.

In the bunker there were plenty amenities to occupy myself and it was not long before there was a knock on the thick steel door. When I opened it, I found the delightful sight of soup and a sandwich of thick bread on the floor.

After I finished eating, I started my search for any clues as to find out where Davie was. In the first locker, there was a hefty selection of arms, most of them old, used or outdated. There were boxes of ammunition and accessories like gun holsters, belts, silencers and other dribs and drabs. I found a box of burner phones and went through them. They were all brand new, never used. After a good half an hour of looking around, I moved onto one of the beds in the last cell and began to relax into a sleep.

Chapter 51

Things You're Not Prepared to See:

I had no luck at all with any leads to help me find Davie so the morning after, I decided to go out and get some breakfast. I had nowhere in particular in mind and drove around until I found a bog-standard café that looked as if it would do a good greasy fry-up, next door to a convenience store, not that far away from the church on Springfield Road. Inside, the walls had layers of grease, a gradual build up over the years, covering a pale festering décor that would win no awards at a beauty contest. I did not have many pleasures in life but one of them was food. I ordered the mega big breakfast and waited patiently for it to turn up. In the meantime, I picked up an Irish newspaper from the neighbouring table and started to scan through it. As I flicked through the pages, the waitress laid down the plate in front of me as I smiled and folded up the paper, putting it back down on the neighbouring table.

I became distracted by something outside. I had a second glance and could not quite believe what I saw as I sliced through a sausage. A familiar man, wearing a black bomber jacket, stood with his back to me. I barely caught the side of his face, hidden by an untidy rag, a turned over balaclava covering his head, with chunks of grey hair falling out. A rollie hung from his mouth as he stood, stone-faced, staring at someone inside a Vauxhall Vectra stopped at a red light. It was Davie! There was no doubt. I recognised his stiff stance.

His rollie fell to the ground as the car pulled away. He leapt into gear and flagged a taxi down.

I screeched the seat across the floor, drawing the attention of the customers as I belted outside. Davie entered a black cab and hastily talked to the driver. He had not seen me and was sternly focused, pointing at the Vectra in front of him. The cab began to move and follow the Vectra as I memorised the number plate and roof number of the cab. I legged it to my car which was luckily parked very close around the corner on a side street.

Once I was in, I ran the red light at the junction and turned left. Luckily, Davie's cab had been stopped at another red light. I couldn't quite believe the chances of what had just happened! I was there to try and find a trace of where he was and there, he had appeared right in front of me.

I kept far enough back, paranoid about being noticed. We drove around for about ten minutes before the cab stopped some distance back from a pub. I noticed the silver Vectra stop ahead of the cab. We sat there for a few minutes. I had no inkling as to why, because nobody had left their vehicles but I assumed Davie was following that Vectra. I would wait until they moved. There, I felt superior to Davie being on his tail and he had no idea. I watched the activity around the pub and nothing suspicious was occurring. Then a baggy dressed, hippy styled fella left the pub and entered a V6 Golf. He pulled away, the Vectra pulling away after it, followed by Davie's cab and then me. What was going on here! I suspected that one of those two motors ahead of Davie were people who could be due him money.

The convoy carried on into east Belfast until it entered a derelict housing scheme with most of the towered blocks of flats and houses boarded up, bar a few here and there. The Golf stopped and the baggy dressed guy left the vehicle, entering one of those towered blocks. The Vectra passed the Golf and turned up a side street, parking at the rear of the tenement block adjacent to the one the baggy dressed guy entered.

Davie's cab carried on past that side street, some hundred metres away and parked. I drove right by it, turning my head as I did so. What the fuck was going on here! There was a trail of people following each other.

I parked and watched Davie get out and hurry up the side street the Vectra went up on foot. His hair was thick and long, tied in a ponytail, and he seemed more gangly with his wide shoulders. He entered the rear of that tenement building which appeared fully abandoned. He followed the guy who was in the Vectra.

I switched the engine off and kept a keen eye. I saw that the block where the Golf stopped was directly across from the block that Davie entered which led me to believe the Vectra was keeping tabs on the Golf and Davie was following the Vectra.

I was left for a good five minutes before I saw Davie leave the back of that block. I was far enough away that he would never see me, and I watched him eagerly, somewhat admiring him and his rise to become The Eidolon. He limped heavily because of his tortured knees.

Behind the tenement block, he had two options. One of them was to return through the side street and the other was to jump into a cluster of trees that could barely be described as a wood.

Being a man who disappeared at every opportunity, he jumped behind the trees, and he was gone. I did not move though because I had a bigger interest in talking to him now. I wanted to know who the guy was he was following.

I hung around a long time into dark. The Golf had not moved and neither had the Vectra. The streetlights were on. It was cold and I was very hungry, but my wait paid off.

From the back of the tenement building, a short man, wearing a woolly hat appeared, looking sketchy and suspicious. He moved quickly with short steps and soon I realised it was not the same guy who had been driving the Vectra earlier. He was half the size of the Vectra driver. I was then faced with a decision: to follow him or stay there. Considering that the whole building was abandoned, I came to the reasoning that those two guys were hiding up there together.

I decided to follow the short guy who got into a different car. The journey was slow. He took us to the Park Inn hotel in central Belfast. He drove in, deep to the rear of the car park, while I reversed into a space nearer the entrance, giving myself the best chance of getting a look at his face. I watched him walk from his car and head to the entrance of the hotel. He had a real leery look about him. As he ambled, he rolled his shoulders and peered at people under his baseball cap, through his beady eyes. He seemed more paranoid than I remembered and a little edgy, shifting his head about like a parrot. As he got closer, he lifted his hat off and passed under the foyer lights of the hotel.

I opened the car door just as he was about four steps from the revolving door. I double checked!

"Micky!" I elevated my voice and made him flinch as he turned to see where the call came from. He stopped but did not answer. "Micky, it's you!" I said, walking towards him. He seemed to pick up on my voice and did not seem so alarmed.

"Holy Christ! Is that…that Max?" It was my old cell mate, Micky Macdonald from the jail. "Check the size of you!" he heightened his raw, northern Scots accent.

"Aye, it is!" I hugged him, amazed at the coincidence that it was him.

"How the fuck? I mean, what the fuck are yi 'doin' here?"

"Small world," I said, struggling to think of a reason.

"This is nuts! Canna believe it's you!"

We reminisced for a couple of minutes before he asked me into the bar for a drink. I made up a story of how I was in Ireland with my girlfriend, but she was away visiting a friend for the day and had left me to do my own thing. He believed it because he had no reason to think I was lying. I told him about my life in Liverpool but remained secretive about the rest of what I got up to. He explained that he had been in and out of jail a few times since I had seen him last, mostly across Scotland, and how he never lived an honest life.

But we were both crocks in one respect or another and I understood that.

Something I never told him about was the reason he got released from Altcourse jail earlier than he expected: because I made a deal with Carlin and Banks to get him out. It was part of the arrangement we agreed on, that I was to keep quiet about what happened to me when I was released, and they would keep quiet about what happened to the Governor.

I was tip toeing around his reasoning for being there and eventually I got around to asking him.

"What brings you to Ireland, then?"

"Listen, on a bit o' a job here. Not mine really. I'm just taggin' along wi' ma mate."

"You going to tell me, then?" I pressed.

"Why not? Nothing majorly incriminating me anyways. We're on the tail o' some cunt. Somebody a man called Steve Dean from Dundee has suspicions of." I wanted to get as much out of him without sounding suspicious about finding out why Davie was following them.

"Wait! Who's Steve Dean?" Obviously, I knew who it was. I was playing dumb.

"A gangster from Dundee, a right ruthless fucker. Never actually met him but he's got a rep."

"How have you managed to get this job?"

"Ahh, no' my job, as I said, just taggin' along. The job's a pal of mine called Joe Marks up in Aberdeen."

Straight away I thought of a link with Davie. I had heard about parts of his life in Scotland. Mostly from Glasgow but stories from Aberdeen did come up.

"This man you're following, who's he?"

"Him, just a medium rate dealer. Mr Dean has some suspicions o' him and we've tailed him from Aberdeen. That has brought us here." It hardly sounded like a reason why Davie would be following him.

"Is anyone else after this guy?"

"No' as far as I know! You're asking a lot o' questions here. Are you after him?"

"Me, no," I said, as his shifty look surveyed my reaction. "I'm just bored, mate. Haven't been in much trouble over the past few years. Lacking excitement, my life is!"

"You know why that is?"

"Why?" I countered.

"Cause you've a bird! You'll be bored oot yer' tits, mate," he said, slapping my shoulder as we both started laughing which lightened those seconds of tension. I became curious as to who Joe Marks was and thought I'd prod away at that.

"So, where's the guy you're supposed to be following?"

"Me and Joe are splitting shifts watching him. I'm on the back shift and he takes most of the daylight hours."
"Did you meet him inside as well?" We laughed again.
"Hey, you no. I got let out early from Altcourse. That shit we pulled went down a storm. The jail got flipped upside down and no' just me, but loads of us got punted
out or moved on."

He avoided answering but then I realised that Joe must be staying at that hotel as well and all I would have to do was wait there for him.

Once Micky went up to bed, I left the hotel and did a U-turn back into the hotel car park. I booked a room and then gauged roughly what time Joe would turn up the next day, but he never did.

The following day, Micky left the hotel with all their stuff. I had never seen Joe and I had to use outside resources to figure out who he was and once I was told, I knew, and I could never unknow. Micky Macdonald was one of those likeable characters like Ringo and it was a shame when I heard about his demise.

Not so long after that meeting, a man called Harry Duncan was released from jail on remand. He had a vendetta against Micky, tracked him down in Aberdeen and murdered him.

Chapter 52

Keep an Eye on the Scar:

After I learned that Micky and Joe were working for Mr Dean, I knew the best person to ask about that was Mr Dean. And I had already come up with a plan. Finding out where Mr Dean lived was not a hard thing to do. I picked a rough looking boozer in a rundown area of Dundee, called Fintry, went in and started asking questions until I found out the location in Dundee.

I knew what I was doing was bold but how else could I have gone about it? I rang the doorbell twice before a pointy faced, stocky, well dressed in black, gentleman answered. It was Lukas, whose face was dry of any reaction.

"What do you want?" He spouted in an eastern European accent.

"Is Mr Dean at home?" He stood mutely, devoid of words or reactions, and closed the door. It opened about a minute later and this time, revealed Mr Dean.

"Who are you?" he growled in a strong Dundonian twang as Lukas stood behind him, his tinted brown glasses covering the coldness of his eyes. His open buttoned white striped shirt indicated that he was either relaxing or deep into something. His prominent scar, running down his cheek if anything, gave him character. He did not have the slightest idea that the scar was my doing.

"I'm Max," I said.

"And I'm a travelling Wilbury. Carry on!" There was a stench of whisky from his mouth and looseness in his tongue.

"I'm the son of Davie Rhodes and I have some questions for you." He was taken aback by my brashness and shared an ominous look with Lukas.

"Are you now?" His hands slipped inside the pockets of his slack dressed trousers as his chest puffed out, aware that not anyone would make that assumption.

"Suppose you better come in." Mr Dean took me into his exotic whisky lounge and sat me down at a round, varnished oak table in the centre of the lavish room, which was decorated with glass cabinets, healthily stocked with whisky, ornamental bookshelves, expensive leather furniture and heated by a wood burning fire. Lukas, a keen observer, sat opposite me and constantly kept an eye on my movements. Mr Dean sat to my left. On the table sat three empty whisky glasses on coasters, around an ashtray with a cigar butt in it.

"The son of Davie Rhodes sits in my house?" he pointed out while lighting a thin cigarette-sized cigar. "And you say yer name is Max?"

"Or The Reaper," I said, attracting their attention quickly, leaving them to inhale deep breaths and gather their thoughts.

Mr Dean leaned into his seat and said, "The same Reaper who recently defeated Belcher Oakley, the Gypsy?"

"Aye." If he knew that, he knew I had killed him which would only enhance my presence and he would also know that I fought under Jack. He gathered his thoughts, drawing deeply on his cigar, allowing the smoke to seep from his slack jaw.

"Ok… Now I can only assume you need something from me. I am not a man who holds a wide collection of friends, who visit for tea and that leads me to believe that you need something."

"I would like some information!"

"Very direct this one, Lukas," he said, without acknowledging him as Lukas kept the same stern mould. It was clear that Mr Dean treated no one with respect.

"And what do I get in return?" Mr Dean hinted.

"That can be negotiated!"

"Negotiated, he says. Well, I am a bargaining chip today."

"You recently had an old friend of mine, Micky, do a job for you in Belfast and I'd like to know who it was with him."

Mr Dean moved his cigar from his mouth and then decided to stand. Lukas remained, absorbing the information I carried with me. I had surprised them. "I don't know how you know this information, but my instinct tells me that you are no threat. If a man, who has done me wrong, decides to turn up at my door and enter my house, he is an enemy, an enemy of high calibre." He sat back down and slid forward from his seat. "Before we get into who he is and believe me, you will be as fucking surprised as I am at this moment, let us discuss what you can do for me. What are you negotiating with?"

"Firearms!" Before I left Belfast, I had filled up a long duffel bag with a couple of automatic weapons, shotgun and a few handguns.

"What man in my line of work doesn't like firearms?"

"In the near future, I can provide more of these at a much cheaper rate than anyone else, provided you keep this visit a secret." This was my leverage to persuade him and Lukas to remain quiet.

"The near future, you say?" Mr Dean repeated. I stood up from my seat.

"I will be right back," I said, as I walked outside to grab the bag from the boot. I returned to the study and dropped the bag on the table. "Here is a down payment."

Mr Dean and Lukas shared an exchange of admiration as Lukas leaned forward and unzipped the bag, had a peek inside and leant back with a gesturing nod of agreement towards Mr Dean. With his elbows on the arm rests and his fingers interlinking, Mr Dean evaluated the situation.

"I noticed you said 'down payment'. Does this mean you have other firearms?"

"In the future I will have many more. Now for your side of the bargain!"

Mr Dean rotated his thumbs through his interlocking grip and then stopped.

"Sometimes coincidences happen that are so distant from each other but so aligned at the same time. What you have just told me has blown my socks off and my socks normally never come off. You say you are the son of Davie Rhodes and that I don't dispute but in the last twenty-four hours, I had the other son of Davie Rhodes in this house.”

Anticipation took control of me. I tensed and eagerly rose from my seat, watching him pause in mid-sentence. My eyes flared, eager for him to finish.

“Twenty-four hours ago, Micky, whom I had not met before, returned from a wee errand in Belfast. With him was the other son of Davie Rhodes, Joe Marks, who was carrying out a task for me!”

My gaze circulated the room, as I tried to understand the actuality of that being viable.

“Perhaps you should have a seat because I have more information to divulge.”

I returned to my seat.

“Do you want a whisky? You look as though you need it!”

“Coffee, I’ll have a coffee,” I said.

“Lukas, make our guest a coffee,”

“Sure.”

“Now, in the world of coincidences, this one is up there with the best. And I mean, fucking up there, right next to the pig on a pushbike, pedalling across the haze of the moon. Joe Marks is not only your brother, but he is also a fighter like you.”

“A fighter!”

“Aye, a fighter, lad, and a good one at that. He fights for me!”

The thoughts of wagering up a scrap between us overtook any ideology I was experiencing at that time. But I still had a need to conquer those who thought they could take me on.

"He's enquired about you, The Reaper, that is. Asked me a couple of times about your reputation, but I've mostly ignored the request but he's hell bent of taking you on. You see, with men like you and him, you have to prove yourself, and to no one else but yourself."

I stood up from the seat again, sending out a firm message to Mr Dean.

"You make it happen but make it happen within four months!"

He tried to decipher the reasoning in making the match in four months instead of next week.

"May I ask?"

I halted him in mid-sentence. "No, you may not!" I said, shocking him with my blatancy as I took a peek into his soul, watching the incensed reaction.

Tense moments of silence separated us as Lukas returned to the room and put the coffee down on the table. Instantly I grabbed it and hoped it would be strong. It was.

"Okay," Mr Dean said. "I will give Joe a test against an ex-boxer called Matt McGregor and if he comes through that, then I will make it happen."

Chapter 53

Was I Really Here:

I absorbed the information, calmly and slowly. Mr Dean filled me in on who Joe Marks was a stand-up guy who looked after his family, a wife and two kids, who had tumbled down the road of fighting in the need for money. Keeping a three-bedroomed house in a town called Inverurie in Aberdeenshire, and two kids, after being made redundant, became too much for an unemployed man with few skills. Once a boxer of great potential and trained by Davie for some of his upbringing, I was sure he would carry some of the ruthless blood that ran in the family.

Now Joe had tumbled down the same road as his father, the same road I had tumbled down. Both men inheriting the callous skill of the fighting manner of their elder. I struggled to imagine the chances of such things occurring in that one weekend and I put it down to fate. Whatever would happen will happen. Now there was an added goal in the equation. Not only did I now want to fight my brother, I had to beat him and play my part in having Jack killed before fleeing the country.

I had been gone for a few days and I had never told Courtney where I was.

I walked into the kitchen, our eyes meeting straight away. I said 'hello' dryly, to which there was no response, and I never wanted one. I was dying for a shower and a bite to eat so I purposely left her company for that shower.

On returning, I walked into the living room to see her sitting on the sofa with her arms crossed in a mood. With everything I had to deal with, I could not be bothered putting up with a woman's mood. I ignored her and entered the kitchen to open the fridge. Inside, I saw a plate of left-over stew and potatoes with mushy peas. I made a 'yum' noise and put the plate into the microwave. When I shut the microwave door, she was standing in the open doorway between the kitchen and living room.

"Are you going to tell me?" she barked, wanting to know where I had been.

"What?"

"Come on! Give me the credit."

"Why don't you ask Jack where I was?"

"He didn't know you were away. You need to tell me before you just fuck off like that!"

"I don't need to tell anyone where I go," I said steadily and waited for the microwave to count down.

"You need to tell me, Max, tell me!"

"I needed a few days' space," I gave her a mediocre answer to stop the assault.

"Why don't you tell me things?" she insisted, which heightened my temper.

"Because of this! This fucking hassle you give me when I leave the flat. I don't need it, woman!" my voice rose and reverberated off the walls of the narrow kitchen.

"If we are going to have a kid then you need to tell me when you're leaving!"

"What kid?" I yelled and stepped forward, silencing her as she stepped back against the fridge, setting it off its legs. I glanced down at her stomach, noticing a small bump. I stepped back, tilting my head, switching my look between her stomach and face.

"Are you?" Her chin tensed and she was near trembling. "Are you?" I asked again.

"I've stopped smoking, Max."

"You're having a fucking baby, and you've not told me!"

"I have told you! You haven't listened!"

"When?"

"Lots of times but you're never here. Your head's always somewhere else!"

I did not know if she was telling the truth. I was confused. I could not have a child; I was a monster.

"Are you hearing me now?" Her voice elevated when I turned my back to her. "Max! Talk to me. Look, I've known for two months now and I'm four gone!"

All that was going through my mind was an extra complication to deal with.

"Max," she repeatedly shouted.

"Quiet, I'm thinking. There's a lot to think about!"

"You can have all the time to think that you want. I'm going to Rebecca's." she said as she grabbed her coat and slammed the door.

Had she really told me that she was pregnant? I wondered if I was there at all. Was I going insane? I was obsessed with Jack and fighting. I was on the verge of exploding. Impulsively, I ran my fist through the kitchen cupboard doors and then picked up the microwave, when it pinged, to smash it on the floor. It was followed by the kettle being launched through the door window.

My heart pounded through my chest as my fists coiled tight. Everything I touched got smashed or broke in the next five minutes as my life of horror flashed before me. Saliva covered my chin and my face was red with fury. But I loved it: every second I had there, I relished, being free from thoughts. The kitchen was destroyed and so was my sanity. There were enough thoughts in my head without the barrage of problems she brought out. I needed peace and some days to think. The idea of having a kid did not register with me. I would be well gone before it would grace my presence in the world, and I would never have to deal with Courtney again!

Later that night, I heard a knock on the door; it was Ringo.

"What do you want?" I asked, as he looked past my body to see the mess in the kitchen.

"Maybe you want a cleaner."

I glanced behind and left Ringo standing there as I retreated to the bedroom. Ringo was in a bit of trouble and needed to hide out so he ended up moving in for a while. He repaid me that night by cleaning the kitchen.

Chapter 54

Date with Destiny:

I received some news from Mr Dean that Joe had come through his test against Matt McGregor. That set up the proceedings for our fight to be made official. I knew that would be the outcome anyway and had already started preparing, physically and mentally. I got back to the gym and back on the steroids. I took one millilitre of dca and sustanon, three times a week, sometimes four. Codie oversaw a lot of my training and pushed me to insane fitness levels. Ringo became a helping hand and accompanied me to the gym, often driving me around and sorting my food out. I ate like a horse, hungry all the time, and I hardly slept. I was bursting with energy and became possessed with the idea of victory.

Mr Dean and I concluded that the only people who would know of our meeting and the family connection were us two and Lukas. I promised him the contents of the arms lockers in Arbs Forest in the north of Northern Ireland and the bunker at the church. All for a reasonable price, of course. But in reality, I would never have to do that because myself and Davie would be long gone. Jack would be dead, and Joe defeated.

Mr Dean contacted Jack and arranged the fight before Jack asked me down to the office. This was edgy for me because Courtney had not been home since our last outburst. I did not want the conflict with her or maybe it was because I didn't want to face responsibility for my actions. I did not want to be made to feel guilty or to feel bad as it would have a knock-on effect on my preparation for the fight. I had never been more serious about anything.

"Good day, Max," Jack said, as I walked into his office and sat down. "What have you been doing?"

"You know, this and more of that. What the fuck can I do for you?" I was becoming more relaxed around him knowing his end was very close. I wouldn't have to look at that arrogant expression ever again.

"Always the romantic, you?" I hoped he was not going to mention my situation with Courtney.

"Get to the point," I insisted. I already knew why he wanted me there.

"You have your first challenger!"

"You're the man to make that happen," I stated.

"I'll make it happen, like always," Jack answered coyly.

"Good," I said and stood up, edging to leave.

"Why do you keep doing that?" Jack blasted while I halted my exit. "Getting up and leaving in mid-sentence."

"Because I have nothing more to say!"

"Don't you want to know when and where and who you're fighting?" It seemed my slack caring and uninterested approach to conversing with Jack had reached his tipping point. But what he did not know was that I had prearranged it all.

"Ok, tell me," I said and crossed my arms. I was making sure he knew the only things I needed from him were his contacts and business ethic.

"Glasgow, early November and you're fighting a Scot called Joe Marks from Aberdeen."

"Okay," I said and walked out. There was nothing more to say to him.

After I shut the door, I breezed past the double doors that opened into the club and stopped. Courtney was standing behind the bar scrolling on her phone. She leaned back, showing a very small bump at five months gone. Vacantly, I watched her, knowing that child would have nothing to do with its father. A fate that I was sure would mean the child would be better off.

At the bottom of the stairs, I bumped into a drunk and irate Calvin who was preparing to unleash another outburst on Jack.

"We need a word!" I said and reluctantly led him away from the door as he slandered Jack's name. I dragged him onto Upper Hope Street where my car was parked. I threw him inside and shut the door. On the floor of the passenger side was a bottle of water. I opened it, splashed it over his face and poured it over his head.

"I have a date. I want to do this now," I said, ignoring the casual nature of what I did.

"What, what are you doing, you nutcase?" he slurred, drawing a breath, spitting water from his mouth. He started slapping me weakly but urgently. There wasn't much strength in his pencil-pushing, elongated body. "You're supposed to be helping me!" he cried.

"I'm ready to do it!" I answered as I gripped his flapping hands and brought them to a stop. He gathered himself and calmed down.

"I've waited too long for this." His desperation was easy to see, afraid at losing his reputation of what Jack held over him. "You know where the video footage is?" "Aye, it's on this hard drive he keeps in one of his locked drawers and I'll give you his laptop, plus whatever is in the CCTV room in his house. I've been in

once, so I know there's a computer in there."

Calvin was relieved and drew a long breath.

Once upon a time, around eight years before, Jack needed a solicitor who would do as he was told and not ask questions. This was for legal contracts to purchase land that secured real estate on the dirt cheap from councils and major landowners, and he needed someone who could manoeuvre around the red tape. He also helped in any debacles Jack had with police and so forth. In order to acquire an individual like Calvin's skills, Jack first had to have leverage over him. To do that, he had to set him up with something incriminating. For this, Jack hired the services of his niece, Julie, on Beverly's side. She was barely sixteen but looked around her mid-twenties. Flawlessly attractive and being deceitfully seductive was her game.

Calvin was twenty-nine and a regular visitor to McCartneys and not a bad guy. He followed the crowd of his work colleges at Donoghue Solicitors who were regulars to Jack's strip joint. Calvin was tall and skinny and had the sex appeal of a Scottish dwarf. He was the kind of kid who was constantly picked on at school because of his looks. He wore thick specs, making him shy and insecure and Jack picked him out like an apple from a tree. He got friendly with him, and one night

Jack took him out on the town and lured him into a gay bar called Pink. Planted inside was Julie. Jack paid her stupid money, money a fifteen-year-old could not turn down. Once Calvin was liquored up, he sent his niece to seduce him and lead him back to a local hotel room that Jack had already paid for and hidden cameras inside. Julie never went through with the deed, but she became a star in Jack's eyes, getting all the incriminating evidence he needed.

Ever since then, Jack had threatened to release the evidence and expose Calvin of paedophilia if he did not do what he was told.

"Calvin, I have to ask again. This will, is it the full shilling?" I had been sitting with Calvin for some twenty minutes, calming and sobering him up.

"Yes Max, everything is correct. I have been over it so many times. I have written the testament wishes, all the assets will be transferred to Ringo, except for the house and one bank account, which will be left to Beverly. Jacks signature is full-proof and the witness signatures of Ringos, yours and mine are good. Not so much as a full stop is missing."

"I have to be sure; you understand I will not be here afterwards and you will be in charge of this. And Jack, he will be dead."

"Jack will be dead!" Calvin jaw turned slack.

"What did he do to you that you want him dead?" He asked and in normal situations I would not confide in someone, but I told Calvin everything I knew about Jack's role in having me arrested and sent to jail and everything that occurred in there.

"That is a better reason than mine." Calvin said.

"Like me Calvin, you will be free afterwards."

A few weeks after that, I heard from Davie with some instructions on two mainland gun deals that I ignored. I had other priorities to hold my attention so The Eidolon would have to get his other dogs to do the deal. I did not want any distractions to take me out of my rhythm. But I did need to talk to him about Jack. I sent him a date in early November that I wanted to follow through with the plan, and he replied with a tick, which I assumed would mean that he would follow through on his part and arrange the getaway out of the country.

Later I would learn it was Panama; I did not know where that was until I looked it up on a map. I had more than one reason to leave and the other was to get away from any contact with Courtney and her baby. I was no man to raise a child, but I was a man ready to take down my brother.

Chapter 55

Safe House in Carnagh:

Two weeks before the fight, Davie had been in contact and invited me to Carnagh, County Armagh, on the border between Northern and the Republic of Ireland. It was what the Irish referred to as 'bandit country'.

For him, it had been a few years since he had seen me last but for me, I saw him a few months prior.

I walked into the small bungalow cottage and clunked across the wooden floor. On my right, the kitchen door was ajar so I peeked in to see the worktops were filled with leftover food packages, empty tins and an assortment of rubbish. I looked at the kettle that had a small brown leather book about the size of a pocket map and a cluster of rolling tobacco and skins beside it. Along with that, the smell of grass suffocated the air.

In the sitting room, where a fire was ablaze, Davie, wearing a cardigan, was sat in front of it, puffing on a rollie while a lone whisky sat on the side table with his tobacco tin and ashtray. Inside the ashtray was a few stubbed-out joints. He used the grass as pain relief for his wounded body.

"Hello, son," he said, without turning around. I did not reply and watched him stand up, stiff with age and tired with burden. His hair grew long past his shoulders, loose and flowing, mixed with white and grey, like an old wizard's. Coarse wrinkles covered his face while his back hunched over a little, showing that even the great Eidolon weakened with age.

"Hello, Davie," I replied, as we shared somewhat of an emotional gathering. "Not met any hairdressers on your travels?" I opened and he laughed.

"There are some things you stop caring for when you get to my age and one of them is haircuts," he joked dryly and held out his hand for me to have a pew on the chair beside him.

"I'm going to make a coffee first." I walked through to the kitchen and put the kettle on, leaving me time to ponder on the state he was in, and look around. Part of me felt sorry for the man I once knew had been full of life. The other side of me was natural, but I still had a sliver of pity for him. I returned to the pew beside him as he eyed my size and I noticed the effect of the grass in his sagging eyelids.

"You've been munchin' those steroids like Smarties, boy. I can tell. Seen it all my days."

He was right, and I was on a bigger dose than normal. "In a couple weeks, you won't have to take that stuff anymore. We will be off on a cruise liner to South America and Jack will be gone. I have everything arranged for a smooth trip." Davie always remained secretive about his gunrunning and never really shared much but I could tell by his shifty body language he had a lot going on and was under stress. "Good. I've waited long enough for this."

Davie transferred his look to the open door and got up. I thought he was about to close it but he walked past and entered the kitchen. He returned to his seat as he slipped that pocket-sized book into his back pocket.

"On the night you fight, there will be a gun deal. Turk and Barb will do it. That will be the last one." I sipped on my coffee while I enjoyed the heat of the fire. The end to that journey was nearly complete. "The operation will be left to 'em, they can have the bunkers, my contacts and Rankin can continue being the information asset."

I sniffed at the thought of Rankin; the slimy rat gave me the creeps. There was nothing Davie did not know about the fight. Through Rankin and other sources, he already knew his two sons were going to fight.

"Why Panama?" I asked.

"There's more corrupt officials in Panama than in Mexico and it's so far out of the loop, we will be left to live like kings for the rest of our lives. If there is anything we are questioned about, we just pay some cunt to keep quiet." I continued listening. "I have bought a mini mansion on a remote part of the beach on the west o' the country. The garage is already filled with cars. I'm still switching siller through accounts but we should have a good few million and 'en, son," he nudged my thigh, "the ladies await us."

We shared a light laugh as the plan sounded idyllic. Ideally the place where I could forget about my troubles and Courtney.

Davie quietened, probably thinking of Joe and if he was willing to tell me that he was my brother. I played poker cool and there was no need to let him know that I knew. I sensed there was something he wanted to say but there was no part of me that wanted to hear it from him. I could hardly say it was his doing that his two sons had both travelled down similar paths to come together on a night that would be the most brutal fight I'd ever been in! With the tense moment passing, he did speak. "Max, is there really a need to have this fight? I've got a bad feelin' about it."

"What?"

"There's no need to take this on. You've proven ye're the best, untouchable. We could leave right now, jump on a cruise-liner and be out of here."

I flashed up from my seat and powered over him. "This is what I do! If this cunt from Scotland thinks he's taking my crown, he's mistaken. I'll squash him like I've done every other cunt who thinks he can beat me." That outburst left Davie speechless. Out of nowhere, I exploded and created tension between us. Not something I wanted to do but I had no control over my temper. I was like a spoiled child that had to explain himself.

"It's up to you, son, but be wary," Davie replied, as if he was not bothered by my outburst, but I knew he had to be. He was hiding it well and his stoned state would have helped that. We sat and discussed how I would let him into Jack's house after the fight. There were a couple of obstacles. One of them was his alarm system and I would disable it from his interface, located inside his security room. The other was his two dogs which were familiar with me. I'd feed them some snacks laced in ketamine that would knock them out. Then I'd open the rear door, show him Jack's bedroom and allow him to shoot him. I would have my redemption for the brutal time I had spent in jail and Davie would have his for his deformed hands, missing fingers and damaged knees.

Beverly would not be harmed if it could be avoided. I had calmed down somewhat and returned to my seat.

"So, the legal document is sorted?" he asked firmly.

"Aye, everything's in place," I answered and reassured him a few more times. Seems he really wanted Ringo to take over from Jack and so did I. "Will you be there?"

"It's risky, son, very risky. I might make an appearance!" he said, full well knowing that he would not miss the battle between his two offspring.

With everything in place, I was left to focus on training for the last couple of weeks. Codie choose to begin to teach me the basics of MMA and kicking. It was for my benefit and gave me a bigger arsenal he said, and I took to it naturally. It appeared like he knew I would need something extra for the fight.

Twice a day, I would be in Rockie's, taking advantage of the two different types of steroids I was on. I never followed Codie's advice about the implications of dosing too heavily or long with the steroids. My mind did not work like that. I had it all, whenever I wanted. On the time off after I fought Belcher, I became rather weak and lost a lot a lot of my muscle mass. I did not like the wailing feeling in that period and I wanted super strength to deal with Joe. He had a reputation, strong, determined, and skilful. No one told of a weakness of his, but I'd find it, or I'd certainly look for it. I was not prepared to lose in my last showdown. The rules had been set out in the final weeks leading to the scrap. Unlike the fight with Belcher when a man fell, he was given a full minute to recover and you could take advantage of that whole minute. You could not hit your opponent while he was on the deck. If you could not stand within the minute, then you lost. The fight was organised by Mr Dean who had a wealth of experience in the game.

In those two weeks leading up to the fight, there was only a couple of people I spoke to because they understood my motives and mood swings: Codie and Ringo, who continued to look after me on the lead up.

Chapter 56

The Beginning of The End:

It was time. The day I had been waiting for since I was released from jail. The downfall of Jack Gallagher. We were parked by a large brown cladded industrial shed in a desolate area of the Clyde docks in Glasgow on a bitterly cold Saturday night in November. I was fascinated by thoughts of Jack's demise and the retribution that was a mere moment away. Holding back on that, I had to remain king and defeat Joe. That was the primary concern.

I gazed out the window, over the tar, at the glint of the sparkling frost reflected off the surface of the shed. The sound of the water was still and at peace, contradictory to what my insides felt.

It seemed as if it was time to leave the vehicle as Jack exited the car.

I followed and hesitated, having that eerie feeling of someone watching me. I carried on following Jack to the entrance, freezing in my long t-shirt and thin jeans. Before I tailed Jack through the door, I stopped dead and turned around to investigate a cloudy windscreen of a car. Someone sat in the passenger seat, staring back at me.

It was Joe. I could feel him. Jack pulled at me to keep going so I ducked my head under the door frame and carried on. Soon enough, I'd meet him officially for the first time in a way no brothers should meet.

On the walk down the corroding brick-built tunnel, my legs weighed heavy as if I was lumbering through sand

I kept having an eerie feeling that someone was behind me, as I continued to cock my head. At one point, I stopped and contemplated going back. Jack noticed this, although ahead of me.

"Max!" He insisted I follow, while I dithered.

The unstable lights kept flickering on and off as I watched rats scurry around my feet, using the stacked ladder racks full of heavy-duty cables as a highway.

"Max!" Jack shouted again as I snapped out of a daze and tailed him. My attention returned when a single dove flew past, frightening and breaking my focus again. I watched Jack, up ahead, as he turned a corner through an archway and disappeared. That was my fate around that corner, and I took a deep breath of apprehension, when my heart crumbled with stabbing pains. My heavy legs buckled, and my palm scratched the ground. It was instant and vicious as I struggled to pass air, as the power had been taken from my body. It passed quickly and stopped. I dragged myself up the wall, before I was seen in that state. I was momentarily stunned because I had never felt a pain like it. Crossly, I disciplined myself, irritated at the weakness I was exhibiting. I shook it off and walked around that corner, into the cathedral of death.

The room stank with a baiting desperation, seeping from the bodies of loathsome criminals, waiting for their source of entertainment to distract them from their own cowardliness. The room echoed the filth of the underworld and it filled with their tense chatter as their consciences were too afraid to admit they relished the sight of other people's pain.

From far and wide the notorious gangsters of the country had come to witness the battle. I could see every worthwhile name on the gangsters' VIP list, from London to the north of Scotland. Word had travelled well and far. Donny Casper looked edgy, standing beside a small collective of his men. A cocked-up Ringo kept a distance from Jack who mingled with Steve Dean, Joe's manager. I boasted to myself of the scar on his face, a scar I'd inflicted, and he had no idea. It seemed my world stood still in the spotlight. I spotted Gregor Palin, Gunther Turner and Bo Pat who, I realised, knew the soaring apprehension pumping through me. The Ghetto Gang was in attendance with Helder Moore looking particularly observant of me.

I gave them all a dry look before I walked between the robust concrete pillars that supported the building, to the rear of the room where I saw a lone stool and sat on it. I wondered how many men had sat there before me. I bowed my head, I breathed deeply, the steroids fuelling my muscles as the anticipation of exchanging fists with my brother drew a different sensation from other fights. There was no fear or no mercy offered to him but I had an unsought quivering of dread scatter and I couldn't explain it. Maybe it was doubt. I couldn't tell because I had never doubted myself before. As I had a momentary feeling of guilt, I was suffocated by what I could only call deja vu. Quickly, I swiped that feeling aside as the pain swept through my chest again.

I turned my head to recover, ashamed to show a weakness and hoping to hide it.

Ringo snuck up and sheepishly tapped my shoulder.

"Come a long way from walking the line," he said, under his breath, concerned that he was bothering my mental preparation.

"And a long way to go," I answered, as he nodded, avoiding eye contact, being afraid of a reaction. I was pumped, visually and internally, while something inside me wished to talk to him. "I have something to ask," I said.

"Anything," he opened.

"If you never see me again, I want you to make sure Courtney gets all my money. She'll need it."

"What!" he replied naively. In that moment of extreme fear, I wanted to find a humble part of me, one who cared.

"I have bags of cash stashed in the mattress and two accounts. All the details on how to get into them is in the drawer on the tv cabinet. You understand?"

"I got ya, kid," he answered childishly, as if he did not realise the environment we were in.

"I keep telling you, don't call me kid," I winked at him, gave him a smirk, and turned away indicating I no longer wanted to speak.

I kept my back to the room as a cluster of strange thoughts overtook my mind. One thing I kept over thinking about was my mother and why she abandoned me. That filled me full of hate. Then I'd reminisce on the Governor and The Gypsy, who filled me full of power, confident in the knowledge I had overcome the biggest adversaries in my life. My childhood of horror in foster homes ignited my frustration which poured fuel onto my rage. All I desired then was my foe and to get the show on the road.

As I focused, I grimaced from another sharp electric shock to my heart. My body tensed as it passed so quickly, nobody noticed.

Without lifting my head, I could taste my foe enter the arena. I began to get rid of the distracting thoughts side-tracking my attack and victory. I wondered if he knew I was his brother, but that wonder could not derail my taste of conquest. His notoriety governed me to turn in my seat and witness him talk to Mr Dean. His body was impressive, his shoulders were thick balls of strength with his muscled upper frame causing his t-shirt to hang loose. Then he talked to a scraggily tall fella, called Tim, as he turned his back to me. I glared at him, inhaling and exhaling deeply to release tension.

When I looked at Joe across the floor of the basement, his eyes spread wide, filled with his own misfortunes of pain that was hidden behind the pulsation of adrenaline. Davie had taught me to remove the fear from my eyes and keep it hidden on the inside, but no matter who you were, you would always show a glint. Joe's eyes held that fear, but that small glint was enough to hold him on the edge. Behind that, I could sense a fuel of notoriety simmer from within them. He wasn't here to fall over; he housed that same rage inside him as I did.

He was smaller with an emerging reputation in the bare-knuckle world and a bucket load of heart at his disposal. In tremendous shape but his fate lay in my hands. His lack of pride in his appearance and look of a man possessed held him in good stead but he hadn't faced a barbarian who was willing to die before victory could be handed over.

I replied by standing with my fists clenched and face solid. He admired my size but had no fear of it. After a stern exchange, I slipped my t-shirt off, showing my sculpture of thick muscle. When I slid my jeans off, wearing shorts underneath, I soaked in the admiration in Joe's reaction but I'm sure a son of Davie Rhodes would not let my size affect him. I began to step around, indicating I was ready to rumble as Joe stripped off.

I heard a shout from someone, "A minute to go." The clock had run out.

Joe's scraggily dressed accomplice stepped in front of him to instil a last drive of ambition as I waited like a gladiator for the gates of the Colosseum to open. His friend departed from his sight when Joe stepped forward. When we locked eyes, I saw a rage that I was only too aware of. In that exchange, I knew he knew nothing of our connection. We nudged closer and closer and the fight had begun!

I plodded around, hovering my hands under my chin, catching Joe's side on the stance of a boxer as he kept his hands tight to his body showing his bulging arms and shoulders. I stalked him like prey, powering over him in size and planted a jab into his hard face. He replied fast with his own jab that I parried down and countered with a solid right onto his lips.

Immediately, I was at home, loving the thrill. I focused on stalking him, I wanted him finished quickly. I could see he was uncomfortable, maybe the apprehension had got to him. He danced on his toes like a boxer does, trying to simulate what he had to do to hurt me. He was quick and I had no time for his boxing bounce. As I stalked him, he threw a blistering quick combo ending with a left hook flashing across my jaw. The fury flashed across my mind and the haze closed in.

He leaped away and went back to moving on his toes, unwilling to exchange with a beast. I hunted him down, feigning going one direction and closing him off on the other until I caught his feet, tripped him up and trapped him back against one of the pillars.

By instinct, I overreached my palm and pushed his forehead onto the pillar. I coiled my elbow around and cracked it across his jaw. He fell. I roared and threw a couple of brash punches in fresh air, missing him. While he lay below me, I coiled over his body with images of stamping on him as the powers that be shouted at me to back off and allow him to stand.

That was the round over and I moved away from him. I had to allow him time to stand. He rose from the dust-covered ground and returned to his friend who fed him water. I did not require water and I stood, drawing long breaths with thoughts of dismantling him. How dare he think he was good enough to take me on?

The minute break was over, and it was time to go again.

Not wasting time, I hunted and pressured him to fight. He danced on his toes and moved quickly, too quick for me, but all I could do was pressurise the slithery fuck. He frustrated me as I tried to grab his face with my open hand. I hissed and growled in annoyance, hunting him down. He was being cowardly and avoided fighting. This was a playground for the hardest of men, not immature boys.

Eventually, I forced him to exchange. He got inside my arm's length and coiled a combination at me, hitting me at will while I replied with my own. I backed him off and he went back to dancing around me. This continued and if he thought I'd tire of it, I would not. As he got closer, I awkwardly tried to kick him; my fury took over the control from my rational thinking. I decided to slow down, still full of frustration, and allowed him to think that he could get closer. He did and I rapidly threw a right hand, watching him weave back to avoid it making contact. He stumbled off balance as my left hand grabbed his shoulder blade, preparing to hit him with my right, when a headbutt crushed into the bridge of my nose. Without notice, I felt a kick land behind my knee that buckled my stance and then a bulldozing right hand clattered across my jaw. The next thing I knew, I was on the floor on one knee. My brother could fight.

I stood up, knowing there was a minute's break. I glanced at Mr Dean who had a mask of arrogance across his face, being the only man who knew we were brothers. I used the time to re-group and as soon as I heard someone shout "Time," I marched across the room, startling him. Catching him off guard, I dived in, throwing thrusting punches, trying hard to hurt him, weaken him or just kill him. I grunted and growled while my hands clattered into his face, rebounding off bone and shoulders. He took it without concern and replied, landing cleanly when he could.

In close, I took a grip around his neck and dug four rapid knees into his gut and let go, leaving him to fall to the ground and shuffle away before I got ideas of stamping on him.

The next round began and I pursued him again. He breathed hard and his body was weakened. That was the beginning of his downfall, in my eyes. Like a hungry hyena, I stalked him, piling pressure on, causing him to live on the back foot. When I got close enough, I managed to hit him in the eyes with two solid punches and a blow to his ribs. He sagged and bent his waist over, isolating his head. I coiled a right hook across his temple, dropping him to the ground. He shuffled away in panic again. The tide turned: I had him.

He came out for the next round and willingly strolled over, holding his fists by his waist as if he was asking me to hit him. I threw a jab that he countered with a right hook, dazzling me, before out of the little vision I had, I could see a leg shuffle around to my side. When I shifted my stance around, a sickening uppercut pinged my head into the air. As my head levelled out, he had moved again and double hooked me. I became blinded to the room, and deaf to anything. I was at sea when a kick behind my knee caused me to buckle again. My knee brushed the ground when a jolting head butt sank into my mouth and then a blow into my solar plexus rendered me beaten on both knees. I tried to suck in the air while blood churned in my mouth of damaged teeth.

I hacked up the blood and spat it out on the dusty soil in front of Joe's feet. He stood adjacent to me, wondering if I was to stand or fall. Fragments of teeth were still stuck in my mouth so I kept spitting them out as Joe glared at me as if I was an animal.

I was taking my minute to gather myself before the next round began when I looked at Joe's face. It flared in a murderous mien as he took a step forward, coiling his right hand behind him. I knew that he was going to break the rules and strike me on the ground. I shuffled off one knee and planted my sole onto the ground, ducked my head under a hook and managed to transfer enough weight to stand up! When Joe looked at me after that, I had most of my weight on the right foot and hit him rapidly with three short punches into the gut. He fell as I booted him in the ribs and stepped away. The look of astonishment was worth taking that pain. He was repulsed that I could take such a beating and stand up afterwards.

While he lay there, I spat out the rest of the teeth fragments, combined with a hook of blood and spat it over his body. I was out of breath and needed time to re-group, so I moved away from him and stood in the middle, awaiting the next round, knowing he would take the minute.

He came bolting out, with tense thoughts and a new determination. Straight away, he ran inside me like a kamikaze pilot and unloaded a heavy combination of punches. His boxing ability was in full show as he dazzled me with head shots and buried his face into my chest, sinking in body shots.

I tried to grab him, but he was slick and fast. He made me step back and fight on the back foot. A relenting assault of punches followed as I was persistently pushed back and he growled with a possessed drive. I was hurt and he stood in front of me battering my ribs; as I tried to return fire, he ducked under the punches and came with more. From the head to the body, he was taking me apart, until I sagged and he piled that uppercut into my jaw, bursting my lip in half.

I had no focus of attention; I was being beaten and could not stop it. Without knowing, I had dropped to one knee again but I was not to fall. I could not allow it. My chin hung out like a washing line when a big hook propelled off it. I had no idea what was happening. I felt him take a grip around the back of my neck and sunk his knuckles into my windpipe. I blanked out, fell to both knees and used a jellied hand to restrain me from plunging flat down. I gargled for breath and panicked, knowing that one hand was stopping me from falling, as I scratched it across the gravel, hoping I could find something to help me.

The clock was ticking. If I was down for more than one minute, I would lose and I couldn't send the signals to tell myself I had to stand. Still, I tried to suck air in, my chest stayed solid and my throat closed as my hand was buckling, allowing my elbow to lean on the concrete. After about fifty seconds, I inhaled a breath of relief and stood up. Joe could not believe it, but he was still psyched, his face open and his eyes engulfed with rage.

He ran towards me with no concern for himself as I dangled on the last string of strength I had. Where was the energy and power from the steroids because I needed them? He stomped in my direction, wide open and uncaring with only murderous thoughts. He thought I was beaten before I met his propulsion with a solid smack into his face, knocking the guts out of him. He fell as I took the time to breathe and come back to life.

While I did that, a shooting pain soared through my chest again. I bit down and hid the pain behind the crowd's attention on Joe taking the minute to recover. Even if I had wanted to capitulate, I could not; I had nothing until the pain passed which it did. I inhaled a huge lungful of air to realise my energy levels were diminished. Joe was close to being counted out and I hoped that would be the case.

I could hear Tim roar encouragement to stand and there were only seconds left. I watched Joe rise to his feet. What was he made of? I became furious that this man was still fighting back. I wasted no time and ran to him. I started to pound him, hoping he would just fall again. He tucked himself into a shell and took the barrage without reply. I continued my assault, watching him take it all. He plodded forward against the onslaught, sinking his weight forward. I used the tip of my elbow to sneak between his guard that connected with the tip of his nose and pinged his head back. I stopped, glanced at him as he smiled back and tucked into a shell again. The pain shot through my chest but I continued to beat on him with everything I had. Weakening, I felt it was inevitable: I could not sustain the pressure.

For more than five minutes, I pounded him without response, as I was persistently pelted by inner shooting pains. He took it all without reply; I was knackered with no strength left and Joe knew that. The pulsating pain drained my strength and rendered me useless.

Joe let his hands drop to his waist and came out of his shell. He smiled at me. At that moment, I wanted to tell him that I was his brother, to stop this madness and I wished I had.

He drew a breath and came for me, in a melee of relenting fury. Punches rattled off me from my waist to my head. I tried to respond but my slack replies were countered by his skilful boxing. The adrenaline that protected me from pain had now diminished. I felt everything from that point until I dropped to one knee again. And then I saw him, in the rear of everyone around the corner from the arch. Davie Rhodes watched his

two sons.

Joe still stood ahead of me, pausing from the barrage as my double vision struggled to focus on him. A savage stab of pain horsed through my heart and I knew I had one punch left; I let it go with all I had left as it coiled across his jaw. It repelled him, momentarily, and then, I saw the end.

I sat hollow over my knees, hung over my waist with my hands drooped by my side. I raised my head as I watched Joe coil his right arm back and beyond him. I saw it unfold, before that bone crunching punch sent me to meet the devil.

Chapter 57

Back to Davies Disappearance:

When Jack opened the door onto Hope Street, I knew the implications of finding Davie again were going to be a hard task. A new challenge had presented itself. Jack rushed us off that street and back into his motor. He got on the buzzer to Bev straight away and asked her if she had seen Davie coming back onto Hope Street but she had not. By the time Jack got to see the footage for himself, Davie was well gone. The footage did show that he had entered a car that was parked outside that door on Hope Street and drove away nonchalantly. You could see me and Jack exit the door where his motor was a mere twenty seconds up the road from us. There was a vein of panic and unrest for the rest of that evening as we returned to the flat to evaluate what we were going to do. The only places I could think of visiting were the arms bunker in Belfast and the Safe house in Carnagh but I was not too sure if I should be letting Jack know about their locations. I slept on it overnight and in the morning when Jack was boiling the water for his cafetiere, I let it slip.

"There's a couple of places we should visit, I mean, that he could be hiding out at," I said, while he had his back to me waiting for the kettle to boil, deep in thought.

"He's a master of hiding, is he not?"

"Aye, he is but these places he frequently visits, I've been to one of them."

"If he's so clever about living like this then why does he keep returning to the same place?" That, I had never thought of before and I wondered why Davie was always safe residing and returning to these locations.

"Because he thinks they're safe," Jack turned around with his cafetiere full and some hope returned.

"Where's the locations?" he asked.

We packed our bags, then grabbed some resources of cash and phones. We both had fake ID's available to us. We jumped in the car, making for Holyhead on the west coast of Wales.

On the way there, Jack stopped in a secluded lay by and stashed his Walter PPK S22 and a couple of spare magazines behind the door card of the passenger's door. He did it quickly and effectively but by the time we got there, we had missed the day's sailing and we waited until morning to sail across the sea to Dublin.

We both relaxed, somewhat knowing we did not have to hide ourselves because we had crossed the water.

We headed for the safe house and on arriving, I could see no cars outside and assumed no one was around. Jack stopped outside and checked the safety catch was off on his gun and prepared to leave the car when I put a hand on his shoulder.

"If there's anyone in there, then I'll go in first." He looked displaced and annoyed.

"Why?"

"Because I know where the key is and if he hears the lock turning with the key then he's going to know it's someone who knows where the key is. You can hide outside, around the corner from the door and I'll lead him out."

Jack agreed and replied. "Okay."

At the door, I slipped my hand behind the gutter where a loose, flat piece of brick lay with enough room to get your fingers into a gap. I grabbed the key and unlocked the door. Jack waited between the door and the living room window.

There were no lights on in the tight lobby and kitchen. There was no noise in the house and I assumed Davie was not there. I investigated the kitchen and turned the light on to reveal a midden of mess. I moved into the sitting room and put the light on. A closed laptop sat on the table, along with a full ashtray and an empty coffee cup. I peered around the room, moving towards the fireplace. On the side table beside the seat stood an empty nip glass and a crushed Export tin. I spied a picture under the tin of export. It was stuck to the table but I peeled it off by scratching my nails under it. The photo showed Davie and another short, bearded dumpy fella, standing arms over each other in a pub, each holding a pint of dark ale in their hands, appearing joyful. In the background, there was a hefty barman and a few others in the room. My eyes then glanced down to a piece of paper stuck down the side of the seat. I bent down to grab it when I heard Jack enter the room.

"He's not here," I said.

"What's that?" he asked, pointing at the laptop.

"That's his laptop."

Immediately Jack moved over, opened it and turned it on.

"What you doing?"

"There might be a world of information on here!" he spurted out.

"Good luck getting into it," I said, as he took no notice. "You'll need to figure out the password." Jack clicked away until it came to the password. "And that laptop will hold no information on it. All it will be used for is getting onto the internet."

His enthralled eyes lifted from the laptop. "Are you sure?" "Hundred per cent sure. He keeps everything he needs to know inside his book and that never leaves his side." Jack closed the laptop, left the room and snooped around the bungalow. I had no idea what information was on that laptop and I did not want Jack looking through it. The only thing he was going to find was rubbish, full ashtrays, old newspapers and bad smells. He returned to the room and sat disheartened by the fire.

"Ok, Kojak, what's the next move?" Jack pondered, as I took the adjacent seat by the fire.

"We can hide out here for a while, but we'll need to think of a way of being close enough to see who comes and goes but far enough away to be unseen."

Jack did not like the sound of that. It was devilishly remote with no other buildings in a five-mile radius, plus it was winter and very cold.

"I thought you said there was a couple of locations?" Jack looked for other actions to take.

"The other one's in Belfast," I replied.

"What is it?"

"It's a church!"

"Let's go to church, then!" Jack insisted and stood up.

Chapter 58

Back to Church:

I was more hopeful of Davie being in the church because the amenities in the basement were more appealing than the safe house and it was a more secluded hideout. In the morning of the next day, I walked Jack into the church as he kept one hand on the handle of his gun.

"This is a church, Jack. You won't need to fire that in here!"

Jack stopped, understood where I was coming from, slid the gun into his chest holster and let his hands hang stiffly by his side. I sat him down in a rear pew allowing him to appreciate the grandeur of the cathedral.

Inside felt more distinct to me as it had done when I visited in the past but I still felt connected to the hollow atmosphere of the vast space. I gazed around, humbled to be inside, blessed even and resonated with parts of it I had not noticed before. I moved, shyly, down the centre aisle, as a white dove unwisely dropped from the air and whisked past my head, flashing back the memory of when the dove flew by, down the tunnel on my way to fight Joe. I watched it fly away down to the altar and felt a wholeheartedly feeling of peace.

I became drawn to the altar and the large cross that hung predominantly with the figure of Jesus tied to it. I halted on the spot as my legs became heavy to lift. I kept turning around, thinking I was being watched or followed, while drifting around in small circles trying to make sense as to why my legs felt so heavy.

The next time I looked in the direction of the cross, I saw the frail, black haired woman at the end of the aisle, the same one I had seen at the rail crossing moments after I came back to life. That time spent in that other place, that place between life and death, returned to me and then I knew who that woman was. It was my Mother, there was no doubt, it had to be. She was watching me, guiding me through the struggle, knowing I was trying to catch Davie.

My concentration was broken by loud clumps of footsteps, offset to the right when the priest, wearing a long white robe, appeared from a far door. He glided past my Mother and stood, at the altar, as if she was not there! He plodded slowly up the aisle, noticing who I was and then turned left towards the elaborate wooden confession box. I followed, shifting my weighted legs in the direction of the box. I entered and waited some seconds for him to speak as I tried to conjure up the reality I was living in, thinking I was going nuts.

"Welcome, child of God, you look lost today!" he said in a shrewd Irish accent.

"I found my way here!" I replied. "You
have finally found your calling?"

I was not sure if that was a question or a suggestion. "I have?" I countered as he slid a key across the wooden latticed opening.

"I have seen the same look on many faces, faces that have been reborn for purpose. I have seen this look in your face today."

I knew exactly what he meant by the 'look'. I did have a calling and I knew that calling was removing Davie from society.

"Has he been here lately?"

The priest mulled over his thoughts for a moment before answering, knowing the thought of Davie being inside the church was a rotten one.

"Sometimes God finds us, and we can repent our sins. Some men are able for this, and some cannot find God for the wrong inside them cannot be replenished by good," he quietened and left me considering the meaning of his words, knowing he referred to Davie. "He was here only yesterday," the priest answered and left.

For a couple of minutes, I sat there trying to fathom why I felt so empowered inside that church. I had been given a second chance, like Lazarus, or had I been brought back to life like Jesus? It was beyond reasoning but one thing I realised was we were always one step behind catching Davie. The weirdly sensations flooding my body were like nudges in the right direction from the other world.

Jack opened the door.

"Well, where are we going?"

I led him down to the basement as he became overwhelmed with the hideout. Once through the steel door at the bottom of the stairs, I flicked the light on. Jack remained quiet and modest as he began to analyse the area, absorbing the environment of a Gunrunner's headquarters. He glanced inside the first couple of cells he could see.

"He has been a busy bastard then," he muttered, meaning he had a level of admiration for Davie as he wandered down the stretch of the room, examining the six cells, all finely kitted out with the means of living underground for many days.

I entered the first one and straight away, I spotted two tins of unopened Export sitting on top of a closed wooden gun create and an empty pistol magazine.

Then my eyes lit up. Beside that was his book, the book that contained all his contacts and snippets of useful information. Without hesitation, I pocketed it before Jack saw it. As Jack continued to snoop around, I tried to work out what that meant. Pretty much every working firearm had been removed from the first couple of cells where they were usually kept and then there were the two full tins of export, plus the book.

I looked intently at the empty magazine that I thought signified that he was finished. The two tins were a gesture to Turk and Bard that they were to take over and the book was the biggest sign of that. Davie was surely following through with the plan that he was going to migrate to Panama and this was his final salute. I had somewhat of a panic there because I had not been told any significant information of that trip or destination. On the lead up to the fight, I was possessed with the idea of destroying my brother and Jack.

I could not be sure he was headed to Panama, as my gut said otherwise. He had just watched one of his sons beat the other to death, and would he not want to confront Joe about that?

Jack returned from his scout around and lit a cigarette, holding it in his right hand, while a half bottle of whisky was in his right. Not often was he lost for words and that was the point he was at. He took a seat on a hardy plastic gun case and opened the bottle.

"As operations go, this is impressive! Are there any signs that he's been here?" Jack asked, as I stood placid and nodded to the tins.

"Theres two tins of export there," I stated and pointed to them. "And he's been here recently: the priest said so."

"It looks like all of his stock is gone; he's sold everything in here."

Jack's business side kicked in. "That means he's getting ready to disappear," Jack stated correctly.

"I don't think he can disappear yet!" I said, as Jack took an optimistic swig of his whisky and a long draw of his cigarette. "There's something I should tell you."

Jack took another long swig from the half bottle before I got down to explaining who Joe Marks was.

Firstly, I described how I came about this information on my last trip to Ireland and then that conversation I had with Mr Dean after I went to his house. It was another kick in the stones for Jack who couldn't believe that he had never known that. He had a lot of knowledge about Davie's life in Aberdeen but somehow, he never made the connection in his head. But as that realisation swept over him, something came into his mind, above and beyond the calamity of having to fight your own brother.

"Wait, Davie watched you two fight, right?"

"Aye, he was there. He seen it."

"Then Davie will want to visit Joe after what he did, will he not? I mean, how can you watch your two sons beat the shit out of each other and for one of them to die, to not want to have a word with him or even kill him in revenge?"

What Jack said was on the money. There was no way Davie could let that lie and that's why my gut told me, he would not head to Panama yet. I glared into a corner of the cell, wondering how I got myself into such a debacle and even before Jack said it, I knew what he was thinking. "Do you know where Joe stays?"

Chapter 59

Turn of the Tide:

We made a bolt out of the cells and jumped back into the car. Immediately we started talking over each other, like small, excited schoolkids organising a plan that was whirling around both our heads. Before we could get further into depth about it, a major news broadcast aired on the radio announcing, C4 Millacky had broken out of Belmarsh prison, and a nationwide man hunt was under way. It also said that he was suspected of trying to rekindle his relationship with Europe's number one most wanted gunrunner, The Eidolon. That put a spanner in the works and dulled our fleeting excitement.

Finding Davie was a mammoth task but right then, it just became harder. It was like locating the corpse of a sabre tooth tiger. In the next few days, pictures of these men dominated the newspapers and tv screens across the UK and Ireland. Regular broadcasts continued to air across many radio stations.

Jack and I checked into the Crowne Plaza hotel that day, where we dined well but slept with difficulty, wondering what we should do.

We decided to continue surveillance on the church and the morning after we re-visited, around nine-thirty, when something miraculous happened. While Jack waited in the car, across the road from the church, I was inside an eating establishment called Hatch, on Cavendish Street, in full view of the church, fetching some coffees with bacon and egg rolls. I walked out, looking at Jack in the driver's seat, the car parked on my side of the road, engine running and heating on full blast, looking directly at me.

I dropped the coffees in disbelief. Across the road, C4 Millacky, wearing a pair of chopper shades, had exited a black Volvo s80, dressed sharp in a pin striped dark suit. He walked fast and heavy and appeared in one hell of a mood. Jack opened the door and stepped out. "You've dropped the coffees!" he announced loudly.

"Shut up and get back into the car!" I ordered and entered the rear onside door.

"What is it?" Jack asked, as I bent down, below the windows.

"Stop looking over there!" Jack picked up on my apprehension and turned around to look forward. He turned the heater off, giving me a chance to think. "That man who just walked into the church is C4 Millacky,"

"Fuck off!" he replied, turning his head around. "Who's the guy in the car?"

"That's Rankin. He works for Davie and he used…Or still does work for Millacky."

"They must be looking for Davie!" Jack stated correctly.

"Aye, and they can't see me. They know who I am and they will know who you are, so stop fucking looking over there!"

Jack switched his gaze back from his driver's window and eyed his mirrors.

"What we going to do here?" I struggled to think of what to do. Should we have followed them? I did not want to take the chance of being seen by either of them.

"We can't follow them, no way. That's way too risky."

"We are after the same man. Should we not try and share information?"

"No, definite no. That man Millacky, Davie cut his feet, stole his operation and he knows who I am. The IRA don't take to kindly to that and he'd shoot me as soon as look at me or torture me to get the information out of me. And we would blow our cover."

As we debated on what to do, we waited. Rankin stayed in the car. Around ten minutes later, C4 Millacky stormed out of the church, pointing a gun at the Volvo and let off four shots, deliberately missing Rankin. I assumed that he had taken a good scan of the cells and realised that Davie had been running wild with his operation.

"Take me to Armagh, you cunt!" Millacky screamed towards Rankin.

"That man has anger issues," Jack said, as I slid further down into the seat.

"Right, take off. Get the fuck away from them!" Jack idolised the size of C4 Millacky's balls momentarily and then calmly pulled away.

"Seems your father is good at making friends."

We drove all the way back to the hotel and pitched up for the day. We discussed an idea we had both already spoken about.

"I think it's the only way now," Jack proposed, without a wrinkle moving.

"It's an insane idea, Jack," I said.

"Sometimes the most insane ideas end up being the creation of genius."

"But it's crazy! How are we going to be able to not be seen by him?"

"Listen, you are looking too deeply into this. It's simple. We find out where he lives, set up close to him, and watch him."

"Then what?"

"Then we wait, and he will appear."

"What about money, Bev, Courtney and my son?" I panicked about being away longer than we had planned. I had amends to make with my family.

"You will see, Max. It will all be worth it, trust me."

Chapter 60

The Journey:

I managed to locate the home of Joe Marks on a street called Baddifurrow in Inverurie, Aberdeenshire. It was so far away from us, it seemed like another country. The plan was to find a property close enough, so we could spy on him and keep tabs on his life. We could not see any other options of finding Davie.

The man lived in obscurity, sure to be in hiding now, scared to surface and suffer the wrath of C4 Millacky or the daunting prospect of facing his biggest fear, spending the rest of his life in jail. There were some sightings of Davie that appeared on the news in the coming day: one in Dundalk in the north of Southern Ireland and another around Dublin. It showed he was heading south, and no other reputable reported sighting followed that. It was official: he had gone underground wherever that might be.

We had to grab onto the last straw and hope he would decide to surface and visit his murderous son in Inverurie. Jack's department was real estate and he got to work on finding a place of residence close to Joe's. Bev assisted him with the task, as she always did, in the background.

We drove up to Inverurie quite quickly having a stopover in Glasgow on the way. Before we entered Inverurie, Jack had a radical change of appearance to aid his disguise. Not seeing it in him to cut his hair off, he tied it back in a bow and wore an old man's styled cap. Still, at his age of late fifties, there was not one tinge of grey coming through. He continued to dress smartly but in more of an `old man, heading down to the Legion smart` with his high buttoned white shirt under a loose blazer. On top of that, he began walking with a stick, pretending he had a bad hip. There wasn't much I could do to change my look. I let my hair grow and always dressed in a way that hid my face with an ever-growing beard, with high-collared jumpers and t-shirts.

We booked into a modest hotel on the outskirts of Aberdeen in an area called Dyce for the first week while Jack started the surveillance and continued to seek accommodation. Bev came back to us who located a two bedroom semi-detached house available for rent on Rashieley Road, the next street from Joe's and we took it.

The back bedroom window looked over the rear of the garden, onto Joes front door and that was good enough for the time being. We both took interest in keeping an eye on this door, but it would only be a short time before we would be accused of being Peeping Toms by someone or being seen. It was evident from the start that the main visitor to Joe's was his close friend, Tim.

Bev got in contact again some weeks later to say that a house had come on the market at the opposite end of the street to Joe. The quiet, mundane street had a line of semi-detached dormer style bungalows that led and ended into a cul-de-sac with a roundabout. Joe's house was tucked into the end of the street at the back of the roundabout. The house that came up for sale was nearer the junction into the street and had a diagonal line of sight to Joes. Jack put in a bid of twenty thousand more than the hundred and sixty thousand asking price on the condition that it was left furnished. It was two-bedroomed house. It took another month for the sale to go through and Jack fast-tracked it as much as he could. He bought it with a fake identity from one of the many aliases that he had and with no face-to-face contact. It was all done through emails and phone calls and my name was never considered.

One point of information that I had gathered about Joe and seeing the comings and goings of people we knew was that his wife and two kids did not stay with him. He had a close friend, Tim, the same guy who accompanied him at the fight, who visited regularly, and they worked together in a scrap metal business they had just started.

Our activity or movement outside of the house was at a minimum, frightened of being seen by Joe. Jack moulded into an old man quite naturally given his late fifties age. He was nonchalant about strolling around the area, regularly making a point in walking around the roundabout past Joe's house. My body started to change somewhat, with no working out or influx of steroids; it became lazy, and I started to lose my muscle definition. It turned to fat and I gained a bigger appetite than ever, allowing my love of food to give me comfort and solitude from regretful memories.

We both knew that this kind of surveillance would not suffice, sitting at the upstairs windows with binoculars poking out the side of a curtain but Jack had already been working on a plan to change that. He paid a security firm to decorate the house with cameras, the very best available so he could zoom in on Joe's house from the outside. The bedroom I was sleeping in turned into a surveillance office, with a PC and a couple of screens installed. For the hell of it, Jack hooked up to his office cameras in Macartney's too where we saw the club and Ringo. It was a means I could use to spy on Courtney too and it broke my heart not being able to talk to her.

She would appear with young Max and show him off to her colleagues and Ringo. It seemed she was often in the office with Ringo. It become a regular occurrence, stopping in on the daily walk and it appeared Ringo was helping her get on with things. Through Beverly, we knew what was happening back home. Young Max was a healthy and happy young soul and Courtney was strict in getting on with life and giving her baby a solid start. She had arranged a private funeral ceremony for me, with around three dozen people turning up. Ringo had taken to his role quite remarkably and looked clean. Like his father, he succumbed to a daily routine of time. We heard that a gang war had broken out in Liverpool after the announcement of Jack's death, in competition for his turf. Regular shootings were reported as crime hit a twenty year high. Ringo involved himself in none of it and ran the club as if it was his sole purpose and future.

Once the camera system had been running for a few weeks, Jack needed something more local to Joe's house. He was anxious to take his surveillance operation further and as he was planning that in the seventh week of being in the house, a new neighbour moved in.

Chapter 61

The Balls of the Man:

One early morning while we were both sharing a coffee, sitting at the desk, we reviewed the night footage, something that we did every day, in case we missed something throughout the night. As usual, nothing could be seen but there was plenty of activity during the day, next door to Joe's. For the past week, his neighbours had been moving out. Something Jack was suspicious of because he had not seen a 'For Sale' sign mounted outside. And that morning, a removals company, in a Luton van, parked over the kerb, and started unloading a host of furniture for the new homeowner. Jack took the telescope lens out of the desk drawer to have a closer look.

"Something's not right here," he mumbled, while the lens was glued to his eye out of the corner of the curtain. "All the furniture being unloaded out of that truck is brand new." I did not think much of it. "It's all brand new. It's all in boxes, boxes of brand-new furniture."

"And?" I questioned.

"When you move house, you usually wait until you get in before buying new furniture and who do you know that buys it all beforehand and stores it somewhere?"

"How do you know it's been stored?"

"Well, that's a removal company, not a furniture company, so all that stuff they are unloading has been taken from one place … a place of storage." Jack put the lens down and stepped back. Something did not seem right to him.

I grabbed the lens and had a look for myself. I watched two lads unload a fridge, a washing machine and a freezer, all still boxed. They were hardy looking men and worked diligently at the task. Watching it made more sense to me: who buys an entire house worth of brand-new furniture?

The houses in the street were only worth an average of a hundred and seventy grand and who had the spare change from that to fit out an entire house with brand new gear?

As I kept an interested observation, a Honda Accord drove into the cul de sac and parked behind the tail lift of the van. An average heighted man with flappy brown hair past his shoulders, wearing dark jeans and a thick, puffy jacket got out. It was not too sunny but he wore a pair of sleek shades.

"Here, look! This must be the owner," I said.

"Really!"

"Aye, must be. He's standing glaring at his house. Ohh …. hold on, he's talking to the removal men now and he's wandering inside. That's him, that's the owner."

"Have you seen his face yet?" Jack asked, as I watched him hover by the front door, waiting for him to walk out, face first.

"He's just aw…"

"What?"

"Holy Christ of Jesus, Jack!"

"What?"

"I can't believe my eyes!"

"Why? What? Who is it? Is it Davie?"

"No, it's…Rankin!" Jack snatched the lens from my hand and looked for himself.

"That's the guy who was with Millacky in Belfast! What the fuck's he doing here?"

"The exact same thing as we are. He's after Davie, too!" "This is getting complicated," Jack said, with accuracy. I was doomed now because there was no way I could be seen by him. There would be little disguise that he could not see through. I knew C4 Millacky would have sent him there. Davie often said that the IRA used any family connection of the fugitive to gain any advantage they could. Normally that would mean torture but, in this case, there would be no point in torturing Joe because he knew nothing of Davie's whereabouts and that is why C4 Millacky had used a different tactic of moving Rankin in next door. Just the kind of task that sniffy cunt would be good at. Rankin would know the appearance of Jack as well and that complicated things even further. Our task, as difficult and challenging as it was, was then multiplied by ten.

"Look. Joe's coming home!" Jack said, while watching Joe being driven home by Tim in a rusty and rundown, silver middle wheelbase Vauxhall van.

I brushed the curtain aside and stood alongside Jack as he gave me a look through the lens. I watched as Tim mounted the kerb as the Luton van had. Joe and Tim both exited the van and Rankin, wasting no time, danced over to introduce himself before they could make it up the path into the house. They shook hands, then Joe and Tim walked into his house. Rankin had his shoulder to us. A few calm moments passed as he began to turn his head in our direction. I darted away from the window in fear of being spotted and grabbed Jack's shoulder on the way to the ground.

I knew then that this surveillance operation we were running would not suffice. Standing, gazing outside the upper bedroom window, taking notes of comings and going of people and relying on an evening camera to record the footage we would miss while sleeping.

Jack was thinking the exact same thing. "We need to make some adjustments," he said, exchanging similar bewildered looks.

Chapter 62

Expansion:

Jack was a multi-millionaire who had the money to spend. Even being as tight as he was back home, it did not influence his spending. His resolve in snatching Davie from his unknowing drove all his ambition, it became an obsession for him because it was the wining and the outsmarting of Davie that was the real victor. Now, there was Rankin to deal with and hiding from him was the bigger challenge. We had to take parameters of perfection to new levels that Jack had never portrayed before and I had to live on that same wavelength. He suggested installing a sophisticated bugging system, envious of a MI5 spy program, on both houses. I did not offer an argument and the first dilemma was getting inside both houses.

"We can pick the locks!" I said enthusiastically.

"No, we can't stand on a doorstep in broad daylight and pick a lock! It'll take too long and attract attention. It must be quick and smooth."

"We could be locksmiths!" I countered.

"On both houses, on the same day! No, that won't work," he said, while quizzing himself about something. "There's another way. There's these things called bump keys. I've never used them, but they work. All you do is slide the key in the lock, pull it out a fraction, hit it with a hammer where it slots into all the tumblers inside the lock."

"That easy?" I replied slackly as Jack went on to investigate the type of lock by using the lens and a pair of binoculars, but he needed a quick walk by the house when they were both next out and he discovered the model of the lock. After, he ordered the same lock to the house and the appropriate set of bump keys that would work with that lock.

When they arrived, he ripped off a cupboard door from the kitchen and fitted a lock onto it, practised for hours using the bump keys and mastered it.

Jack knew we had to get into Rankin's house first and quickly because he was erratically coming and going, during day and night while he was moving stuff in. Jack had the idea of fitting hidden cameras, disguised as smoke alarms. The chances of Rankin recalling what his smoke alarms looked like so early since his house move were low. We struggled to think why Rankin was appearing for a day then disappearing again but we both knew it was something to do with orders coming from C4 Millacky.

We hired a van and disguised ourselves as electricians, with a cheap tool kit, carbon fibre yellow steps and half a dozen smoke detectors. Disguised under thick collars, bump caps and boiler suits, we approached the door at nine am on a Tuesday morning, after Tim had picked up Joe.

Jack bent down and pretended to remove a key from under a stone at the side of the footstep. I had the hammer at hand, ready for his request when he slipped the bump key into the lock and drew it back a tiny fraction before twisting it to the right, so that it was lodged. I passed the hammer and hid him from any onlookers.

With one hit, the key slipped into the slots. Jack turned the key, and we were in.

The house looked modern, with tasteful wallpaper and carpets from the previous owners. All the furniture was brand new so it looked more like a show house than someone's home. There, we ran the gauntlet because we had no idea when Rankin would be coming back. A slack move by both of us.

Jack had all the understanding of how to fix and connect the detectors. I only assisted by handing him tools and keeping a look out. All the smoke alarms in the house had already mains power in them. That was the genius part of the installation because that served to power the cameras. The camera system had an internal SD card that recorded on a loop, so once it was full, it would rewind to the beginning and record over footage. It used a sim card to send the footage, and recorded sound, to a software system so we could hook up to it from the comfort of our house. With that one prepared, we repeated the same technique in Joe's house about three days later, but his smoke detectors were much older, worn and discoloured, compared to our new ones.

This time I took our motor and parked a good distance from the house on the incoming route from Aberdeen, at our side of the bridge that crossed the river Don. Tim and Joe usually entered from that side. I was on stakeout in case they appeared, and I could inform Jack to get out. But I had not heard from Jack for far too long. He called around lunch time after he had been in the house for three hours.

"There's a problem with these," he said. "I'm having to take the guts out of our smoke detectors and put them into the original detectors, cos he will notice the new shiny ones." He did not look panic-stricken but seemed confident.

"How long's that going to take?" I asked, worried about how much time we had.

"I've just managed to do the first one. I'll need a few more hours."

Joe and Tim never returned home at the same time so it would be an anxious time.

"Okay, keep your phone close. If it rings at all, you'll know you need to leg it."

Jack carried on and I waited patiently.

A few hours had passed and I had not heard from him. At around two forty-five, I could see Tim's van at the other side of the bridge. I tried to call Jack, but I had no signal; I panicked and tried again. I could not get through; it would not ring. I had to think fast as the van was coming across the bridge where it would take a left onto the road I was sitting on. I flopped up my hood and started the engine. I began to do a slow three-point turn to block the traffic on both sides as I repeatedly tried to get through to Jack.

Tim and Joe stopped in my eye line and started sounding the horn as I continued to do the turn at snail's pace. I avoided looking to my right, devastated should I be recognised. Still, I could not get through to Jack as I reversed to the kerb, knowing I had to move and knowing that they probably recognised our car from the street.

My heartbeat accelerated into overdrive as Tim peeped his horn frantically and I caught sight of Joe waving his arms in the air, becoming agitated. The whole operation was on the line if either of them recognised me.

Joe jumped out of the van, a cigarette hanging from his mouth, and stomped over angrily as I watched him from my side view mirror. Less than a couple of metres away, I thought the sting was up as, finally, Jack's phone began to ring.

I sank my foot on the pedal and pulled away. It was a close call as I drove past the street where our house was, allowing Tim to turn in. I gave it half an hour before returning to the house to find Jack peacefully sitting upstairs, setting up the cameras on the laptop, providing views of Joe's house.

After that, we decided we needed a GPS tracker on Tim's van. We fixed it to the chassis using a magnet and bounced a live signal from the satellite to the laptop through some downloadable software. We ordered four so we could swap them round when the batteries failed.

Chapter 63

The Task:

The enduring task became a monotonous drag of boredom as time passed like that screeching noise that occurs when you drag chalk across a board. For Jack, he loved it; the thrill of the chase and he quickly adapted to the new way of life.

I took the opportunity to get my teeth fixed, so I booked an appointment at a private dentist in Aberdeen and had two broken teeth removed. I got three crowns fitted and I felt great afterwards for it. The distraction was welcomed and I took advantage of it by having a few days stay in the city.

My thoughts rarely drifted from Courtney and young Max. To think I had a family in Liverpool and was missing the early stages of my son's life, infuriated me. Jack regularly talked to Bev, but I couldn't talk to anyone. I think that's what kept him sane. I was missing my child growing into the world and even more, I missed Courtney. I had stacks of regret over the last months we were together and my inability to give her the emotional connection that she needed. Why she stuck with me, I did not know and could not work out. But I did realise that I had taken her for granted for many years and I needed to tell her that to make amends. I longed for Davie to turn up and I doubted that would ever happen every soul sucking day after day.

I kept a close eye on my brother trying to form an image of what kind of man he was. He smoked like a chimney but I had never seen him drunk. Once or twice a week, he went out jogging but seemed happy gaining a gut from somewhere. He kept himself private and didn't seem to have much of a social circle, apart from Tim bringing his wife, Dawn, over with their twin kids. An older lady called Margaret also often visited; she owned a pub, the Fountain, in Aberdeen where Joe used to work and stay. The other person who kept himself heavily involved in his social circle was his neighbour, Ben! There was one thing that entertained and fascinated both of us and that was Rankin. It became evident that he was a double agent to C 4 Millacky. He had his own gunrunning operation going, one making Davies look pathetically insignificant and went by the name Lucille. We were picking up all kinds of conversations to heads of Interpol, MI5, G2 and various crime syndicates throughout Europe, setting up transfers of arms between gangs, armies and countries. Often the goal was to capture and arrest these gangs. Rankin was a dirty snake, playing both sides to a remarkably high degree. And there was us, spying on him from a house at the end of the street, with more information on his activities than anyone else.

We did not realise this for a good four months, but Rankin was not alone in the area and had two shifty associates who were in the vicinity. They visited the house one day, and we recognised them both as being the two removals men that unloaded the Luton truck full of brand-new furniture. I followed them and marked their location at the other end of Inverurie, shacked up in a bungalow. These two men were backup to Rankin if Davie did appear. They held the standard, dubious low-key attitude of the IRA in operation and we hardly saw them, but we had been made aware of them, so we got a GPS tracker on their blacked-out Range Rover. They were Turk and Barb, the other members of Davie's stable, loyal IRA men. They were probably under the spell of C4 Millacky and I would use that to my advantage. My suspicions about Rankin were confirmed. On two gun deals I had partnered with him, one with Mr Dean and the other in London, there was a quick influx of the authorities charging in. I think that he was trying to get me busted to get me out of the picture. To think that not long after getting out of jail, I was so close to returning.

I did not have that much more hate to give but a slab of me wanted payback for that.

Rankin had an office area in an upstairs room where we watched him on his computer on various arms sites and news reels. He had a wealth that could not be imagined, and various offshore bank accounts scattered everywhere. Using a lot of patience with mixed frustration, time and zooming into Rankin's laptops, Jack had acquired the usernames, passwords and pin codes of Rankin's accounts. He birthed a new ambition where he prepared to take all his wealth and he predicted the death of Rankin.

He had disguised himself as a computer programmer called Ben, who kept his Irish twang and said he had moved across from Belfast to a new job for a start-up software company in Aberdeen. He had a whole divorce story to go along with that, all fabricated bullshit. He became friendly with Joe, becoming a regular visitor at their house and a good shoulder to rely on.

As time passed, slowly for us, Rankin became so friendly with Joe that it got to the point where Joe had revealed everything about his life one evening and told the story of how he defeated and killed me in a fight.

I had listened to it all and heard the remorse in his words of how he let his addiction to fighting go that far; it had ruined his marriage and took away his children. His wife, May, had left him and took the kids where he was battling to see them again. That broke him apart. It took eight months of negotiations between solicitors and the social services before he was blessed with the company of his kids again. I admired that and watched a man share real love with his kids. The kind of love I idolised sharing with mine one day.

Rankin was an actor and the best one Jack had ever seen. His relationship with Joe was remarkable; like a manipulating girlfriend, he slithered in and out of his life at will.

Every now and again, Rankin would receive phone calls from C4 Millacky where he had to update him on Joe's activities. Millacky himself was looking for Davie, sure that he had recently been filled with the knowledge that Davie was the one who grassed on their operation that got him and a large quantity of his IRA troops arrested. He had been searching around Ireland with no luck. Word had it, that he had already reinforced his confederacy of willing soldiers, using their devoted loyalty to aid him in his hunt for Davie with a bounty on his head.

The pains in my heart came and went, and at no point did they seem like stopping. The years of steroid abuse had caught up and it looked like a lasting side effect that would not leave me. I lived with it, and I lived enclosed inside those house walls. I used the late evenings to go for walks, to clear my head and get a break from Jack. My time in jail hardened me to isolation and compared to that place, that type of reality was luxury. Nothing seemed to affect Jack. He was solid twenty-four seven and was always confident that Davie would surface from hiding, requiring retribution for my death.

What we were going to do with Davie once he was captured formed a lively debate between Jack and me. Jack wanted to shoot him and bury him in a forest somewhere. He did not require him to suffer; he only wanted him dead so the rotten stage in his existence could end. I was adamant that was not the answer. As much as I now loathed him, I did not want his death on my conscience and I did not believe in any kind of violence anymore, but I would commit one more atrocity for the safety of my future. Who would want the death of their father on their conscience!

It took some time, but Jack came around to my way of thinking, of having him jailed. My decision, that I withheld from Jack, was to have him inducted into Belmarsh where a welcomed reunion with the IRA members he grassed on awaited him. That sounded far more satisfying than a quick bullet. There was no way Davie would see the outside world again with the abundance of terrorist charges that were about to be levelled at him and that's what convinced Jack.

After a year and a half into our sentence had passed, my addiction to steroids had firmly subsided and had been replaced with food. My ripped and bulking frame had sagged and withered which curdled with a dense state of depression. I went through chronic slumps because of the frustration that mixed with the solitude. I felt, as time went on, I got closer to the edge of giving up and many times Jack had to talk me out of leaving. One evening, well past the hour of ten, I was sitting on the sofa with a bag packed full of my clothes at my side, hearing Jack stride downstairs, whistling. He walked past the opening on the way to the kitchen and then returned, tilting his head to the bag.

"What's this?" he asked although he had already worked out what I was doing.

"I'm done. This is fucking madness!" I belched out

"You're not done, and neither am I until he makes an appearance." Jack had been here before and talked me out of leaving half a dozen times. That time I was dead serious. "No, I'm not asking," I said, as I stood up. "I'm going home, to see my kid." My voice started to rise.

"You will not go anywhere!" Jack countered, while he pointed his finger into my chest.

"Who the fuck lives like this? Who the fuck does this kind of thing?" I backed away from Jack, taking me further into the room.

"Max, how many times do we have to do this? Take yourself out for a walk and come back when you've calmed."

I huffed and puffed, prancing around the room with my fists tense. So, I did what he implied and went for a long walk. That walk that evening saved my sanity and calmed me right done because I gained new hope.

For the following weeks, I was thankfully calmer and more assured of what we were doing would work out in the end, even though it was approaching two years   in that house. For a long while, for me, it seemed as if that was going to be our lives for as long as we lived but I had hope.

It was around mid-afternoon on a warm Sunday. We sat in the sitting room having a coffee with the blinds open a slither, enough to see out and pick out cars and people. Jack's seat looked directly onto the road as he talked about how Bev and how Ringo was getting on at the club after they had a lengthy conversation the night before. As ironic as it sounded, they seemed to live more uplifted lives without Jack there, but I was not to say that to his face.

"Ringo gave the place a decoration, suppose it needed it. I can always change it when I get back."

"When's that going to be, Jack? How long are we going to do this!"

Jack rolled his eyes. "Again, this conversation." His mood became aggravated. "You think, I want th…" He stopped in mid-sentence as his jaw dropped to the floor.

"Jack, you all right? Looks as if you're having a stroke."

"You think I want the same thing," He finished his sentence hesitantly and stood up, holding his coffee cup waist-high and walked over to the window. He pulled the blinds open a little, staring down the street towards Joes.

"There's the fucker!"

I followed him to the window and watched Davie thumping down the road!

Chapter 64

The Last Lap:

Jack burst out of the room, grabbed his shoes and his gun. He ran back into the sitting room, sat down and put his shoes on, foaming at the mouth with excitement. He returned to the window.

"He's nearly at his door," Jack explained. "Right, are you ready, Max?" he barked, as I stood remarkably calm. "This is it, the time we've been waiting for."

We had discussed this moment several times and never did we agree on a solid plan. The one flaw in his operation was the invisibility of what would occur at that moment. We knew Rankin would play a considerable part when Davie arrived at the door, and we were right.

Jack returned to the window and right on cue, Rankin exited his house discreetly. He passed over his garden and arrived at Joe's door. Rankin sneaked up on Davie from the rear and lay his gun at his head. Seconds later, the door shut behind them.

In Joe's backyard, he was having a barbeque. Tim, his wife, and kids along with Margaret were all there. An added dilemma to the situation.

Jack's idea was to hijack them at some point, whether it would be at the door or from the inside of a motor vehicle. Jack's plan was vague and unprofessional, and I had a better one.

"Right, start the car and drive it closer to the house. I'm heading over to the door and waiting until someone comes out."

Jack had become delirious, retreating from any kind of rational thought. He was desperate but I was not. The entire sacrifice of my life came down to that point.

"What are you doing? No time for second thoughts. Let's move!" he said, as he edged to the outside door.

What I did next was rational in my mind but not in Jack's. I took my phone out of my pocket and sat down. "What the fuck are you doing? Move!" He yelled in my face.

I waited for him to quieten down.

"I'll do this myself, you cowardly cunt," Jack said. "That would be irresponsible, and we have to wait a few moments before we leave."

Jack was bamboozled at my attitude. "We have to wait until Rankin sends a message for pickup!"

"What?"

"There's no need to panic. I have it all sorted." It was then that Jack knew I had been doing something deceitful, so I proceeded to tell him.

With my growing frustration of living a deserted life, a few months prior, I was gifted with an idea and a radical one at that. I was in the same mood then, that I was in that day. I was boiled up and ready to go back to Liverpool without Jack's approval. On that evening, I had gone for a long walk according to Jack's instructions to try and calm down. I did not know where it was taking me until I realised, I was in the vicinity of Turk and Barb's house which was close to the local swimming pool.

I considered an idea that sprang to my mind right on the spot there. Desperation can sometimes make you do silly things. I approached the house and knocked on the door. It took a few knocks but eventually Turk opened it up.

"What can I do for you?" he asked, in his distinguished Irish while his face stiffened up.

"I was hoping we could have a chat!" It was not until after he heard my accent, that he knew who it was.

"Jesus, Mary and Joseph. You're supposed to be dead." Turk said, as Barb appeared behind him.

"Fuck me," said Barb, gasping for thought.

"Don't suppose you know where your father is?" Turk asked. They invited me inside the house where I was interrogated, peacefully: firstly, about how I was still living which they accepted quickly; then, I had to explain why I was in Inverurie and where I was staying and who with. It was a lot of information to absorb and I had to repeat it many times. They were good listeners and detached from any need to panic.

"So, you're up here living on the same street as the brother, the same brother who thinks he killed you!" Turk stated.

"That's right."

"I've processed this information and I am struggling to come to no other arrangement than to say you are waiting for your father to appear!" I was glad Turk arrived at that conclusion.

"That is correct!"

The twins blithely exchanged fascinated expressions, and both sat down after a marathon of striding back and forth. They had been reprimanded by C4 Millacky for their actions of working with Davie, as had Rankin, and their punishment was to live a mundane life with no excitement, waiting for their old boss to turn up. My guess was that would be their last task in this life before C4 Millacky ended their lives for their discourtesy towards him and the IRA.

"Combining all my years of experience, I take it you are here for a reason!" Barb insisted.

I then explained that Rankin was a grass and outlined the operation he was running from his house. I made up random bullshit, that Rankin had a bunch of incriminating evidence against them, kept in a digital file, ready to use if necessary. I used this to try and enlist their aid.

"That's Lucille!" the twins uttered with revelation at the same time. They then explained that there was this Rogue informant who was the cause for so many deals being busted and men landed with long jail terms. It was the first I'd heard of the name as the twins continued. "I know a man who would require this information a bit more than us," Turk said.

"I know that man is Millacky and that's the reason for my visit," I said.

"Go on!" Turk barked. I explained the fact that both of us were waiting for Davie to appear and both of us wanted him. I was bargaining with them to let me have him in exchange for all the information I had on Rankin. But that was not their decision; that belonged to Millacky. I was then in too deep to retreat, as Turk entered the kitchen to make a phone call, leaving me with the quiet Barb, who said nothing. Turk returned.

"Be here tomorrow evening," he insisted.

I returned the following evening to be escorted into the living room and greeted by the infamous C4 Millacky who sat in subdued lighting, dressed in a suave, dark navy suit and open buttoned shirt.

"The son of Davie Rhodes! This is a delicate surprise for me. I know you worked for your father and that is not nearly as serious a situation as it should have been in other circumstances. Sit down!" I obliged and sat. He had an aura around him. He acted and smelt of wrongness; he carried that murderous stench with him like a sour whiff of sweat. As I sat, he fixed his agitated emerald eyes on me, unwilling to draw away. "Leave us alone, boys!" C4 Millacky ordered as the twins left the room.

"Now, I have been informed by the twins that you have invaluable information for me."

"I do," I answered, going on to explain all the information that we had found out about Rankin which completely surprised him. His insides flamed with revulsion, but his outer attitude never changed; soon enough, he wanted to know the bargaining which led to this information. I went on to suggest that things be left as they were until Davie turned up. When that happened, then I would give him Rankin and I would get Davie, but he was not sold on that idea.

"You put me in a difficult position. Your father is the reason I rotted inside that jail and he infiltrated my gun-running operation. Normally, men don't get to bargain with me and neither are they allowed to live to tell the tale. I only know of your father's influence in my arrest, due to an anonymous letter I received in Belmarsh. You have brought information to me that everyone in the circuit will be glad to hear of. This Lucille entity has floated around for some time and I, along with a collection of people, will be very glad of his demise."

"It was me," I replied, as Millacky observed me with some respect. He uncrossed his legs and sat up.

"You sent the letter!" he asked.

"I did!" I knew that would help my cause.

"Mr Rhodes has caused me a considerable amount of aggro but your dedication to finding him is somewhat admirable. I dread to think how he's influenced your path."

"He has to pay for what he did to me!"

"And how shall he pay?"

"Once I catch him, he will rot the rest of his life in jail." Millacky bit his lip, disagreeing with my ethics.

"Jail will not bring him much pain, Max. You have to think through the minds of the IRA. Prolonged torture is the way with the stairs to Hell at the end."

"I do believe it will be the way because he's going to Belmarsh, where a lot of your associates have been imprisoned because of him." He caught me out by standing up suddenly, firmly knowing that Davie, being sent down to Belmarsh, would experience a life of torture with no fairy godmother to save him.

"Stand up," he ordered and offered his hand to shake. Sheepishly, I did stand and I took his offer, feeling the coldness of his hand, reverberating chills up my spine.

"There is a place in the IRA for you," he said, as a corner of his mouth lifted with glee, showing the darkness of his character, full of scorned pride for his beloved IRA. He drew away his hand and walked towards the door.

"What about Rankin?" I asked, as he stopped and squared up to me.

"My only demand is that you kill him, Max," he said coldly and walked out of the room.

C4 Millacky left at that point as Turk and Barb returned. We went through the scenario if Davie turned up. Rankin was to message or call when it happened, Turk and Barb would scoot over with the vehicle that Davie was supposed to be thrown into and transferred to C4 Millacky.

That would not happen now and a new plan was formulated. When Turk or Barb received the call or message, they would inform me and then drive over, as planned, in their blacked-out Range Rover where we would do a switch over into the vehicle. Jack and I would replace them and appear to be Turk and Barb at the door of Joe's house.

Around three days before we saw Davie, I received an unexpected phone call from C4 Millacky on the landline. It was fortunate that I answered the call and not Jack.

"Young Rhodes," he said. "Aye!" I answered, knowing who it was.

"I have just received a very interesting phone call from your father. He tells me that Rankin is Lucille and I acted shocked. I expressed my wrath on both him and

Rankin over the phone." Vibrantly, he explained how the conversation went. "Now, we struck a deal of neutrality and he thinks he will get off scot free for bending me over backwards and fucking me. But we are no different and what I'm telling you is that he has surfaced from his seclusion. I felt he was filled with an expectation of salvation." The line went quiet as he prepared his last message. "Remember and do as I requested or else I will have my own salvation to seek…Young Rhodes."

What I gathered from that conversation was that Davie was on the way.

All of this was explained to Jack while I got the message from the twins, and we waited for them to arrive. We were to meet them well before they came into vision off the street to avoid Rankin spotting any movement. Before they did, I needed to confirm something with Jack as I looked to the gun in his hand.

"Do you have a silencer for that?"

"It's upstairs," he answered, as I took the gun from his hand. After telling him that story, he had lost his superiority in the relationship, and I was allowed to take the gun from his hand without question.

"Get it. I'll need it."

Chapter 65

The Gamble:

The formidable gamble played by Jack and myself had paid off in a spectacular way. We lived as dead men for too long, sacrificed so much, but the day of reckoning had arrived. The cost to our lives and the desolation of leaving our loved ones behind became worth it. Davie Rhodes, my Father, was handcuffed, duck taped, and shocked to his core sitting in the back of the Range Rover, next to the treacherous and deceased rat Rankin. Davie was more confused over the fact I wasn't decomposing at the bottom of the Mersey, than Rankin's death. And then there was Jack's heart, which supposedly packed in a few days after my demise, was still beating, and a satisfying beat at that.

My intangible Father had finally turned up at my brother's door. It was a calculated gamble and the circumstances of this plan to phase out was so miraculously farfetched we doubted ourselves from the minute go, but two emotionally draining years had ended. The thoughts of returning to our own lives, seeing loved ones we missed, and no longer having to live in patience of a certain presence to appear, was utterly brilliant.

We played the long game, a game Davie liked to play, and it materialised better than we could've ever imagined. Davie's worst nightmare of decaying behind bars for the rest of his days was close to fruition. Even though Rankin had planned on handing him to C4 Millacky, where a punishing end to life was forecast, I intended on delivering that harsh end to his life, but in more poetic way. All we needed to do was hand him in to the authorities where a cruel motive drew my desire for Davie's sentence. Knowing he'd get homed inside a maximum-security jail because   of his reputation, Belmarsh, the same one as C4 Millacky and all his goons served time in. A bleak future awaited him.

As Jack started the engine, I turned to double check Rankin, or should I say Lucille, had no pulse. Sitting latent with his head tilted back and eyes pulsed open holding a surprised gaze, he was dead alright. The bullet I fired landed straight into his heart and the aftermath spurts of blood glistened across Davie's famous bomber jacket and grim face as he gazed at me like a phantom. I'm sure he reckoned we were inside the motor to save his life; how wrong he was. There was no sorrow or guilt of having to kill Rankin, he deserved it for being a rat.

The initial shock was passing as Davie began mumbling through the duct tape. At first Jack and I ignored his call of attention but after only a minute it pissed me off, I knew he wouldn't stop until he had his say. I shared a glance with Jack.

"Don't do it kid, you'll regret it." Jack insisted. He was aware I was thinking of removing the gag. After all, this car journey would be the last moments I'd ever spend with my Father. Jack was right, Davie had a habit of slithering out of unforeseen situations and this was one of those he'd be typical to riddle out of. I wanted to gloat toward his misfortune, so I hesitated no more, swung round in my seat and ripped the tape off in a quick swipe.

"What kind o' game you playin' here boy?" His tone was sharp, his question being more of a statement indicating he thought I'd saved him from his impending doom, or should I say Lucille. No hello or how are you son, just straight into his desperation to be unconstrained.

"Game! This is no game, and if it was, I've learned from the best." I turned to look out the windscreen and focus on the road as it signified the end of a loathsome journey. The closeness of our bodies wasn't filling me with pleasantry. I could almost hear his deceitful thoughts, running through scenarios of how this was possible and how he could attempt to wriggle out of his dilemma.

"So, come on 'en boy, tell yer old man, what's goin' on here?" His voice crackled in aggravation and again Jack and I shared a look of wondering if we would play his game.

"You'll find out soon enough," I answered, absent of any empathy.

Davie leant forwards and his coarse breath on the back of my neck made me shiver. I waited for him to shout abuse as that sentence surely indicated we were handing him over to the authorities. There he knew, his capture from Joe's house was a well-constructed plan, so implausible, so mind blowing, so finely calculated, Sherlock Holmes himself would find it most improbable, and all Davie was trying to do was fathom out what the fuck just happened.

"Son, I don't know how ye've pulled this off, but I'd suggest not handin' me in just yet. And where's Millacky?" Davie asked, making an attempt to squirm his way inside my head, but I wasn't letting his conniving ways affect me. I'd waited too long for this moment. Davie somehow thought C4 Millacky was part of this plan, and he was right about that.

"You don't have to worry about him," I answered coyly, and took a slow swivel around on the leather seat.

"Why don't you get comfortable Da' and I'll tell you all about it."

Chapter 66

The Last Ride:

It was almost done; we had the bastard. The jubilant feeling that was sailing through Jack was vivid with joy. My satisfaction was purring but the task was not yet complete. What we had to do now was rendezvous with the police branch in Aberdeen. Before we set off, I put a baseball cap over Rankin's head and squashed a rolled-up jumper against the window, to make it look as if he was asleep, and wiped away any obvious blood splatters.

Turk and Barb were following us from behind as we left Inverurie, making for Aberdeen.

"Old Davie Rhodes," Jack gloated as Davie's eyes burst wide with a confused outrage. "This is an emotional day in my life."

"Are you still a tight cunt Jack?" Davie said, hoping to tilt the gloating tone of his voice but there was nothing that could be said to tilt Jack's joy. Right there my heart went into a spasm again as I gipped my chest and groaned.

"What's wrong son?" Davie echoed from the back and demanded, "Jack, stop the car!" Jack checked me, sure it was going to pass, as the rest of them did. He had seen it happen for two years now.

"Don't stop," I mouthed to Jack as the spasm receded.

"Yer no' in a good way son, you need to see a doctor."

"We should've left that duct tape on," Jack stated.

"Let's stop playin' games here, yer supposed to be dead an' so is Jack! What's goin' on?" Davie was rightly desperate because he had no idea how long he had to talk himself out of this. I chose to keep my feelings to myself pleased that it was almost all over. I allowed Jack to spout the story of what happened after the fight and he did with so much pleasure and authority. Davie quietened during that time, amazed at the dedication Jack had put in but more surprised with my deceitful nature, but I learned from the best. Davie had seen what admiration Jack had for me and he thought I replicated those feelings towards Jack.

"Was that cunt part of this?" He referred to Joe. "Or this cunt?" he insinuated towards the body of Rankin.

"Joe had nothing to do with it and Rankin was merely and inconvenience," I answered.

"You talk smart now-a-days, surely spent too much time wi' Jack." Davie said and took a remote silence, knowing his life as he knew it was dissolving but he did need to know one thing. "You've got ma money have you boy?" He wondered and he wondered right.

"Aye, I've got it, every cent you had in that account is now in my name," I answered as Jack cocked his head to me in surprise.

"It was you!" He muffled. "How did you get into ma account?" Davie wondered.

"It was as easy as opening your book and taking pictures of the pages inside it!" The time I travelled over to Ireland to visit Davie in the safe house in Carnagh, I walked into the kitchen, where there, amongst the mess, his book sat on the counter, and I took as much pictures as I could with my phone. After analysing it for months

I figured out what his passwords were. Davie was deeply miffed and became distant only to speak a few minutes later.

"Has he told you Max; Jack have you no' told him?" I looked at Jack who avoided eye contact.

"Told me what?" I turned to Jack as he drew his eye.

"I can't believe it, he hasn't told ya!" Davie said solidly.

"What?" I countered to both men.

"Your mother Max, Jack knew her, didn't you Jack!"

"Whatever he's about to tell you, remember he is trying to get out of this!" I became perplexed and concerned. I did not oblige anyone to talk, and I could not ask again.

"Jack will tell you the story son, or at least he should but he won't so I'll crack on wi' it." My heart vibrated with a nervous shiver.

"This is lies Max, remember, lies." Jack repeated.

"She was one of Jack's girls, worked in his brothels and was kind o' keen on the brown." I looked at Jack's wrinkled face as it hardly moved and avoided taking me on. "She got pregnant see and hid that from her mighty boss. She kept it a secret, even from me. I liked her, she was sweet, and so did all her punters, and there was a lot o' 'em." A tear retracted from my eye.

"Max, don't react," Jack said.

"She disappeared without tellin' her boss and turned to me for help. I set her up in a wee bedsit and made sure she had enough money to see her through. Jack looked for her, but he never found her until after you were born. I couldn't be around all the time cos I was in Aberdeen for most of it. I sent her some siller and that was all I could do. No' known to ma at the time but you were ma son, the chances o' that were out o' this world and I didn't know until Jack here did a DNA test without tellin' anyone."

I kept a tight hold of Jack who was still unwilling to take me on.

"The bad thing about ye're mum, she liked the brown, a lot. Jack became short o' girls and once he found her, he put her back to work, against her wishes of course. She was a mess and I saw it wi' ma own eyes when I returned to do a job for Jack that he couldn't be arsed doin' for himself." Jack opened his nostrils and marginally shook his head. "Now, on complete coincidence, when I visited her, at the brothel, I found her comatose wi' a needle sticking out o' her arm. I tried to revive her but there was no chance o' that, she was gone. Died on Jack's take!"

"Is this true?" I pierced Jack solidly.

"Some of it has truth but he's manipulating you," he answered while keeping a hard focus on driving.

"And you were there, in a spare room cryin' yer lungs out, only a couple months old. I couldn't leave you there, so I took you to a church!" The motor was approaching a checkpoint, Kirkhill Forest. I had texted Turk and Barb and asked them to follow me in.

"Jack pull into the next left; we need to get rid of some dead weight!" There were a few other cars parked in a single-spaced row of parking slots on the edge of the forest. Jack parked and I jumped out. Turk and Barb arrived behind us. I opened the back door and waited for the twins to head over. I let Rankin's weight sag and then lifted him out with the twins help.

"You pair o' cunts in on this too?" Davie moaned as the twins did not so much as look at him, annoying him further with their blatant uncaring and disrespect for him. Rapidly we got Rankin into their car, on a one-way delivery to C4 Millacky so he could do what he wished with the leftovers.

"Thanks for the help," I said to Turk and Barb honestly. They both nodded and returned to their car. I watched them drive off, took a deep breath, and braced myself for the final journey.

We were approaching Queen Street Police headquarters in Aberdeen, the final destination for Davie Rhodes, the number one wanted man in Europe. Jack squinted his eyes on approach as a convoy of participants waited on our arrival.

"Jesus, are they expecting us?"

Jack became edgy.

Chapter 67

The Arrival and Departure of a Legend:

There was a convoy of vehicles and a collaboration of authorities all keen to witness the arrest of the fugitive. It portrayed a carnival of hungry civil servants, dubious and longing to witness the arrest in person. Davie had accepted his forthcoming arrest and knew he would not get out of this one. Jack became alert because he knew nothing of my plan.

"What's going on here?" Jack enquired, as he pulled into a large car park at the rear of the Aberdeen Police Headquarters.

"Get out and I'll show you," I answered and left the vehicle. I ran my eyes over the crowd and spotted Inspector Carlin standing with the female inspector Banks along with a transport convoy of specialist firearms officers. To the front of them, there were three tactical armoured vehicles sent from London, governed by MI5, and around twelve armed men with semi-automatic weapons. Hastily, they spread around our vehicle in a circular formation.

To the side of those vehicles, there were two formally parked prison vans, ready to transport the prisoner straight to Davie's new five-star accommodation. The female executive director of Europol stood beside the ageing male director of the G2, both requiring confirmation with their own eyes, of the arrest of such a high-profile target. Also in attendance were the heads of the Aberdeen police network, in particular an inspector

Magill who had a keen interest in Davie Rhodes who had slipped his grasp in the past.

Jack lifted his hands in the air, being held at gunpoint and noticed the fact I was not fazed by it. As I opened the rear door, I heard guns being cocked by the armed officers taking a defensive stance in preparation to fire.

Davie stepped out and stretched himself. "I never knew I was this popular!"

Carlin and Banks strode over to us. "Are these the two who are getting the glory, son?" Carlin asked as Banks grinned. Carlin gave Jack a check, shocked he was alive. "Aye, Banks there, the blondie, will get most of it!" She had approached as Carlin retraced his steps and admired the show, looking his unhealthy yellowed self. Banks continued to move forward and embraced me. Jack looked on, perplexed at the affair as Davie's face was sourer than the granite buildings of Aberdeen.

"Strange circumstances bumping into each other again!" said Banks, who grinned wide and free

"Aye, it's not your everyday event," I replied. "Fuckin' hell, get on wi' it," Davie spat out, as a cautious Jack onlooked me with disagreement.

"I suppose I should officially do an introduction here," I insisted, as Davie turned away in defiance.

"Davie, meet Felicity Banks, daughter of Nancy Fowler and adopted father, Sam Bryson." Davie registered a stillness and closed his eyes. His jaw line dropped, before his face tensed with the corner of his mouth curled up. Regretfully, he turned towards Banks and then switched his miffed attention to me. Jack had walked around and joined us alongside Carlin, who was amazed to see him.

"Thought you were dead!" Carlin stated, as he puffed his chest out.

"Not anymore, Carlin. I'll be claiming my territory back in a day or two," Jack said under his breath as Carlin sighed. I carried on with the introduction!

"Davie, your daughter!"

Jack started laughing hysterically, aware of the irony of Davie being nicked by his own daughter.

"Hello, Dad. Finally, we can start bonding!"

Davie stood open mouthed and had nothing more to say than, "Fuck!"

The deal with Banks back in the interview room:

When I had first met Banks, sat inside the interview room, I was preparing to be convicted of murdering the Governor and spending the next twenty-five years in jail. Carlin began the explanation of why I was going to be let out and when Banks appeared, she began her part in the explanation. When Carlin left the room to take a phone call, Banks carried on the conversation. But there was no phone call to be taken.

"So, what's it to be, Max?" she asked in her Glaswegian accent, enquiring whether I was to speak of the horrors inside Altcourse prison when I got out.

"It'll be, that I'm walking out of here. You're all bent, you lot. Disgusting cunts, give me the shivers."

She leant back in her seat, astonished at my language, and seemed concerned about my situation.

"I've asked that we can have some time together before you leave," she said.

"For what? I've had enough abuse. Leave me be and let me out!"

"There will be no more abuse, Max, not on my watch. There might be a favour here and there!"

"I don't do favours with pigs, never!"

"You are pretty fiery, you. Well, that can be expected from yer family stock!"

"What the fuck's your problem, missus? Shut the fuck up, do one and let me out of here." I still had the Governor's blood on my hands; I was still trying to fathom what I had done and how to live with it.

"I'm going to tell you some shocking information, Max. I'm not just a disgusting pig. I'm also your sister." "Fuck off!" I said, shaking my head. Banks gawked and stuck her nose in the air, allowing me to understand what she had just said. Her solid expression told me she was deadly serious.

She went on to explain, in detail, that Davie had killed who she thought was her real dad, the hardened Sam Bryson in Glasgow. In the early eighties, Davie had had a brief fling with Nancy Fowler, Sam's other half, which resulted in a pregnancy and the birth of Felicity Bryson. Felicity had spent her whole life believing Sam was her real dad but after he was murdered, Nancy told her otherwise.

Banks showed me photos from the investigation into Sam's death as he lay in the lobby of a house in Glasgow with two bullet holes in his body. This had happened when Davie was rescued from his torture, the episode in which he had lost fingers. Davie had not killed Sam but his rescuers did. Banks knew that but Davie was still good to take the blame for that.

I allowed her the time to explain it to me without interruption. She was the first person to treat me well after two years of hell. She described how she had entered the police force under a false title, so the reputation of her criminal dad never caught up with her. The reason for her introduction into the police force was solely to find her biological father and make him pay for the murder of her dad. The love she bore for Sam could not be questioned. She worked her socks off and quickly headed up the promotion ladder, categorising herself as a career woman; she had secured a transfer to the Merseyside police service because that was Davie's last known whereabouts. It seemed the offspring of Davie Rhodes all held the same deceitful trait.

"I want you to help me find him!" she had asked, sitting in the interview room. At that time, I still very much admired Davie and had no interest in helping her but I knew it was a condition of being able to walk out of that jail so I played along, like a good boy.

"I'll message you if I hear from him."

Felicity was street smart and far from stupid, knowing I was only saying what she wanted to hear. Felicity gave me her card with her phone number that day; I had never called it until I needed to find out where Joe stayed. In return for that information, I told her of who Joe was and that opened communications between us.

As time passed, living in Inverurie, I decided that I needed her help in disposing of Davie and ensuring that he was sent to Belmarsh. I kept her in the loop with mine and Jack's operation and in return. I promised Davie to her. When C4 Millacky made that phone call to me, I contacted Felicity afterwards, telling her to get up to Aberdeen and arrange Davie's arrest. It all worked out very well and Felicity would have her way.

Back in the police headquarters car park, I was to have my last words with my father.

"You've ruined my life from the minute go you bastard and you've destroyed the rest of your kids' lives. You deserve nothing but to rot inside you cunt."

He halted me. "I saved you, boy. I took you to that church after yer mother fucked herself on that bad batch of smack. I gave you life and look at you now!"

"Bad batch?" I questioned as Davie lifted his head towards Jack whose palms turned moist, while he hid them in his pockets trying to appear calm, but he was so badly itching to get away from the surrounding of authorities.

"Ask him. He knows and anything he tells you will be a lie."

I ignored Jack and carried on staring at a desperate man who would do anything not to be jailed. "The file, there's a file. If Brian hears of my arrest, he will leak it! It has everyone's names on it. Everyone will want to know who leaked it." He referred to the file that Brian was holding in the south of Ireland where he had been hiding out for the past two years; however, that was insignificant to me, and it pulled no strings in his favour.

But Banks had heard of it.

"The file is not of any importance to us. We know of it and have seen snippets of it. Now that we know there is a man called Brian who holds it, we will locate it and deal with it."

That last hope of Davie's sank into the drain as I wanted to continue.

"My mother, Joe's mother and Felicity's father, you've taken their lives without grief and now we are taking yours. You're finished, and you're headed for Belmarsh." I stiffened up, tensed my body and leaned into his breath. "C4 Millacky's men will give you a warm welcome."

His face sagged like a melting candle. He tugged his duck tapped wrists in an irate tantrum, attempting to free himself. He knew then that he had been a hundred per cent outsmarted. Banks's pokey face, usually vinegary, gleamed with smiles.

She walked to Davie's side and gripped his elbow.

"Come on, Da. Let's go have a wee talk about your upcoming accommodation, shall we?"

Davie was led away from me, despondent and gutted, closely escorted by half a dozen armed guards. They led him to the rear of a prison van and put a set of handcuffs on him. He took a step onto the back shelf, stopped and gazed back at me. His irate manner ceasing there, he admired my intelligence and capability. He nodded his head in a 'well-done' kind of gesture. That was the last time I'd ever look at him. Jack snapped me out of my fix when he wandered over to me.

"You planned all this?" he asked.

"I did!"

"You could've let me in on it! You did good kid!"

"Well, I could've, you're right, but that would've spoiled the surprise."

Jack sniggered quietly, being remarkably uncomfortable in the company of so many members of law enforcement. Banks began to wander back and was joined by Carlin.

"Right, we are done with him," Banks spoke confidently as she rerouted her attention to Jack.

"Mr Gallagher, Liverpool will be glad to hear of your return from the grave. Won't they, Detective Inspector Carlin?" Banks swivelled her head to her partner who was caught unaware. Banks had kept him in the dark.

"It will certainly be a revelation!" Carlin revelled. "We are looking forward to getting home," I said to Banks.

"Are you using 'we', as in a collective, or just you?" she asked.

"I can only speak about myself, Banks. Jack will have to adjust to where he's going!" Jack's lacklustre shoulders slouched, quietly figuring out what I was insinuating. He fixed a wondering glare as I refused to remove eye contact with a changed, grimly fierce look. Jack calculated what was about to occur and without the necessity to argue or resist because there was no scenario that would get him off the hook.

"You are truly a ruthless man, Max. Somewhat admirable! I used to see a lot of your father in you. Now… I see a lot of myself!"

Some local Aberdeen constables approached Jack and put the handcuffs on him. They pulled him away and put him In the second prison van as I watched with pride. His arrest was a necessary evil. He had put me in jail and had a part to play in the murder of my mother. He, like Davie, would rot inside.

Two suited gentlemen from the anti-corruption unit of the national crime agency approached Carlin and slapped the cuffs on him, quickly and forcefully. "What the hell's going on here!" He resisted. "Get those fucking things off me, Banks, what's going on here?"

"You can go start your new career inside, Carlin. You've cut so many corners and taken so many brides that you make the Mexican Cartels look like stand-up guys."

"You bitch! To think how much I helped you!"

"You never helped me, you tolerated me. Take him away." Carlin was unwillingly dragged away and chucked in the same prison van as Jack. That was everyone dealt with. I stood, untouchable, and absorbed the best feeling of redemption I'd ever experience. Banks was harmoniously pleased that she was tasked with the arrest of Davie and her corrupt partner. The female director of Europol, who wore circled shades on a dull day approached Banks.

"You are congratulated," she said, in a Dutch accent. "I am staying in this god-awful place for another evening. I am residing at the Hilton Hotel. Here is my card." She handed it over. "Come and have dinner with me tonight. I need another female like you in my department."

Banks was taken with the invitation while the director walked away.

"Well, brother, I bet you're glad of this day," Banks said, with a gloating satisfaction that she could not hide while glancing at the covering of blood splatters across the back seats of the range rover.

"Should I know anything about that?"

"Its best you don't know," I insisted.

"Simpson!" she shouted. "Get me that paperwork!" She ordered a fellow lanky detective who went into a car and removed a file from the back seat. He hurried over with it and handed it to her.

"And Simpson, get this car indoors and covered over immediately."

"Yes ma'am," he answered and then Felicity handed me the file.

"In here is all the information about your mother. There was an investigation into her death when you were a few months old. But thought you'd like to know, she also had a sister. I'll leave you to mull through it. I've added a page with my own opinions on the investigation. If there's any questions, give me a call."

I took the file from her hands. I had asked her to find out all the information on my mother that was available. "Maybe there is some goodness in the police force, Felicity."

She nodded her head in appreciation, the first time I had used her first name.

"I'll head off now, I have a brother I'd like to visit, a little boy and a Mrs that I haven't seen in a good while."

"Can you tell Joe I will come introduce myself when I get a chance."

"I'll pass on your message and we should have a get together once the wind dies down."

"I'm sure we could Max."

Chapter 68

Hello Joe:

The unyielding satisfaction whipped me for six. I had done it. From the dumfounded street kid abducted and manipulated by his father at the age of fifteen to an intelligent criminal.

I had one more journey to take before the elation of returning to my family could be achieved. Banks lent me a car and allowed me to leave with my freedom intact. I wanted to press on before the capture was leaked to the press. Banks granted me a couple days of secrecy so I could get back to my family.

There were a couple things I had to do first. One of them was to visit my brother who would be perplexed to what was going on. I knew the whole meeting would be surreal and it would be stranger for Joe than it would be for me. I knocked on the door. A rugged haired Joe looked at me through the window of the sitting room and came to open the door.

"What the fuck is goin' on!" After some vibrant pleasantries, he invited me into the sitting room. There sat, his gangly shaped friend Tim, wearing a ragged checked shirt under a mop of hair. They were surely gossiping over what had happened a couple hours earlier. I brushed Tim's shoulder as I walked past him and sat on the sofa.

"It's no' every day I see a ghost," Tim said and shared a stern stare with Joe.

"It's not every day that one can stop living like a ghost Tim." Tim judged my manner that I was a civilised person and not this beast everyone knew me as. Joe stood square to me with a growing gut, with his arms crossed, wondering how to start the conversation. "I suppose I should offer you a cup o' coffee," Joe insisted when Tim gestured with his hand to sit down.

"I'll make the coffee but it's probably whisky I should be pouring." Tim left for the kitchen. For the next couple of hours, I filled Joe in on everything that he needed to know to explain, why on that Sunday, Davie, myself, and a crazed neighbour he thought was his friend, had infiltrated his life and flipped it upside down. I described it from the night he thought he killed me to Davie's knock on the door. Then I had to fill him in on the challenging life I had led, his sister Felicity Banks, and my mother's death. There were plenty of questions from Joe and Tim but no aggression or aggravation. Joe realised his father was a worse man than he had already imagined, and his neighbour was a snake. His biggest shock was how we managed to abide at the end of his street for nearly two years without him noticing. I filled him in on the surveillance system we installed and the GPS trackers on the vehicles they were using. He was in so much of a disbelief about this he ripped off one of the smoke alarms and tore it apart to see the camera inside.

Joe explained to me that he had conspired with the police, an Inspector Magill, to aid in capturing of Davie on the night of the fight between us and how he stood with a gun in his pocket, as Turk and Barb conducted the gun deal with Bobby Munroe and company. He proudly told me he had some people who had double crossed him, set up and arrested. Then later he used Lukas to conduct hits on them through the compliance of Mr Dean. One of those people was someone he referred to as Skinner. The same guy I had met years prior in that Indian restaurant in London. We also had a lengthy conversation of how I followed him and Davie in Ireland where he explained the job he was on for Mr Dean. He shocked me when he told me of the murder of Micky Macdonald after I informed Joe I shared a cell with him. There were no moments of silence, and many cups of coffee were drank, where we ended at the same conclusion. It was strange how closely our lives were related being so many miles apart.

"I woke up this mornin' wi' no family, now I have a brother and sister. As much as I'll regret this but we should keep in touch," Joe announced.

We exchanged phone numbers and agreed that we would meet up in the near future and I would introduce him to his sister. After some pleasant goodbyes I left to do one more thing before I could return to Courtney and my son.

My Mother was named Carrie McCabe, and she was the sister of someone called Danielle McCabe. The same Danielle that died in my arms and that meant that Davie had a sexual relationship with both my mother and aunt. Danielle would have been too scared to tell me who she was in fear of both Davie's and Jack's reactions. The investigation into my mother's death was brief and deemed a suicide by none other than a young Inspector Carlin. Banks had secretly investigated the case herself and began to question everything she had found.

Forensics were run on various bits of evidence that were still left with the case file, including cash, banks cards, and the syringe used to inject the heroin into her arm. Davie's fingerprints were found on all those items. The syringe was sent away for chemical analysis and the results showed there was large traces of fentanyl that indicated the dosage had been tampered with and that was the cause of her death. I believed Davie about one thing; he did not issue that dose of heroin. He was caught red handed holding Carrie's arm with the syringe in his hand but that was a coincidence. They say there are things in this world you cannot explain but it did go some way to justify the images of the frail woman I was haunted with after I came back to life. It was My Mother checking up on me, willing me for redemption. Her death was down to Jack who had informed Davie that the baby me was his, after a DNA check. Jack assumed Davie would have done something to get her out of the prostitution ring or he hoped he would. He never and she became a big nuisance to Jack, because of her insistence on taking myself to work with her and her constant questioning about Davie's whereabouts and demands for money. So, Jack did what he did best and got rid of her. He disguised the murder as an overdose so Davie would never know. His goal was to remove her from his life.

On a pure coincidence, Davie had left his comforts of Aberdeen and travelled to Liverpool for whatever reason. Maybe for a job, maybe to check up on me, who knows, but he arrived at the brothel minutes after she had passed. He could do nothing for her, but he did rescue me and take me to that church. If not, then who knows what would have happened to me.

I had found out the truth and that was closure for me, it had to be or else I would forever punish myself. The revelation of what I had achieved soothed me. I had returned from the dead for a purpose and I had achieved that. The man without an education had outsmarted everyone and now, I had all Davie's money. That day I picked up his book from the safe house in Carnagh I took pictures of as many pages as I could where I got the passwords and usernames of his offshore accounts. Davie was rearranging his cash into one account at the time when I emptied it. I was a millionaire more than once over. Money I would use to give my family a proper future away from the callous Liverpool environment we were involved in. To top that even further I had Jack's notes on Rankin's accounts that he was preparing to empty. I had more money than any man needed. All the pieces of the puzzle were completed, all conveniently laid and dispatched superbly.

Chapter 69

The Walk over the Landing:

I had been through an endeavour that no one could predict. I had suffered my whole life. I had taken the lives of three people and that I had to forgive myself for because with no forgiveness there is no solitude for the conscious. Before my Fathers capture, I dragged the remorse of the Governor and Belcher Oakley's death around with me like a burden. I had to end Rankin to the request of C4 Millacky and I did that for two reasons. One: I hoped he would not investigate where Rankin's fortune went. Two: He would leave me alone to go about my life how I wanted. The fact I hated the dirty rat made the task that little bit easier. But it was my desperation to end that part of my journey that made pulling the trigger that little bit simpler. The Governor deserved his fate, he abused his power in the prison system to feed his insecurities and bitter redemption for his life. The vendetta he carried towards Davie was an added bonus to seclude me to a torturous time inside. The method of how it happened was not something I would repeat. That savagery had died when I was re-born. Belcher Oakley was a death I did not wish. The haze took over me like a tornado, the ferocity of anger oozed with a temper of unstoppable rage. But the Gypsy had took the lives of others and he knew the risks. The tide of repetition was a cruel one and it was one I wanted to end. This revolting family repetition of living burdened lives had to end. I wanted young Max to become a good honest man who would forever be unfamiliar of the world in which I lived.

The moment I had waited for, for over two years had arrived. I left the elevator on the fifth floor with a huge draw of relief. I had a smile stretch the length of my face that I had never had before. The emotion overwhelmed me as tears of elation dripped from my moist eyes. My thinking went into overdrive knowing I had a lot of explaining to do but I was prepared for that. I'd tell her everything she needed to know. The thoughts of meeting my son, my blood, and something that was part of me for the first time was making my endorphins erupt with joy. There were zero thoughts of regret over Davie and Jack's futures. I felt I had redeemed my sins by completing my journey and hoped eventually, once I explained that, Courtney would agree.

On a late evening, as dark as any night, I joyfully leapt across the solid concrete landing as a man stood, gazing out at the lights of the city, around three quarters of the way down the landing. As I got closer, I noticed he lazily puffed on a cigarette with his head nestled under the high collar of his heavy coat. He leant over the balcony wall over his elbows as I passed him, seemingly unbothered from the world. I did not wish or want to converse with anyone. It would derail the moment and I hurried past him.

"I ponder why a man with so much money would choose a place like this to stay," the cloaked man said as I halted to the spot and sank my head.

"Sometimes we don't get choices." I wondered what to say and replied drearily.

"And today you have made a choice…you return to your family." C4 Millacky said, drawing on his cigarette, holding a vison of the city in front of him.

"I've done what you asked." I said frankly as he turned with a moulded seriousness, absorbing me with his sullen eyes.

"You have that Mr McCabe; you have indeed done that and I can express my gratitude." He thanked me in his formal and versed Irish accent.

"What do you think men like us are made for?" He asked.

"What?" I replied as he made me wonder what I was really built for.

"Men like us are the lions of the world, we don't conduct our lives like the others who adjourn to work and sleep while they piss their weekly wage up against the wall." He stepped closer to me as his facial expression relaxed but remained deadly serious. "We are kings, we rule the worlds that they are so naïve to think does not exist."

Remaining calm, I replied, "I'm no king and this world is dead for me." Behind me, we both heard a door open that drew our attention as C4 Millacky overlooked my shoulder.

"This world is the only place you will ever feel at home with and that world," he nodded past my shoulder as I turned to see Ringo exit the door of my flat, "is a world that will strip you of any goodness you think you may have."

I became taken at seeing Ringo as Courtney stuck her head out of the door. I felt a seizure of happiness as I flinched and began to walk, almost about to shout, to announce my return as he gripped the back of my right tricep uncomfortably hard.

"Watch!" He asserted hardly. Courtney leaned in and kissed Ringo passionately, wrapping their arms around each other, romantically taken with each other. My heart plunged to the ground. It felt as if someone had blown my guts out with a shotgun. As he whispered in my ear.

"Love is this world's greatest weakness, for any man. A woman can rip your soul apart in a heartbeat. That pain is uncontainable Max. Each man finds his way of dealing with it."

I continued to watch, gobsmacked, as Ringo walked to the staircase exit at the opposite side of the landing to us. Courtney briefly drew her look our way, catching a sight of us as I bowed away from her. C4 Millacky kept his gaze on her while he took a deep draw and waited until she walked inside.

"Your boy in there will have a good life if you're not involved, cos inside you, the devil lives, I can see it in you. One day, not in the next week or the next month, it will resurface and there is nothing you can do to stop it, it's a matter of time."

I growled and stomped away from him.

"You're vermin!" I said. "Fucking vermin, you are."

"That's right, that's what I am and unlike you, I live knowing that. You have to accept who you are Max."

"I did what I was supposed to do," aggravated, I screamed. "I got rid of them, both of them. And I'm supposed to be here. I'm supposed to come back to her." He allowed me to have a momentary hissy and continued.

"Have you ever considered how convenient it was for you to fall for Jack's barmaid, his shining girl." He caught my attention. "Did she ever question what you were and what you did?" I took seconds to think with a rapid answer.

"No, not once." He flicked his cigarette off the side and stepped into me.

"Don't you think that's strange!"

I had never thought it was but now I did. I relived my entire life with her at that point.

"Jack played you like a puppet, he put her into your life so he could use you, keep an eye on you!" I shook my head, denying it, but the realisation that it was true began to become evident. All those times I disappeared for days doing Davie's gunrunning work and stepping in the door bruised and battered at all hours, she never questioned me until she fell pregnant. I offered nothing to her in terms of companionship and not once did she question that.

"And your child, do you think she wanted that child, that was all Jack!

I could not fully admit it but deep inside my soul, I knew what he was saying was true. My heart rotted, sucking the goodness from my body. I wanted to erupt, approach the door, and bust it down so I could unload my wrath. But he gripped my wrist and stopped me.

"I'm here to give you an opportunity, a very appealing opportunity Mr McCabe. The war for me is dead. The men of the IRA are not who they say they are. They fantasise that they are hard men but they idolise a role for which they cannot act. I would still like to live as a rich man so now I must turn my morals to ash so I can adapt to the new world." I listened to his words that were distracting me from my heavy heart.

"Look down there." He insisted. I hesitated and then peaked over the wall. "See that motor down there with the lights on?"

"Aye, what about it?"

"Turk and Barb are inside that motor and they await my return. The British Government are more corrupt than any organisation I have ever dealt with and they have contacted me, the head of the IRA, to dispatch their unwanted arms to Togo in Africa. They need a mongrel, who am I to deny who I am, and naturally I am their best man for the job so I have obliged. Now, I will become their number one arms trafficker so my future has…let's say, entered a new chapter."

He choose to have a moment to himself and gestured his head over the landing.

"I'm heading to that motor and then we will drive away. If you so do choose to follow me then please be obliged but know this if you don't. This opportunity will never appear to you again because us as men will not exist."

I turned to look into his eyes once more as they gloated with opportunity. He had a new lease of life, rosy with optimism. I had enough money to never have the need to earn again but I was drawn to his proposal. Ringo and Courtney changed my outlook on the future. C4 Millacky broke eye contact with me and began to talk as he walked away.

"You are a dead man that never existed Max; you have nothing to lose in this world but a legacy to gain." He said as he continued walking and then halted to the spot. He turned around. "You now have your own connections we could utilise. Your sister Inspector Banks will receive a vast promotion into a lucrative position in Europol and then there is your brother who would be a good hand." He rushed a breath through his nostrils and took a sly step forward. "Hell, you could make it a family business." He said no more, turned the corner and headed to the elevator. I ignored him at first and began to head towards the flat door, tentatively. I stopped and thought about the excitement of being a gunrunner, those moments in the church bunker when I dressed like Davie wondering what it would be like without his restraints. It inspired me and then I continued walking until I reached the kitchen window. I could see through, into the living room where young Max sat on a playmat in a onesie, surrounded by vibrant toys and glued to something colourful on the tele. His innocence floored me, I had love for him, lots of it. It refilled my heart with happiness as I became swamped in the moment. His head turned to the window and we met eyes for the first time. He seemed to pause as he looked at me and smiled with a chuckle. I waved to him as my eyes watered. His beauty weakened my knees. Courtney kneeled and sat on the floor beside him. Their shared love was envious but an instant hatred floored me as I imagined her love for me was all a lie. But she loved him and he loved her and that's all he needed. I could sense that as they both smiled effortlessly, in a playful bliss.

There was no part of me that wanted to disturb them and there was no part of me that felt I belonged there. If I involved myself in their lives, it would only bring a disease into their world. He would grow up with love and peace being brought up by a clean-living Ringo.

I turned away and looked over the landing, to a different life that would not fill me with so much pain. C4 Millacky was right, I was an animal of the world, a beast not fit for a mundane life of normality. I believed I was brought back from the dead for the purpose of having Davie sent to jail for the rest of his life and the better good. But I now believed I had a different fate.

I opened the back door of the blacked-out Range Rover with Turk and Barb in the front and took a seat beside C4 Millacky.

"I had no doubt," he said.

The End.

If you enjoyed this book, please
be kind and leave an honest
review on Amazon.

You can follow the Author on social media
for all his updates on future books in the
`Fighting's in The Blood` series or visit his
website Leecooperfighterwriter.com

Facebook
Lee Cooper-Author

Twitter
@leecooper84_lee

Instagram
@Fightingsintheblood